BY RICHARD LLEWELLYN

Sweet Morn of Judas' Day
A Man in a Mirror
Up, into the Singing Mountain
Chez Pavan
Mr. Hamish Gleave
A Flame for Doubting Thomas
A Few Flowers for Shiner
None but the Lonely Heart
How Green Was My Valley

SWEET MORN OF JUDAS' DAY

SWEET MORN

DOUBLEDAY & COMPANY, INC.

OF JUDAS' DAY

by Richard Llewellyn

GARDEN CITY, NEW YORK, 1964

*All of the characters in this book
are fictitious, and any resemblance
to actual persons, living or dead,
is purely coincidental.*

SWEET MORN OF JUDAS' DAY

1 It was the sort of morning when you might expect to find the Heavenly Father off in a corner and doubting His Own Self, and nothing to be done but wait, God love Him, and His Own patience save us all.

Arquimed Rohan O'Dancy Boys, using each moment of life as if it were draught from Grandfa Connor's own champagne, tried to open only one eye in red dust to see Democritas Pereira, and grinned, mouth tight shut not to be getting the teeth of himself full of grit, a hate from childhood, in food or water, chewing or drinking, even if every grain thereabouts was part of his own Inheritance.

Dem, poor man, seemed not to be walking, but only pushing the hugeous ball of his stomach with his hands in the crimson sash behind his back, and the white jacket rolled in creases between the crooks of his arms, and the panama over his eyes bouncing on the ends of his mustache, and his feet just seen, though *he* never did, pattering away down below there, a dozen steps to anybody else's one.

A few hours into Judas' Day they were, and not a splendid mother's son looking for anything more than sweet bad luck, which was no less than what any of them were getting, and abundantly, perhaps from the very paws of Iscariot, that Kissed one, yes, patron saint of any sinner, accursed suicide only the night before and not yet still in the heels of him from the spin of the rope.

But even if all the dust, and the earth underfoot, was part of himself, still there could be too much of a good thing, and The O'Dancy, called so because The Tad and Grandfa and Great-Grandfas before himself so called themselves, he, ah yes, he, with each foot to the ankle in hot red earth, wished himself at rest and cool in The House, or going down the stairs to Giuseppe's Bar for just a little more of that fine whisky and O'Dancy coffee in the high glass. But he rathered himself up the Rua Augusta, that artery of mixed blood, in Maexsa's place, all hanging fish nets and seashells pinkly naked with lights behind them, for another bottle or two of that icy champagne of hers, some more music and, just as likely, another fight, and perhaps, but only perhaps, an answer to a terrible question, one, yes, that had himself on edge.

There was worth in thought of it, if Maexsa, that true mystery, met that very night and never before, would talk to him, would listen instead of laughing, would show those marvelous tall legs again, that she said were never in anything except scarlet silk stockings and black garters, and perhaps a wider hand span or even more of her own self's white-milk, and the skimp of scarlet frilly drawers to hide the Secret, seen only by the girls, more the pity, for Maexsa told him she was no man's woman, and the whiskers of him bristled to think of her, going over the bar counter in a cat roll, and tearing the machete from the rack under the till, and swinging it around the long black plaits, and screaming like a good one, and everybody jamming the doors to be out and away and to hell with that.

But poor Dem was slow and he got a puffed eye from somewhere, and a slash on the right shoulder, though not from Maexsa. In that crowd and little candle power could nobody tell what was anybody doing. Out, to blue daylight and the doctor's white room, but it was no stitching job, by strength, Dem swore, of his wife, on her knees all night, beads in hand, waiting for him to get back from the city and a stranger from her bed until he did.

Then the poor, brand-new truck was sitting there only a mite off the floor, wheels away, everything inside stripped, a month's stores gone, the cases of bottles, everything under the hood, spare wheel, headlights, radio, you might say, picked to the graveyard bones, and not a loving soul in sight. So they manhandled her out of the yard, and rattled a fair marvel of an old iron tune along the Avenida Rio Branco to the dealer's place, and him shuttered for yet a few hours, and still in snore when he answered the telephone, but coming in at once, naturally, nothing too much for The O'Dancy, and to sit comfortable in the corner bar with a bottle on the house till he got there.

It was then The O'Dancy found his inside jacket pocket picked, wallet gone, and the hip pocket slit out of his trouser, a fine, handy wad flown to someone else, and nothing between his arse and the air except his shirt's own tail.

Dem had loose change, but the other two were drunk out. The boss in the all-night bar on the corner gave them credit, and why not, because everybody knew The O'Dancy, by name at least, and it was no less than an honor to have him in the place at all, with his overseer and a couple of his cattlemen, drunk, sober, or anyway else.

So, while they stood there, politeness done, and the glasses getting a polish, the coffee urn blew up.

"Well, now, for the dear love of the holy Infant Jesus," The O'Dancy said, while steam blew, and voices roared, and leaning on an elbow under a table where himself had rolled or been flung. "Isn't the only safe place in this whole distressful world Giuseppe's? Ought we not to go back there and hole up for the day? Father Miklos said the evils were mounting, and piling, the way he never saw in all his life, and him three times at Rome, and twenty years wiser than myself. Would we disbelieve the reverend man, then?"

"When that misbirth of a dealer shows his miserable carcass, we can be fitted and out in the hour," Dem said. "There's little traffic so early, and we can be asleep by, depending on how we drink for luncheon, noon, should we say? Depend on it, that's where the razor worked, in Giuseppe's. Not in Maexsa's. Women are not skillful pickpockets. They work best with a pillow."

"I'd pay her anything," The O'Dancy said.

"A dry tube, believe me," Dem said, and it took the three of them to pull him upright. "The girls pay her more. There are more of them."

"I never understood it," The O'Dancy said, looking at the boss cursing creation in the steam. "Never did. Mind, I'll say this. I never tried to. What a woman can do to another when she hasn't what I have, well, there I'll confess me, I'm in a welter. Will we ever be getting a drink? Is the man standing there, seething his crabs, or what?"

"The water's off," Dem said, looking over the bar. "The gas pipe's soaped in and safe. He's suffered some fine damage. Iscariot doesn't hang himself every day."

"Glory be to God," The O'Dancy said, and crossed himself, and kissed his fingers. "The year's day of all misfortunes, and every affliction, preserve us, now, from the misery. Why's myself not at The House, doors locked, blinds down? Ah, the comfort of that."

"We could fly," Dem said, holding ice to the purplish puff. "There's a helicopter at the club. And the little two-engine. Forty minutes, we sleep as sucklings."

"On this day, fly?" The O'Dancy said. "Would you implore the Accursed One to deal with us? Were we not lately on our knees at the chancel to avoid that very thing? Let's have the drink and be on four wheels, joyful, and cool, without fire, as Christians ought to be."

Clovis, the Number One cattleman, went behind the bar and took the bottle and slapped one glass into another to make a jiggle of four, and came back. There was just enough sense in the man to see what he was at. He poured the whisky with never a miss all the way to the brim, and took off his hat and bowed to The O'Dancy, bowed to Overseer Democritas Pereira, and poked out his tongue in a horse's blast of rudeness to João, his second man.

The O'Dancy drank two gulps and put the glass down.

"Nothing like it," he said. "Been saying it a long time, too. There's still nothing like the *uisce beatha*. I'm feeling that push along the Avenida. I'm glad the truck wasn't loaded. My shoulders are sore. Am I getting old?"

"I'm seven years older," Dem said. "My eleventh son last year. A daughter next."

"Not that I'm feeling old that way," The O'Dancy said. "How much would Maexsa want?"

Dem raised his mustache, like a spread bat, with the back of his hand, and winked at the other two.

"She'd give it to you," he said. "Ask her. How could she refuse The O'Dancy?"

"But I did ask her, yes, that's the very thing I did, of course it was, for I've never been backward with any woman or anybody else at all," The O'Dancy said, in a spittle rush, and the whisky well into him. "And what did she do? Pinch me titty. That's what she did. Bring me a pair of these, says she. Titties, says I? Titties, says she. I've a man's pair, says I. Get some air to 'em, says she. Swell 'em up. And me in me sixties?"

"Sixties, fifties, forties, thirties," Dem said. "You're a better man."

"I look at me white hair," The O'Dancy said, soft for him. "Me soul turns away in disgust. And if I do that, and living, what'll a woman be doing, and only looking? Except to pinch me titty."

"She didn't pinch anywhere else," Dem said. "Sense enough for that. Why didn't you pinch her?"

"Wasn't that the very thing I was doing all night when I had the chance, then?" The O'Dancy said. "Don't I know what she's wearing? Don't I know the mortal wonder of every palpitating millimeter of herself? But only with everything on. And it's thick stuff. It's that knotted silk. Shantung, is it not? But she's got a magic beard, there, be Christ, it's to her knees. What I'd pay to see it. Ah, what I'd pay."

"It'd put the talons in you," Dem said.

"Clawed and bloody," The O'Dancy said. "Bloody, then, bloody now."

"You have your pick of more than seventy unclipped and unshaved virgins on your own place," Dem said.

"Have them," The O'Dancy said. "And that's a thing I never said before, too."

He sat back in the small iron chair laughing the ear-thrumming O'Dancy HA-A-HA-A-HA-A, and they could hear the echoes play touch in the growing skyscraper's slim bones across the road and flutter off in morning breeze among the billboards.

"I'm old," he shouted, and smashed the glass in a wide sweep of fist and arm. "Old. A gift of virgins. Have them. What a thing to say. I'm old. That's what it is. Tired to think of them. Old."

"But virgins are tiring," Dem said, and filled Clovis's glass, signed to him to share with João, and put it gently in front of The O'Dancy. "A thrust that hurts, if it doesn't skin you, the warm stream, and what? God's Perfection, I was skinned to the muscle once, but never again. "The open one, running her own wine, yes. A pure, sainted pleasure. But what would you expect from Maexsa? It's a length of bamboo."

"Her, it is," The O'Dancy said, sobered a little. "The gentle her."

"The bamboo, and a fist-size gourd on the end of it," Dem said. "A fine girl to caress you, and the squirt, and what did you pay for? Wood it was, wood it still is. Dear master, you overprize a thought."

"Ah, but the gentle her," The O'Dancy said, trying to focus lettering across the street. "I'm too old to court. That's it. And she won't have the paying. So if there's no courting, and no paying, how will I know the gentleness?"

"Who finds gentleness in Maexsa, finds his mother in a tigress," Dem said, and without lifting his fist from the table pointed two fingers of the right hand at the dozing cattlemen. "I'll take these two, and bring her from her bed and you can tell her when she can go home. That's what your father would have done. And often did."

"But where would then be her gentleness?" The O'Dancy asked, and reached for the glass. "Besides, now there's the law. A round dozen of senators and deputies and judges, and how many score of lawyers and newspapermen in the family, police or soldiers wherever you turn, where's the sense in that?"

"Or in an apparatus," Dem said. "Beard or not."

"I'd pay anything," The O'Dancy said, and drank.

Clear glass widened in the tumbler, and then it was gone in a blue flash and red flame, and an explosion that left them clearheaded and on the floor, listening to spraying water and groans.

"Will nobody ever be getting a quiet drink anywhere about, at all, then?" The O'Dancy asked gently, from behind the tipped-over table. "Did they make up their minds? By The Man's own shoe, I'd swear it was a conspiration."

"The other urn blew up," Dem said, holding the handkerchief to his eye. "This is the morning to expect it."

"Could they not have picked another if I was coming in?" The O'Dancy asked a stream of water flowing past him. "Has he any more urns to be getting out of hand?"

"That was the last," Dem said. "If somebody doesn't help me, I shall be inundated, and my wife's prayers were for nothing. If she prayed. Or if she stopped praying at this moment. You note the time? The water main's burst."

The O'Dancy watched a glass turning circles on a veering axis, come to rest, with its mouth taking in and giving back water.

"It was good whisky while it lasted," himself said. "And a good talk. If I could remember a word of what it was about."

"Getting old," Dem said. "I'm wet through."

"I was never old in all my life," The O'Dancy said, and got up on hands and knees, holding onto the edge of the table, but it cycled away, tipping him in a stream, and he raised up on elbows. "You see how it is, here? Half a drink, and me hat's not me own."

The sirens' voices in mesh of terror outside seemed to be coming in at them, and the floor shook with runners, and hands took them, lifting and carrying them, and they were put down under the shop front among the feet of a gathering crowd, not many, but enough to raise a fine dust.

"Let's be out of it," The O'Dancy said, and held the wall, raising himself to stand. "I never had affinity with other than the sacred breath of God Almighty, His Own Self, and that's the clear, quiet air."

Other men pulled Dem on his feet beside him. Clovis lay coiled and rapt in a doorway, and João slept with his back against the wall, legs straight out, hat over his eyes, hands in his lap.

"Happy men," The O'Dancy said. "Happiness, that's a serious business."

"How can happiness be serious?" Dem asked, trying to see through the swelling, tipping his nose to look over. "A contradiction perhaps?"

"Some people are born and taught to be in pursuit of it," The O'Dancy said. "If you're in pursuit, why wouldn't it be serious? They're not satisfied to have it, or know about it. They've to pursue it. If that's not serious, what is?"

People were crowding at the corner, and firemen unrolled hoses down the side street where the walls were in blush of pale rose and red, and some of the windows glittered crimson.

"Oh, but we're not missing a good fire?" The O'Dancy said. "Come on. This one's costing us nothing. Not a hundred and twenty-eight thousand bags of coffee."

"One hundred and twenty-eight thousand, four hundred and sixteen," Dem said, pattering beside him. "And the barn, and the carts and coaches. Why should I forget such a night?"

"Be quit of it, now," The O'Dancy said. "The wound still open, and you'll pick at it? No insurance. Dead loss. But we made it up, oh yes, we did. Did we not show them what we could do? A hundred and more bags in place of every one lost, and fifteen barns, not one, and how many trucks?"

"Forty-four, counting this one," Dem said, turning to look at the wreck outside the dealer's. "You see? He's there. They're working on it."

"Let them," The O'Dancy said. "I wonder do I know the fire chief to get us good places?"

They pushed through the crowd, Dem in front, for the man had the size and weight, and The O'Dancy, slighter by another two pairs of trousers, putting his good shoulder in behind. Fire trucks closed the narrow street and the pumps were praying for air. Every window opposite nested three or more heads, except where the flames reached out, and the firemen stood in groups, holding shining copper nozzles with a long tip of spraying white water.

"A game we used to play," The O'Dancy said. "I'll piss you for the highest. Or longest. Or most. Could you ever reach it in those days?"

"When I stopped carrying hundred-kilo coffee bags, and cutting pineapple and bananas, that's when I took the weight," Dem said. "You were too young for me. Seven years is nothing when you're older. When you're young, it's the known length of history. I was good enough in my time. Nothing tremendous, but adequate. Did you ever know Amaria Curupaiti?"

"I'll go to me grave regretting I never did," The O'Dancy said, and off with his hat in a wonderment, and staring the palest gray-blue eye, that his father had told him was mark of the best men in the Honor of Leinster, that he ever used to fine advantage since the moment. "Be telling me, then. What was the woman's pride?"

"She stood a little shorter than you," Dem said while somebody scrawled in the air to them that the house they were passing might fall in the street. "She could put a fount over her head. She'd pull her skirt up and play on the pipe like a clarinet. Pressure, that's all. Of course, no direction. Your eye or your pocket, all one to her. That was the champion."

"Think of that, now," The O'Dancy said, taken with a whisper.

"Amaria, yourself'll maunder in me mind, micturant, from this day on."

Screams were rising under their walking feet. The gratings in front of the shops were open, and the hoses curled over the edges and hid their nozzles in the cellars.

"There's women down there?" The O'Dancy said, or asked the question, or both, at the sun's rising light filling the end of the long street, lustrous in his face, shining in his hair and pinking out the red, the remaining youthful red, in the whiskers of his chin and cheeks. "Is there nobody giving them a hand, then? Women?"

He jumped into the nearest pit, and fell among water and hoses, and rolled through a window on to a stone floor, and stood in thick smoke, silvery in the light of an electric beam from a fireman's helmet. He ran, doubled up, with his head near the floor in clearer air, toward the screams, and tripped over a barrier. Smoke thinned, and a fan blew toward him, and a bulb gave white light from the ceiling.

Three women crouched before a row of candles in front of a table, screaming themselves raw, and one he saw when she moved, a little to the side, kneeling, with her face to the wall.

"Come on, now," he said. "Be giving me the little hands of you, and we'll be out in the fresh air while the Holy Mother watches ward and counts the steps of us."

"I'm Mother Mary," one of them said, but quick, and gave him a hand like a child's, knuckly and supple. "I was praying for a guide, and here you are. The saintly mother *iemanja* will follow us. She speaks to other lords."

The other two stood beside him, screaming done, calm as that, not a tear, not a stare, not a mite of fright. The mother *iemanja* stayed on her knees with her face to the wall, though something in the set of her haunches, in the stiff turn of her swathed head, told out, in loud language, all part of smoke and silence, that she was looking at him, and not only just looking, but she knew him, perhaps, or not even perhaps, by name and place, by hand and foot, in or out of the cradle, as well as his own mother ever had, and she, a floral thought to her, lost in a grief of gray marble, iron-railed and badged, ah, hang your head now, these fifty odd years, where himself would also be one of these fine days, and be turning your back on it while you can.

"Be stirring, now," he said. "Death by fire is not the shortest. In hell, they're burning yet."

"Leave her," Mother Mary said, against the loud shouts of the firemen outside. "The lords speak soft, and she must listen."

But himself had seen the sway of the walls outside, and felt the shaking ground, and heard the warning note in the shouts, and he tore from the child's hands, and went to the kneeling woman and put a hand under her elbow.

"Do your praying in the sun," he said. "That's where the Bright Ones are, him that latched the shoe, and Him that wore it, and she, sweet creature, that poured the ointment and raised in all of us the ghost of love. Come now, while the Light's in us."

She stood, and walked in front, and passed the other three, and all of them went through the door, and a masked fireman ran them over to the grating, and hands waited to pull them through the smoke, and into the flat of the street, and policemen shouted and put their arms about them, and half-ran them down to the corner, into the crowd, and nurses and doctors, and ambulances, and what all besides noise.

"At last," Dem said, and the relief holding out an embrace in his voice. "The truck's ready. Here. The other two'll carry you. Did you have to voyage into a chapel of heathens? Must you bring the Touch upon you? On such a day? Wasn't the scent enough?"

Only dank smoke deep in paining lungs and hardly a known thought of clear breath in himself, but a memory of incense. Tired, too, not because of the work or the rush, but knowledge of the kneeler down there, the mother *iemanja*, the one in white, nobody else, he was certain, except she of the scarlet skimp of frilly drawers tight over the Secret known only to the girls.

That was who she was, no doubt of it, in his blood or hers, none other than Maexsa, that one, that made the whiskers of him bristle.

"I'd pay anything," he said.

They put him in the truck, and was it the whisky, or what was it, but he saw nothing more till the tire burst, and he opened his eyes to see Dem pulling at the wheel as though in a bout with a young stallion, but they were across the road and turned over in a dry flame of dust.

So they walked, every one of them whole, hardly a bruise, in a flowing wind toward the gate to The Inheritance, and passed through, and Clovis slammed the iron till it all shook, each one expecting something to fall on him, and The O'Dancy opening one eye at Democritas Pereira, and grinning, mouth shut, for the grit tapped at his lips, wanting to ask what more they might expect to glorify among the matins of Judas' Day, and the sweet bad luck no more than begun for one long clock-around of it.

But wanting most to open his lips and ask if she had been Maexsa he had seen, and afraid, not really of the grit that he hated, getting in his teeth, but of the answer, because he knew beyond all telling.

2 "The luck that the Hanged One's given us this morning's taught me a lesson I'll never learn about taking care of what's me own, anyway," The O'Dancy said, breathless at the top of the slope. "Put in a radio telephone at the gate, and have a shift sleeping there from this day on. A stables was there till Grandfa Shaun suffered his attack of pride, and we got the trucks. He said horses were no longer the extra legs they were, if you please. Why'd we be walking, and all them trucks up there, and no way to get one down here outside of a smoke fire to send it? You'd think we were living a hundred years off."

The Inheritance, as it ever did, came broad and brave to the senses. Miles on, it went, sweet with the sweat of five generations, fling after fling of green leaf and brick-red earth, curving and twisting this way and that, with the terraces of coffee trees the darker green almost to the halfway, and down near the river, the electric-blue spears of pineapple, and bright squares of pasture, and farther off, a froth of bananas, all in straight lines, with the red earth tilled in sugar cane between groves and rows, and driving lanes in a loop and swoop here and there, and not a sound, and sun on the surface of the leaves in ragged quicksilver banks, one risen above the other, with always the red earth below, his own, every grain and meter of it, blade and branch, his, nobody else's, only his, a hundred ten kilometers on each side, and far more to the mountains and beyond.

Up on top of the level ground, highest point of any till the mountains began, five celtic crosses carved from green granite marked where the first man of five O'Dancy generations kept company in the Long Watch.

Leitrim O'Dancy, and God long kind to him, that paced out the land in 1811, lay at the brink, looking across almost a day's walk at the house he began. Behind him in the narrow way, Phineas his son, and happy whispers from his trees that were still quiet-shadowed there, could see the barn he built and the garden he planted. Shaun, a wondrous thought to him, came next, fallen sleepy in his hundred and third year, watching wide awake the fencing he posted in his century, and the coffee groves, his own pride and that of Connor, praise his name, next in line, dead himself a year later when a colt fell on him. The fifth, Cahir, oh yes, The Tad, be gentle-thinking and gentler-speaking, when Satan tiptoed across resting angels, died in a knife fight at forty-four, but he took three with him, nameless men, thieves looking for meat in a hard winter, that he offered them, coming on their camp at night. But he saw they had a prize cow hanging in her quarters and the hide still on her, and grief of griefs, the finest father any man ever had went in at them, and with the dying breath of him asked that three hungry ones might be buried in the same place, washed and combed, and dressed as himself, with the cow's limbs, and the fire's ashes, and the sanguine earth, all together, boys, all together, God save us all and forgive the hard words and bloody hands of us, all together, boys, all together, now, forgive me, forgive The O'Dancy, boys.

O'Dancy Boys the name had been from that moment, because nobody listening had soon forgotten that voice, woman-high and bubbling in scarlet foam, through the chapel and across the yard and patio, or the screaming of his wife, darleen, *mavrone!* and worshiped mother, that cut her wrists that night and went the journey with him. But nobody could say plain Boys, except The O'Dancy and Brother Mihaul, and the sons and daughters, for only they spoke the Other Language, though Boys or Boy-ess was all one to himself or them.

But all the O'Dancy women and any, except the eldest sons that wanted, were buried down in the garden. Only the First Men came up here.

Clovis waved a match under a pile of fronds and blew himself dark in the smoke.

"Today, last year, my mare broke her leg, and a ewe threw a monster with three eyes," he said. "Today begins well. We're still alive."

"Keep your eyes on the stables, or you spoke too soon," Dem said.

"I shall follow the master down to the river, and the shade. Find us when somebody comes."

A shallow rock stairway, built by The Tad, scythed down between great clumps of show flowers all planted at her order—and see, O see, the gentlest, dearest daughter, Hilariana, see the smiling passion, the strange light, Etruscan could those eyes be?—or Attic Greek?—well, Celtic, yes, of Maeve or Boadicea, perhaps, even of Theodora—and see her smile in bloom of blues and whites, reds, mauves and golds, to the horse walk along the river laid flat for The Mam's evening canter. Everywhere about, some one of the O'Dancys had built something for somebody, nearly always a wife or daughter, or sometimes, like the bridge to the only island out there, for a first-born son. O'Dancy women had always been either Portuguese or a mixture, or indigenous, of one people or another, nobody minded much so long as they were beautiful, and that they always were, trust an O'Dancy. At first they lived too far from everywhere to mix with many people, but when the world found the blessing of coffee, and the trade shipped out of Santos, and the see captains came up on the plateau to São Paulo to bargain for cargoes, the O'Dancy women went with the children to their own part of the house, and let the men discuss their affairs with a bottle or so, and later, when a city grew from a village and agents drove out in cars, the men and their sons ever stayed with the guests. So there were two O'Dancy houses, and everyone knew the difference except those with no right in either.

That was the way of it yet, and it was one reason why The O'Dancy had little hope of being rolled in a blanket anytime before next day, because nobody in the women's part could look out on this side to see smoke or anything else, and the second was, that everyone had gone off for the day to be out of the bad luck, and far more than both, himself was in black certainty that the careful misery of Judas' Day, in the way it began, was not by any manner of means over for himself or any nearby.

There was nobody to tell him that, and no sign anywhere about, or up in the plain sun-sky, or out in the red earth, or along the river's rush-stuck green, but with it all, himself felt sure in the way a man with an excellent toothache knows he has a head.

They climbed down to the pavilion built for Great-Grandam Aracý by Tomagatsu, the first Japanese to land for work in Santos, and taken on trust for his smile, knowing no words, by Grandfa Shaun, as a gardener first, and then for his brains and goodness as headman in the coffee groves, until the Grandfa gifted him a tract, and he walking many a splendid year afterward into the Rising Sun with a regular dynasty of Japanese families all about, and leagues in tidy furrow where swamp had been, millions in his own bank, and a city named after him.

The pavilion was hand-carved, built as a gift of love so that Great-Grandam Aracý might rest and make tea, or drink coffee, or picnic with her children. All very well, but this was taken ill by Puxe, the O'Dancy carpenter at the time, and he swore to teach the infidel something about the art of raising a roof, and chose a spot farther down, and there built as dear a little place as you might dream, with a chapel just big enough for four women to enter and kneel without the skirts of them touching, and since they wore the crinoline then, there was plenty of room for a dozen as they dressed today, and their men, too. There the matter sat till the colt fell on Connor, and Tomagatsu, almost another father to him, kept a vigil for five days and nights and had to be carried to his bed nearly dead himself with the tears still shining in the lines of his face, and Grandam Xatina ordered a place for him set at the family table while she lived, and when he was better, there was no finding him, till he came back one morning, early, and took her along the river to another pavilion he had built for her, of timber lacquered scarlet and black, and gold leafery about, and gave her a key, and said it opened a door to a place of the heart where she might think of her only man. By that time, old Puxe was himself on the other side of the iron scrolls, but his son, Manoel, head carpenter in his father's place, found affront to his office in timbering going up anywhere on The Inheritance without a word or will-you-let. Off he went, an hour here, a couple of minutes there, though never absent from his own job, and put up a house that was poetry with tiles on, a little room, carved in different colored woods with bouquets of all the flowers that were planted about Connor, and a chair wide enough for two, where Grandam Xatina could sit, with her ring hand resting, waiting for somebody to come along and take it up, as Connor always had, and kiss, because there was great love between the two, and without him she was salt. There were always special favors for Manoel till the morning she joined Connor, but it was no full satisfaction, because the order to set a place at table beside Tomagatsu's was never given, and only, she said, for one reason, that though Manoel worked himself blind in hours all his own, and raised a marvel from his craft, he did so because his spirit put him to it for a prize on the end, but Tomagatsu built in the heart, from love.

Into the house of Grandam Aracý The O'Dancy went, and left his boots outside, not to mark the floor. Cedar roamed the air, and fine rattan mats turned off the drafts and let in the airs blowing fresh off the fountain's spray.

Dem took off his panama, and slid the fat of his spine slowly down the jamb to set himself in a plump on the outer step.

"We could walk," he said, meaning Clovis or João. "It would take them until tomorrow. We must hope somebody will see the smoke. No woman will ride on Judas' Day. No man would try."

"A man and a telephone at the gate," The O'Dancy said. "A lesson, that's what this is, in catching up with yourself. Do we all live yesterday? How shall we live today and tomorrow?"

"An electric mill to cut the timber on Lot Twenty-one," Dem said. "Axes and handsaws are the costliest tools, today. They waste time."

"Save it," The O'Dancy said. "Get it."

"Hydraulic power for electricity," Dem said. "We have the river. Candles and kerosene should be in those tombs, up there."

"Put them in," The O'Dancy said. "While we're at it, what else?"

"Concrete roads," Dem said. "Straight roads, well drained. We could walk to The House from here in comfort, without dust, in twelve hours. Or fourteen. On these tracks? A day or more."

"Build them," The O'Dancy said. "I'm talking more business here today than I ever did."

"You sit still today," Dem said.

"You'll make yourself a percentage on it," The O'Dancy said.

"Less than many," Dem said. "While I do, nobody else will. At least, it will be well done."

"I'll say that for you," The O'Dancy said. "I haven't moved a finger, but I've spent millions. I'll remember this Judas' Day. Tell me, then. Was it Maexsa?"

Dem looked out, across the flowers and the fountain's white head, along the riverbank toward a grove of cypress planted where Grandfa Shaun had killed a jaguar, and skinned and buried it with a dozen torn dogs.

"The weight of the day's curse is in this," he said. "If we must be sure, we ought to go back and ask her. She looked like Maexsa."

"She felt like her," The O'Dancy said. "That's thin stuff, that white linen."

"One woman of a size feels like another," Dem said. "Hands are blind."

"The pelvic bones," The O'Dancy said. "A chalice of bright jewels. It was her, no doubt of it. The firemen took her out of my hands in a moment of limpid emptiness I've never known. I was in furious melt with only the feel of her. I must, but I must find out."

"Not this day," Dem said. "And if she was not Maexsa? Then?"

"This day, never tomorrow, I'll look both in the eye," The O'Dancy said. "Depend on it, the two are one."

"With utmost sensibility and delicacy, I approach another matter," Dem said. "The Lady Serena and the Lady Hilariana. I am also servant to them. And less, to the Lady Divininha, and Belisaria. And accountable. I have no wish to be beaten with thin sticks to the color of a ripened plum."

"It'll never happen again anywhere I am," The O'Dancy said. "My mother was part Tupinamba. I'm part of a part. I don't have the Indio habit of mind, either. My wife'll do as she's told. My children, too. When they want to make decisions of their own, they can leave The House. If that's understood, we've a clear way."

"Delicacy, once again," Dem again. "What's to be my attitude when the scandal becomes known? I say when, not if. I hear the tone in your voice, dear Master. I say scandal, because it cannot be hidden. The stigmata, even now, stains the air. The Lady Hilariana, for one, will not accept gossip. Nothing can be hidden. A word in the mouth of a Bahaiana today is two in the mouth of a Carioca tomorrow, and five in the mouth of a Paulistana the day after. Thousands of kilometers separate them, and every natural barrier. But a word has its own nuclear force. It kills as stupidly as lightning. Maexsa could harm the Lady Serena. The Lady Hilariana. Who is Maexsa?"

Dem turned farther into the room, but his bulk was fast in the narrow way, and it was more comfortable to sit back, and look past the fountain, and drop the panama on his knee.

"A drink of anything'd be a great treat at the moment," The O'Dancy said. "The river's crawling, and the fountain's only pretending. Not a pipe of clean, and not a potable drop from any spring."

"Cut a reed and drink the nectar," Dem said. "We could find a wild-bees' hive. A comb of thin honey is food and drink together."

"I'd give dearly to know who she is myself," The O'Dancy said. "She runs a bar? Does she own it or not's beside the point. Is she twenty? Not more than thirty-five, a box of gold on it. From her talk, she's schooled. Her way of English is superior to me own. That was no pleasant surprise, either. French and Italian. I've heard her."

"João spoke to her in Guaraní," Dem said. "He thought himself back in his village. Her mouth to me was truly aristo. Why does such a woman own a bar? Or supervise? Or herd female cattle?"

"In industry, she'd be an executive secretary," The O'Dancy said. "She'd earn a high salary. A tithing of what she earns in that club. Or bar. Or whoreshop. Whatever it is."

"For women," Dem said. "João followed that girl in. We followed him. You paid for how many dozen champagne? Then the girls began to undress each other. So? We were shown out. Diplomatically. With a machete? A little too immured in wine to know it."

"When I die, see to it I'm walled up in wine," The O'Dancy said. "There's a rare sound to it. Where was the place?"

Dem raised a lax balustrade of fingers, and set them on the panama.

"Augusta Street, somewhere," he said. "Those places all look the same to me. Where did we leave the truck? Which reminds me. The total loss will be paid by Clovis and João. That's what they were with us to do. Guard the truck. Does it matter if I was drunk?

Does it excuse them? Anyway. We came down Avenida Rio Branco."

"See the firemen," The O'Dancy said. "Ask where the fire was. Then we shall find that *iemanja*. We'll ask how a mother of the mysteries so cheapens herself. A bar for women?"

"The cult is for believers," Dem said. "Others work in laundries. Seamstresses. Housemaids. They all earn their daily bread, believing or not."

"A fine Hebrew custom," The O'Dancy said. "By the sweat of thy brow. Christ was all for the lilies of the field. I know little enough about these whisperers and screamers. But I sniff burning bones. That I do."

"They are not Hebrews, neither are they Christian," Dem said. "Their father is Exú. He carries the trident of Satan. Any saintly mother is his wife, and dam, and sister."

Dem twisted all the way around while the jamb creaked under strength, and he was looking up, and the man was running tears and no sound, not any.

"If these bones are yours that burn, dear Master, what then?" he said. "Shall we who are left, in turn, revengefully burn theirs? If a devil's hunger were to put a worm in your mind for the Mother Superior of the Sacred Heart, would you lay hands, break the beads and strip the habit? By prayer, or pay? Forgive me this thought. She has thighs. Pelvic bones. A chalice of bright jewels? Brighter than most, that no man ever saw, or handled, or ever will, except in the thorn brake of his mind, where a wisp of the beard might catch and blow, if she is unshaved, or shorter if she clips. Sacrilege? Blasphemy? Indecorous, certainly. But apart from mental maggots, the reverend woman is secure in her sanctity. Why not this mother *iemanja*? If mother *iemanja*, why not Maexsa? Bamboo, all of them. Dry tubes. Apparati. Does a dream grow in a stink of burning bones?"

"There's the gentleness," The O'Dancy said. "Dry tubes and stinks are in the minds of us, where else? What's outside's beyond, and untouched. It defies the thought, and all talk. It's the gentle, wanting woman. That's it. I'd pay anything. This life, or the other."

Dem had the place in a squeak and creak.

"I turn from imponderables," he said. "But I ask, what is to be my attitude to the Lady Serena? The Lady Hilariana? I can be silent, and so, half an enemy. I can speak against you, and so, a whole enemy. Or I am your champion, and so, their enemy. For a sow I could devaginate with thumb and finger?"

"That's no choice of mine for copulation," The O'Dancy said. "I once saw a fellow get into a goose. I'm not sure there was any great merit to it. Feathers and fleas are no just reward for the male effort, in my opinion. Asses, calves, goats, sheep, all the other primers, what are they? Butt of farm boys. Not in the same mind, or level of living. Yes. There's a small agony in thinking of Serena and Hilariana, is there not?"

"They should not be hurt," Dem said. "Nobody must be hurt."

"You love them," The O'Dancy said.

"No," Dem said. "I love my love for them. That's dearer. It would make me your enemy."

"God damn us all," The O'Dancy said. "I'd pay anything."

"I am your enemy," Dem said.

"Tomagatsu, you built this house only to cage the ugly flight of those words," The O'Dancy said, and looked up at the lines of the roof. "I wonder is there an uglier meld in any language? To save your poor feelings, you're my enemy?"

"Any help I must give you will be for their sake, because they would wish it," Dem said. "How could I agree to impossible conduct in one I respect? Or condone it to one I love? Not as I love my wife. As I love an early morning, or thirst before lime juice."

"Wait," The O'Dancy said, and stood, looking along the river. "Hold on, now. What's the movement near the bridge? Is the water on the rise, or has the land taken a turn?"

Dem kept his back to the jamb, dug in his heels, and pressed himself to stand, humped and rigid, looking between the fountain's froth and boughs of myrtle.

"A visitation," he said. "They chose this day. The day of the accursed. *Latrodectus mactans* has decided to migrate. I thought at first it was the fountain. But now, what do you hear?"

Spray fall held the quiet at arm's length.

There was, there was in surety, some other sound. Not a whisper or anything so gross. And not a breath of leaves. No patient sough of heavy boughs. Neither the wing whisp of passing birds, nor

scurryings of two legs or four, or rilling of water in wander, or
shift of duning sand. Not any other small song that an ear could
be turned to, and a word picked to put it in proper place.

Here was delicacy of millions in purpose of six-legged skitter,
with none to judge the purpose, or look inside the minds, or see
from so many eyes, or guide, or speak. Yet all followed the same
way. Somebody, ah yes, a Somebody there must surely have been
inside those skulls, a Somebody had to be thinking behind the
gloss of all those eyes, flamant in black fur, looking, and knowing,
aware of being guided, even of being spoken to, and speaking. No
reason why not. The way was direct, over from the island, across
the bridge, along the path to the house of Tomagatsu, and up the
slope to the hilltop, no pause, no hurry, no turning aside or about,
holding an exact front perhaps ten paces wide, close together,
closely followed behind, without space or gap, all the way down
to the riverbank, and all the way over the bridge, that, once the
eye was calm, heaved in its roadway, heaved black, heaved su-
surrously, heaved and moved, and the heaving was motion of
bodies, all obeying, all guided, and all, each one without exception, able to kill man or beast with any lick of a cogwheel tongue.

"Fancy that, you know, and on this, of all other mornings," The
O'Dancy said. "I expect we'll be safe enough in here, doors shut,
lattices down. But what of the two boys up there?"

"The column will go over us if they don't intend to swarm," Dem
said, white about the nose and chin, smoke-black in the eyes from
stifling fear. "No more movement than necessary. No sound. They
may take a day to pass. Or more."

He whistled, four fingers in his mouth, undulant blasts that
hummed in the timber, and João came to the edge of the hill holding the echoes in his arms.

"Come down," Dem sang. "Down, you and Clovis. Down, down.
Immediately."

João raised hands to his ears in a question.

Dem pointed to the island, swept to the bridge, and along the
riding path.

"The kiss of the unloved," he screeched. "The spiders are march-
ing."

"The black widow gratifies with a swollen, bulging kind of death," The O'Dancy said. "And not a tint of *uisce beatha* to pass an idle hour. Now, why wouldn't we stay at Giuseppe's? Or considering the day, anywhere else, at all?"

3   The cattlemen were barely in, fear-struck into jerks and blinks, and sobbing breath through dry rims, and Dem was quietly closing the door, and they heard Steb's voice, from heaven or the river was all one. Head-raised, they looked at each other, a moment of happy paralysis, hearing the dryish scrape getting louder, and The O'Dancy flipped the lattice catch on the river side.

"Would it not be like us, impoverished devils we are, to forget the water, the very stuff of life," he said, as it were, to himself. "There's Steb in the boat. Come, now, let's out of it, and praise a Blessed Man, not yet nailed up or dead Himself, and unwilling for us to go before."

He stood aside, helping the sweating cattlemen out first and then Dem, on one leg, and him sitting astride the sill, trying to stand on the foot outside, and the two of them pulling on his left arm to coax his fat beyond the frame, and The O'Dancy ramming him until he fell out in a soft, bouncy squelch, with the liquid in him splashing like water in a rubber bag. They upstood him, and dragged him to the low wall, and manhandled him over and down to the reeds, and Steb turned the boat stern on, and there was no trouble to it, at all, climbing in one after the other, The O'Dancy last, and himself getting never a sight of a single black thing.

"God be praised, and all the angels about Him," he said. "It was not, after all, anybody's burning bones I could smell. It was high scent of those ladies, that's half of them gents, was it not?"

"Spider smell," Dem said. "They must be destroyed."

"As good a day as any," The O'Dancy said. "Gasoline'll do it."

"We must call out the men," Dem said. "Two barrels and a pump to each truck. Mark their limits, spray and ignite them."

"Poor unsuspecting things," The O'Dancy said. "Doing no harm unless you get in their way. Will something bigger than myself

ever get the idea of igniting me? What's the Father of us all to
say about it, I wonder? Or does He squash us as we squash the
flies? Why do we have to kill everything, for God's sake? And
then live ourselves out? Kill ourselves with time. Why's it laid on
us?"

"Your father gave you health, and your mother made you a gift of
free will," Dem said. "I crawl to think of death by the black widow."

"Any death's enough for me," The O'Dancy said. "It's no pretty
matter."

"They must be eradicated," Dem said. "That island's been a
sanctuary of death for every animal and insect for the past five or
six years. Now they've conquered everything. So they turn to the
mainland. We may have to burn down Tomagatsu's house."

"Never," The O'Dancy said. "Never let it rest in your mind. I
give fair warning. Poison, and the house untouched, yes. Fire and
destruction, no."

"No poison will affect them," Dem said. "They're stronger than
any rat."

"Then they'll live, and so will the love of Tomagatsu," The
O'Dancy said. "When it touches principles, to hell with the death-
dealing."

The boat glistened unmarked, and the engine did no more than
make the soda in the glasses quiver and roughing the river's silk
only a little, but they were doing about ten miles an hour and
three hours would see them tied up at The House jetty, all healthy
Christians, and never a worry.

"Perhaps the Hanged One let us off all he'd plotted back there to
put us in something worse," The O'Dancy said. "Which reasonable
natural calamity would we ought to be looking out for? Or is it
the business of the faithful to seek not to know? I shall not want,
Thy rod, and etcetera."

"Master," Steb called from the wheel.

"Well," The O'Dancy called back, and saw himself, almost, in a
youngest son, O God, that took the heart of himself, yes, and
wrung, wrung, almost a pain, yet really not, but ever a great
pleasure to see, to be near, his own self in looks and, most said, by
nature, Stephen, it was, in the Other Language, and Estevão in

Portuguese, and Steb to everybody on The Inheritance and of course all the girls. "God love you, and myself, too, what then?"

"Hil-oh's working in the plant house," Steb said over his shoulder. "Sir, should we call on her and take her back for the midday meal or she'll have none?"

"Let's call for my only darleen, why would I not?" The O'Dancy said. "Why would the joy of my heart be working on this day, of all others? Is she so defiant? Of her father, God save him, and all else?"

"Defiant and dedicated both," Steb said. "The orchids are ready. Coffee's fit to bud. Bananas are in flame and waiting. Pineapple's in the burst. And she's been there day and night for the past three weeks. And she'll be there till she's rich in her mind that she's done all she ought. According to the way of her training, and the word of her dominie. And her own self's communing, which is all that matters, or has any substance. Plants wait for none."

In flower of the twenties, a physician of talent, so they all said, yes, with a mind in him it might have been thought for sure was a full forty years of age, and why not, considering his training under Brother Mihaul, an Associate of Jesuits, the second O'Dancy, own brother to The O'Dancy himself, by blood and exertion of dear Pater Cahir and the suffering Mam, and, in any case, a disparate one, a small gray-eyed importunate, but ever himself, steady right hand of the Father, the Lord God Almighty, and be careful, now.

"And how many slaves has she, working under the lash of her beauty, the Magi preserve her with royal gifts?" The O'Dancy asked. "Are they worth their salt, all of them?"

"Five more graduates last month," Dem said, looking at the groves in deep green glow on brick-red earth passing by. "Eighty-two men and sixteen women altogether. Twenty-three of the men work in the plant house. The others in the garden. Seven men and all the women work in the glass room with the Lady Hilariana. You pay for the most useful plant laboratory in South America, dear Master."

"If it's worth the money it's taken, all right," The O'Dancy said. "Knowing little, I say little."

"It fattens your Inheritance," Dem said. "Not one unhealthy plant."

"Talk to me loosely, then, of coffee or bananas or pineapples, or about any tree, or anywhere in the garden at all, and I'll be giving you a strong entertainment," The O'Dancy said. "But if it's about any of the marvels she's mysteriousing in there, well, I can't remember the names to start with. And I don't care what they do. I'm reminded of Grandfa Shaun, himself long in the love, going on a hundred and seeing that airplane. It was in his eyes. He could hear it. But take it in? 'Don't be discommoding me,' says he, and that's me and this plant business. Pay for it, yes, and pay the people, yes, but I'll never go near it. I'll not be discommoded."

Current came strong from everywhere, and Steb handled the boat like any ancient mariner and he had to, for there was little depth to the water and rocks big enough to found kingdoms on, all in a bubble and splash. The two cattlemen sat staring at the deck boards, and if the boat pitched even a foot out of true, just enough to take them from one cheek to the other, their eyes slid to the wheel, or to the little flagpole astern, and back to their toe tips, and you might almost hear their prayers to be away and on the back of any unbroken shaghoof ready to kick them free of any little brains they happened to have, rather than endure the dip and twist of a new boat, thrust in her way by a hundred-horse-power motor, with the new paint unscarred, all safe in the hands of as fine a fisherman-pilot as might ever be met in the entire Occident, that, yes, and useless at any other thing except his medicine and cutting people up.

"Where had you been on such a day?" The O'Dancy asked. "Did you not think you had a duty beside your mother?"

"They got back late so they were sleeping," Steb said without taking his eyes from the river. "I took home Yoshi and his sisters."

"You mean you took home Koioko, and the others went with you," The O'Dancy said. "And a nuisance from three sides of hell, they were, too. And you wished them back in the fourth, and Koioko and yourself alone on the water, and nothing between you and the dearest kiss of your life except your conscience, if you have any, which I doubt, Brother Mihaul and all his breviaries to the contrary. Isn't that the blessed way of it?"

Even by the back of Steb's head he was smiling.

"She'll wait for me, sir," he said without turning, and a breeze throwing the dear boy's voice ahead, that might have come down from another, ah, those years ago. "When I'm back with my degree, then we'll marry. Would you see her father, sir, and make it so?"

"You don't come first to ask me, I notice," The O'Dancy said. "Does your mother have nothing to say? Or is it all put together by the pair of you and to hell with us?"

"Ah, sir," Steb said, and almost turned. "Mãe gave her Grandam Xatina's ring and bracelet. There was no asking, there."

"Settled in the cradle," The O'Dancy said. "Well, the best you could have picked. From the best. Yes. I'll talk. I'll see she gets the right bit of property, too."

A voice came tiny over the water and Efram stood beyond the trees, waving his hat. Not a big man, but the best workman on The Inheritance, though impatient of learning the language and unable to supervise, woeful, misguided one, because, though the Brazilian boys were poor of goods and oftener barefoot than shod, they were all the richer in spirit and pride, and a loud voice and a threat of fists only made them laugh and turn away, careless. Thus, there stood Efram, unmarried, unloved, in blue cottons he washed and patched himself, sandaled and hatted in a width of straw, laughing gappy teeth to see the boat turn toward him, hopping from root to root to catch the rope, a good one in conscience, with love for the land and any animal, but little or none at all for his fellow men except those of place or property.

"Well, then," The O'Dancy called. "And why would you be working on such a day?"

"This day has no meaning," Efram said. "You make your own rules, you Catholics. We have the Law. We work until the seventh day, and then we rest."

"Very good," The O'Dancy said. "But was not Judas Iscariot himself a good enough Hebrew?"

"More a Roman, and so was your Jesus," Efram said, and tipped the boat with a jump on the gunwale to come aboard. "The pair of them of no worth to us."

"You'd speak so of the Son of God?" The O'Dancy said. "Have a great care now."

"Two thousand years of great care and many wars changed nothing," Efram said, and took a glass from Steb and nod-bowed his thanks. "Iscariot hanged himself. Christ had Himself crucified. What's the difference except that Iscariot made his own decision, and Christ let the Romans take all the blame? And the Romans shifted the blame to us. We have far more sympathy with Iscariot. At least, he admitted he made a mistake. He was honest. He hanged himself. In private. The other had to make a public show of it. He knew the value of suffering. It inspires pity. That's next door to sympathy. Throw in tears, and a miracle or two, and it's a business."

"Brother Mihaul, you should be here," The O'Dancy told the river. "This heretic deserves a fine, thick stake of seasoned timber."

"Destroy what you cannot remedy," Efram said, and raised the glass. "The O'Dancy Boys. The best man I ever met."

"Be listening to him, now, will you?" The O'Dancy said to his son. "It's a raise he's looking for. Himself, the anti-Christ."

"Not," Efram said. "Altogether too much energy to waste for a small matter. As to the raise? Again, no. What I want are a few more Japs. We should be ready to plant in ten days."

"Dem, see to it," The O'Dancy said. "Everybody has his own way of thinking, I suppose. I wish I knew why. Things are very plain to me. I wonder why they're not to others?"

"Perhaps a little time in Auschwitz made a difference," Efram said. "Where would you find such a place in this marvelous land? Where do you find here the people to create it? You never heard men praying to be dead. Or children screaming for their mothers already in the oven. Every day was Iscariot's day. Who forgets? Why should I? Millions in the bone yard. White lumber. Stacks of frozen feet. Should I mention this? Forgive me, it was an awakening. We have to be grateful. Have you carried dead children? They have doll's eyes. They stare. Ah yes. We were made a favor. We were made to know ourselves. The children of Jehovah had become footstools. A favor. By, of course, Christians."

"I listen against me will," The O'Dancy said. "It's like having to pass a place where there's a stink. You'd rather not breathe. But you must. Wouldn't you like a piece of land of your own, now? Isn't it time?"

Efram shook his gray crop-head.

"Two years more of saving, and I'll have enough to go to my own people," he said. "That's what I dream about. If I can grow coffee here, I can grow it there. And cotton. And grapes. And so many other things. I shall work with people I can talk to. Instead of these bean-eaters."

"Is there anything wrong with beans?" The O'Dancy asked.

"Forbidden," Efram said. "Pork, forbidden also. Blood meat, forbidden."

"Your life's cluttered with signboards," The O'Dancy said. "I'm not the one to envy you."

"As an emperor, why should you?" Efram said, and drank the lemonade in gulps-ulp-ulp-hmp. "But I shall soon speak in my own tongue to my own people. I shall have my own house, and a car. What more could I want? Only a Brazilian could be happier. And I cannot be."

"Yamoto and his team will be here tomorrow, with two tractors," Dem said, putting his pen away. "You tell them what to do. You'll have no trouble."

"I never have trouble with anybody except these bean-eaters," Efram said. "They don't deserve this country."

"I've a great fondness for a dish of beans myself," The O'Dancy said, watching a fine expanse of growing sugar cane. "Any variety at all, cooked well, there's nothing better. A slice or two of bacon, green or smoked, or a cut of ham, can you match them at the time of hunger? And as for the country, I don't doubt we'll come out of the right gate one of these days. When everybody that wants has gone back to wherever. Could I be lending you the money to go now?"

"I shall work two more years for the car," Efram said, and gave Clovis the glass. "I never borrow."

"Forbidden," The O'Dancy said.

"What I have is mine," Efram said. "Nobody can take it away."

"Nobody," The O'Dancy said. "But wait till you get to your people. They have taxes, there. You never paid a small coin's worth here."

"At least they pay for an efficient system," Efram said. "For roads, light, schools. These are still in the way of Africa. Sacrificing goats and chickens. Drinking hot blood. Worship of Satanas."

"Where at, was this?" The O'Dancy asked, and stood. "Be sure of your ground, now. Not on The Inheritance, for a start."

"On The Inheritance," Efram said, and pointed to a roof beyond the fig trees about a mile off. "There, in the house of Romulo. Singing and drumming all night. It's not the only *candomblé*. But it's the one that keeps me awake."

The O'Dancy looked at the top of Dem's head, downbent, trying to see across the trousers' bulge.

"What do you say to this, Mr. Overseer?" he asked. "Will I be sending Brother Mihaul on a bell, candle, and cross, here? How did it start? Why didn't I know?"

"People come in from the outside," Dem said, still looking down. "It doesn't last. I find out, and they go."

"They don't come, and they don't go, and Romulo was born here," Efram said, looking at Dem square in the averted forehead. "So were the rest. There's nobody from the outside. You're rotted with *macumba*. Don't argue. Or pretend I'm wrong. Don't blame me for telling you something you've known all your life. Twice a week, here. Other nights, other places. All your own people. They can't work in the mornings? Naturally. I don't get on with them? Of course not. I don't want to speak to them? No. Why? They are of the devil. Satanas. That's why. Good day, best friend. Come and see what I shall do with those Japanese. Clean people. Decent. Strong. With them I speak very well."

"Go with God," The O'Dancy said, and nodded to Steb. "Up to the plant house."

Dem stuck his heels in while the boat turned, and the city shoes with the pointed toes and fancy stitching gave him an air of untrustworthiness, as if the fancy business down below, chosen with care and paid for with careful money, might be repeated elsewhere in his character and in everything he did.

"You never told me about any *macumba* here," The O'Dancy said.

"There has always been *macumba*," Dem said, and looked sideways at Clovis and João, and they nodded without a look anywhere at all. "It's in the people. The families also go to church."

"Church is proper," The O'Dancy said. "*Macumba* in any form is for the devil's own. There, Efram was right."

"No, dear Master," Dem said gently, with a smile. "There is more of the devil in any church than with the true *macumba*. We cast out the devils."

"We," The O'Dancy said.

"We," Dem said, and sat up, hiding the shoes. "Why should I deny it? You'll find out, after this. I may just as well tell you. Most of us on The Inheritance, we are part of *Umbanda*. It is stronger than the Church."

"No more," The O'Dancy said. "On such a day I'll not discuss it. I'll take it up with Brother Mihaul."

Dem laughed huh! in the air, all his teeth shown and closed eyes, and bent his head, laughter gone. But the other two shook in the shoulders, faces hidden under cattlemen's hats.

"Brother Mihaul'll want to know what's comical about him," The O'Dancy said. "I never found a single smile, or my father before me."

"My better side is ruined with drink," Dem said. "I'm sleepy. And the spiders talk to me. How should we deal with them?"

"Hilariana can tell you," Steb said without turning at the wheel, and such a clear, steady voice, yes, with authority, that strong gift. "She's been catching them. They do no harm if they're allowed to be."

"Neither do I," The O'Dancy said. "But if I'm not allowed to be? What, then?"

"There're two opinions, and a fight," Steb said. "They don't compromise. They're not diplomatists. They can't put a case. Or argue. Or go barging into oratory. They do as they were intended."

"By whom?" The O'Dancy asked.

"By God Almighty," his youngest son said, in his wisdom.

"No comfortable idea," The O'Dancy said. "He has His bad ideas, too. Or why would they frighten the cold air into my heartbeats?"

"Your conception, not God's, that's plain enough," Steb said. "They live and die, and so do you. Keep out of their way, they'll keep out of yours."

"At the moment they're filling the tombs," The O'Dancy said. "How will I sleep well, knowing it?"

"They've good shelter and traditional hospitality," Steb said. "Why should they complain? Would you want to occupy their place for any reason?"

"Be damned," The O'Dancy said, and spat a frothy circle into green water. "I'm sorry to think of the First Men bothered."

"They were here before the First Men," Steb said. "They are part of The Inheritance. I'd never permit them to be touched unless they threatened other animals. Then I'd divert, not kill."

"I like your thought, boy," The O'Dancy said. "Bad ideas have a place with the good? Demonstrably true. Without one, would there be the other? Debatable. Wake me when we get there."

The O'Dancy lay down on the rubber seat with his ankles on the gunwale, and tipped his hat and pretended to sleep, but he, Arquimed, yes, himself, no less, was horrified, was appalled, and the others, seen in a fog of half-closed lids, himself was aware, readied their senses for life to collapse about them.

Macumba on The Inheritance, dear Redeemer of the Thorns and Bloody Nails, could only mean that himself, not anybody else, had failed the First Men, and the Faith was not merely in question, not only in jeopardy, but wrenched by brutes—oh silently! —out of place.

Anti-Christ, a word at any time before, a joke, at any rate among certain minds, a spurious thought without any substance, was real, was near, was part of himself in fact with the grains of sand, with the leaves, with all he owned.

"Sir," Steb called, and The O'Dancy sat up. "Isn't it Jair in that truck? Bring him over here, you'll be there the quicker."

He flashed the red light, and here the truck came, bouncing off the track and over the short pasture, among the anthills, sending the cows in a prance. Clovis daintied like an acrobat testing a worn rope, watching the prow move toward the gravel. Four of them helped Dem off, but his weight pulled them all to their knees in a shout, though he was on top, a clothed octopus and laughing, yet in the time it took for him to offer a hand to The O'Dancy, his eyes were ringed in fright and his mouth was a small o.

"Jair is cut," he said. "Quinto's in the back. Cut?"

"Three of us," Jair said, with the truck door open. "Two came in from Mouras Bentos last night. They sat up, with wine, playing dominoes. They lost. They drew their knives. They never put them back."

"Dead," The O'Dancy said. "Would you not know it, on such a damned and bedamned and thrice-damned day? And how was it taken by the Lady Serena?"

"She knows nothing," Jair said. "It was all in the men's lodging."

"Did Brother Mihaul give them a shriving?" The O'Dancy asked.

"It was late for that," Jair said. "Besides, he was not there, or in his house. The Lady Hilariana attended us. If we live, we shall put our lives on the ground in front of her angel feet."

"How was she there?" The O'Dancy asked.

"By telephone, dear Master," Jair said. "There was so much blood."

"It frightened you," The O'Dancy said.

Jair nodded.

"How did three take two?" Clovis asked.

"They cut Jacinto, first," Jair said. "I came in with Quinto. They cut us. But I shouted. Julião came in. He slit them both."

"No harm to him," The O'Dancy said.

"Not a scratch," Jair said, pulling at a shoulder. "This aches. He settled them well."

"Over dominoes," The O'Dancy said, waiting for Dem to be pushed up in the back.

"There were other matters," Jair said, and used one arm to pull himself over the side.

"Women, of course," The O'Dancy said, before he closed the door.

"I came in at the end of the discussion," Jair shouted. "So did Quinto."

The O'Dancy nodded to Clovis, and the truck bumped over pasture, and among the anthills, and again the cows pranced. Twenty thousand head of Charolais, zebu, black Angus, and Holstein gave meat, hide, tallow, milk and butter, and the far more important manure for the groves, and from any hill the five-kilometer grass squares made equal checks with the greens of coffee, cotton, citrus, cane, pineapple, and banana.

"Who were these two from Mouras Bentos?" The O'Dancy asked. "A dirty village I've left only horse droppings in. What are they doing all night in the lodging?"

Clovis shook his head. There was still plenty of drink in the man, but he knew enough about a wheel to drive, and though the truck had fifty times more movement than the boat, all four wheels were on the ground, and he was comfortable.

"I must say what I would rather crush under my teeth," he said. "The two men last night? The dead ones? They came for the *candomblé.*"

"Have no fear," The O'Dancy said. "I'd guessed at it. Why would they come?"

"One of them made sacrifice of the animals," Clovis said, steering for a white post where the wire fencing could be dropped to pass through. "Goats, dogs, chickens. The other one was saintly father."

"You're assaulting my ears," The O'Dancy said. "The man's dead. His saintliness has been in question for some hours, all glory to the Judge."

"His spirit will be among us," Clovis said, and stopped the truck in spacious silence. "Now, or soon, or perhaps in years. But his spirit will come. Julião. What will happen to Julião?"

"First thing is a little present of three months' wages," The O'Dancy said. "If I find he made it one clean thrust each, I'll make it six months'. If he opened the tripes of them crosswise, in the old tradition, he'll get a year's wages on the spot."

"We shall have to watch the animals," Clovis said. "They've always first to show The Touch."

"Open the wire and close your mouth," The O'Dancy said. "We've veterinarians to attend anything on four legs."

Clovis looked as if he had plenty more to say, and he walked half sideways toward the fence as though he would shout, but then he might have caught a sign from someone in the truck and he nodded, and turned, pulling at the wire fastening.

The O'Dancy looked through the cabin window. Dem was standing up, a hand on João's shoulder, holding a forefinger toward

Clovis and frowning a command that should have been a shout.

"Would you believe it?" The O'Dancy said through the glass. "I never found the smallest deceit in you. And on this day of days, am I finding anything else?"

Dem took off the panama with both hands and held it over the sash because his arms reached no farther, and leaned against the bags, a penitent, from the tears in his eyes, well on the way to purgatory.

"Only on such a day I'd expect to hear it," he said. "With to-morrow's sun, a cleaner day, and a better thought."

"I can wait," The O'Dancy said. "Where was Jair going with this truck?"

"Taking back beans and rice," Dem said. "For the funeral guests."

"Buried at my expense, of course," The O'Dancy called before Clovis slammed the door.

"Dear Master," Dem said. "There is tradition in other things, besides the use of the knife."

The O'Dancy sighed a deep one, down in the dark crypt of himself.

"The plant house," he told Clovis. "The cure for some of this is in Hilariana's smile, God have an arm about her."

4 Down, deep, in the dark crypt of himself, where the priestly voices hummed, and a host of naked women danced for none other, and dreamed with him when he desired, and populations unseen were obedient, and enemies died, and friends were lauded, and selfishness spun gross filaments to hide the Altar, and duty was never in balance with what he had a mind to do, and love was perfume of the unknown Eve, or only a shouted word, there The O'Dancy met the self he knew was ever part, seldom seen, and then horrid, unheard except at times, and then hated, there, where the shadows wept, they met.

Not face to face, or at distance, or in comfort of words.

The two became one, and truthful.

Too much property, and power over small people and misusing both, never mind the work of later years, that, yes, and he would never get away from his voice, the accuser, even if the denier had many a fine argument. But if he had to go through it again, he was unsure if, or how, he would change his ways. Grandfa Shaun, himself, in the old coach, sounding as if what he was saying came from the squeak of leather, cursing Uncle Bohun for going off to travel the world instead of working for what he spent, well, yes, unknown and unheeded at the time, there was a lesson of sorts.

"The man has his work here, and work he will or he'll get no share of mine," the voice said, out of the shadows. "For why would the man go away to see what's to be seen, so he said, a stable of curses on him, and my own brother? Shall I work in my hundredth year, and him spending it? That I'll not. He shan't have two red pence of me. You get your travels done early, as I did. Didn't I go to Rio de Janeiro, and meet all those fine black bitches there? I did. Did I not go to the old country and think little of it, except for Dublin, and drunk for a month on stout and whisky, and a fine flaming red-haired one. If I haven't forgotten her name, now, but does it matter? Well, then, London, a top-hat city, and the lights, but a cold lot. Paris, yes, I went a dozen times there. Was anybody not in that bedroom? Have you never felt a woman's breasts in a bath full of champagne? You'll be an O'Dancy when you do. I'll willingly pay for that. But that Bohun, great Christ in the Sepulcher, what right's he to go off, throwing money about, him only a couple of better legs younger than my own self?"

Uncle Bohun had been dead for twenty years at the time, but it seemed useless to say so, though when the will was read, Grandfa Shaun had left out Bohun's family, and though everybody helped, it was never what it should have been, and Aunt Gloria drank three bottles a day and died in a hut.

A boy was not to know the end of that, but it was a lesson of sorts, though if he ever learned it, or did anything with it, there was no real evidence, and Mr. Claypole was a fine example, yet if the man had listened, it might have been different. The Tad and he, sitting in the Dark Room, with the glasses shining in the lamp, and Mr. Claypole talking about the DaSouza coffee and the price in reis against gold sovereigns, and himself coming from behind The Tad's shoulder and saying the coffee was not worth the bags it was put in.

"Shut up," Mr. Claypole said, looking into his glass.

"Outside," The Tad said, and the strap whipping in the voice of him, God rest him.

"Sir," himself was saying, and looking at Mr. Claypole's red face and shiny, pitted nose, and the long beard. "But didn't I hear Silva telling Tomi?"

As far as he got, for the hand caught him a spinner.

"Outside, and let me never hear you call Mr. Tomagatsu anything else except his name," The Tad's voice was saying, even now. "What Mr. Claypole's going to make of us I'll never know."

"All the same at that age," Mr. Claypole said, and drank the tumbler dry, yes, dry, to the drop, and breathing in—hear it now —with a catch in the breath of him. "Bloody nuisance till they're twenty-one, then they go mad. I've got a pair of them."

He also got a bad bargain with the coffee, though had he asked the right question, he might have been told that Silva found the beans musty, and a dangerous buy, and so it was proved, and Mr.

Claypole never came again, and The Tad never got paid a single real for his own crop, either.

"Should have told me," The Tad said.

"You knock the child's head off," The Mam said in no great humor. "Why should he open his mouth? To be killed?"

"Come, now," The Tad said. "A push?"

"Push," The Mam said. "I know your pushes."

"Thank God," The Tad said. "Will I be having another cup of your exceptional tea, then? Speak your mind, boy. Always say what you have to."

"Watch the push," The Mam said.

Was it The Push that made him a hypocrite, never to say what was in his mind, except after, when it was too late, or was it, as Brother Mihaul said, plain good nature and not wanting to hurt? Ah yes, but the two were different, for one was cowardly and he knew which one. This business of the *candomblé*, now, and *macumba*, and *khimbanda*, of course he knew about them, and spoke of them, and listened to others, though never seriously, but casually, in the way people might be chatting of bad habits. There was no profit in such talk, and nobody ever had any good of it, so any knowledge was mere smatter, and the subject came up to be dismissed in the moment.

In truth, it was of the Devil.

Listen, now, at the shadows, weeping for the spent, the useless years.

If he remembered a day, it was when The Tad was buried, and The Mam with him, the day himself became The O'Dancy, and old Mr. Carvalhos Ramos read a long paper from beginning to end, with everybody in the family standing about, and so much sniffling that half he said was never heard. But he was a fine man, long in the love and rest his soul, and he had a duty to a small fellow suddenly knifed into an empire, and well he carried his cargo.

"The boy will go to school in Europe," Uncle Kiernan said. "We'll look to the place."

"The O'Dancy will go to school in his own country," Mr. Carvalhos Ramos said, and put his spectacles with grace and care into the case, and closed the lid—whap!—and looked up at Uncle Kiernan—one of the exemplary drunkards of all time and unsteady at any time, especially then, after two days and nights at the barrel—and there was no smile about him, or any kindness, but only the hard, *brasileiro* stare. "If you were listening while I was reading, you must have understood that I was made sole executor until the boy is a man. He will be tutored here, and he will go to school here, and when he finishes school he may choose his university. It will be his choice. Until then, he and his property are in my charge."

"And you'll make a fine thing of it," Uncle Kiernan said. "Will he ever see a whole coin?"

"Outside," The O'Dancy said. "You and your family, out. Come back sober, and beg the pardon of Mr. Carvalhos Ramos."

The Tad had said it to Simeon, out in the men's lodging not long before, and it was simple to copy the tone.

Mr. Carvalhos Ramos sat back with his finger tips together, and smiled at the inkwell, but everybody else seemed to say Oh! and then laugh. All the women perfumed him with arms and kisses, and the men shook his hand or patted his shoulder and said he was a chip off the old block, or a colt from the same stable, or some other prattling stuff. The Kiernans got into their Ford and never came near the place again, perhaps because they moved to Paraguay, but nobody ever heard a word, except when young Kiernan, the only son, was killed in 1940 with the Royal Air Force and there was a bit in the paper, but the family seemed to have died with him, for his sisters married out.

"That's how the true blood goes," Father Miklos said, a severe, hectoring man at the time. "And these about us, they breed fifteen or twenty, and ten live, an incubus to themselves and everybody else. You oughtn't to have said what you did. You were talking to kin, not servants."

"He spoke as a man," Mr. Carvalhos Ramos said. "The other took offense. It was his choice. By his silence and departure, he concurred with The O'Dancy. I wish I were executor for many more like him."

"Speak in those terms in front of him, and nobody will ever have a chance," Father Miklos said. "An opinionated little humbug will grow up to be an impossible mule."

"The more trouble for you, eh, Father?" Mr. Carvalhos Ramos said, and laughed. "I'll make you a promise. The moment I find the humbug, I'll tell you. But he's The O'Dancy. You'll never find a grain of it in him."

"A monster," Father Miklos said. "We shall have to choose the school."

They chose five in all, and they were wrong each time. The first, two months, and out, for bringing one of the local maids into the dormitory, to do nothing wrong, but only to sing for them, though nobody else seemed to understand that, and he remembered looking at them, and wondering. The second, five months and out, for going off to the carnival at Rio de Janeiro, staying away eleven days and bringing a troop of boys and girls back with him, and all of them drunk on sugar cane. The third was a little better, but only a little, of two years, and out, for going off in a sailboat with a couple of friends, and finding their way down the Amazon, almost to Manaus with the entire police and armed forces looking for them. That might have been smoothed over, except that one friend was a girl, and when the police took her back, her father had a stroke and died there and then, and poor Sonia had to be put away. The fourth was a real prison of a military school, but he did well, and even liked the discipline, though the end came at a sports meet, and he went off with a band of drums and maracas for a couple of weeks, and, instead of getting himself found, went home, and done with it.

The shadows were starting to weep, even then.

The Tad was not there to push, or hit him the spinners, and The Mam, God save her loveliness, was only blind eyes and tasteless water whenever he thought of her.

But if everybody else minded, Mr. Carvalhos Ramos never did.

"You'll never be a common one, or a European," he said that time. "You were born The O'Dancy, and *brasileiro*, and as long as you're able to speak and act intelligently, and write a legible hand, that's all. Your duty and your life are on your inheritance. If you take care of that, and leave it in finer blossom than your forebears, well and good. Not all of us are giants. Some of us pray to be merely human, sensible, of wholesome instinct. Remember, you are The O'Dancy."

All that time Tomagatsu controlled the work and the harvests. Dem was bagging coffee, or manuring the groves, or cutting cane, or clearing ground, or loading banana carts, or carrying pineapples. Everybody did something to bring in the money, or brighten The Inheritance, even the Indios, who did only a couple of days' work and got drunk for the next three on their pay.

Only he fed, and drank, and thought the idiocies without stint or any control.

He was The O'Dancy, was told so, and treated so, and knew himself so, and that was all.

Perhaps the women of The House were just as much to blame, though "blame" seemed a silly word. He was the fondling of their lives. Never could he walk by any one of them without a hug and a kiss, till the soft roll of unbound breasts and whispered, fierce joy of the female, herself not long from the jungle, became a passing thing, expected, taken, forgotten till the next. But he was growing, and they knew it, and they watched him, and fondled—ah, motherly, every one of them!—until the morning he was felt to be a male by Creonice, herself about twenty-five or so at the time, a tall strapper of a girl, and there, on the turn of the stairs, she put him into her and he thought the top of his head was off. He fell in love with her, if that was never the stupidest euphemism in any language, and night after night, she tiptoed into his room, and taught him all there was to know, and she kept him to herself, wise girl, because every woman waited to fill herself with The O'Dancy's baby, not to be married or any such fantasy, but to be part of The House forevermore, with her own space, and the child, boy or girl, growing up on The Inheritance as all the others had, with the jobs always ready for them, more money than anybody else, and all the food and clothes they could ever want. There was worth, and ease lifelong for the mother of an O'Dancy child.

Then the morning when Tomagatsu looked at him, once, across the sorting table, over the sliding mounds of beans.

Once.

Never before had anybody looked at him through the bone of his skull, through all adulation and nonsense, piercing, destroying, and yet affectionate, and gentle, though the beans never stopped in the slide, and the hands were just as quick to throw out the rejects.

That night he was put in another room, and a man slept outside the door. Next morning Mr. Carvalhos Ramos and Father Miklos took him into São Paulo to the O'Dancy House, and there he stayed with the same bodyguard and two menservants, but no women.

Nobody said a word and he asked no question, but he thought himself being punished. A few days after, Mr. Carvalhos Ramos came in with three men, one to teach mathematics and general science, a second to take him through history and geography, and the third in the arts, all of them to be off on the two-o'clock train to Rio de Janeiro, with the menservants. In mathematics he went as far as learning to calculate how many of various sized bags will go into this, that, or the other type of truck, and he never forgot. In history, he remembered that the Dutchmen should have owned Brazil and that King Pedro of Portugal had once been their emperor, and that it took the weight of three armies, their own, Argentina's, and Uruguay's many a year to defeat tiny, mighty Paraguay, which disgusted him, and he wanted no more of history. In the arts, he went on a traipse about the museums and galleries with Mr. Corriss, the only one he remembered, because the man spoke his mind.

"I'm doing this for the fee because I want to get on a boat and go home," he said one morning in the heat of the picture gallery, where even the nudes seemed to be sweating. "If you'll be taking my advice you'll leave one ear open and listen to half I tell you, because if you get an exam, and you don't have enough marks to keep me in the job, I'll knock your brains out. That's till I've enough to get on the boat."

"And after that, what?" himself asked, all blithe.

"You may all go and shit in your hats," Mr. Corriss said.

Himself had thought it worth translating for the benefit of Sergio, The Tad's manservant, at that time looking after him, yes, but Sergio must have thought differently and told Mr. Carvalhos Ramos on his monthly visit.

Mr. Corriss left with the other two, and none of them said good-by, and himself had often wondered since if the man ever got on the boat, but the odds were against, because Sergio said enough liquid had been in the empty bottles found in his room to float one.

Shadows wept for others, too.

Mr. Corriss, with the snuff stuck like cinnamon in his nostrils, and the smell of a sweet cachou trying to hide the liquor on his breath, scratching the fair fringe of beard and looking sideways at a Boudin, whether he knew it or not, had left a few marks that lasted.

"Here's one of the masters of space, dimension, and color," he said. "He even seems to be able to draw the light in sea air. When they can't draw, pay no attention to anything else they do. The pencil's more important than all the color. The rest is art critics' flummery."

He met Morenne, yes, on the morning he was first allowed on the beach by himself. He saw her under the shade of a pink tent the housemen were putting up, in a costume frilled below the knees and at the neck, with long sleeves, and a mobcap over her eyes, all of linen, and pink, her favorite color, and as a banana skin shows the exact shape of all within, her body proclaimed a marvel of glowing gold in glitter of sea drops. She stood with her face in the sun, and sent away the men in a flick of fingers, and he watched her for moments, looking at noded breasts outlined in wet cloth, at the shadowed navel, at the hips, at the mount of Venus, until she opened her eyes and saw him a few paces away.

Perhaps even then, unknowing, down where the small shadows wept, he began to curse Creonice. He knew too much and understood too little. He had to look at himself to find out what he felt, or thought. All women were not Creonice, that was certain. He could look at any thousand walking by and no memory was touched. But if any woman had Creonice's color, or hair, or smile, or movement of arms, legs, thighs, then he felt the heat in his eyes, and the swelling filled his mind, and there was nothing to think about except her, or anybody like her, and going into her.

Morenne was about the same age as Creonice, had the same strapping marvel of a body, and most of the color, and the shape of her mouth when she laughed was truly Creonice. But by her eyes as she looked at him, he knew she was not the one to put him into her. No warmth or heed of him was there, but amusement, because Sergio had lent him bathing drawers that almost reached his ankles, and the waist was corded, with most of the cloth bunched over the binding.

They were alone. The housemen had gone between the gardens, beyond the beach. A few tiny people walked down near the coffee bar, a few farther off the other way. White sand, too bright to look at without wrinkled eyes, sun almost overhead, and the ocean rising in a green curving, froth-topped wall that fell, shaking the sand, and another following at about the time it took to breathe, and he standing without a move, looking at her, pink and deep gold against white sand and a mauve sky.

She told him afterward that nobody had ever looked at her like that, and at once he thought of Tomagatsu, and knew he had borrowed a certain way of judging by knowledge, though what knowledge he had, at the time, was confined to Creonice.

"Why do you look at me?" she said. "Go away."

"I am The O'Dancy," he said. "I go when I choose."

The white skin, dark red hair blown in sea drift, and the voice of one used to ordering, she told him, as well as a strange name and an indefinable accent, brought her to smile instead of telling him she would scream for the housemen.

"I wish you'd choose now," she said. "I want to change this costume."

"You're beautiful, so," he said. "Without it, there'll be no word."

She turned her head until she looked at him from the corners of her eyes.

"You're only a little boy," she said. "Where did you learn to talk like that?"

"In my own place," he said. "And I'm no little boy."

He pulled the knot of the cord, and the drawers fell and he walked toward her. She crossed her hands over the frills at her throat, though no fear was in her, for there was no threat in his eyes or in his manner, but only in the shock of the nude male, and she had to smile.

"I must have been mad," she told him after.

"But why?" he said. "I wanted to be in you. The moment I saw you smile, I knew I could."

"I was frightened to death somebody would see us," she said.

"Somebody," he said. "We're afraid of God-knows-what for the same reason. We're forever off in some corner or other. But we were there in the sun. I'll love you till I die."

She always put his head on her shoulder because she was never far from feeling protective, but he hated it because he always thought of The Mam. Creonice had been altogether different. Once she found him capable, then she savaged. But not Morenne. She would never touch him except to kiss, and then only fondly, shortly, on the cheek. He did as he pleased, and she seemed a stone until he heard the deeper breath and kissed an open mouth, and her thighs moved, and quivered and she whispered as though in a faint, and her arms tightened and then fell, but her body shook for moments, and she was crying, though Creonice never had.

The first Sunday he raced back from church, but he was too late. Towels and mats in the tent were still damp, and there was a bottle half full of mineral water, which he drank with greater fervor than he had the wine at Mass, hungry for her, pleading for her, making sounds in his throat like a whimpering dog, fitting his body into the sand where she had lain, trying to feel where her thighs might have been, imagining the buttons coming undone, the linen whispering over her breasts, the soft of her nipples between his lips, the taste of salt for a moment, and then the taste of her, which he had never forgotten. But half in his madness, he saw Sergio looking at him, an eye around the flap of the tent, and knew himself called to lunch with Father Miklos and Mr. Carvalhos Ramos.

For a week after he wandered the beach and never saw her or the houseman, but the tent was there, and even sitting in its shadow was salve of a sort, though he ached in the throat, denied any food or drink, sat up long after midnight had struck, thinking of nothing, dreaming of nothing, except her, until he slept.

Sergio took no notice, but Mr. Carvalhos Ramos came twice that week to take him to the polo matches, and Father Miklos went with him to see a man fly a wooden insect he called an airplane. But nothing put Morenne from his thoughts for long. He told nobody. He could remember no questions.

Early on Monday, under a sun still clouded, he saw her turn a corner, a straw hat, a mauve costume, and he ran, ran, ran, ran. She put up a hand to stop him, but she might just as well have ordered the heavens to be less cloudy. He caught her, sobbing, dry, and fell to his knees, arms about her, feeling the muscle hard under satin beneath the linen drawers. She raised him by his knot of hair and looked back.

"Don't you ever think of other people?" she whispered, eyes wide, wet, smiling, frightened, breathless, and yet content. "Couldn't you have waited there for me? Don't you imagine people might see us?"

"I waited a week of fifty years," he said. "To hell with people."

"You're The O'Dancy," she said, and took his hand to walk. "I've heard about you."

"Come on," he said. "Run. Where have you been?"

"Home," she said. "I told everybody about you. A lot of people knew who you were."

"As long as you do," he said, and led her into the shadow of the tent, but she put him away.

"Morais is coming with towels and mats," she said. "We'll swim, and then he'll have gone."

"Morais is a loutish nuisance," he said, feeling for the buttons, but they were changed. "What's here, now?"

She laughed and kissed his cheek and ran for the water, throwing off the straw, kicking away slippers, and into the foam, and they swam in the quiet pools, or dived through curving, glistening walls, and lost each other, and went up in a mounting wave to look into a trough, diving to catch a hand, an ankle, until she tired, and crawled out on the sand and the maid came down with a robe and towel and said it was time to go. Morenne pitied him with her eyes, and smiled, patting herself over the robe, which maddened, which he never forgot.

"It was pleasant to meet you again," she said in a voice toned for a servant to hear. "Perhaps I shall be down again tomorrow. Until then?"

He could say nothing in front of a servant. That, at least, he knew.

"I shall accompany you to your residence," he said.

"It will not be necessary," she said, and turned. "My father has provided an escort, as you see."

He bowed—he remembered the movement of his head, as if his

neck might break—let her go, and watched her to the edge of the beach, and followed to the turning between the gardens, and she waved, and he held up both arms. He saw where she was staying, and waited, and she waved from a window on the second floor. That night he bought an armful of carnations and tied them about his shoulders like a cape, and climbed up the low wall, onto a terrace, up the cornice, and spread-eagled along the wall to the window, and over the balcony, in. A long room, not wide, a bed big enough for a family, with blue silk valances, blue carpets, a screen, and a toilet stand, table of crystal. He put the carnations on the floor beside the bed, and listened to a maid talking to somebody in the next room.

"In the big basket," she said, louder, and a light became brighter under the door. "We'll have no time to pick and choose."

He walked behind the screen and pulled the leaf closer, and the door swung, and candlelight bobbed over the ceiling of grapes and small angels. Bed linen whispered. She hummed a song he knew, pillows were slapped, stroked, sheets were folded over.

"Everything in here, too," she called out, a good-humored voice bubbling with crunched sugar.

"Why not now?" the woman shouted from another room. "Save time. He won't come back tonight."

"By the Sacred Cross, he'd flog us blind," the maid said, and laughed. "It stays till five. If he's not back then, we pack. Doesn't take long, with Morais to help."

Sugar crunched, a tooth was sucked, light bobbed, the floor creaked, and the door closed.

He sniffed the air near the table of crystal bottles.

Nothing there reminded of Morenne. He was sure he was in the right house. He walked to the door, opened it slowly, and looked along the corridor. A doorway showed candlelight. He walked there, on the rugs, and looked in, to a woman's room in white and pink. The maid he knew. She knew him, great-eyed, openmouthed, drawing breath to scream, but he held out money.

"Tell me where she is," he whispered.

"Gone," she mouthed, and pointed below.

"Where," he asked, and she took the money.

"Recife," she said, more with lips than voice. "Go. Three house guards downstairs. Go."

Her face and the extravagant fear of her fingers miming death for both of them earned her the rest of the money. He could hardly be responsible for the punishment of a maid. He looked at the stripped bed, half-full traveling chests, flowers dying in pots and vases, sniffed the faint sweet he knew, that tore his throat, blurred the light to glitter of diamonds, and nodded, and walked back to the balcony, over, spread-eagled, to the cornice and climbed down, and carnations pelted him as he passed, and the dark shape of the maid flung out the few more, and she went in, slammed the shutters, and the street became an open grave of silence, loss, misery. He walked, thinking of dark hair, thighs that felt like a satin bowl, eyes that pitied, the pleading voice, ardent, frightened, ah yes, Morenne. Perhaps it was those hours with an absent woman, that vigil for love recalled, through the lanes of the city among the stalls and the squatting basket vendors, in blue gas jets and flares and candles, in the long night when he knelt before the shrine in armor, resting on the shield, perhaps then, yes, the crypt within himself was opened, and memory piled the first dry leaves to whisper dun regret.

5 "But, you know, if it's to be marriage, you must think very well about it," Mr. Carvalhos Ramos said, in the white shirt, laced at the collar, and cuffs. "Your father was a year older when he married. You were a long time arriving. He never regretted his marriage. Now, listen to me. Do you want to marry this girl if I find her?"

"Yes," himself had said simply, yes, ah yes, and no time lost.

"Very well," Mr. Carvalhos Ramos said. "We shall discover who she is and what property we may expect with the contract. You have, you know, many a sweet pluck under your hand. Daurina Oliveira de Santos, for example. She's two years older than you, which could be an advantage for the next twenty years, and she'll bring the whole of the south side of the river. All the rice, cotton, and coffee."

"Morenne," himself had said, and he remembered how he had said it. "Only Morenne."

"You know your mind," Mr. Carvalhos Ramos said. "Meantime, you will attend the office of Mr. Heitor Delmonico from eight o'clock tomorrow morning. You will learn the fundamentals of shipping freight all over the world. You will stay in Santos at the house of Mr. Leandro da Cunha, his general manager, and Sergio will look after you. Do well."

The roof of the long shed on the wharf at Santos still shimmered silver to think of it, and his face still burned in the heat under it, and his shirt stuck to his body in the main office, and a fan cooled in the private office, and in Mr. Delmonico's office, and in the coffee parlor, and the countinghouse, and in Mr. da Cunha's room, stacked with lading bills that always felt hot to the knuckles. Himself had a table in the main office, next to Miss Kazakian's desk, that rocked when she typed, until he balanced all the legs with cut cork and she smiled, and surprised him, for it was no custom of hers.

She was first to teach him that all women are not the same, that a smile is not an invitation, that stupidity leads inexorably to regret. Miss Kazakian must have been one of the first women to learn how to use a typewriter, one of the very few women working among the dockside staff, and plainly of great courage, because every morning she walked, white blouse and long skirt, white veil over white hat, through thousands of half-naked stevedores, any one of them able to break her spine with one hand, and, by her attitude alone, inhibit remarks, gestures, certainly those incidents which the smallest familiarity could have provoked. Only once did a man shout a remark, and he was so quickly kicked into a pulp that the police were never able to find out who he had been. The stevedores, too, had their pride.

Himself knew the proper course of conduct well enough by her manner, strict, scrupulous, and serene. She was industrious, eight in the morning till eight at night, and worth any three of the men, as Mr. da Cunha said. She controlled the entire business of consular and legal inquiries, and all the documents up to signature by agents, masters of ships, and the company. Her desk in the main office was for the typing work, and the entire shed shook when she used the machine the way it would be if cattle went on a gallop outside. She had another desk, in Mr. Delmonico's office, where the documents were checked and stamped, and another in the countinghouse. There was nowhere to go without seeing Miss Kazakian, or hearing the starch of her petticoats talking in whispers as she walked in laced boots, arms always burdened with documents held at the level of her belted waist, slightly away from the high-collared white blouse, head up, eyes always half closed, always looking down to step over uneven boards, brown hair, reddish in sunlight, piled on top of her head and pinned, generally with an orchid that she grew in tins along the shelf in the countinghouse.

Himself never knew much about her, or thought much about her. He brought her coffee when the manager was out, and got a nod, or he sharpened leads, or carried something for other nods, sometimes a smile that stayed at the mouth. She rarely spoke to anybody, and those who spoke to her got a yes or no. The rest was discussion of business. She seemed to have no more feeling than her typewriter. Himself never heard her exchange a word of small talk with anybody, not even Mr. Delmonico, and he was a breezy man, used to dealing and drinking with seamen, though he always called her Miss Kazakian, but to Mr. da Cunha he called her "that Armenian sherbet."

Himself, meantime, had been everywhere with the messengers, the checkers, dispatchers, and agents. The docks were miles of wooden wharfs along the banks of the river, and most of the freighters unloaded out in the stream. After a few weeks he knew coastal shipping from keel to truck, all the flags, signals, types of cargo, and manner of loading and unloading. He started at four o'clock in the morning by choice, because then the first shift of stevedores went out on the lighters to unload, and the ships' stewards served a breakfast for the agent and himself, a great banquet, of many strange sorts of oatmeal, and fishes from all the oceans, and eggs, sausage, bacons, hams, cold meats, steaks, jams, marmalades, jellies, and a dozen sorts of bread, and it was like tasting all the world on plates. Himself had no trouble with the work. He could take control of any job after a time, and often did, and the agent went home early, knowing the other name for trust was The O'Dancy. Sometimes at night himself went about town, but there was little to see in narrow lanes, except the scores of drunkards, and fights, and little to hear except bawling sailors and screaming women. On any Sunday he went to Mass, if not on early shift, and afterward walked along the beach to São Vicente, and swam, or visited Mr. Delmonico and his family, or else Mr. Carvalhos Ramos came down from São Paulo, and they strolled the afternoon, dined early, and went early to bed, to be up early. If any thought of women bothered him or not he never could remember. Hard work and long hours are the finest killing of fancy. He might have gone on with Mr. Delmonico for months longer, except that in the afternoon of that last, hot day, a pencil rolled under Miss Kazakian's desk.

Santos was a hellion's boil that summer. The wooden shed quivered in heat. Sweat dried to brine flakes. Down at the shed's end stevedores grilled half chickens on the tin roof. Miss Kazakian sat at the desk, blotter beneath her elbow, casting figures. Her white blouse showed patches where the voile stuck. Sweat shone under her eyes. Her lips moved with the count. She turned to crosscheck, and the pencil tipped, fell, rolled under the green baize cloth that covered the desk almost to the floor all the way around. Piles of paper hid the top, almost hid her, and her left shoulder was turned away from him. He picked up the baize fall, and crawled under. Light flooded in the inch or so between the cloth's tasseled hem and the floor. The pencil shone, and he reached for it, and then sat on his heels, feeling his heart suddenly punching at his ribs.

Miss Kazakian's skirt was pulled back, and her many petticoats were over her knees, and the lace-framed white thighs, with the faintest blue vein running down on the inside of the right leg. As he watched, her hand appeared, and in the quietest gesture, rubbed a middle finger under the knee where sweat ran, perhaps, or some itch offended, smoothed the part he could see, dabbed it with a little of the petticoat, put the petticoat back, and the hand went, and the thighs opened wider, the laced boots moved wider apart, and she sat forward a little farther in the chair. Himself was ever certain she had no idea he was anywhere near. He crawled nearer, carefully evaded the boots, stretched his face to kiss the thigh, felt the warmth against his cheeks, set his lips to the flesh, moved his tongue, on the instant felt the sudden rigidity, sniffed the scent of woman, myriadly more delicate than a fine, unlit cigar, and there was light above him, a tremendous crash! and the table was over, and she stood for a moment while the chair fell, and kicked at him, but he went flat on his face and the boot went over his head. He was on his feet and out of reach before she could kick again, but she ran to the door, and through, toward Mr. da Cunha's office, and the door closed, quietly enough, behind her.

He heard no voices, but then the door opened, and the heavy tread in slippers and the clack of her heels came along the corridor.

In shirt sleeves, smoking a cigar, Mr. da Cunha looked at him over thick glasses.

"Go home," he said. "Don't come again. You're finished here. Understand?"

Himself took no notice, but looked at her, and she looked through the door.

"I meant no harm at all," he said. "I saw the beauty of you. That we never see. There's no gift anybody could make me that I'll treasure more. You're beautiful. Why would I be saying anything less?"

"Go," Mr. da Cunha said. "Don't talk. Go."

Himself saw the jewel-flash in Miss Kazakian's eyes before she turned her back, and he smiled.

"That's the way of it," he said. "Good-by, Mr. da Cunha. You've been kind. I've learned a great deal. My regrets and respects to Mr. Delmonico. I'd been here long enough, anyway. Miss Kazakian, there's no apology. A warm, white wonder is what you are. God love you. Good-by, now."

Even if Mr. Carvalhos Ramos knew about it, he said nothing except to tell Sergio to pack.

"Tomorrow morning you'll start in my office to learn a little about the law as it affects an estate," he said. "A couple of months will be enough. I think you should have a little time with a coffee exporting house. Learn something about grades, and prices, zones, and so on. Then you'll go on the coffee exchange and pick up a little about bulk sales and futures. After that, I think you'll be ready to travel. A glance at the world will do you good. Now, as to this Morenne."

Not that thought of her for any moment had stopped being sharp. In some way she and Creonice seemed to have joined hands. Thinking of one brought memory of the other. But in that, Mr. Carvalhos Ramos was flat stone. There would be no going back to The Inheritance until he entered the gates as The O'Dancy, ready for responsibility as well as title.

"We've done everything possible," Mr. Carvalhos Ramos said. "She's not to be found. The house was taken for the season. You say they went to Recife. Inquiries up there brought nothing. The surname isn't known. They might have gone to Europe. Anywhere."

It never occurred to himself that a lawyer might have found out she was already married, and that he would fence and parry for a while until it came time for the world tour, and bank heavily on that to push her out of mind.

"If I'm to stay on at the house, could Creonice not come to cook for me?" himself asked, ah yes, heat in the throat, and a burst of desperation.

"Creonice is properly married, and working for one of Tomagatsu's daughters," Mr. Carvalhos Ramos said. "How could she leave her husband? And remember, the 'rights' of a master are still not part of the law. We're growing more responsible. That ridiculous dangling thing has had enough to say. It's time we started thinking with the other end of our bodies. Men. Using a mind instead of tissue."

"I wonder whether you'd do me the blessing," The O'Dancy said. "While using the mind, what would you be telling the tissue? Will it be listening?"

Mr. Carvalhos Ramos put down his port glass, and sat back laughing.

"Very well," he said. "Remember, when you travel, it will be with tutors. I believe it necessary that you consider the possibility of entering a university. In your present state, that means work. But you have the brain. Will you try? Far more to your eventual happiness than all the tissue nonsense."

Himself had no thought of it, one way or the other. As it happened, the new tutors were far better men than the others. Latin he had from Father Miklos since a child, and together they rarely spoke anything else. French he had from The Mam. English from The Tad. Portuguese he spoke daylong, in The O'Dancy style perhaps, but the tutor was highly satisfied and should have been, because The Mam had seen to it, first. In mathematics himself was dull in some aspects, bright in others. Physics he needed from the beginning. History and geography were scrappy but not hopeless. There was time.

"All in all, splendid," Professor Riskind said at the first meeting. "We shall start the morning periods. In the afternoons you attend the office. In the evenings, a short period. You will enter a university, have no fear."

Professor Riskind had been born in Poland, spoke ten languages, and seemed to carry every known detail about any mortal subject in a small, bald head that he had shaved every morning. He wore cream linen suits, white shoes, and high, starched linen collars with a broad black silk cravat, and very soon after they began work the other tutors got into the same uniform, each of them crowned with a broad-brimmed panama. Curiously, as the months passed, they began to look the same, because they all wore pince-nez on black ribbons.

Of course, even then he could slip out to some hotel or other where Sergio had put a girl, but if it was relief of a sort, it did no good except to take away the need for a time. The hunger was always there, some kind of hunger that became most unbearable at the moment the seed was jolting out of the flame-tip of himself, and that was why he never remembered any of them, Chinese or Japanese or Arabs, whatever delicacy Sergio picked, himself wanted nothing more, once it was over, than to swill his mouth and bathe, and get his clothes on and be away, yes, away, away, away, as much in pity for the woman he was leaving as disgust with himself.

That sense of disgust was ever a torment, for the women were beautiful, well taken, and often, afterward, well remembered.

And yet.

The stories he picked up in Mr. Carvalhos Ramos' office were sometimes funny enough, though he never remembered them. They seemed to slip his mind. But the tales, the air about the tellers, the look in the faces of those listening, all seemed too much for the traffic they were picking over, and the cause, he knew now, was only the same hunger, exactly the same, for something more, something, anything tangible, retainable, which might palliate that sense of disgust with themselves. Failing, they had to laugh at the act, at the woman, at themselves, to provide some basis or any reason or excuse for the agony of not knowing they had misspent a force, the anguish of the unknown, the lost, mourning in a fleshy wilderness for love of a son, a daughter, indolently, in false affection, tawdry emotion, thrown sweatily away.

But then was the other Godforsaken hunger, for the woman herself, before the waste, before the sweat, that hunger which brought the acolyte to spend unsteady hours in smoke of the censer, trying to raise the spirit from a slough, to remind, to recall, to reclaim. But himself was no acolyte. He loved the dream, savored the hunger, admired the swollen rod, Thy rod, Thy staff, ah, so, and then, in a moment, cursed himself, the woman, the hunger, and asked himself what it was worth. Fun, it was called, and sport, yes, very enjoyable, and away to the next. Presently the age is on you, and

God be merciful, for the muscle refuses, and Sweet Jesus in Thorns, then what is there, except a dream of Maexsa, or *iemanja,* that one, of the magic beard, and Almighty God be merciful, for that, only that, in all compassion, that was all.

And a sixth cross ready-carved, and waiting.

"Master," Clovis said, and changed down. "The Lady Hilariana won't permit trucks inside. We cut the paths."

"She has the right of it," The O'Dancy said. "It's high time for hard-surface roads. Stop here. I'll walk."

6 Hilariana in cherry linen came into the office those years before, and put a roll of drawing paper on the desk, and looked at himself with the smiling brilliance of gray eyes for just the moment, and bent to kiss him, and the love for her winged in her perfume, a marvel in the head the way it ever was, God be praised, and himself knowing the high estate of a blessed man.

"This is what I want for my birthday this year and next, and Mr. Lacerda says it can be built," she said, and unrolled the paper, taking out the inkstand and her mam's photograph, and her own, and the bowl of roses. "The cost goes into millions, but I'll earn that in a couple of years. It's needed. I want it. São Paulo wants it."

"Why doesn't São Paulo pay for it?" himself asked, looking at her, possibly, he thought, in a long-distant part of his mind, the most beautiful woman he had ever seen, if the thought was only out of pride, a jubilating wonder that himself was her father, indisputable progenitor, and protector, and worshiper, luxuriating when she was near, and in constant yearn when she was not.

She clasped her hands in collapse of patience and leaned her weight on the heel canted out in front.

"They have institutes, and all sorts of laboratories and gardens," she said. "That's not what I want to do. I don't simply want to take everything to pieces. I want to find all sorts of things."

"All I have to do is find the money," The O'Dancy said. "What is it you want to find?"

"Come and look at this," she said, and pleaded, opening her hands over the drawing as a mam over a crib. "Let me tell you what I want to do."

But himself reached over and took the paperweight galleon off the edge of the paper, and it sprang in a roll back to the ash tray.

"Anything you want to do is mandate," The O'Dancy said. "I've no wish to see anything at all. It's yours. Give the order."

"Tad, you're hopeless," she said in the Other Language, that was only dear music of vowels and aspirates carried on a voice that might have loved the soul of all mankind. "Please come here, and hold my hand, and let me tell you what I want to do, first, and then tell me I'm right. I might be a perfect fool."

"Tears, then?" The O'Dancy said, and out of the chair, and around there, and taking a dearness, ah yes, a beauty itself of warmth and sweet and tenderness, and kissing the hand that suddenly took his fingers tight and held them to her lips. "No, now, no, God take a life, never tears, listen, now, to me."

"Tad, you know our Brazil," she said with a rasping passion that shocked by the suddenness. "You know São Paulo. You know that beyond the city, a bare kilometer from the last cocktail party, it's savagery. Barbarianism. Civilized a yard on each side of any road. The rest?"

"We have to grow," himself said. "Everybody else did. And took a long time about it."

"This is my part," she said, and tapped the drawing. "I want to find what puts the aroma in coffee, first."

"Did Almighty God not put it there, to begin with?" himself asked. "Did you ever taste any without?"

"It often smells better than it tastes," she said. "Why? What makes some coffee bitter, and others with more of the aroma we think of as coffee? If I can find out, and put into ours what's missing, don't you think it's worth while? It may take years. Am I a fool?"

"Any money spent'd be worth it," he said. "Tell me who'll make you a fool, and I'll be dealing with him. Only coffee?"

"Ah no," she said, picking a corner of his handkerchief, leaning dear weight on his shoulder. "Pineapples are sometimes a block of sweet wood. Sugar cane's often sweetish cotton. Bananas taste like what? Pulp of some sort? Oranges? Some are sweet, others are knots of rag. Lemons and limes are always bitter. Why? What helps them to hold the astringency? If it were found, couldn't it be added to the orange? Perhaps to any other fruit to retain its sweetness? If we could find what, exactly, causes sweetness? If it could be grown? Bananas from Ceylon are the most wonderful I ever tasted. I want to grow them here. Add their quality to ours. Oranges from everywhere, especially India. And the shaddock. That's a fruit from paradise. We don't even know it. But we could grow it here. I want coffee from Colombia and El Salvador, and tons of their earth. It's glorious coffee, and don't look like that, Tad, you know it is. And there's rice. And cotton. And beans. And all sorts of flowers."

Himself felt her weight that fraction more while she leaned in a dream, knowing that her mind, her imagination, the entire marvel of the real woman herself, was off in some joyous glade where every color and a thousand simple scents of wonder fused in sober drunkenness.

"Flowers," himself said, soft, not to waken her, for the weight was dear. "Cahir's stairway's a picture. It is, that. Will we never be having a few of a sort in the garden, then? It's been many a long day, has it not?"

She stood away and folded the handkerchief in careful squares and put it back in his pocket.

"Not this month," she said, rolling the drawing. "Next month will be time. But next year you won't have to ask, Tad mine. And never after that, either. I promise."

"Better than any hundred-year treaty signed by the noblest," The O'Dancy said. "Where will you put this place?"

"Along by the river, for water and power," she said. "On the turn."

"Would you not be knowing it, then," he said, "above Shaun's Landing?"

"Yes," she said, and rolled the drawing tighter. "On Daniel's Flight, that's where it will be."

There it was now, a long box of green and blue glass on thin legs of concrete and steel, and planted about by every tree she could find, in a garden filled with plants in bloom for the past few years that looked as if they all had been there for centuries. Far over, the plots were in mist of irrigational vapor, with a rainbow over all. Nearer, a couple of men clipped shrubs. Under the building a line of men were planting sprouts in pots, beating out a rhythm with their feet, and softly singing an old slave tune himself must have learned not long from the cradle.

Now try, little one in a shawl, to remember the words. Luisa, yes, nurse to The O'Dancy, God suckle her kind, a freed slave, had whispered that song all the time, even while they were carrying her off, after she slit the laundrymaid open, and pulled out the kidneys, wrapping them in her apron and walking a couple of kilometers to put them in church, bloodying the edge of the font. Nobody ever knew why, because the maid's brother broke into the shed that afternoon, and took Luisa by the hair and chopped her into gobbets.

Somebody in the plant house rang a bell to warn upstairs of visitors.

All sorts of people were always going there, himself was ever reading and hearing, and not giving a damn. Great ones from the Government, and the United Nations, and learned ones from the universities were never out of the place. Himself had been once, when it was opened, but the whole fuss, the look of it, seemed beyond the time of himself, the smell of it, all new sprays and insecticides, and rooms of new plants in darkness, and others growing in red light, and some in black light, or so they said, and himself never bothered to find out. If he faced himself, direct, now, in the eye, the entire place, start to finish, was not a real kettle of the sort tea himself had any care for. There was no question of being frightened or distrustful.

It was simply that himself saw within it a Brazil of the future when The O'Dancy would be somebody else. Arquimed would be gone, and hate grew in thought of it, even if there was far more of envy, or jealousy. The mind of himself was clear of doubt why Grandfa Shaun would not be discommoded.

The discommoding was fateful knowledge of the waiting grave.

Ah, but the true worry was who else except Hilariana, herself at the wrong end of her twenties, and no husband or any sign of him. The usual crowd of chasers, brothers of school friends, doctors, chemists, politicians, and other idiots, met in the course of her work, and receptions, and travel here and there, but nobody, not a single one at her side, and himself remembered some very good property standing about. There had been one, lately, but not even he seemed able to take her out for a drive on a Sunday.

"Tad, you're so old-fashioned," she told him. "Who goes for drives on Sunday?"

"Begod, now, if I were any age at all, and yourself anywhere near, we'd see who'd be old-fashioned," The O'Dancy said. "What's wrong with a drive, and a picnic on a Sunday? Out in the air, and stretch your limbs."

"I stretch my limbs walking about here every day," she said. "Nobody could possibly have any more air. And we picnic every day. There's no time for a big meal."

"You'll ruin your health," he said. "You ought to eat more."

"And be a porpoise like Vanina, or carry a fatty droop in the upper arms like so many others," Hilariana said, and shook her head sharply, once, a habit she took from himself, so he knew what it meant. "There's no time for anybody except the people I'm working with. Sometimes I feel like the Mam and Grandam of everybody, myself."

"You ought to be a mam truly," he said. "I'm looking for The O'Dancy. I'd like a word or two before it's late."

"There's Stephen," she said, and the eyes of her with the great tears.

"He'll do for the years he lives," The O'Dancy said, and wide sadness about him. "He'll be the one in my place. But he won't be The O'Dancy. That could be your own son."

"I shall be careful to choose his father," she said. "Should I take the first bull?"

"I'll not be quarreling if he has the blood," The O'Dancy said. "Don't be telling me your son won't have the brains of yourself?"

That was a year or so ago, and lately there was this somebody. Himself had met the fellow two or three times, once at the office, once at the São Paulo house, and once for Sunday lunch at The Inheritance. He was not the sort himself might have picked for her. But she had to live with him, nobody else, and if she knew her own mind, let no man put asunder. He was good-looking, yes, and junior partner in the chemical firm owned by his father, so the property side was safe enough. But for all that he still looked like a rain-jacket potato, and without saying so, or even looking in her direction, Hilariana knew what was in the mind of himself, but she never said a word, and it rested there. She was taking prizes all over the place, and her name was ever in the papers as a botanist, or scientist, or whatever, and she always came to him with the scrolls and gifts, showing them, not with pride, but almost as if

she acknowledged they were his by right of paying for the work of
the O'Dancy Foundation, as it was called. If he ever looked at any
of them, it was only to please her. Himself was proud enough of
her and all she could do. For the work, he was impatient of interest.
She had an apartment of her own on top of a new skyscraper in
São Paulo, and another in the O'Dancy Building in Rio de Janeiro,
and her own place at The Inheritance. Her old nurse was still with
her, and a governess, and she had other maids. Nobody was in
her way, and there were no rules in her life except those she made
for herself.

Often enough there was wonder in the mind of himself about
what a woman going on in her thirties did for the sake of her body,
though it was delicate thinking, and uneasy air, and it was not for
a father to mistrust. Her temperament was very much O'Dancy,
but her mother was strong in her, ah yes, the nun, that beauty of
many a transcendent memory. The night she left her life was
when himself took to the whisky.

Daniel, it was, made the cure. For that moment, at any rate.

Nine, at the time, the boy must have been, Daniel Leitrim
Arquimed O'Dancy Boys, and he came in the room and sat on the
arm of the chair, and put the strong little right hand in a grip on
the shoulder that himself could still feel.

"Dr. Moise says I have a sister and I shall have to take great care
of her because you have work to do," said Daniel, and listen to that
voice. "And it's not good for you to sit in the darkness, and to take
you at least once a day in the garden."

"What will we be doing in the garden?" himself had asked, a
whisper from a charnel house.

"We shall talk," said Daniel. "Dr. Moise said The O'Dancy will
ever talk to the one coming after him."

"Very well," The O'Dancy said. "To the garden, and let us talk."

Ever since that afternoon, when there was no business, or when
Daniel was not in school, they walked in the garden and exchanged
the coin of the day.

But a sunny morning still felt warm in the mind of himself when
Daniel, in the white suit, and the red hair of him still dark from the
bath, said he was off to the war.

"No quarrel of yours," himself had said.

"Every man's quarrel I take it to be," Daniel said. "They're running roughshod. Wouldn't they try it with us, later on?"

"You're looking too far in the crystal, now," himself had said. "You don't happen to remember who you are?"

"That's why I'm going," Daniel said. "I'm old enough."

"True," The O'Dancy said. "I can't stop you. But supposing they take away your citizenship?"

"If they do, I'll be in good company," Daniel said. "A fine parcel of us are going."

"You'll be needing a few pennies," The O'Dancy said. "I'll be looking to it. What will you go in?"

"Whatever they say," Daniel said. "I'm a better sailor than anything else."

The next news, a fine photograph of Second Lieutenant Daniel O'Dancy Boys, and an address in figures and numbers, and after that, three letters saying nothing three times over, except that he was well, and everything was smashing. Then, the pause, and weeks of going every night to Hilariana's room to hold her hand, and listen, while Madame Briault read her a story, and then her prayers, that he still heard, and turned his head away not to lose blood.

At the office that morning came the telegram from the consulate. His Majesty regrets.

Himself was never in the old O'Dancy office again, never in sight of the building. It was razed and rebuilt.

Back to The Inheritance, blind through the dust, and a loll in the head, without strength in legs or hands, into Grandam Xatina's room, and over to the piano, and a sweep of the photograph into his right arm where the boy, oh, dear Christ now, let be, the best one, had last stood the moment to say good-by, and blind, blind, out from the open windows, down the stone path Grandfa Phineas had cut—"Will I not go dry of foot into my own house, then? Oh yes, but I will"—and to the darkness of Grandam Aracý's jacaranda tree, and down, without help of knees, in the shadow, and now, cough out the bitter blood.

It might have happened to himself those years before.

But instead, the consul down in Santos asked to see his documents, and that was the end, because the finger tapped the birth date.

"I fear you're a little too short to put a lever into this, you know," he said, looking at the pages.

"What lever?" himself had asked.

"Arquimed is Archimedes, you know that, don't you?" the consul said. "He found out how to move a stone by applying the force of a lever against another, didn't he?"

"I suppose he did," himself had said. "He had a head on him."

"True," the consul said. "Come and see me in a couple of years. There's plenty of time."

A fine-looking man he was, with a mustache creeping from above his ear, down the cheek, over the top lip and up the other cheek to the top of the other ear, but his head was bald. There were not the barbers these days to dress a man so.

"The Germans'll take me," himself had said.

"If, of course, the Royal Navy permits them the opportunity of getting you there, which I beg leave to doubt," the man had said, and laughed up at the picture of his king. "His Majesty'll be most pleased to take you when you've grown a couple of inches more, d'you see? One has to be just that much taller than usual to serve with the Irish Guards."

"Would I not do as well anywhere else?" he asked, and all of life slipping away from him.

The man tapped the documents.

"Not with a name like that," he said. "Thank you for thinking of us, and do please come again."

It might have been that story, so many times told, which years later put the idea in Daniel's mind. But there was the other morning, not long after the regrets, that the consulate sent up a note to say his presence was requested on the cruiser taking oil aboard in Santos. Down he went in the Cadillac, and surely no man ever went that road faster, full of a wild, sobbing, ridiculous hope the boy was alive, or some mistake or other had been made. Ah, tell yourself a tale. But, no. The ship was ribboned with ropes and slings, and holes gaped, and she was bent here and there, patched in many places, and hundreds of men were at work in a clatter of hammers. Himself had never forgotten the smell of her, of soap and linseed, paint, iodine, and new jute hawser, and the scorch of steel against steel that stung in the nostrils and burned high up in the head, and a cleanliness in the air beyond the brush and holystone of the ship herself, braving out her own strict scent, that primal odor of a male company stripped for battle, sane perfume of the hero.

Ever since, thanks be to God Almighty in His mercy, himself was able to think of Daniel, yes, steady, among the Shining Ones.

Up in a small room on top, from the stairs they climbed, himself went through a little door like those in Alice in Wonderland he was reading about to Hilariana, and a tall man in a white uniform not well laundered or pressed, with a badge in his cap that was black and verdigris instead of gold, gave himself one look, and smiled at a chair.

He put a bottle and two metal cups on the table.

"Your son served with me," he said. "Not on this ship. I promised I'd give you these if I had the chance. Enough?"

He held up the mug, and himself nodded.

The little package on the table was what was left.

"Your health, sir," the officer said, and drank.

Himself ever tasted that whisky.

"I lost my own son at the same time," the officer said, and he might have been talking of the weather. "Daniel was a very fine boy. Very popular aboard. Great courage."

"Glad of that," himself had said, well, and it might have been the price of coffee getting a pleasant word. "Is that all there is? Were there no uniforms? Or a cap? Or anything?"

"Those are all the personal possessions," the officer said, and drank a little more. "As I tried to tell you, he was killed in action."

"No wreath, then," himself had said, with great thanks to the whisky.

The officer might have smiled, but then, it might have been when he lifted the mug.

"No," he said. "No wreath."

The O'Dancy called on his fathers for the tone of voice, or any voice at all, and, God love them, they answered.

"Would yourself, sir, do me the honor, not like to be taken out to Daniel's place, with every man on this ship, now, and see where he lived his young day?" himself asked, hearing the words, and the quietest ever spoken, and clear even to himself. "There's accommodation for as long as any of you please, and I'll bring every man of you back, as my son would have done, sound of limb and sweet of temper, whenever you say. They're working very hard down there. It looks as if there might be time?"

The officer looked at the little clock flush with the steel wall.

"In twenty-eight minutes we put to sea, time or not," he said, and got up, raising the bottle. "A little more?"

"Just to take me down the stairs," himself said. "You'll drink with me?"

The officer smiled and poured for both.

"I know what it is," he said. "I've got a daughter left. But the name's gone. Unless there's a filly who wants me."

Himself held up the thin tin mug.

"To that very filly," he said. "And I can see her now. You'll put your blanket across her, and nothing from her except the whinny. Do you not know it?"

"I'll look forward to it," the officer said, and drank. "Thank you for dragging all the way up here."

He held out the package, and a sailor came from somewhere, and they were going down the narrow clanging stairs, no good-by or good luck or a handshake, nothing, except that smell, and the little package, and somebody whistling.

Himself never looked inside the paper. Hilariana took it, but she never said anything about it. Himself never asked.

That first anniversary, the room about Daniel's photograph was filled with flowers, ah yes, and himself got raving drunk and smashed all the vases and flung out every flower to the smallest leaf and tore up every flower in the garden, and wept himself sober in the greenhouse.

Ever since, nobody had bothered to fill a pot, and the garden was left to grass.

That slave song got in the heart of himself, and the drums and maracas got into his feet, and again he was carried across the thigh of Luisa, and heard the voice of her, tremulous through her ribs, and felt again the grip of The Mam pulling himself away from gentle brown hands that suddenly turned into claws and tore at his clothes.

"Daughter of Satan," The Mam shouted at her. "Dare to take my son to such a den of sin? Dare to bring him under the Touch?"

"Oxalá has him in keeping," Luisa screeched, like a branched bird, open mouth and chipped teeth. "No harm comes to him. I paid the price."

"You paid for nothing," The Mam said. "Go back to your house. Never enter here again."

Himself crying for Luisa, and all the women howling and beating their hands, and that canto wild in the head of himself even now.

Of course, there was no not-knowing at the heart that the business of *macumba* went on. It passed from father to son and mother to daughter. There was no way for it not, just as people wipe their noses as their fathers and mothers did. But there was a place for it, and that place was not, by any consent of himself, on The Inheritance or near it, and neither had it ever been in open knowledge, at any rate for the past twenty years, that *macumba* was in practice among the people. Himself knew them all, man, woman, and child, all the hundreds of them, and a thought of them in quick scan of names and faces brought no whisper of anything in the air.

Especially not Democritas Pereira, and if him, then also Ephemia, his second wife, though Creonice must have been, even if she had never said a word of it, for when she died, the *macumba* procession was far greater than the one from the church taking her to the cemetery, and Father Miklos refused to go on.

"But the woman must be decently buried," Mr. Carvalhos Ramos said, leaning out of the coach, and shouting over the drums. "We could wait until all the noise is past."

"We shall wait a long time," Father Miklos said. "I cannot permit the ceremony to be profaned. I shall go to my church. When they are ready, then I'll go back."

But it was four days before somebody went to tell him, and when he got there, the grave was set about with sacrifices of flesh, and the holy man turned away. Democritas cursed him, but he could afford to ignore it.

"The man's not baptized and was never of the Church," he said.

"Creonice was. I married them because of her. And Tomagatsu insisted. Anything in the nature of a ceremony that man loved. It was the best wedding I ever officiated at. Even then, they had a three-day *macumba* that Tomagatsu never knew anything about."

"And did you not tell him?" himself had asked.

"I found out in confessional," Father Miklos said. "Would you expect me to?"

"What, then, in the Devil's own name, is *macumba?*" himself asked, and the tone of voice surprised by the fear, never for any moment thought or felt, though it must have been at work, unknowing. "It's a slavish thing, that I'm sure. And what else?"

"I hate to bring the stink about me," Father Miklos said, and held the crucifix by the beads. "It's a mixture of African fetish, Indio ritual and what's left of the diabolic before the Christian epoch. Before the message of Christ permeated the courts and the countries. When the Roman gods were still supreme. The slaves came from Africa with their own horrors. They found here, where the sailors had been coming for years, vestiges of the old European religions, and, of course, the native Indio blood ceremonies. The slave quarters became seedbeds of hell. There was nothing to stop the fetish masters from borrowing the names of saints from the ritual of the Holy Church, and using them and the ritual to worship their own gods. On the sly. Who'd suspect it? That's what they've been doing for generations. Imagine the spiritual desert, then, in our own time. Why should we wish to discuss it? We deal with souls and the Spirit. But there are other spirits. We know it. Save yourself, now. Pray diligently. Go in peace."

"Amen," himself had said, and obedience was all.

But the slave song had changed when himself was near enough to be seen, and in mid-line the men were all turned around, boxing the pots in rows, and filling the spaces with moss.

Innocent, ah yes, with a curve to their backs, like dogs that know they have done wrong.

"Why would you mouth that gibberish?" himself called, and walked across the short grass toward them. "Do you not know you live as free men? Did nobody ever tell you? Or will I be putting a boot behind a few of you?"

"Now, Tad, Tad," Hilariana sang, over the balcony rail. "Such a fine temper on a wonderful day? You're looking a little bedraggled. Is that the journey, or the passing of the flask, or was it the spiders? Steb telephoned from the landing. Come, there's a luncheon we can order. And a drop of the Creature, for sure."

"Hilariana," himself said, looking up at the world's only smile. "There's music, ah, there is, in your name. And an anthem in what you just told me. And isn't that what I came for, God be praised, and a full court of all His angels about Him, then?"

7 "What's the business about a couple of dead ones" he asked her while the men closed the glass partition in a sound of slow thunder against dark rooms filled with green sprouts. "Did it have to happen on this day of all others?"

She looked at him with the eyes that seemed to have their own extraordinary light inside, that made them a darker or paler gray, or blue sometimes, even, just now, under the strange lamps in the plant rooms, a green that startled, that almost made him feel it was not herself but somebody else, not looking at but watching him. There were black pencil lines at the corners that tipped them up, and there was blue color along the top of the lids.

"I've shown you tens of thousands of some of the world's rarest plants," she said, half laughing, half pretending to cry. "That's the thanks I get? Coffee that possibly will sweeten itself. Coffee with all the aroma of the African varieties, and a far better savor. Pineapples all solid meat, tender as *filet mignon*. Grapes as big as your thumb, not a seed, not a half ounce of waste in a pound of fruit. And you speak of dead ones?"

"I don't know why not," he said. "We've had no dead ones of that kind on the place since the Revolution. And that's a few years. Why'd we start now? Did they choose their own date for it?"

"Poor things," she said. "I did what I could. It wasn't much."

"You didn't go to church," he said. "We were looking for you."

"I shan't leave here for at least another three weeks," she said. "We're following progress moment by moment. I know if I were to leave somebody'd forget the thermostats and ruin years of work."

"Wish you were taking this kind of trouble with a child," he said. "We could do with one."

"Plenty of time for that," she said a little impatiently. "Pupi's at The House. He's looking at the greenhouses."

"Has the fellow nothing else except Pupi in the way of a name?" he asked. "The sound of it makes me peevish, so it does. Pupi, be Christ. How could you put your tongue to it?"

She laughed, the silent, graceful paroxysm that made her shake, rolling back on the divan, never a sound, only the breath, the famous laughter that collapsed her friends.

"Aristides Lhme da Silva," she said. "His mam called him Pupi. It won't do for you?"

"It will not," himself said. "I suppose it's pleasant enough in Portuguese. To this ear, it's all right for a lap dog. It's on the top of m' mind to tell you that's what I think he is. But I'll not go that far."

"He's not here to bother you," she said, and took his arm. "Let's have a little something to eat. We've got fish—"

"To the devil with it," himself said.

"—and a small steak—"

"—that too—"

"—and a slash of green bacon—"

"—that's it. No fat. And two eggs. And put the loaf on the coals. Why do you put that blue on your eyes? Aren't they blue enough?"

She called the order through the trap, and he watched her putting glasses on the tray. There was something unusually thoughtful about her that day. He tried to imagine what it might be, or if she was getting a little of the mature businesswoman about her, or just a passing headache, or if it was the wrong part of the month.

"You know what those men came for, don't you?" she said quietly, quickly, as though she was glad the words were out.

"No, I don't," he said. "But I'll be damned, I'll find out. It was a macumba, was it not? And what's a macumba doing on my place?"

"It was not macumba," she said, putting ice in the glass. "It was khimbanda. That's much worse."

"Khimbanda," he said. "I've heard the word. What's it? African? How's it worse than macumba? Is the Devil worse than Satan?"

"Macumba calls to the baser spirits," she said in the same quick way, and without looking at him, as if she had rather be rid of what she had to say. "Khimbanda's black. Black ceremony. Black sanctus. The mass of Satan."

"Be quiet, now," he said. "I might think you were contaminated."

"You're not a believer," she said. "It's as well. At least, you're safeguarded. Faith makes you immune."

"You're talking nonsense," he said. "Will you now be so good? Talk sense. This *khimbanda*. Where did you hear of it, who told you, and where's it going on? Not on The Inheritance?"

She nodded.

"It may be," she said. "It's hard not to be able to deny it. But I know enough to be sure of one thing. Where there's *macumba*, there's bound to be *khimbanda*. One leads to the other. There isn't one without the other."

"For the love of Jesus, girl," he said, and looking at her back, long, slim, in the laundered nylon overall, and the piled hair, all tinted green by the glass. "How would you know so much about this, and I next to nothing?"

"I've lived a little closer to them," she said. "One thing I'm sure of. *Khimbanda's* dangerous and it's being practiced. Here."

"Bring me the names," The O'Dancy said. "Don't be just idling your mouth. Tell me who, and where, and I'm your man. They'll last till I get my hands on them. Why did you let it go so long before telling me? How long have you known?"

"Since the night you knew about Daniel," she said. "There was a *khimbanda* that night."

"You never told me," himself said, and only just.

"Were you in any condition?" she asked prettily, as if it had no importance at all. "Then, or for weeks after? Remember, I was what?—ten?—and I was frightened of a lot of things. If it hadn't been for Bri-Bro, I don't know what I'd have done."

"Did dear Bri-Bro have anything to do with finding out about *khimbanda?*" he asked.

"Nothing," she said. "I went down to get Daniel's photograph you'd left under the jacaranda. I heard the music and went over there."

"With Daniel's photograph," he said in misery.

"They put it on the *khimbanda* altar," she said. "I probably fell asleep. I woke up next morning and the photograph was on the piano downstairs. That's all."

"It was never purified," he said. "I'll have to get Father Miklos to it."

"Now, Tad," she said. "Listen to me. This was years ago. After all, there's a big difference between religion and superstition. I can be patient with one. I won't tolerate the other."

"Oh well, now, wait a moment here," he said, and stood up. "Your patience and tolerance, my darleen only glory? Am I supposed to change an opinion in the light of either one? Let me tell you, now. I am the master here. Everything will be done as I say."

She was laughing at him. In the silent way, her own, the graceful, helpless groping for breath, showing the perfect teeth, the pinkest tongue, holding herself at her waist, yes, the laughter. But suddenly it was no longer childish, or funny. There was nothing comic in the helplessness.

Hilariana, well-named, because she laughed so at her birth.

In that dark moment himself knew that her laughter was something to guard against.

"Am I seeing with other eyes?" he asked her. "Is there something new I'm thinking?"

"We've been speaking of *khimbanda*," she said, ice, ice cold. "The spirits are near. They come at call. You must be careful."

"Never," he said. "To hell with all that sort of thing."

"But you believe in the Holy Ghost," she said, and got up, and stretched, and there was never a finer cat in white silk, even to the quiver of her jaw. "Holy Ghost is spirit. If one, then others. If others, then many. How many?"

He looked at the painted eyes, and in a freeze within himself felt her contempt.

"I'm seeing you for the first time in these past years," he said. "I believe I'm seeing somebody I never saw before."

"Now, Tad," she said, with the new, mature impatience.

"Don't, for God's sake, Tad me," he said, and stood up. "Keep your lunch. I'm off in the fresh air. I feel I've been in a sickroom and every window shut. Would you not know it on such a day? Yes. The day when The O'Dancy must protect himself more than on any other."

"That's your superstition," she said, and she was talking to one of her men downstairs. "I don't know why you persist in this O'Dancy nonsense. You must know everybody's laughing. It's out of date, Tad. In fact, it's a good thing there's Steb. He'll carry it on. I won't.

I belong to another country. Another world. I'm a little tired of make-believe."

Well, there was a big difference in talking about being an old man, and suddenly, for what reason, feeling like one, with weights in the legs, and pains in the arms, and a lightness, something like a balloon in the plexus, that might take him up, and then again, he might fall down. There was no strength in himself to prevent the one or other.

"I wonder where did you find the goodness to say it," he said.

"Now, Tad, do stop the sentimentalities," she said in the same superior, or mature, if that was it, sort of voice that was so strange to her, and yet, he knew, it was part of the green and blue glass and the odd business going on inside there. "Fact is quite another thing. We have to deal with facts in these days."

"Aha," he said. "And while we're dealing with facts, what about these spirits we've been talking about?"

"They're facts too," she said, whipping it at him, a tall woman he knew only by her looks, rigid, staring the shining eyes, at the moment grayer than his own, out of the blue window. "What I'm talking about is this O'Dancy business. It's been embarrassing for long enough. Airs and conceits not in keeping with the times we're living in. The name's been venerated only because dear old Leitrim was a blackguard. He burned the Indios out of their land, and his sons followed his example till crooked politics gave them title. Then they were lords of a fairly large part of this earth. The O'Dancy? It's an accusation, not a title. Rape, pillage, banditry, never acknowledged. Always excused in the most groveling terms of hypocrisy. What I'm doing here will make up for it, in some part. Steb's going to do a little more. He'll use the name only to please you. But he'll drop it as time goes on. There won't be another. Be quite sure of that. When we're entitled to, this estate will go back to the original owners. If we can't find them, we'll make them. We're agreed on it."

"I'm glad of that," he said. "There's nothing like a quiet agreement. Especially when there's nobody there to give you a fight. Your warning's taken to heart. When you're entitled? You mean, when I'm dead?"

Rave and curse was what he wanted to do, but there seemed

no need. What she said, in that tone of voice, came from her brain. She meant every word. He wondered in which year the thought could have grown, or what had caused her to change from being that daughter of so many sunlit days to the cold heart in front of him, turning the pages of some damned magazine as if nothing was going on.

"When I'm dead," he repeated. "On the cards, it won't be long."

"Or for any of us," she said, making a flip! with a page. "It'll be less for you, the way you're behaving at the moment."

"Would you not explain that?" he asked, catching great hold.

"Look at yourself," she said without looking up. "The O'Dancy. You come here for the first time for years. Your appearance is disgusting. What do these people think of my father they've heard so much about? After rolling in every gutter in the city? Reeking of drink?"

"Well, yes, for one reason or the other, I had a few," he said. "And we were in a fire. Perhaps I'll go home, and have a bath and a shave, and put on some fine fashion and come back. Let's see what they think of me then."

"They won't forget what they've seen," Hilariana said, and put the magazine on the divan beside her. "They won't forget that in the state the country's in, one of its multi-multimillionaires walks about in worse condition than any stableman in his employ, and I'll guarantee you don't know how many. But you know how many of your cherished race horses there are. And when are you there? If it weren't for old Fazelli looking after them, or somebody in his place, would you dream of working there? A box at the Jockey Club, a little equine chatter among friends as useless as yourself, and what are you? The owner. Paying for what? A social grace? A plaything? Box of toys? Your estate—"

"The Inheritance," he whispered over coals, if she heard.

"You know nothing about it," she said. "It goes on, in spite of all you make quite certain you don't do. Other men are far more entitled to its product than you are. Or have ever been. When were you of the slightest use to your country? As a colonel? A tourist. You curse the politicians? Did you ever dream of entering an election, or raising your voice in places where it might matter? In

bars, in night clubs, in the stables and cattleyards, yes. Among
your own kind?"

"I've kept things together," he said. "There's more now than when
it was given to me. It produces a thousand times more."

"Other men's work, not yours," she said.

"That I pay for," he said. "Take this place. Which I think's the
worse crime I was ever in, and serves me right. I let you have your
own way. I was wrong."

"You always had your own way," she said. "Was that wrong?"

"My responsibility," he said. "I've done what I thought was
right. But I never heard anything like what you've been saying
here. It's the right place for it. Where poor plants are made to do
what was never intended. Twisted this way and that. Tied up.
Injected. Put under horrible lights they never saw before. Poor
things. And helpless."

She was laughing again, a gentle warp, without sound except
in the quiet, indrawn breath, and the whisper of nylon against the
divan's fabric. The lower button of the overall was undone. The
bare legs sprawled helplessly, but white, of classic form, he admitted and reproved himself, but the judge of horseflesh was also
judge of women and a daughter was not exempt from inspection.
He wondered again why nobody had ever been to see him about
her, some lawyer, or a friend of the family's, asking about the business side on behalf of some shy boy or other, out to set the ground
before trying his luck. It had never happened even once. But he
saw very clearly that if anyone got that laugh, especially in the
middle of saying something he might think was serious, then that
would be the end. Himself was surprised, but only thoughtfully,
that nobody had ever thrashed her. Her nurses and the governess
Briault had brought her up. Himself had gone in, day after day
to see her, and every night he was at home he spent a couple of
hours with her. She had never been other than a well-behaved,
beautiful little girl. There had never been anything but praise and
prizes from her schools. In the holidays they roamed the land or
went down to the sea. He could never remember tears except
when a pet died. Then was, oh, tragedy. Three years she had in
Paris and eight times he went over to visit her. Except that she
was grown more, with more beauty than he could have dreamed,

she never seemed to change. She was ever his only darleen glory, and himself the single light in her sky.

So, yes, so himself had thought.

"What made you suddenly change?" he asked her. "Tell me that."

"It hasn't been sudden," she said, lying back, showing the long line of thigh, tightly molded in shining green-tinted nylon. "Drinking. I always hated that. The way you've treated Vanina. And then running after those little streetwalkers."

"I was photographed with a few starlets," he said. "Now, wait a minute."

"Whatever they're called these days to carry them into print," she said. "Wasn't Iralia the perfect specimen?"

8 It was a set world, of boxes and circles, everything with a place, in place, and it was no use trying to explain, especially himself standing up and ready to go, and she lying there, talking in that cool way, the grown-up way, the way of the world-famous directress of the O'Dancy Foundation. A Woman of the Year, by the grace of God and somebody else's money. There was no way, except to sit down, even if it had to be over a pot of coffee, for the whisky seemed to have gone, and go back to the beginning, and tell her about the flower market that night, and seeing a girl quietly walking from stall to stall dipping the soul of herself deep down in all the colors, and putting her face into the buckets of roses, and at last, after the fifth time around, buying a little bouquet of colored daisies, and himself just left the restaurant, and on a lonely way back to the echoing house, following in the shadows, loving the selfless shine in her eyes.

"Wait, now," himself said, and pointed to the roses. "What have you got at home that you could put those in?"

"I'd find something," she said without surprise.

"Give me the lot," he told the man, and looked at her. "Where do you live?"

"Not far," she said.

"We'll take a taxi," he said, without thinking.

"Waste of money," she said, and took the roses in a wax paper torch almost bigger than herself. "Would you like to buy some champagne? The national's good enough."

He paid the man, and turned to stare at her. There had never been any notion in his mind other than giving a lover of flowers a bouquet for herself, and walking home the warmer for it. Far back an African was part of her. She had the large, dark, smeared eyes of those whose tears have run and run, and long dried. A small head of close-combed, clean bronzy hair, and a fine structure of bone to her face, a rich crinkled lower lip, no jewelry, and a country girl's complexion, movements, and a massive health that shone out of her.

"How many bottles?" he asked.

"Two'll do," she said, making nothing of it. "If you can afford three, it'll last longer."

They went down the hill to a bar, and he bought six bottles and had them put in a box, but they were heavy and the cord was thin. He put the box down to stretch his hand, and she gave him the roses, picking up the box in a sweep and putting it on her shoulder.

"A taxi'd save all this," he said.

It would not, because she ran up a short stairway and put her handbag down, feeling for the key. They were in a dark street of small houses, all shuttered. The door opened in darkness and she went in. They had barely spoken a couple of sentences, but she seemed to have made up her mind about him. Himself was uncertain what he wanted to do. There was no idea in the bone of his head of so much as taking out his handkerchief. But then, it was something to do, and when she came back and took his hand, he went inside with never a word, along the passage, to a room at the back. Three candles were alight in tins on a shelf. He ever remembered three candles over the narrow bed, a table and chair, and a toilet bucket filled with scarlet roses, more in a cooking-oil tin in a corner, and the rest on the floor by the bed.

"Pour the champagne," she said, and pulled off her dress and she had nothing else on, a beautiful, small girl she was, too, and her body untouched by blemish or sign of handling. "I won't be a moment."

"Look here," he said, taking charge. "I didn't mean this, you know."

"You're a kind man," she said. "You're lonely, and so am I. Couldn't we sit for a little while, and drink champagne, and talk, and look at the roses?"

"How do you know I'm lonely?" he asked, knocked aside by her matter-of-factness.

"Look at yourself," she said, and went out.

It was no matter of falling in love, or of an old fool becoming a real old fool, never mind the tears in his eyes, now. In those six or more weeks they did little except buy champagne and roses. She loved being flat and naked on the scarlet heads and drinking champagne, pouring it in little drops over her body and laughing when it tickled, and he simply liked watching her, and talking to her, and the whole idea of anything so beautiful happening in a São Paulo slum seemed like a new sort of life, especially in company of a girl barely out of school whose instincts went back true to Ptolemy's queens. She came from Minas Gerais and she had a job in a *boutique*. Her father looked after a stone quarry, and she had two brothers, a policeman and a bus driver, and she was in love with both of them, and she said it simply and unmistakably, without a tone in her voice or any move of her face. Her mother never spoke a word in her life, and they had a sign for everything. Somewhere she read in a book about the roses and champagne. Once before she met him she tried it, but the bottle of champagne had lost half its gas, and there were not enough roses. He took her to small clubs and *boîtes,* and they danced. She talked, he was not always sure what about, but she was thoroughly happy. He wanted to put her in an apartment. She refused every single thing. She had no use for a maid. He bought her clothes, nothing expensive or the girls might start talking, she said. But then people began to notice them, and they were photographed a couple of times and shown on the front page, with a caption about the "multimillionaire playboy never grows old or cold." After that he took her on weekends to Rio de Janeiro, and they stayed in the same hotel. A mistake. One evening, after going down to take a call from São Paulo, he went back to find the suite crowded with jazz musicians, noise enough to bring up the manager, and Iralia singing to the crowds in the street. He tried to stop her, but the musicians played him down, and anyway, it was all amusing until the police came. The rooms cleared of noise, crowds, smoke, and Iralia had gone with the musicians, and so had all his clothing, toiletries and trinkets. Next day, the papers were full of him, her, and the jazzmen, and the front page showed him grinning, like Mephistopheles, looking down on two photographs of Iralia, one in a white Communion dress with a rosary, and the other in two strips of lace, with a caption which placed him among others, not named, as corruptors of innocence and voracious devourers of modesty in minors.

Young Nestor Carvalhos Ramos saved the day by paying the paper for a long-term advertising campaign for O'Dancy Enterprises, and it was just as well he did, because the police had been after Iralia about the loss of his trinkets, a few watches, cuff links and some money that himself would rather not have thought about. But he was awakened at five in the morning at São Paulo by the chief of police, and told that she had been arrested as a cocaine seller. The little room in the street behind the flower market was a pick-up point for the touts. She had an apartment not far from his own house, a car and chauffeur, an apartment by the sea down in São Vicente, and during their trips to Rio she passed millions of cruzeiros' worth of cocaine taken from sailors off the boats in Santos. While himself sat up in bed listening, she was held in detention at the city prison and asking for him as a witness.

Young Carvalhos Ramos begged him not to go.

"You must think of your family, sir, and all the people involved here," the image of his father said, bloated with sleep, in a great-coat over pajamas, and an umbrella that ran a silver streak across the parquet. "Think of your relatives. They run into hundreds. Business connections? Thousands. Your banks. Shipping company. Airline. Construction. Everything is affected in the grossest, most damaging manner. This isn't the first time, unfortunately. It won't be shrugged off. It's not, after all, a young man's prank."

He meant that The O'Dancy had behaved like a lunatic. That was what it came down to, and the worst of it was there could be no other way except for himself to agree with every word.

Except.

Always except.

Iralia was the first woman for a long time to insist on taking pleasure in making himself know that he was still a thoroughly healthy normal male. There was the pull of those memories, and the tug of wanting to go back, and both, together with the instinct that only half-breeds desert their friends, gave himself a mind.

"If you're coming with me, say so," himself said. "If not, send another lawyer down there. The girl needs help."

"She'll ruin you," Young Carvalhos Ramos said, to the face of himself, leaning on the umbrella, with the pajama cords hanging under the raincoat. "With you, your family. I call on your sense of responsibility."

"I was something like a couple of months with that girl," The O'Dancy said. "I never had more pleasure in the company of anybody. And I suspected nothing. If she's guilty, then I'm guiltier. I should have seen through it. I never saw any single thing to see through."

"Rats build underground and between the walls," Young Carvalhos Ramos said. "I've seen this woman's record."

"At her age she can't have a record," himself said, and walked out.

"She's twenty-eight, looks sixteen, and she's known as the Free Ticket," Young Carvalhos Ramos said, in the elevator. "She admits anything. For nothing."

"There's nothing you can say that'll keep me away from that prison," himself said. "Now, if you're done, get in the car."

Half the skyscrapers they passed had been built by his own company, or his bank had financed them, and Young Carvalhos Ramos amused nobody by naming them, and the many companies interested, and looking up at the bank's electric sign that told the time and the news, and commenting on the initiative that could raise most of a city and, without thought, plan its own destruction.

"If I ignored that girl's appeal I'd deserve it," himself said. "You're a lawyer. Very well. Handle your own business. You're not the man your father was. You say too much. If you'd said less, I might have left you at it. But I know what you'd do with this girl. We stopped throwing people to the lions a long time ago."

"They still send bitches to the moon," Young Carvalhos Ramos said.

She was still half drunk when the policewoman opened the cage door to let her out, and all the other women inside screamed and sang and stamped. The place was dark, down a dark stairway, along dark corridors, to the space with a bare bulb, a scratched table, rickety chairs, barred windows, and a smell of misery and human grime. The policewoman, brisk, in her early twenties, dark hair bunned in the peaked pillbox, seemed a vision, no less, of starched blue linen, pressed serge, and a bath lotion that dominated all the talk.

"I knew they'd call you," Iralia said, older, and for the first time frowsy, without the shine of health or any light in the eye. "I didn't want you here. I don't need any help. The stuff was planted. Jacob told me so. They were going to blackmail you."

"How?" Young Carvalhos Ramos said, and clearly he was wishing he had washed and dressed, instead of having to meet the policewoman's cool eye in his purple- and gray-striped pajamas. "The entire gang's been arrested. What was there to blackmail for?"

She sat sideways on the horrible little chair that was probably crawling, looking at himself in the way he knew, ah yes. She wanted to take her clothes off and lie on roses.

"The room was cheap," she said, with more strength in her voice, because the policewoman was watching her. "I didn't know the house was a filling point. I answered the door, took messages, parcels, anything. That's why I got the room cheap. I never saw anybody else living there, except the woman upstairs. But I'd met a few people before I met you. I went to some clubs and sang with the band. Earned a little more. And a couple of hours' music. I met a few of the boys in Rio. I couldn't stop them coming up."

She looked at her hands, that were dirty, and put them down, holding the seat of the chair, swung a black satin slipper, tried to rub marks out of the black satin sheath, and looked at the policewoman and shook her head.

"I hope you'll let me have a bath soon," she said. "That room. I could die in there. Even the floor moves."

"I'll look after you," the policewoman said.

"I'll take care of any expenses," The O'Dancy said.

"Don't do any more than you need," Iralia said, loud and shrill. "It's my fault. Nobody was ever kind. Nobody looked after me. I thought you were sent from God that night. I was wishing for roses. Roses. Only roses. Wishing. Praying. And you came behind me. It was the voice I expected."

The tears ran down her cheeks, shone, ran, and she caught them with her tongue.

"After we went to Rio, the first time, a man came in with the woman upstairs," she said in the trembling voice. "He only nodded.

The woman told me. He listened. She showed me the wire under the bed. She knew who you were."

The policewoman touched her arm, and looked at the clock.

"In five minutes, the night judge will be in session," she said. "She'll have to be ready."

"Get bail, get anything," The O'Dancy said. "Get her out. Take her to my place."

"No," Iralia said. "Never. You won't suffer because of me. Nobody else was ever kind. Nobody ever made me feel so much. I love to feel. Feel."

The fists, body on tiptoe, tightly shut eyes, head back, teeth in a grin, and the policewoman took her by the elbow, and she went down on her heels, and blinked.

"Till the next time," she said, and followed the policewoman, with the black satin drawing the silver lines of her grace in darkness.

"You heard it," The O'Dancy said. "Do what you can."

"If the judge wants you, I'll call you," Young Carvalhos Ramos said. "If the reporters know anything about this, keep away from them. Say nothing."

He waited in the wide, glass-roofed room of worn white paint upstairs that had been a salon for ambassadors in the days of velvet and plumed hats, but even the cigar tasted the same as the smell. Young Carvalhos Ramos was a long time, and it was daylight beyond the doors, but he walked easily, an uncombed head and an overcoat in silhouette, swinging the umbrella, and the pajama trousers had been tied tighter, showing his calves.

"She's out," he said. "I just sent her off to the hotel. She made me promise you wouldn't know where."

"You're saying that," The O'Dancy said.

"I promised," Young Carvalhos Ramos said, in the eye, eye to eye, the eye of his father.

"Splendid," himself said, and put a hand out. "You did well. When's she got to appear?"

"I'll make a case," Young Carvalhos Ramos said. "There's something I don't like. I don't think she's what she appears. The record I saw isn't hers. Dismiss it from your mind."

"You see what we get for coming down here," himself said.

"Illumination. Do they never clean anything here? Or is the place greased with the prayers of so many lost souls it won't wipe off? Is that it?"

"Would The O'Dancy pay to have it all scraped and painted?" Young Carvalhos Ramos asked. "The state hasn't the money for it."

"A thought worthy of your father, and God love the idea of him, too," The O'Dancy said. "It'll be done."

Standing there, in the green light from one window and blue light from another, in the reception room. Well, it was painted in gold letters on the glass doors, though nobody guaranteed the sort of reception anybody might expect, especially not the father paying for everything, and himself particularly hated the slosh of paint by some idiot hanging on the wall, even so, a little crooked, and so was the price, whatever it was, crooked, from a crooked mind, a crooked soul and damn it all, only a crooked buyer would fling money away on it.

"Who chose that infliction?" he asked, looking at the swabs of no color and blobs and dishonest dabs.

"Everything in this building was chosen by me," Hilariana said, and picked up the magazine. "That's a Tamish. Probably the best painter since Picasso. Are you interested?"

"Disgusted," he said. "Apostles of ugliness, the pair of them."

"They tell you the horrors of your world," she said, looking at photographs. "You helped to create them. You persist in their creation. You do nothing."

"I don't hang the stuff on walls," he said. "I'd never spend a cent on it."

"You prefer a condominium of prostitutes," she said.

"What are they, except prostitutes?" he shouted. "Paid-for essays in disgust. Is there any single line or tone that'd ever give you a quiet moment? At least my prostitutes settle a hunger."

"Hunger," she said, laughing again, quietly, showing more of the long leg.

"Hunger," himself said with the sadness heavy about him, and quiet. "Oh, dear Christ, such hunger."

Remembering the narrow white bed, golden in three candles, and the glow, the edged, lit, petaled warmth of scarlet roses.

Gentle hands, a luscious mouth, the tongue, and a cool, smooth skin, and muscle, oh, and God be praised, life, the marvel of a mighty pulse, and a woman's gentle hands, and the soothe of whispers barely heard, the gentleness, the guardian-sweet gentleness of a woman in love, tenderly, wholly of love, with love.

"God damn it," he said over two quiet bodies. "You never knew love between a man and a woman. You don't know what love between a man and woman is. Or hunger. That isn't for bread. Or gifts. Or anything. Not for money."

"Simply for another body," Hilariana said almost to herself, while she looked at the pages, passing her hand down her own body, tight in nylon, greenish in the window glass. "Of course, I do know. Yes, I do. But how to find it?"

"Ah, sir," Young Carvalhos Ramos said over the telephone. "They just found her. The room hadn't been used. She was found in the building next to the bank. The half-finished one. She was strangled. The police will do everything. I promise you, so will I. She was quite innocent."

"But who would do that?" he said, looking at the crucifix, and believing nothing.

"Sir," Young Carvalhos Ramos said. "We have many people who would, for a price, in our country. Unfortunately."

"Find the man or men," himself had said. "Cost is nothing. I'll pay anything."

"Money is no use to the guilty," Young Carvalhos Ramos said. "It accuses them. She's dead. Was it the police? They could make money. The other people? She's a mouth stopped. Let it rest. One more dead. Does it matter?"

Nothing mattered. All the reports and the lawyers hurrying came to nothing. No relatives came to find her. No policeman or bus-driver brother, in love or not.

"Nothing to do except bury her," the chief of police said in his sympathetic way. "Would the illustrious gentleman care to identify her?"

"I don't advise it," the policewoman said. "I identified her by her feet and her hands. She took great care of her person."

"I'll ask for a Mass at the cathedral," himself said. "Do many go like this?"

The police chief turned down his mouth, and the group of officers moved in a sort of shrug of the feet.

"She's not the first," he said.

"What's being done about the people behind her?" himself asked.

"We've got a few of the outer ring, that's all," the police chief said, and straightened his tie, and pulled down the lapels of a gray silk suit. "We'll never find the big fish. They're too deep in the ocean."

He rubbed finger and thumb.

"This does everything," he said, and smoothed his hands about the air. "All settled."

"Offer a ten-million-cruzeiro reward," himself told Young Carvalhos Ramos. "I'll bring them to account."

"A hundred million won't," Young Carvalhos Ramos said. "Where are the witnesses? Alive or dead? If they appeared in public, how long would they live?"

"As bad as that," himself said.

"Worse," Young Carvalhos Ramos said. "The judges, the police, the lawyers, my professional brethren, how many would you trust?"

"There's yourself," himself had said.

"Perhaps," Young Carvalhos Ramos said. "Perhaps. Only perhaps."

"This hunger you speak about," Hilariana said in the repressed voice, as though she spoke with sweet fruit in her throat, and oh, she was like the marvel of her mother then. "Do you suppose it's any easier for a woman? Are we talking about the same thing?"

"I'm getting tired of standing up," he said. "It's when you feel you want another body. That's what I mean, and God forgive me for talking like this. I never thought I'd say anything of the sort to my own daughter."

She lay back and laughed, and swung her legs away from him, and the magazine fell on the floor.

"I wonder what your hypercritical staff'd say if they came in and saw you," himself said. "You're half naked. Are you wearing anything under that?"

"Not much," she said, and lay quietly, looking sideways through the window. "I envy a man. He can go with anything. We can't.

Unless we want the name. I don't. Even if I could, I wouldn't. Couldn't. Is that the Irish?"

"You could marry," himself said, struck with sorrow, and suddenly, because the young Hilariana was in her voice, and the woman lying there was all but quickly, in that moment, defenseless, seeking, crying for protection. "For the love of Jesus, now, I suppose in many ways I've been a bad father. I don't know what more I could have done. I can tell you I've been proud enough of your looks. Proud of what you've done. I hate this place, but others think it's a wonder. I suppose I should. Where did I go wrong? What did I do? What didn't I do?"

And standing there, in the cathedral, asking himself, a little one before the high altar, and the choir screeching, if there was anything he could have done to save Iralia. But there was the selfish way, and he had taken it, because the days were filled with thought of a naked girl lying white on scarlet roses, and the drip of champagne gold in candlelight, and happy, laughing talk forgotten, all in a little room in a slum, and himself in the careless, yes, the selfish dream.

In the priest's voice, a saintly whisper at that distance, he knew the viciousness. He wondered what the few people there would think if he stood up, now, and denounced himself as a part-murderer.

A bearded man in the front pew told his rosary over both hands, kneeling, following the service, word for word with the priest. A ragged man, a beggar, in an old raincoat torn under the arms and at both overfull pockets, wearing broken shoes too big and tied with string. But the back of that head, rough as a gray terrier, called out. The back of that head he knew. He wondered if the man had been in his employ, or if a beggar had come to the gate. But when the Cup was brought down, and he knelt at the rail, he saw the bearded face from the side, and the spirit of himself seemed to falter, for there was no doubt of it, but the beggar was Horacyr.

Horacyr, kneeling at the rail as any prince, taking Hope with the gestures of the Palace, and walking back, in the broken shoes trailing string, as emperors approach a throne, to kneel again, and in his face the authority of priesthood.

They went in line, after the blessing, to the flowers piled where her body should have been, and the file of quiet people took the silver dipper, sprinkled water in the Name, and himself saw the drops, golden in candlelight, and prayed within himself, without words, for peace, O peace, for a dear girl with no fault except that she felt, yes, felt the flight of wonder in her senses, and adored her Creator in the miracle of His orgasm, trumpet blast of new souls, of birth the harbinger.

The beggar knelt, arms folded on the end of the catafalque, staring into the lights.

"Horacyr," himself had said when everyone was gone.

Only the eyes looked at him.

"Princess and beggar," Horacyr said in the same voice. "Won't you disturb your pocket for the beggar's prayer?"

"Of course," himself had said, and passed the notes. "You don't remember me? Arquimed?"

"Arquimed," Horacyr said, putting the notes inside that raincoat, with the rattle of metal pots somewhere in there. "I remember nobody, except my love."

He spoke loudly, and the echoes went up, up, past the statues of the saints, above the bishop's crimson canopy, seeming to make the altar's lilies tremble.

"Where you not called to the priesthood, yourself?" The O'Dancy asked, for the young priest in his vestments stood not far away, watching them. "Surely, you were going to Rome to the college, were you not?"

"Sonia is my church, and my love," Horacyr said. "I worship a virgin."

"Sonia," The O'Dancy said.

9 Two youths, a girl, in a sailboat, and green days in the mangroves' shadow along the Amazon. Silence in the darkness of nights flecked in static snowstorms of stars, the stir of fish, and the three of them lying face down, looking into water lit by mystery, watching schools of luminous shapes in chase or fighting. Dawn, pale green again, and faint rose, mauve, and a naked girl, the first white girl he had ever seen naked in the clear air, curling her toes on the bowsprit, with the mists of morning passing in caress, and rising light touching fair hair in a flame cloud, itself a sun, with her hands enclosing a bauble of golden froth at her thighs. And ever, yes, for them, a virgin.

"I never found out what happened to you," himself said, but Horacyr was walking away. "Will you not speak to me? Will you not let me help you? Come, no argument, now. We'll find the car, and go home. My clothes'll fit you."

"This is my chapel," Horacyr said, turning at the door. "Every child, every beggar in São Paulo helped to build it. The widow's mite, the school child's toffee, the beggar's rice, and the women. Without the women, this would be space. Four walls, nothing more. The night I found her, I prayed here. I conducted the service of thanksgiving. I give a little of everything I receive. The beggar and the prince, or princess? They die? I pray."

Except for his genial quietness, there was nothing sane about him.

The O'Dancy tried to find any part of himself in a dry mouth. The young priest made a sign that he would help, and himself shook his head, but in sorrow.

"God love you," himself said. "What's this about Sonia? The last I heard, she was in a convent."

"She's here, with me," Horacyr said outside on the step, and nodding across the narrow street. "We are together. It took time. But prayer and love, what shall withstand them?"

"Your father had millions," himself said, desperate, for the poor man was walking across the road, showing bare heels. "How are you brought down in such a state?"

"The rich are sent empty away," Horacyr said in the middle of the road, raising his arms and swinging the rosary. "I gave everything for Sonia."

He walked to the shape squatting in the dark doorway, and knelt beside her, talking, taking her hand.

Himself went over, slower, hoping.

But there could be no doubt of those eyes, the blue eyes, bluer in ghastly strip light from the bar a little way down, looking at him, but not knowing, never knowing, without hope of knowing, but only freezingly, merrily, mad, and chin on fist, looking at him, past him, and good-by Sonia, good-by memory, good-by, there was no more awful word.

"I must help you," he said. "Please, dear Christ, let me help you."

"We have the Vespers, then they put out the candles, and I shall have one," Horacyr said, holding up a space between thumb and finger. "Even that's enough for wonderful light, and we wash, and say our prayers. I shall cook a good rice, tonight."

"Listen to me, Horacyr," himself said. "For the sake of old times. Will you not please let me put the pair of you in the car, and get you taken care of? Won't you allow me the plain duty? We could talk things over, and find out what you'd care to do. Let me help you."

"Yes," Horacyr said, and held the hand to his cheek, and looked at her, but she still looked the merry smile up the hill. "In a few days we shall walk to the lake. The peace that passeth all understanding, you remember? My love's a blessed woman. Who could be more beautiful than my love?"

The O'Dancy waited for traffic to pass, and went across to the steps. The young priest stood in the doorway talking to Bulhões.

"I'd like to do something for those two," himself said. "They're friends of mine, more than forty years ago. Think of that."

The young priest nodded.

"The man could be a nuisance, but he never is," he said. "People don't like the unwashed. But there again, we can't discourage him. Christ washed a beggar's feet. They say he was a priest. He seems to know a great deal. They're both mad, of course."

"Nothing to be done," himself said. "They were both beautiful. But if you know they're mad, why do you permit one or other inside?"

The young priest rapped his knuckles on thick timber.

"These doors were made wide enough to admit all souls, at all times," he said. "They're perfectly quiet. They've forgotten there's sorrow in the world. Isn't that as well?"

But standing there in the blue window light, looking at Hilariana on the other side, in green, himself wondered if he had ever remembered that the world had its sorrows, or had ever been conscious of a sorrowful moment in any life except his own, until, of course, it was too late.

"You can't answer me, can you?" Hilariana said. "There's no one rule for us."

"Why don't you write a list of the men you know," he said. "Or let me make a list. A long one. The best I can find. Run a pin down it. Stick one, and let me go and talk to him. Any man in your bed, and you'll be a happier woman."

"How many women have you had in your bed?" she asked. "When were you a happy man?"

"A man's different," himself said, and not believing it, and cold, yes, sent empty away.

She sat up, swinging her legs over, pushing her feet farther in the sandals.

"Your meal ought to be ready," she said. "I'm afraid you'll have to excuse me."

"I'll have something at The House," he said. "One bite here'd be poison."

"You should have let me marry Hiroki," she said.

"You were fourteen years of age," he shouted. "Great God in His mercy, what's a man to do?"

"I was old enough, and just as ready as I am now," she said. "That's when I began to hate you, I think. I didn't know it, though. Hate, real hate, takes time."

"Ah, Judas," he prayed, eyes up, almost seeing The Shadow.

"Are you listening? Did you ever know greater triumph on such a royal day, then?"

"There's Father Miklos just coming in," she said, and put her hands up to tighten hairpins. "Probably about the two last night. He'll be glad to talk to you about dear Judas, and all that black-bog nonsense. It's heresy, you know."

"What's heresy, now?" himself asked.

"This nonsense about Judas' Day," she said, half through a coil of laughter. "It's not in the liturgy. Africans weren't the only ones to introduce curious ideas. Irishmen helped, didn't they? It must have been old Grandfa Leitrim. That bandit. What a horror he must have been."

"I wonder if he was ever half the horror you are, yourself, at this moment," The O'Dancy said.

He had to push the glass door open, and while he went down the stairs, she was still laughing at him.

With no sound.

10 White sunshine made Father Miklos look brilliantly younger, in the clean white habit tipped by the shine of the nimbus, which was what he called the rim of short white hair about his ears, which almost gave him the halo he deserved, though the tan of his face was still pale against the black skin of Democritas, and the eyes of him a clear brown, perhaps a light madeira, and white whites, but the eyes of Dem looked all black, and very sad, or at any rate bulbously unwell.

"The patron of us all," Father Miklos said. "And what's first to be told this day?"

"Nothing, except praise God and all about Him we're alive," The O'Dancy said, and kissed the held-out crucifix, and half-knelt and crossed himself. "Would you not know some devilry'd be in preparation against the day? Two of them. Where will you bury them?"

"There's nobody to bury," Father Miklos said. "They've both gone home."

"But didn't Hilariana think they were dead?" himself said in a regular stare. "Would she make a mistake?"

"Evidently," Father Miklos said, and no great interest. "I came to borrow some plants for the chapel. No excuses, now. You'll be there in the morning?"

"I will," The O'Dancy said, and turned himself about, facing the green window up there, and saw her looking down. "Hilariana, would you kindly come here, please?"

"What a nuisance," Father Miklos said. "I didn't mean to disturb her. She's a very busy girl. But I fear she intervenes where she oughtn't."

"There's nowhere anywhere near where she couldn't intervene, if that's what took her mind," The O'Dancy said. "When I'm not here, she's the boss. Let's be having it right, now, shall we?"

Hilariana came down the stairway wrapping the overall a little tighter. She looked no less than tall, and cool, and wonderful, and his own darleen glory, and so she was.

"The two you treated last night," himself said. "Were they hurt at all?"

"Hurt?" she said, and stayed where she was, a smile, perhaps because she wanted to please everybody, a stare at the question, and a frown on the way. "Of course they weren't hurt. They were dead."

"They're both at home," himself said. "Back home in Mouras Bentos."

Hilariana looked at all of them, and away at the rainbow, and back, through the massing pink-and-gloriously-blue hydrangea, to himself.

"I don't believe it," she said, and shook her head, but gently. "Neither had pulse or temperature. And it isn't much use bandaging a ten-inch wound, is it? The other had been knifed through the liver."

Father Miklos looked at Dem, and Dem looked down at the edge of the bulge.

"I'll tell you how we settle this," himself said. "Get in the truck. We'll go there, and find out."

"I'm coming with you," Hilariana said. "I want to see who can make a fool of me. After all, I do happen to know a little about nursing."

It was a day's journey by horse, and less than an hour by truck, and the ride was pleasant enough, through the coffee groves, across the pasture, and Clovis, by old custom, pressing the button for three hoots to bring people out of the few houses they passed to wave greeting to The O'Dancy, along the river and over the log bridge, into the village, outside the narrow part of The Inheritance, where freed slaves had once built huts and Arabs had settled to open shops. The place had never grown, because no roads were near, and the land belonged to the state, a poor tract not likely to be sold. The fifty or so people living there made a little money by odd help in harvesting or planting, or working with cattle, but most of them grew sugar cane to make spirit, and sold the bottles down the river.

The only street was hollowed by the rains and rutted with the dried mud of generations. A dozen houses and shops built on stone plinths to keep the floors out of a flooding river were of mud laced with bamboo, whitewashed, and painted about door and window frames in wide bands, each house a different color. The place on a quiet day of sun had its charm, The O'Dancy was forced to admit, but himself knew the murk of soul and corpus behind the quiet and the color.

Clovis pulled up in the dried ruts at the end of the street, and went to a closed door. Not even a child came out anywhere. Shopkeepers moved in shadow beyond bead fly curtains, and chickens scratched in heaped refuse, but flies were the liveliest creatures anywhere.

The door creaked open a crack and light wrinkled the eyes of a crone smoking a pipe. She looked one to the other, a moment, and swung the door wider and nodded them in. An earth floor was clean swept, and a fire sparked in a corner. The table held washing and sewing, and there were hats on chairs carpentered from cane. Coffee sent its savor through the place, taking edge off the smell of years of living stuck to smoke-dark walls and cobwebbed rafters.

Except for Father Miklos they went in a group, through to the next room, and an earth floor, clothing on pegs, a saddle, boots, and a fall of slippers in the corner, a shuttered window chinking moted sunlight, and in a hammock in deep shadow a dark face watched them without fear or any sign of illness.

"Glicerio," Democritas said. "You were at The Inheritance last night?"

Glicerio nodded.

"You played dominoes and you drew a knife, you and Afonso," Dem said. "You cut three men. Julião settled both of you. Yes?"

Glicerio seemed to shake only his eyes, slowly, in steady denial.

"Wait," The O'Dancy said, and looked at Hilariana. "Is this one of them?"

She was staring at the man, but as if stricken in the very soul of her.

"I ordered him sewn in a blanket and taken to his family," she said slowly, to be heard. "The other as well. This one has the wound across the body. He wasn't alive."

"Supposing you'd buried him," The O'Dancy said.

"HE-WAS-NOT-ALIVE," she said, and bent a knee a little with every word.

"He looks all right," The O'Dancy said, and turned to the old woman. "Take off the sheet. I want to see the injury."

"He's in a pudding of herbs," the old woman said, pipe in mouth. "But the worst is over. He won't hurt."

She folded the sheet down, and carefully pulled off a cloth stuck with a green mess. Under shreds of leaves and stalks, they saw the broad wound.

Hilariana straightened, looking at the wall.

"Very well," she said in all acceptance. "I believe it. Now that I've seen it, I believe it."

She went outside, and she was calling for Father Miklos.

"Where's the other one?" The O'Dancy asked.

"He lives beyond the pool, in the swamp," Clovis said, running his hat through his fingers. "You'd have to walk, Master. It's a long way."

"I've seen enough," The O'Dancy said, and looked down at Glicerio. "Why were you over there? Why did you fight?"

"We went to see Brother Mihaul," Glicerio said, and no harm in his quietness. "We played dominoes and drank coffee, and the others came on us. There wasn't a fight."

"You're telling the truth," The O'Dancy said, sure of his man.

Glicerio held up his right hand.

"Let this burn," he said.

"Why did you want to see Brother Mihaul?" himself asked.

"We wanted candles, and other things," Glicerio said.

"Could you not buy them here?" himself asked.

"We don't burn the Devil's light," Glicerio said, and turned his eyes toward the old woman. "Come forth, Mother. Out. Not a word, or any sign."

The old woman seemed to be shivering, and her arms were twisted stiff about her neck, with the finger joints bent against the backs of her hands, and as quickly she opened her eyes, and took out the pipe, and smiled at them.

The O'Dancy walked out to the street.

Hilariana sat in the truck, leaning back, eyes closed. Father Miklos stood outside one of the shops, talking to a little girl. The O'Dancy went up and took his arm, and turned about to look at Democritas, a ball of a man taking up almost half the road.

"That woman was on her way into a trance, was she not?" himself called out.

Dem nodded, staring over his head.

"*Macumba*, then?" The O'Dancy said.

Dem frowned, and seemed to take other strength.

"Not that, Master," he said, loudly, perhaps for listening ears. "*Umbanda*."

"*Umbanda*," The O'Dancy said, impatient. "*Macumba, khimbanda, Umbanda*, what's the difference?"

"A far greater difference than between Hinduism, Buddhism and Christianity," Father Miklos said. "Those three are cleanly. The three you mentioned are of Satan."

He raised the crucifix.

"I forbid you to speak," he told Dem. "Not a word. Wait until I am not in your company."

Himself squeezed the holy man's arm.

"If you know, why don't you tell me?" himself said. "Why should I be breaking my head against this, if there's something I can do? But what can I do if I don't know?"

Father Miklos looked along the ruts curving into the treed edge of the swamp.

"There have been many visitors here today," he said, and pointed his stick at the tracks. "These are not your vehicles. These are private cars, and how often do private cars come here?"

"Find out who these belonged to," himself said to Clovis, pointing at the tire tracks, and looked at Father Miklos. "Have you nothing else to tell me?"

The holy man went off in a long stride to the left, up a stony rain drain between two houses, along the overgrowth of broken-fenced gardens, through the stench of ordure and refuse, and up a clean path, to a low wall of stone, and looked through a banana clump at a small house, shaped like a chapel with a bell tower. Flat columns framed double doors in the Gothic style, the walls

white, the door red, and the columns blue, all massed with flowers
and fruits about the pediment, with a smell of rot in the air. Feathers, and red flesh going black littered the three steps leading to the
doors, and blood in black satin, and the pelts of cats, a goat, and
sheep.

"Blood sacrifice," he said, staring as he did when he read the
Mass. "*Khimbanda*. It floods, it engulfs. You see how near you and
your people are to disaster?"

"I'll have the place burned down this very day," The O'Dancy
said, cold. "I never knew a word about it. Clovis, you and
Basilio, get the cans of gasoline. Hurry."

Democritas put out a hand, but Clovis had not even moved.

"Master," he said, and took off his hat. "Please. Spare us this. The
property belongs to somebody else."

"I'll build a fine chapel on the same ground," The O'Dancy said.
"Nobody'll suffer. But I'll burn out this plague spot here and now."

"Not as simple as that," Father Miklos said. "You burn bricks.
The evil persists. Where is the root? Who owns the ground?"

"Very well," The O'Dancy said. "Who?"

"Brother Mihaul," Father Miklos said. "And he built this."

The O'Dancy walked backward, away. Himself looked at the
beaked, brown ball of a priestly head in silver rim, and the white
habit throwing up light in the lines of the face and shining in the
peaceful brown eyes.

"Oh, God, now," himself said. "What are you saying to me? My
own brother, too? Is that why Hilariana cried the tears? For him?
The plague rat. He wouldn't dare whisper of it to me. Or bring
his filth anywhere near us. He had to sneak over here. To the
swamp. Very well. This day he goes. Bag and baggage. Purify his
house, first. Then I'll have a tractor smash it in the dust. In any
case, what's his is mine. Clovis, get the gasoline."

"Clovis has gone, Master," Dem said in a shaking voice. "But he
won't bring the gasoline. None of us will. Not one. We bring The
Touch upon us. The Touch, Master. The evil. The howl of the
dark places."

Father Miklos raised the crucifix.

"Peace," he said. "Here is nothing to fear. Nothing. Let us go
back. Arquimed, I suggest you speak to Brother Mihaul. At last we

approach a nadir. But it's been going on for more than thirty years. Since he left the Order.

Hilariana had gone, with Dem, João, and Basilio. The street was still.

"Never mind," Father Miklos said. "You can talk to her afterward. But remember. There were visitors here."

"I'll see him," himself said. "By God, I will."

"Wait, now," Father Miklos said. "Let me explain."

"Nothing," The O'Dancy said. "Let him do the explaining. I'll do the burning."

11 On the other side of the bridge it was simple to tell they were back in The Inheritance. Green order in pastures and groves went on for miles. Far off, sign of fine weather, the mountains were an even, deep, brilliant blue, fair in promise, fairer in work, with quarries deepening as national highways grew, and lumber coming out for pulp, timberyards stacking a greater variety of rare woods than any other country in the world could show, and ore fields of so many kinds that the trucking fleets were painted a special color for each.

If himself asked a question about the balance sheet of O'Dancy Enterprises, there could be little in the answer but deep content-ment. Nobody sold more coffee, fruit, sugar, wine, peanuts, or cotton for a better price, or carried as much tonnage in his own ships. No cattleman on the continent had finer herds, and there was never a time when anybody had outsold him. With the elec-tric rail completed from the mountains to São Paulo, the output of timber would increase fifty times or more, and transport of everything else would cost far less. There were unsung mineral deposits up there that few would know about until the Govern-ment was ready to issue a loan for a third steel foundry. The other two had cost O'Dancy Enterprises nothing, and both were doing well, though they could have doubled or tripled output except for the Army's cold clutch on the board of directors. The generals themselves seemed intelligent enough, but their trading policies were brutally limited, possibly because optimum yield might create a flourishing economy and a happier people, with less worry about national security, which could mean smaller military budgets, less power to move men and arms, less regard for gold lace, and fewer paunches to wallow in decorated idleness.

Farther north, almost unexplored, were veins of precious stones. Yet the oil fields, about midway, could make himself another prince of the Arabian Nights. If, that is, the Government would help instead of hinder. The right price for the terrain, and a percentage on each barrel, and everything would fall pleasantly into place. Any scheme for expropriation, or working without royalty, and himself promised war on the responsible politicians, whether by newspaper, radio, or television, or simply by closing shops and factories in their electoral areas. Most of the state legislators did as they were told or they knew what to expect, whether then or at the next election. A bottle of wine, free beer, and a few cruzeiros did wonders at the polling booth, and that was how Hiroki, a third-generation Tomagatsu, was put in his place.

A fighting samurai out to remake the world was what the fellow pretended to be, forever spouting about reapportionment of land, production by collective farms, a basic market price and daily wage, Government-financed housing at ridiculous rents, new schools, technical colleges, universities for "poor" men's sons and daughters, oh yes, the young fellow fairly sweated his nonsense, though, of course, the money was to come from taxation on capital or some other cheap-jack way.

"What happened to young Hiro Tomagatsu?" himself asked while they bumped across pasture. "Did he go back in the bank?"

"He joined another man on the coast," Father Miklos said. "They're growing camphor trees. Very profitable. He's happier than in politics."

"I'd hope so," himself said. "Probably a little saner by this time."

"A very good man," Father Miklos said, keeping his eyes on the road. "We could do with many another."

"We'd be bankrupt the sooner," himself said.

"We're in peril of it now, and no help from him," Father Miklos said.

"Have you any idea of the profit we made last year?" himself asked.

"I'm not talking about you, but the country," Father Miklos said. "You and your sort of people have had your hands on the wheel the whole time. We've gone nowhere else but down. And down. What's the cruzeiro worth today?"

"No business of mine," The O'Dancy said. "That's the Government. I attend to my business, and I can tell you, it's thoroughly healthy. There're too many of us putting our noses into matters that don't concern us. That's where we go wrong. But any harm the politicians do by day, dear Mother Brazil grows back and covers over by night. That's one satisfaction."

"We're becoming known as Strike Land," Father Miklos said.

"They should take the Army to them," himself said. "That's what we pay for."

"Would you let me off at the chapel, please," Father Miklos said. "I'll have to go back for those plants."

"I'll have them sent," himself said. "I'll come in with you. You can say a little prayer. I don't want that thought of Satan hanging over me. This day's not far longer to go. Until now, no great trouble. Enough. Not too much."

Father Miklos rubbed his chin and leaned an elbow on his stick until Clovis turned into the chapel garden, itself a wonder of color, planned and supervised, of course, by Hilariana, and herself in a smile everywhere.

They got down in a warmth of scent, and walked to the postern. Father Miklos went through the belfry door toward the altar, and himself went into the family pew and sat still, a boy again, and The Mam and Tad beside him, and Grandfa Shaun in the leather chair with his feet up, and Bobo, his man, squatting beside him near the rail, and the family and everybody else behind it.

The paneling came from somewhere north, brought in on carts by Grandfa Phineas, and it was told that all the pieces were black when they got there, but after a polish they came up in a shine they had ever kept since the day. All around, to twice the height of a man, bas-relief silver figures showed the Birth of Christ in the Manger, the Coming of the Three Wise Men, the Flight into Egypt, the Teaching in the Temple, the Scourging of the Money-changers, the Agony in the Garden, the Judgment by Pontius Pilate, the Stations of the Cross, and behind the altar the Resurrection. The ceiling shone in gold and silver, put up there by men brought especially from Rome in Grandfa Shaun's young day as a birthday present for Grandam Xatina. The pulpit was made of black and white marble, and the font came from a church in Serbia, bought by The Mam on one of her trips abroad.

Peace settled there, and all hallow in memory of those at rest, please God, and pray for the dear souls of them all, now.

Incense bloomed, a prayer itself, and fondled the scent of flowers.

Father Miklos sat in his chair by the side of the altar, in shadow.

"O God," The O'Dancy prayed, sitting out, tired. "Help me, now. Help me, for I've been a fool. But I have. I've tried."

Himself wondered if he had ever tried as hard as Grandfa Shaun or any of the others. He was uncertain about the others, but Grandfa Shaun had worked most of his life with oxen and wooden plows until the day they got the steel shares, and thousands coming from all over the land to see the teams all going forward in a long, long line, and Grandfa Shaun one of them. Even as an old one, and shaky, the hand of him was hard and glossy as wood. Grandam Aracý spoke for him. She sat in the front pew, with a white mantilla pinned with a flower. When she left the chapel, old Tunta, her maid since a child, took it off and put on the black, with another flower, fresh from Grandam Xatina's garden, every plant and bulb, from all over the world, a gift from Grandfa Shaun. His son, Grandfa Connor, was another sort, a tall, broad man in dark suits, given more to brain than the plow. He changed the breed of the cattle, and bought stud animals long before anybody else thought of it. He was first to supply the city with butter, cream, and cheese in quantity, and when others competed, he was first to put the butter, cream, and cheese in tins, and then fruit and vegetables. After that he found cooks off the ships to make soups and stews and cooked meats of all sorts that could be tinned. From there to a cannery industry was not far. It was one of the strongest arms of the O'Dancy Enterprises, especially after himself signed with the fishermen. The world wanted flour made from fish, now. Himself had no idea of it, but it was supposed to be good for the system, and the O'Dancy Cannery and Mills could supply any amount because Mother Brazil had a long coastline and every fish in the world loved swimming near her. There was no end to it.

But if Steb was to be a medical man, and God put an arm about the boy, there was nobody in the place of himself. Hilariana had her own work, and it seemed that any idea of marriage was far from her way of thinking. In any event, no son of hers could be

the true O'Dancy. Steb was, as son of a second wife, an O'Dancy
of a sort.

Paul was the true heir, but himself turned from any thought of
it, or of him, a dirty, drunken animal, no less, and no right to the
name. But second true son of himself, nonetheless, and in law, if
he went to court, the heir of himself and not much argument.
Upward of forty he must be, never a day's work in him, not a
thought of anything except the bottle and women. Not every
woman or any woman. Only the black ones, and the blacker the
better, for him, and the house pulsed with his litter, and he
sat among them and laughed.

Hilariana laughed, but Paul laughed in another way, out loud
and happily, and his women thought he was God, and the children,
generally coffee-colored, some with red hair and gray eyes, climbed
all over him, and he loved them and they loved him. There was
never so much love in any family. But the man had never earned
one cent, and never intended to, and never would, and said so.

"I'm born a man, and these are women, and this is Brazil," he
said. "Why should I work for you or anybody else? You brought that
nonsense from Europe. Take it back there. We can grow beans and
rice and mandioca. If we can't, there are bananas and nuts and
animals and fish. The world managed to live before you were born,
O'Dancy. Before your fathers were born. What did old Leitrim eat
when he came in here? Jaguar steak? Monkey? Plenty of birds. It's
you that's mad, O'Dancy. Building those skyscrapers? The people
are living in them, floor on floor, and the cess pouring down through
the walls all about them. If it was glass, or if you could smell what
was pouring a few feet from your nose, could you live there? What
you don't see you don't miss. Fancy living in that sort of cascade.
Part of it. To hell, man. I live on the floor. We're healthy, and
happy, and there's love anywhere you look."

The truth, no less, and little room for argument or reason, at any
rate, on his terms.

But it was strange that a man so against everything rational
should be just as unpleasant with Brother Mihaul, another fellow
without sense of duty, or responsibility, or any affection at all for
anyone of the family, not even Steb, for the moment, or except
Hilariana, and that was no more than a grunt now and then when

they met. Two years younger, Mihaul was, than himself, and that was the root of the trouble because the man was greedy, unscrupulous, and ambitious beyond his gifts or station. As a boy he had taken all the prizes. He went to only one school as a minor and left there the prize scholar, and became prize man again before he went to the university, and then he graduated as a classical scholar and went to Rome. But whatever happened there, or elsewhere, nobody ever knew, and the Church never tells, but a day came when he got back to The Inheritance on foot, a thin, deep-eyed, silent scarecrow of a creature in a patched habit, with the shoes hanging off his feet. All he wanted was a roof, running water, and food. He never used his bank account, where his share of The Inheritance profits mounted with interest during the years, and he never moved more than a few miles outside, and then on foot, or if he felt like it, he might nod a ride on a cart or truck. What he did with himself, beyond read, possibly nobody knew, for there was no woman anywhere near him. Housework in the mud-and-bamboo shelter, and the garden, was part of his toil, and sometimes washing swung on the line. He never ate meat, he grew most of his vegetables, and fruit he was given, with salt, coffee, rice, and beans from The Inheritance store.

Only Stephen had ever gone near him.

In the years as a child, the moment he got away from his governess he was off to Brother Mihaul, and, wonder of all wonders, the uncle started teaching the boy. Himself made no objection. Stephen showed him the pages of Latin and Greek exercises, and recited poems, and Father Miklos talked to him, and said the boy was becoming a passable scholar, and that was reason enough for allowing him to go across there for hours every day. It told when he went to school and started romping away with the prizes. Mathematics, Greek, Latin, French, and Portuguese, there was never anybody near him, and he graduated from the university under age and with more prizes than anybody else since its founding.

But instead of coming into the business as the potential right-hand man of himself, the boy chose medicine.

He stood there and said so, and yes, a razor wound in the heart, no less, in thinking of Daniel.

That was no disappointment, but a great shock, and a lasting hurt. Himself had ordered an office designed for the boy, and engaged three beauties as part of the furniture, and a door engraved with "The O'Dancy, Son, Inc.," and in smaller letters "Estevão Leitrim O'Dancy Boys." The night he heard the word, himself got drunk and burned the drawings, and the firemen came through the window and took him home, and he opened a case of scotch and they all got drunk together. They were goodhearted men.

Steb and Koioko, now, that would be a fine match, it would, no doubt of it, a good boy and a dear little thing himself had known since her christening. The family was Buddhist, though in later generations many of them, and all of the youngest women, had gone into the Church because in studying at convent schools they could hardly be different from the others and, as old Tomagatsu had said, a blessing twice a day did nobody any harm except Satan.

The old man had been a great watcher of Satan. Whenever there was bad luck, it was proof enough to him that Satan was present, fork, tail, and sulphur, ready for mischief. Incense burned wherever he worked, and each room was smoked at dawn, and the sticks burned all through the house every hour of the clock.

"All decent men worship God instead of themselves and the thing that encases them, that dies," the old man said that day, over in his office, which was Japanese even to the absence of any chair in the place. "They forget Satan. But if there is a God, there must be a Satan. No God, no Satan. God creates in love, Satan destroys in hate. These are our poor human reasonings. These are our beliefs. You believe in God? Remember Satan."

It seemed nonsense at the time, and it was good to come out in the sunshine and light a cigarette, and walk across to the plane and fly up, over the lake and artificial ponds, above the coffee groves, and home.

But sitting there, in a glow of silver all about, and the poor Christ struggling up the hill with that cross, himself had to wonder about it. There had been enough in his own life to put up a fair score for the Other One. The thought made himself itch. It was not lost that an itch was touch of Satan, but after all, there was superstition, as Hilariana had said. It was a fair word, a condescending word,

and an excellent wrapping of knowledge about a vacuum of ignorance. Himself had not forgotten a wrapping of pretty paper, and
bows of plastic tape about a box that had only two stones and a
rotten banana in it, gift of Vanina that Christmas, because he
refused to let her go to Paris alone.

She went anyway. Himself followed, the moment he found out
she had gone, and there she was, having her face lifted, and her
breasts lifted, and everything else lifted except her spirit, that
secondhand thing she got from somewhere, that made her the life
of the party for a couple of hours, and death, nothing less, in the
house. There was no more children after Steb because she wore a
cap over the most gracious part of her beautiful aphrodisian body,
and when himself found out he told her that never again would he
go near her to have the best of himself washed down the drain.
That was when himself went out and found the girls, so many of
them the memory never stayed. Where the difference was between
putting it into them for them to wash, or into Vanina for her to
douche, he never quite settled with himself, but it was a sour time,
and he turned away from any memory.

Vanina had enough money of her own to do as she pleased, of
course, but so far as he knew, then, she had never had anything
to do with anybody but himself, perhaps because he had told her,
plainly, that if he ever found her with somebody it would mean a
bullet for both. She could have got a divorce, or at any rate, a
brasileiro divorce, which meant an end of marriage, but without the
right of marrying again. She never had once suggested it, and he
thought he knew why. It would be an end to being mistress of The
Inheritance, an end to being queen of the social season, and never
again could she command a private plane, or a banquet for a
couple of hundred or anything else in the O'Dancy name. She
loved power, and she had no intention of losing it. That accepted,
there was nothing himself could do. She was blameless in law. She
told Young Carvalhos Ramos, when he went to see her about a
separation, that she wanted only to be the wife of The O'Dancy,
and the bed in any of the O'Dancy houses was made and ready,
and she was naked and waiting in the middle of each, and always
had been, and would be until she died.

There was no more to be said, and all finality was in the voice of Young Carvalhos Ramos, putting his papers away, a married man, but susceptible, and plainly impressed by her beauty and by her tears, which himself knew were lies founting from the salt pit in the heart of her.

But there had been no haste about their marrying. When he came out of the shadows after Fransisca died, it was sudden, like waking up on a Sunday afternoon and wondering what day it was. There was never a question in his mind that he had to devote himself to the children. In those years he never knew any woman for more than a week or two, generally dancers or singers met in clubs. Gradually he got tired of the same body, the same chatter, the same restlessness. They were not women to bring peace. There was no peace in their own lives. They had none to bring into another's. They knew who he was, knew what the gifts would mean, and set about love-making as maids clean a house, those, that is, with any knowledge of what they were about. Very few he could remember were any more than listlessly inclined to patronize an old man's whim. But he had no whim. All he ever wanted was a woman, in her simplicity and beauty, moved in love, for the sake of love, not only to passion, but even to charity for somebody as willing to pretend as herself. But unless they were trained, very few women were actresses, especially in bed.

No doubt about it, himself, the very one, was lost. In London and Paris and Rome he strolled, and in Tunis and Madrid and Cairo. Faces were beautiful by night and ugly in the morning. Bodies were sumptuous in shadow, in sunlight of the damned, veined, raddled, bruised by other hands, other mouths. Perfume covered them for the waking hours, but nothing stifled the odor when light came bright. Fransisca, impeccable, *brasileira* supreme, was the measure, and nobody approached, or if they did, they suffered. In any event, the girls who consented were rarely on her level, and any comparison was stupidity. But with a nose above the bed sheets, it was difficult not to compare, and far more difficult to be courteous, or kind, or even attentive to what himself was there for, and if his partner was making private reservations about his age and the level of his energy, very well, then, he knew and sympathized with them when they lay there, and so many of them did, with that expression on their faces, and fell asleep. Generally he waited till then, and got up, and left them ten times what they had asked, which was ten times what they would dare ask a younger man, and walked out in blue streets, wherever it was, trying to think of some way of drowning or damping for a time the pain that was no pain at all, at least not in meat or nerve but only in memory.

Gradually, perhaps because of business, and luncheons, conferences, dinners, he got back to the women of Fransisca's style and social environment. Between São Paulo and Rio de Janeiro, and Mexico City and New York, and Caracas and Buenos Aires, and London and Paris, wherever he flew, private houses were open, the cards were on his mantelpiece or stuck in the mirror, or a secretary came in at seven o'clock to tell him that he was due somewhere or other in twenty minutes. It went on like that, a sort of mobile drunkenness, himself never certain where he would be during the next hours, and giving not a curse anyway, since he knew that every twenty-four hours O'Dancy Enterprises, under his control, was the richer by at least two hundred thousand dollars, on some days far more. If thought of the money gave himself any satisfaction, he was unsure. Himself was even unsure if thought or act of being a multimillionaire gave any sense of security.

Himself was himself, and there was no other way to be.

From childhood the family had been taught never to talk about money, and never to bring any topic to do with wealth or property into any conversation. Other children were taught in the same way, and it was acknowledged to be a mark of thoroughly bad upbringing to mention anything to do with finance or its offshoots and all about it.

So far as himself was concerned, money was ever only a usefulness.

It was in Paris, one evening, on the Rue de Rivoli going toward the Ritz. Darkness was on the way, and the lamps bloomed in their everlasting strings of pearls, and under the arcade a woman hurried in front of him, a black shape carrying a box, and without premonition or warning he was attacked and held and stabbed in the groin by Fransisca's perfume. Instantly he was back in the *souk* stall in Marrakech, and he knew that the woman in front must have been there, because the old Arab made the perfume only for the hand it was tested on, never for an absent one. At the moment he stood there, somebody bumped into her and the box dropped and the cover fell off, and while she picked up shoes and slapped tissue paper, she cursed loudly, healthily, some of the staunchest words in the language, but with the accent of Rio de Janeiro.

"Well," he said. "Carioca. Now, where did I put the maracas?"

She was nothing like Fransisca, of course, but while he helped her to wrap the box, he knew she was exquisite in her own way, with the huge, palest of pale brown eyes, almost an amber, that could only have known the Brazilian sun. The tone of a ripened peach—ah, Fransisca!—tinted her skin, the only comparison possible, that held down to the day, not a white or an ivory, no touch of gold, wheat or maize, for all those he had known, as well as the black, and bluish black and dark chocolate, and milk chocolate, and a patching that sometimes happened in many crossings, of black and pale brown, and bronze and copper, and a mauvish bloodless paleness, none of them, and nothing else except the ripened peach. A mass of hair about the color of new coffee berries washed in henna fell lower than her waist, and if her figure was a little heavier than Fransisca's, it was still of classic Greece, the rounded, marmoreal splendor of flesh and bone that almost seemed to have been hand-carved and polished, that could barely be imagined as sweating, or of carrying the wastes of eating and drinking, or of being the temple of other than a goddess. Only to feel that body brought a lour of drunkenness. At least, in the beginning.

She carried the box into the women's lavatory in the Métro, and came out laughing and took his arm.

"The dresses and underwear are for a niece of mine and her friend at school here," she told him. "They've broken rules to come out and enjoy themselves at a party tonight. At eleven-thirty I meet them here, they change clothes and go back. They've often done it. Poor things. Locked up all day. Girls at that age need some life."

"Isn't it dangerous?" he asked.

"Perhaps for you," she said. "You're a father? Then certainly, for you it's dangerous. For them, for me, no. I know where they're going, and I'll see they get back to school."

"Why don't they change in a more convenient place?" he asked.

"What's more convenient than getting out of a window, running fifty yards to a Métro station, getting out here, changing into a party dress, hopping into a taxi, and *voilà?*" she said. "Isn't it simple? Besides, they're both horribly ugly, they'll never go anywhere, so they may as well make the most of it now."

They strolled around to the Ritz and she told him that she came from Belém and went back to Brazil only for her mother's birthday, and for ten years Europe had been her life and love. She shuffled him through a crowd of her friends from embassies or banks, and a few travelers, most of them known to himself by sight or through business, and in a moment he had her background and many a detail. The family owned mineral rights, shipping and rails, telephone and construction companies. She lived in her mother's suite, and had a house of her own at Antibes, a yacht, her own racing stable, and she was financing a team of cars for the Monte Carlo run. The party was in honor of the drivers, whom she regarded as demigods, though himself had no opinion of them or their noise, and held that driving a tractor was a hundred times more demanding, and she bounced up in a huff and went off with the crowd. Himself took one of the girls to dinner and afterward she went with him to the Métro and they waited till after midnight, but without seeing Vanina or the scholars. His partner went in and asked the attendant, and came back laughing, saying that the girls were at the Marietta, a night club that catered more to women than to men.

"She's making it up," he said. "They're schoolgirls."

"A thousand, cash, Vanina took them there," Dirah said, dark and smart, a model for Tezé, about to marry an Arab car dealer and move to Phillipeville. "She loves odd changes like that. She isn't that way herself, at least so far as I know. After all, she's single. I could find out."

"Uninteresting," he said. "At any rate, for me. I'd rather find out about you."

"But we've discussed this," she said very softly. "I've told you. I'm on the shelf. I shouldn't even look at you. Even for daring to go to dinner with you in full view of everybody, my precious Arab would kill me."

"Your precious Arab is in Algeria," he said. "You're not yet a prisoner of the zenana, or what they call it, there. Besides, an addition to your dowry, wouldn't that be more sensible than going home alone?"

"Ah, far more interesting, I agree," she said, and held his arm a little closer. "I saw a pin in Van Cleef and Arpels."

"Which, of course, you will wear no later than tomorrow morning," he said, turning toward the hotel.

"Ah yes," she said, matching her steps with his and managing to bump his thigh with her own at every other pace. "But promises made with the night's starch are lost in the morning dew, as we say. How do I know I shall wear that exact pin?"

Himself knew her doubt, and felt in that moment deep sorrow for those without the means, or worse, with no intention, of keeping a given word.

"I'll show you," he said, and they echoed across the Place Vendôme, talking about a diet for models, which seemed to be only steak cubes and black coffee, and he knocked on the grille till the night watchman came, and gave the man a card, and she pointed to the window.

"Have all the pins in that window sent over to the hotel in the morning," himself said. "Send a few bracelets, too."

"A watch would be useful," she said.

"To guard the time between now and when you meet this precious Arab," he said.

"No," she said. "I always wanted to know a man, not a European, because I detest them, and not an Arab, because I shall live with one, and only one, for the rest of my life. I'd like to know a stranger, somebody who's lived a completely different life, among different people, in different air. I've never been able to. I had to think of my figure first. I couldn't live with anybody, because I wanted my own life. I had to take every precaution, and I hate rubber and detest grease. And I don't think it's right, if you're not going to be part of him, to live with a man. A weekend, that's for starvation. You can get rid of a lot. But it's nothing to you or to him. Unless you're a fool. If he dominates, then you're finished. If you dominate, what have you given? Besides, these Europeans, they think they know. What monsters they are, don't you think? Little schoolboys, pretending such knowledge, such philosophy. Café pimps."

"I don't think a great deal of their existentialism," himself said. "How do you know I'm not one of them?"

They were going through the swinging doors, and he ever remembered the beauty of her laughing face half-shadowed in turning, flashing glass.

"We shall see," she said in the silence of the foyer, which ought to have been part of a cathedral. "I have nothing to wear, no cosmetics."

He took her down the hall of glass cases filled with the world's prettiest arts and she chose this and that, and somebody unlocked the cases and took the things upstairs while they drank champagne in the bar. They must have had a couple of weeks together, dear days that ran into each other, and late one afternoon he got back from the office and found an enormous bouquet of white roses on his pillow, and a bridal bouquet on hers, and on the dressing table she told him she had been called by her precious Arab, and naturally, she must go. Think of love when you remember me, she lipsticked in capitals on the blotter, and if you think of me, kiss me exactly as we have kissed, and I shall always think of you with that kiss. My heart, until later. And I was right, you see.

He sat on the bed while taxis called in the blue evening, and oh, Christ, now, wait, but did the tears run or not, nobody outside of hell cared. The flowers were only the ghosts of those on Fransisca's pall, that day, and she, wrapped in thick lead, a shiny relict, it might have been, from Egypt, with the folds open just enough to show the calm glory of her unmarked face, a thousand hymns of thanks for that mercy, and the rest of her fevered by typhus, only a little after Hilariana was born, and himself not with her.

But that was a Judas' Day of those years ago.

12 Father Miklos prayed in the soft Latin that himself preferred as lofting wings for other, purer thought. So he had prayed on the day Fransisca was brought home, a shape, no more, and shining in the silver casket, shining among shining walls and every white flower, and the whole world in tears.

But at that time there were no more tears within himself, dry, at distance, and apart, far, far away, and himself knowing the space, and sorry for it, and without desire or will to do more than listen, yes, in patience of contempt. They all showed forth in grief, but none of them knew the grieving that shows nothing, feels nothing, sees nothing, hears nothing, wants nothing excepting only the silence, the darkness, that Self existing then, and Being then, only because it cannot die.

So, Hilariana.

But there were so many small questions, little matters himself had never quite understood, that seemed unimportant at the time, and yet, whenever they came to memory, they disturbed a little more. Most of them about Vanina, of course, had been understood for long enough. Others had told him even when she had not, or himself had found out. Doubtless the woman had been honest enough in her own way. But it was a dishonest honesty, the way a drunkard will confess drunkenness when found drunk.

"Come," himself had said, under the lemon trees that night, and the deep greens of leaves gilded in a light of oil wicks, and the fruit staring like a thousand virgin teats, and the fragrance all about. "Have you not chased enough? Is there anything about these people you could stand for more than a night or two?"

"Years," she said. "But I agree. It's empty."

She had that sense. There was indeed a core, and hard. She had eaten not a mouthful or touched a glass. The telegram about her father's death was on her plate, two squared lines, and a signature.

"I know nothing of business or anything else," she said. "But it's wrong that he and the family should have worked for so long for somebody else to take away. I'm frightened of those lawyers. I don't know any of his men. Nothing about what he did. If we marry, will you control his business as you control your own? It's something I respect in you. So does everybody."

"Wait," he said. "I've enough business. I'm not marrying business. I'm marrying you. I want children. What do you say?"

She shrugged. She wore a black dress without any jewels. Her hair fell over her shoulders. There was no color in her face, no make-up, and her cheeks shone, and her mouth was beautiful, pale.

"It's worried me, or it's been a sort of brake," she said. "You know, your wife dying with a baby. I don't particularly want to die like that."

"It's your decision," he said, and got up. "You should have told me. What killed my wife was not the birth, but a devil's itch of a woman who opened a window in the next room to talk to her lover, and left it open all night."

"Whatever it was, she died, and I don't want to die," she said, a little girl, frightened. "I don't think I'd make a good mother. I don't like children."

"Be thinking it over," he said, looking across the balcony wall at the fisher boats roped together in the harbor lights' sequins a hundred feet below. "How about a swim?"

"You're so romantic," she said, and took the telegram, and went toward her room. "At least, a proposal of marriage ought to be made in a certain manner, don't you think?"

"It was made two years ago, on the train from Monte Carlo to Rome," he called. "You were on top of me, and you were calling on God, remember? That was when I asked you."

"But what a moment to ask questions," she said, and went in, and shut the door.

He left early the next morning by fishing boat for Athens, and it must have been two months or more later that she walked into his office in London, and put a little leather box on the desk, and showed him a diamond engagement ring, an egg, it seemed, and the secretary said Oh!

"I don't want a ring somebody else might have worn," she said. "I bought my own. I also bought a wedding ring. If you want to marry me, when?"

"In Rio, next week," he said. "I'm signing a wheat contract there, and afterward we'll go to New York."

"You go," she said. "I'm going to stay at home. The other life is finished. The day we marry I am your wife. I shall never leave Brazil except for visits."

Himself had never been happier than on that day, though he would have preferred buying the rings, but he bought her diamonds and emeralds instead. The thought of somebody so beautiful and graceful as a wife, the hours of happy companionship, an intelligence to confide in, an intimate opinion to seek and listen to as he might to himself, and no more of the wandering at nighttime, and the stray, doglike looking about for somebody else off the leash altogether seemed too good to be true.

And it was.

She married him because her friend married somebody or other.

Nothing wrong with the man or the marriage, but the friend kept it to herself and told the newspapers first. That was the shape of it, that reminded him of a piece of metal sculpture, dead, contorted, without dignity or decent form or ghost of vital beauty or semblance of respect for life.

"But isn't that a very extraordinary reason for marrying?" he asked her, cold as the ice in the bucket.

She tipped the wine and swallowed, and licked her lips, and kept silent, looking down at the empty glass.

It was the first time he had seen her drunk in the morning. Then he understood why a luncheon cocktail made her lightheaded, still more why a few before dinner made her just a little poutish, although she could pull herself together and last through the first half-dozen dances at a night club, even if she had to be helped to the car, and home, and to bed, all in a beautiful, helpless, almost ballet-like grace of arms and legs and nodding head. She was not an untidy drunkard, but she could be loud, and at those times it was plain that she had explored the roots of language, and not only her own, in company of experts.

He went home that morning with no thought except to have a bag packed for a trip to Recife and to invite her to go with him, instead of simply telephoning. She was in the bedroom with only a cerise nightdress on, and a young footman was sitting on the edge of the bed smoking a cigarette. He was dressed, although his neck-cloth was crooked, and her bathpowder covered his shoulder, small details, painfully seen, and a retch of murderous anger in one gesture that put the fellow in a run for the door.

She smiled with her eyes, and dandled her leg, and told him, as if she enjoyed every word, what she thought of him, slowly, and in detail, and himself had never forgotten, or forgiven, or touched her since the moment.

"To hell with you," himself had said, but it was a lean voice coming out of him. "This is your apartment from this time. I'll find one of my own. If ever I find a man anywhere near you while you still pretend to be my wife, I'll kill the pair of you. Be warned. And go to hell."

The rest was a social charade until Daniel had been gone about a week or so, and his childhood playmate, Leonor Alameida da Cunha, tall and slender and just the girl himself would have picked for the boy, came to the office with her mother, and said, there, in the big red chair, that Vanina had been trying to bed him, and that was why he had gone, rather than have the displeasure of causing his father an unhappiness.

"Displeasure?" himself said. "What unhappiness? Why didn't he come to me?"

"He was simply tempted," Leonor said. "He told me. We are engaged. The night he left, he said I must be careful of her. She became friendly with him, she told him, to try to make you return to her."

"Friendly's a curious word," himself said.

"Daniel was not fond of her," Leonor said. "She knew it and she tried for a long time. She sent presents to the university. Many things. You didn't know?"

Himself shook a tired head.

"I wondered why he went off so suddenly," he said.

Leonor cried, gulped the sobs, looked for a handkerchief, took her mother's.

"She waited in his rooms at the top of the house," she said. "He was afraid to go home. You might have suspected him. She was always innocent, that one. That witch."

"Always," he said. "Witch, in Portuguese. There's a better word though. Why have you come to tell me?"

"Because now she's sending me flowers and wants to 'know me better,'" Leonor said, with the wide, wet eyes.

"Stay away," he said. "Say I told you to. Have nothing to do with her. Bitch. That's the word."

Then came the consul's regrets, and he cleared the house, and had it torn down, and a skyscraper went up on the space. Vanina seemed to know why, and made no complaint. Everything was moved out to The Inheritance, and she lived in Grandam Aracý's house for a time while her summer house was built, and except for trips here and there to friends, which himself cared nothing about, she stayed at The Inheritance. Himself had no interest in anything she did, unless it was her will to go to Europe, which he forbade, because he was always afraid she would end in a scandal. And that came, of course, as it had to.

It was only natural that she should go to Lisbon to meet Hilariana from school, take her to Paris for a day or two of shopping, and himself to meet them in New York and fly home together. But there were days of waiting, and then Pinheiro called from the office in Paris to say that Hilariana was still there, with her governess-companion, and wanted permission to go to Rome to meet Vanina.

"Tell the young lady to stay where she is until I get there," himself said. "Why didn't you report this before?"

"I was told not to," Pinheiro said, wavily unhappy over the air. "Madame chartered a plane for sixty guests. A jet. I was told you had given permission."

"I'll see into it," he said. "See that Miss Hilariana is followed and guarded wherever she goes. Let me have a complete report. Find out where Madame is staying in Rome. Have the report waiting."

"In Paris, sir?" Pinheiro inquired. "Ah, wonderful."

"In Milan," himself said. "We'll be in Paris later."

Himself caught that night's flight, but the office reported no trace of her. Torresiani, the director in Milan, had taken charge of inquiries, but even so, with help of police and the bureaus, there was no report on Madame and sixty people, except that they arrived in Rome, got into cars, and vanished.

"By the time you get there we should know every detail," Torresiani said. "If I'd been warned she was coming, I'd have met her myself, of course. Morillarto, poor man, he's going mad. He called every hotel in Italy, and then got me out of bed at three this morning."

"I was over the Atlantic at the time," himself said. "We're suffering in a splendid cause. Madame is probably staying at the home of friends. With sixty people?"

Morillarto had a long report of her arrival but no idea where she was at that moment, and no information about her guests, except that most of them seemed to be artists, but the detectives were checking and would have a report that evening.

Himself had never been overfond of Rome since watching people howl while Blackshirts tried to goose-step. Even without that, there seemed a mark in the very walls of fumes from crooked minds over the centuries, and streets still rang with the screams and prayers of those early Believers, dipped in pitch and hung to light dear Caesar's way. Even looking out of the hotel window, he imagined he could see the miles of posts and flame, and in any cookshop's smell he sniffed the burning martyr flesh, and any drink tasted like blood.

"You're run down," the doctor said, a youngster, but he knew what he was playing at. "You'll take B-12 and calcium, and Vitamin C. Stop your sugar. Use honey where you can, or saccharine. Nothing wrong. You're simply doing too much. Take the pace easier. An hour's sleep in the afternoon. In bed by eleven at night as a rule. When you're late sleep late. What do you eat?"

"Anything that's put in front of me," himself said, with the thermometer taste still in his mouth. "I never eat much, though. Haven't the patience."

"Probably what's saved you, so far," the young fellow said. "Breakfast, fruit and coffee and milk. Fruit, remember. Don't poison yourself with juice. You can do without acid and fat. Lunch, one rice dish. Meat or fish, and rice. No bread. No spaghetti or any fillers like that."

"I love good spaghetti," he moaned.

"You used to love it," the young fellow said. "Now, you never heard of it. You can't see it. Dinner—"

"Wait," himself said. "Did we finish lunch, yet?"

"You are now lying down, after one plate only, of meat, or fish, and rice," the young fellow said, writing. "Sometimes an omelet. Or poached eggs and fish. Poached eggs and minced steak. Cooked vegetables. A soup. No bread. And only one dish."

"I hope I live," himself said.

"I'm giving you another thirty years of healthy life," the youngster said, as if he knew. "X-rays, clear. Blood, everything else, optimum. How late do you dine?"

"When I've finished work, or when I'm at the table," himself said. "Will I be getting anything for dinner? A nice bone, or whatever?"

"Meat, of any sort, not underdone or overdone," the young man said. "Liver, either lightly grilled, or minced and lightly cooked, at least once a week. Squeeze half a lemon over fish or meat. Any green vegetable. No potatoes."

"I love potatoes," himself said. "I love bread. Crusty bread."

"You've loved a lot of things," the doctor said, and folded his glasses. "Now you will turn your strict attention to things which love you. A soup, yes. Minestrone, yes. Well made. Grilled fish. No sauce. Grilled meat. Nothing fried. Stewed in wine, yes. With vegetables."

"You'll let me live," himself said.

"Within limits," the youngster said, and himself was beginning to listen. "Be careful of salads. Many crimes are committed in the name of lettuce. Grilled tomatoes at any time."

"Pizza," himself said. "It's my other name."

"It was," the youngster said. "Wonderful for boys and girls. They have the digestion. You, make certain, have had your share. Pizza is a memory."

"It isn't going to cost much to run me," himself said. "No chicken, and such?"

"Any bird, roast or boiled," the young fellow said. "But not fried. No fat."

"Chicken, Southern style, in the basket?" The O'Dancy said. "Great God, now, look, I'm undone here."

"And healthy," the doctor said. "Try to drink red wines, clarets, a half bottle, no more. That's food."

"I knew you were human somewhere," himself said. "What about The Creature, then?"

"Creature," the young fellow said, and put the pen down. "Your wife?"

"Whisky," himself said. "Whisky's called The Creature in our language."

"Two ounces, after six o'clock at night, and no more," the youngster said, poor boy.

"Wait a minute, now," himself said. "I can put that in my eye and never blink."

"Until the moment you never blink again," the young man said. "Be careful of your 'creature.'"

"If we're discussing the same matter," The O'Dancy said. "You mentioned my wife. Twenty years younger."

"Excellent, but again, caution," the young fellow said. "One too many times, or a little strain, you ask for cardiac trouble. A stroke. Paralysis. Parkinson's disease. The nerves withstand so much. They are not steel cables. Your wife is of calm temperament? Sensible?"

"Very calm, very sensible," The O'Dancy said.

"All you have to do, as a man of common sense, is to live fully, but quietly, without the exuberance of your youth," the doctor said. "Remember that the sexual power is also of first importance, and the sexual thought must be explored, and the sexual act also, but with caution. If you neglect the act, the reproductive system begins to fail. It weakens. Any part of the body requires exercise, or it deteriorates."

"You mean, I won't get a hard," himself said. "It's been no trouble so far."

"So I had deduced," the young man said. "I shall ask the nurse to give you a vessel."

"If it's the one I saw when I came in, I wish you'd give me the nurse," The O'Dancy said.

"She has other patients," the young man said, without looking up. "When were you last physically examined?"

"In applying for renewal of a passport," himself said. "Normal."

"Before that," the young man said.

"Every time I leave the country," himself said. "I'm never out of a doctor's place. It's one of the reasons I think twice before packing. Them and their damned rubber stamps. Every lazy bastard ever born's in the passport business or customs. One or the other, hounds in a garbage bucket."

"Why did you call me?" the young man asked, and stood looking down, and himself saw Steb, God love the boy, because he would be the same sort of physician, kind, and sharp, and knowing a great deal, but ready to listen and make up his mind. "Were you simply tired?"

"Yes," himself said. "Tired, and flat, and discouraged."

"This prescription will attend to the physical side," the young man said. "Spiritually and mentally, you must protect yourself. That's where you're discouraged."

"You're one of the best I ever met," The O'Dancy said. "You should come to São Paulo. If ever you have the thought, let me know."

"Where did you learn Italian?" the doctor asked.

"In bed," The O'Dancy said. "Will you suggest better?"

"A vessel is in the next room," the young man said, and never a smile. "Please do your best."

That night the reports were in from dozens of officers. It seemed that the party had split up, and most had gone to Rome's artistic quarter, where everybody lived in the same room, and pictures, sculpture, and all else were sold in the street.

"Where's my wife?" The O'Dancy said when all the paper had been looked at.

"Must be staying with friends," Torresiani said. "She's not on any hotel register. We could advertise."

A wonderful state to be in, and himself sitting there.

"Continue your inquiries," himself said. "A hundred thousand lire for the first lead."

Sergeant Borretti won it within the hour by telephoning to say that an artist's party was being given at a night club on the north side of the Tiber, decorated that morning with Brazilian flags and orchids flown from Rio de Janeiro.

"That sounds like it," himself said. "Have it watched, and when everybody's there, let me know."

"Sir," Torresiani said. "You mean if Madame is identified?"

"Would I, for Bloody Christ's Own Salvation, be wanting to know about anybody else?" himself said. "I'll be ready to leave in the moment."

Just before midnight he got the call, and drove out, through the wide, bright Roman streets, and over the bridge, into a darker part, and they pulled up in a new square, and a string of blue lamps outside an arcade. Dozens of cars were parked, but there were very few people. Walking slowly toward the doorway, himself heard the muted braze of a trumpet, and the doorman lounged in shadow humming the tune. But while he held out a note and the door was being opened, headlights swung around the far corner, one after another, and the doorman let the door swing, and ran down the stairs. Himself hurried down behind, past all the photographs of legs and teeth, and through thick curtains, into a long, loud room, with a band in full thump, and the floor crowded with men and women, all pink or brown, whitened by light one moment, that flashed blue, and green, and magenta in time with piano chords, but they were all naked. Opposite, on the raised floor seen between bobbing heads and shoulders, men and women were all over each other, and so were lipsticked effeminates and groups of women. Strings of dozens of flags were thick with orchids around the walls and overhead.

Torresiani came to him at the stair foot. He looked like a small boy caught with a cigarette, half smile, half grimace, not sure whether to brag or be sick.

"I wish I could have saved you the journey," he said. "The party was ordered by Madame a week ago. I have destroyed the details. She has the table on the rostrum."

"Get all the flags down immediately," The O'Dancy said. "Rip them down. Put them in the car."

"It may cause trouble," Torresiani said. "There's been a lot of champagne."

"The police are outside, if I'm not mistaken," himself said. "That's what the fellow was shouting for."

Torresiani spoke to the headwaiter, a fat one, with eyes that had seen everything long before his mother bore him, and he went off, grabbing waiters, whispering. The police were a fair time making up their minds, but the ropes of flags were most of them untied, and coiled, when the first files of uniforms came through a side door, and blocked the stairway, and an officer went up on the bandstand and music stopped in mid-beat. But the feet went on shuffling, and the sounds from the couplings on the rostrum, the half-shrieks and moans, brought loud laughter from the naked ones on the floor and there were shouts for music.

"Here's music of another kind," the officer said into a microphone. "Line up at this table to give your names and addresses, with personal documents. Those without proof of identity will be taken to central police headquarters. These premises are closed as a house of ill-repute. Everybody here is under arrest as a person of indecent habits."

Whatever else he said was waste of breath. Everybody in the world started screaming, and everybody seemed to race for the stairs, clawing, pushing, punching, wild in the eye and weeping, most of them, vicious and snarling, some, and a few giggling. The police had no trouble with anybody. Men behaved or they were cracked on the head. Women were lifted up and passed upstairs to be put in the wagons. By the time the place was quiet, and everybody was lined up and the police busy with their writing, Torresiani had managed to get Vanina and the flags away, and he came along to the office mopping his neck.

"You did well," himself said. "I hope you spent enough."

"So much, that your name won't be mentioned," Torresiani said. "Everybody else's will, though. Rome's upper crust will erupt many a cooked bird. When I tell my wife about this, do you suppose she'll believe me?"

"Your wife's a nice woman," The O'Dancy said. "At least if it's the one I've met."

"The same," Torresiani said, and bowed.

"It'll make the girl curious," himself said. "There's a lot here we all respond to. The Greek isn't dead in most of us, thank God. If you give her the details, you might go home one night and find the neighborhood and herself practicing in your own drawing room."

"Possible," Torresiani said, watching two naked girls, trying to put their dresses on back-to-back to steady themselves. "I think I'll tell her."

"Oh now, castigation of martyrs, what 'ridiculous' behavior," Vanina said, half tearful. "We were only enjoying ourselves with a little grown-up fun. We're not children. I get so bound and chained with that damned convent existence. There's a place for loosening. Relaxing. I like it. I love watching it. And you're not such a priest yourself."

"Anywhere and anything," himself said. "But never in the presence of your flag. It's a dishonor."

"It's the mental and physical freedom of our land," she said. "I asked them to be Brazilians for one night. To accept and enjoy the adult hospitality of the New World."

He whipped at her with the cord of the flag he held, and she fell against an armchair and crumpled, hair glossed over nakedness, and beautiful, drumming her pink heels on the carpet, a child.

"A flag's a monument to those gone," he said. "It flies in honor because somebody lived before us, and produced, as we live and produce to maintain it in honor. You'd make it a hand towel for whores and queans. Hilariana's waiting in Paris. I'm seriously wondering whether you and she ought to meet."

"Don't poison her against me," she said, looking up through shining hair. "In any case, when did you become such a puritan? You've put on better shows. Was it because you weren't invited? Why should I? I wanted to see men and women again. Bodies. Mouths. In a few years time nothing'll waken me."

"That's all that saves you," himself said. "I can't very well apply for a divorce on the grounds you're going into the menopause."

She lay back screaming, thighs wide, pulling her hair, and himself turned and left her.

But in the morning she had flown to Paris and he said nothing. Himself had given many a party of the same kind, but not in sight of any flag except the underwear of women guests. There was zest in such a gathering, and laughter, and a sense of being mature enough to enjoy the fruits of health and realize a love of life, and there was breaking of habit in public show of what was ever done in private. No heart was in himself to hold the folly against her. Part of himself sympathized, and a part ever wished she had let him know. That was the source of his anger, he knew, but the flags had been the cause of the real, the absolute rage. No sententiousness, no self-righteousness, no patriotic humbug interfered, but the flag was sacrosanct, and in a church, or on a public building, or in front of disciplined columns, or wherever there was heart or pride, that was its place. At the same time, there was surety that Vanina had never thought in that way. She had meant no harm. She was proud enough of being a Brazilian and she liked showing the mob what a Brazilian could do. But that sort of gesture at root was childish at best, tawdry at worst, and always, and too often capable of being twisted by the foul-hearted into something else, uglier, cause of disgust. In all, it cost him a few days of talk, and some money, and a lot of diplomatic pressure and ironing, but the "artists" went back to the streets of Paris, the Romans went to their rustic haunts, the newspapers outbawled themselves, and through it all Vanina was never mentioned. But if ever he dreamed of representing his country abroad, that was the graveyard. Everything he had done, everything he had paid, was known.

"We came out of that very well," Torresiani said. "I'll split the cost between Milan and Rome. The only people who really suffered were some of the youngsters. Of good family. Society names. Families that lost their money. The journalists say what they please. They know there isn't money to stop them."

"Get the best lawyers you can for them," himself said. "Sue those newspapers, smash them, cram the filth down their sewer throats."

"Unfortunately, they go bankrupt and start again," Torresiani said. "We might retain a public relations man to represent the women. The men, naturally, think it all adds to their reputation as lads-about-the-village. A village is what it is. It's the girls' mothers and fathers I'm sorry for. They don't deserve that sort of publicity."

"Who gave the game away?" himself asked. "Who warned the police?"

Torresiani looked down, eyebrows up, wagging a foot as if examining the graceful line of his moccasin, a triumph of Milanese saddlery.

"You will forgive my surprise, sir," he said without looking up. "We thought it was yourself."

"It was not," himself said. "Find out."

If there was any shock in the name, himself was unsure, but when he showed it to Vanina in Paris, she simply threw the paper in the air and laughed.

"Well, what are you going to do?" she said. "There were a lot of people there who'd invited themselves, and I knew they would. There were a few of the diplomatic scum I've never particularly liked. Many of the others deserved all they got. But they'll remember me. I wanted to be all over the front page of every rag in the world. But they missed it. That was you and your office boys, I suppose. I'd love to tread on that Torresiani. He'd do nothing I told him. I did everything myself."

"You'll never get another opportunity," he said. "At least, not with my name, or my money. Did you see that your Greek friend and her husband had a fine show of pictures? They painted out the details, but it's plain enough. It'll finish him, poor man. It's plastered all over Athens."

"I'm glad," she said. "If she divorces him, I've invited her to stay with me. It won't interfere with anything you want to do, will it? You'll never see her if you don't want to."

"Your life's your own," himself said. "Try to remember others have theirs to live too. And from this time out, I'm not letting Hilariana spend any time with you."

She laughed the high, hooting cackle and turned, leaning against the table, and light on blue lamé showed the slenderness of line and the flat front of her, and he regretted, then, that he could never go near her.

"She's intelligent enough, don't worry about her," she said. "When she's old enough she can make up her own mind. If you must act the villainous father, very well."

"I don't like the way you treat your friends," he said. "Your relatives might get worse. So I'll stop it now. Find your own way home, and from this moment, use your own funds. You can sign nothing in my name."

She turned her back, flipped up her hand, and walked out.

Himself was not aware that two male secretaries, the footman, a caddy, a hairdresser, a masseur, and two chauffeurs were part of her suite, and he was uncertain what he might have done had he known. It was just as well he never bothered to inquire, but he knew, some time afterward, that a lot of people had a curious notion about a man calling himself The O'Dancy and considering himself somebody in finance, and coffee, and minerals, and one thing and the other, and yet letting his wife run loose all over the place, and live with anybody she wanted, even her servants, and himself with never a word to say.

Himself never knew because he never troubled to think, and anger is very little good after the damage is done.

There was sooth of sorts in the Latin prayer, and Father Miklos' white soutane fell in folds that seemed carved, and his stillness made him a statue, something solid in a fluid universe he had always been, somebody ever the same, trustworthy, dependable, immovable.

Suddenly the heart of himself went out to the man, to the spirit and soul of him, for the body was almost not corporate, so far into age, into the years, so dried by time and sumped of energy. But whatever was thought, the man appeared to have more spark and light than any dozen others about him. That was the miracle. Nobody even thought of saying that the Thursday Mass for the men in the mountains was too much for him, or the Wednesday Mass over in the timberland, or that three services on Tuesday at the ore fields might be taken by a younger man, and certainly not that six services in his own church every Sunday were much too much. Nobody said it because nobody thought of it, and if they had, they would never have dared put it into words.

For more than sixty years the holy man had lived on The Inheritance. He knew everybody into the third and fourth generations, in birth and baptism, in Communion and confession, in life and death, and what was in death was secret to him, just as what was in life remained a mystery. There had been no spending of wealth, or concupiscent hours with women, no bedding of whores or pretense of love, or enjoyment of vice, no drunkenness, or shouting in quiet streets, no fighting by night or day, no scraped fists or bloody nose, or blades whipped or pistols drawn, no cursing in the lees of language, no hate, no anger, no envy.

The white habit, the breviary, the silver church, the Bread, Wine, Love, and, yes, This is My Beloved Son.

In one shining, seeing moment, then, those years ago, no wonder the Iscariot hanged himself.

"Master," Democritas whispered, behind there. "Mr. Paul would like to have a conversation, please. He presents filial compliments. His first wife promises hospitality of the highest order. Sir, I have the truck outside. Permit me to interrupt blessed thoughts. I have asked forgiveness."

13

"You're getting breathless," himself said in the truck. "You were always a great log. What's behind you?"

"Ah, Master," Democritas said, a sad man, and sadder for the blue, swollen eye. "So many terrors. I can work. I like to work. I want nothing more than to work. I like to see things done. Piles of timber. Lumber in seasoning stacks. Oil barrels lined and squared, each one in place. These are very little things. To me, they are the part of my life I like best. Trucks of pineapples properly loaded, plumes out. Coffee berries bagged and heaped square to the corner. Banana sticks in array. Even milk churns I like to see squared, in squares, so that the count is simple."

"Very well, Dem," himself said. "We share the dream. I'll raise hell for the same thing. What's extra?"

"Other things, dear Master," Dem said. "We have been so happy. But it becomes worse."

"Where did you leave Ephemia?" himself asked. "Was she with the children?"

Democritas watched the avenue of hibiscus and shook the dark head.

"She is with the Lady Hilariana," he said. "Sir, we have shadows about us."

The man crossed himself and kissed his fingers.

"I just came from a place of light," himself said. "I've no doubts anywhere. Where's the trouble? Tell me a little thing first. You're an unbaptized one. An infidel, even if I never knew it. If you're not of the Church, or Ephemia, why do you cross yourself?"

"We are both of the Church, Master," Dem said. "We are both children of the Healer. We don't enter the temples and synagogues of others. We have our own church. We make our own devotion. White people have their way. We have our way."

"We, you mean the Negro?" himself said. "What do you mean,

your way? Our way? What are you telling me? You know there's
never been a difference. What's the difference, unless you make it
yourself?"

Dem laughed a great, deep seat-shaker, and the driver looked
at him, and laughed too.

"Ah, Master," he said, and pulled out his handkerchief, which
was whiter washed than The O'Dancy's own, and himself knew
there must be a word or two with Didina. "If you were not the
master, would I be overseer? If you, God protect and strengthen
you, left us, how long do you think I would be allowed in charge?
Do you think, even now, that any of the whites notice what I say?
Do I ever bother to tell them? It's my own brothers and sisters
who obey me. Without them, what work would I get done? The
whites would ruin everything."

"It's not true," The O'Dancy said. "I won't believe it. Now, Dem,
you're going to make me very angry."

"Master, I will make you greatly angrier," Dem said. "It's told
there is no color in this country, and every skin's *brasileiro*. I
agree."

"Now you make me a happier man," The O'Dancy said. "Of
course it is."

"It is *brasileiro* if you want to put a girl on the bed," Dem said.
"If she is Negro or Indio or Japanese or Chinese or whatever she
is, yes, certainly, the color of the skin is acceptable. Where are the
Negroes and Indios among the men? In the universities? In the
schools? In the service of our noble country? In industry? In politics? A handful? Less?"

"A matter of brains and ability," himself said. "Schooling. When
enough of you've had an education, you'll be happy enough."

"We are four hundred years old as a country," Dem said. "We
have been out of slavery for less than a hundred years. Who are the
leaders among us? Who has the message of hope? Who listens? If
we listen, shall we hear? Whose is the voice? Who is he? Where
is he?"

"No politics, now," The O'Dancy warned. "You're not talking
politics, are you?"

"Politics, facts, color of skin, earning enough to eat, and I am
the world's most fortunate man, and a Negro," Dem said, and

shrugged his weight. "Where you touch, the bruise is painful."

"Would you like every one of us to be the Master Paul?" himself asked, and holding his temper, for there was no real anger for the man. "Fornicating his life away with any color at all except his own. Knowing there's me behind him to send his brood to school?"

"He is a wonderful man and a brother," Dem said. "He is truly *brasileiro*."

"Then I'm not sure what you mean," The O'Dancy said. "I don't want to be angry. Is it *brasileiro* to sit the whole day and eat your own dung and drink your own piss? It's what some of them did, there, in the Bible. Isn't it what he's doing?"

"He is taking the color out of us, and training his children," Dem said. "None of his children are black. None of his grandchildren are black. They will have an easier life. They are all properly schooled."

"Say no more," The O'Dancy said. "I'm listening to stuff I never knew was in your head. Or anybody else's. What you're saying is that most of my people are not happy. They've never been happy. In all the years. And when I'm gone, they'll be even less happy. Is that it?"

Dem nodded his head.

"They are finding out they are unhappy," he said. "Who is unhappy until he is told? Who is sad until the word is known that describes it? Tell me the meaning of 'sad.'"

"Are these 'teachers' on The Inheritance?" The O'Dancy asked.

"At times," Dem said.

"What d'y'mean, at times?" The O'Dancy shouted. "God damn it, talk as if you know who I am. Who are these people?"

"Mr. Paul will tell you, Master," Dem said. "He knows from the beginning. From the Lady Hilariana. And the Lady Xatina. And the Lady Aracý. I am overseer, Master. But Mr. Paul is O'Dancy."

"I knew that'd come to howl at me," himself said. "Where's Father Miklos in this?"

"Between Satan and the fire," Dem said. "But we shall take care of him."

Himself sat back and laughed.

"While I'm in a chatter with Mr. Paul, would you ask them out in the kitchen to grill a little beef for me," he said. "A glass of wine wouldn't come amiss. Or cold beer."

"Everything shall be prepared, of the best," Dem said. "All our candles are burning for you, and our smoke even now supports our prayers."

"If I knew what you were talking about," himself said while the truck went quietly to the gate. "If only to Christ's own hell I knew. But I will, I suppose."

Dem looked at him with the eyes so dark that there were no whites, but only the deeper darkness in the middle, and they were far out of size, and sad.

"Yes, Master," he said. "You will. Remember our prayers."

"To hell with your prayers," The O'Dancy said in the Other Language. "There was a time when I'd have soon as said to hell with the Pope. Now to see the son I hate."

Paul's garden was the largest on The Inheritance, of every seed, bulb, and plant in the country, growing in a glorious wilderness, it seemed, but a closer look showed the planning and the mind of the gardener. Flowering trees patched in great clumps, and in the shade beneath, the flowers that liked the gentle light, and in the branches, all the orchids. Out in the open, cropped grasses of many types made spaces of different greens, and beds of blossom scented and shone. Rock ponds fed by stone gullies flashed a fountain, and lilies pleaded in little lakes, and birds were everywhere. The house had to be looked for, because the paths went off here or there, and no car would get near, so the only way was to watch for signs of use and follow the worn track until the great hedge of hibiscus, and walk down, looking for the gate, which was only a hole with wire across to keep the dogs out.

The building had been Grandfa Leitrim's storehouse and later Grandfa Shaun's plow shed, part of the first group of roofs on The Inheritance, of logs, mud, and bamboo, all thatched in rush. Paul had done little except to make rooms along the veranda so that each of his women lived her own life, with a wide space behind for everybody's meals. His own rooms were on the end, away from the children and noise, and everything else, kitchen, stores, laundry, and servants, was at the other end. It was only a little smaller than the main O'Dancy house, planned by an architect unnamed, but a master in the use of timber columns, bamboo supports, and roofing, for an airy structure that had stood for more than two hundred years and still had the appearance of being new. Paul clearly saw to it that every square meter had a coat of varnish now and again, and the roof got a regular thatching and, from light in the leaf growth, the place was thoroughly sprayed every week.

No doubt of it, but the fellow lazed his career in a mansion.

The O'Dancy stood outside in the overhang's shadow, looking at a polished veranda floor in patterned woods, and varnished bamboo walls, plaited rugs, chairs and tables splendidly carpentered on the place, and into the deep shadow behind open double doors, where reflected sunlight showed the raftering forty feet above, and all the hams and sausage and drying fruits and vegetables hanging, and the panniers of stacked fruit gleaming on the long table axed from one tree, and the log chairs about it, and the nearby cluster of small tables and chairs for coffee.

"Well, then, be giving welcome to The O'Dancy," Paul said quietly, from shadow of a doorway along to the left. "What do you think of the best part of your inheritance, sir? Would you like to burn it down?"

"No," himself said. "I was thinking, you live in a beautiful place. Far more sensibly than I do with all that modern stuff. I'm getting to hate it."

"There's little comfort to it," Paul said, and turned inside. "What I've seen is all theirs without an argument. I don't belong to the age, or they don't. Will you be drinking a little?"

"I will, and that's the truth," himself said, and Paul took his hat, and stood aside to let him pass into a room alive with books, and a ladder to reach the top shelves, and a table cut from one piece in the middle, and chairs like beds, with covers of jaguar hide. "You have a rare comfort here, that's a fact. And all of a decent time, too, when it was no crime to speak your mind. If you could fight."

"Did you never notice it before?" Paul said. "Or were you not here often enough?"

"It's cooler than my air-conditioning," himself said. "Asthma boxes is what they are."

"Double roof of thatch," Paul said, over at the bottles and glasses. "Would it be The Creature, now?"

"Was it ever anything else?" himself said. "Cane and rum are very good in their way. The Creature's a friend. I'm in need of one."

Paul nodded, and bottles spoke and a siphon blew contempt.

"Enough soda to flatter the color," he said, and put the glass down with a magazine under it. "Mark the table and Cleide'll murder us both."

"Here's rumors of peace," The O'Dancy toasted, and drank. "The world's going to hell. I'll not be part of it."

"Stay with us," Paul said, and drank. "There's plenty of room. One more mouth's an extra couple of plates, that's all. The cost of living's going up. I expect a revolution. We could be attacked here. They could have the lot. I'd not move a finger."

The O'Dancy drank a little, and put the glass down, and clasped his hands.

"Was ever there an idler bugger born in Christ's creation?" he asked at large, but mildly.

"I doubt it," Paul said, and lay back. "I've trained a talent for it."

"Is there nothing you can do except process your arse day after day?" The O'Dancy asked.

"I seriously doubt that, too," Paul said. "After all, there's been a lot of practice."

"Did you never do any work?" himself asked.

"I believe I did," Paul said. "I found it inimical."

A flight of parrots came to screech on the rail outside, and they watched, and the screeching went on, and The O'Dancy looked at his drink and put it down.

"They'll go away," Paul said.

"You wouldn't think of slinging something at them," himself said.

"And why would I do that?" Paul asked in mid-drink. "They're friends of the house."

"You've some noisy friends," The O'Dancy said.

"I've some quiet ones, too," Paul said, and pointed to the shadow beside his chair.

A large gray snake lay coiled, about two feet high, perhaps asleep, but there was no sense in asking.

"He has family about the place, somewhere," Paul said. "We don't have many visitors."

"Democritas seemed to think there was something you wanted to say," The O'Dancy said, keeping an eye on the coil. "Could you not have come to The House?"

"It's a fairish way," Paul said. "And you might not have been there."

"Is that damn' thing going to be moving while I'm here?" The O'Dancy asked, watching the coil. "If so, I'll be that much quicker."

"He'll harm none," Paul said. "Fear of serpents is bad conscience. It has a silent language all its own, the conscience."

"I suppose you've a fair control of it, yourself?" The O'Dancy said.

"I talk to the children," Paul said. "They teach me."

"How many is it you have?" himself asked.

"I believe it'll be sixty-eight with this morning's arrival," Paul said. "Everyone in splendid health. And a few bright ones among them. There isn't one of them, Adam or Eve, above the age of ten, who doesn't speak, write, read, and sing in the Latin. The only true language on earth."

"Amen to that, and what's more, I'll drink another one to it," The O'Dancy said, and passed the glass. "You were uncommon heavy with the soda last time. You mean it's a light in our darkness?"

"It's a light of faith," Paul said, and held up the glass. "Would that be enough?"

"Enough's like beauty in a woman, that's never enough, but even a little will do," The O'Dancy said. "Go steady now, with that soda. I was never one to mix drinks. Have I seen more than a dozen of your outpourings?"

"You've never bothered," Paul said, and sat back as if he cared less. "Every child of mine will be proficient in his own language, and in English for expression, in French for grace, and Russian, that has expressiveness and grace as well, and it's bound to be a predominant force by the time they've grown. Brazil's nothing but a village country for the moment, and Brazilians are a village people. We haven't yet lost the curse of Europe. But we'll be a power in the world. My children are going to be as strong as I can make them. Spirit and brain, that's what I look for. When it's there, I'll train it."

"Would you mind telling me, then," The O'Dancy said. "What's the curse of Europe?"

"Thinking we're a lot better than we are," Paul said. "Europeans give themselves a furious lot of airs. We borrow the hocus. We're most of us bastard European. What we ought to be is American. South American, at that. A lot of Indio, but we don't like to admit it, a great deal of Negro we'd rather not think about, and rag, tag, and bobtail European. Not worth a damn."

"We've some very old families," himself said. "You have to give us that."

"Very old, and the names are golden on the escutcheon," Paul said. "Put the lot down a hole, and what difference will it make?"

"You'd find a difference in the tone of things," himself said. "They fight for many a cause."

"The cost of living's gone up two thousand per cent in the past few years," Paul said. "Have you heard any of those fighters saying anything about it out in public? Have any of them come out in print? If the price of bread and rice goes up, will I hear The O'Dancy saying anything about it? Except being the first to put up his prices?"

"That's business," The O'Dancy said. "Don't be confusing things. Do you want everybody bankrupt?"

"I'm not remotely concerned," Paul said. "Bankruptcy's another Europeanism. It's ridiculous to mention bankruptcy, and in the same breath, Brazil. It's the same as calling a millionaire a pauper because he hasn't any money on him. Our money's yet to be used. When it is, I hope it'll be by my children's generation. It can only be misused until."

"You're talking about in twenty years, then?" The O'Dancy said. "It's not a long time. Looking back, it's like this morning. You think it'll all come our way by then?"

"Not that it'll 'come' anything," Paul said. "For those living and using their brains, what's present will never be right. It'll be better than now, let's say. Now we've got the moneylenders in power. But they won't last. They're dead in half the world. They're dying in other parts. They'll last longer here because a few people need money and they'll pay for the use of it. But if most of the people can't get enough to eat, they'll fight. That's when the moneylenders will die."

"I'm something of a moneylender myself," The O'Dancy said. "Some of your dividends come from moneylending."

"Study my accounts," Paul said. "I've never touched one cent."

"You're worth a fortune," The O'Dancy said.

"My children can use it," Paul said. "I've a feeling they never will."

"Are your children such great ones they'll never need money?" The O'Dancy asked.

"They're being brought up to live simply and well in the land they were born in," Paul said. "If everything's taken from them, they'll still be thoroughly civilized people. That's my prayer. Brazil's not a body to be carved up. It's not a bank where you take out money and spend it elsewhere. It's not a bourne for get-rich-quickers. To hell with all of them."

"We're producing a fair lot," The O'Dancy said. "We're beginning to show we've got the potential. We'll soon be exporting. You'll be here talking, and a few miles away the country's beginning to mean something. We're going up year by year in cars and trucks, alone."

"Not for the people," Paul said. "Not for any one of us. For people with the money. See the difference?"

"I wish to God you'd talk sense," The O'Dancy said. "You'll tell me next you're a friend of Mr. Castro?"

"Why not?" Paul said. "He's told everybody to go to hell. His people are with him. I don't see why I'm not a friend of Mr. Castro's."

"Is a son of mine a communist?" The O'Dancy said.

"I'm much better than that," Paul said. "I'm a Brazilian. Do you not yet know the meaning of it? Whatever you half-bollocked Europeans do, and your skyscrapers and factories, we shall one day be the masters. Simply because it's our land, and as you said just now, we have the potential."

"But who the hell are you talking about?" The O'Dancy said. "We? You mean us?"

"I mean Brazilians born, the Indio and the Negro and the Euro," Paul said. "I don't mean just you and the rest of you. You're only a handful. The Japanese are going to help. The rest of you are condemned to death. You're thinking in terms of factories and production. The rest of us aren't. We're thinking of living. You'd like to tie us up in a prison of wages and just enough food to live. An extra month's pay as a sop? That most of you dodge paying? Then you'd like us to come rampaging out in the streets so that your great soldiers can shoot us down. That's a splendid lesson for misbehaved animals, is it not?"

"If you've nothing better to tell me, I'll be going," The O'Dancy said, and pointed the glass at the coil. "Is it that thing putting the ideas into you? I can understand it. After all, it was present when the ructions began in the Garden."

Paul reached down and passed the tips of his fingers over the creature's head.

"He's not annoyed unless the rhythm of his day is interrupted," he said. "Then he's a terror."

"I never had less gratification from a couple of drinks," The O'Dancy said. "Did you hatch all this tomfoolery your own self, or did you get some help?"

"Considerable help," Paul said. "We've friends all over. We'll wait our time. May not be in my time, but the time will come. That's the important thing, isn't it?"

"Fill this," The O'Dancy said, and held out his glass. "I'll see how it strikes me. Would you take a great umbrage if I told you you're wasting your life in a ridiculous little world of your own? In other words, you're cracked."

"You're the originator," Paul said, measuring a good one. "All it is, is hereditary strain, blood and so forth, education, and living with eyes and ears open."

"You've had your trousers open most of the time," himself said. "Sixty-eight of them. Well, by the Lord Jesus."

"He may have helped at the appropriate moment," Paul said. "You've whored and frigged and flung your seed into any hole at all. It went out with the laundry soap. Mine didn't. It went where it ever ought. And it did what it was meant to do. And never one that was deformed or unhealthy. That's because I loved the girl. Yes. Loved her. Every woman in the house is loved, and knows it."

"It's against every theory I ever heard," The O'Dancy said. "But you might just be correct about all the frigging."

"This isn't theory I'm talking," Paul said. "You don't get sixty-eight boundless wonders on theory. Women have to suffer for them. If they're loved, they'll suffer silently, and you'll live as you were meant, in paradise."

"How do you keep all of them strung on the rope?" himself asked. "Don't they ever present an argument, or a word or two out of place?"

"There's no rope," Paul said. "There are no arguments. The woman wants to live here, or she doesn't. If she doesn't, she can go."

"You're a knockout," The O'Dancy said. "I'd never realized it before. This has been going on all this time? I don't blame you. If you can find women to live with you, I don't see much harm. But your thinking's damaged, somewhere. What does your sister think of you?"

"I have five sisters," Paul said, looking out of the door. "Three brothers."

"You've one sister," The O'Dancy said.

"Five," Paul said. "Why don't you finish your drink and go?"

"I thought you wanted a word with me," The O'Dancy said, and leaned back, resting the glass on his chest. "Bedamned if I'll be thrown off my own property."

"Bedamned if it's your property," Paul said. "It belonged to Grandam Aracý. She gave it to Daniel. He gave it to me."

"I never heard of it," himself said. "I'll want to see the papers."

"They're here," Paul said. "I could easily throw you on to your own property, if that's what you want?"

The man was about forty, a year or two back or forth, but he looked thirty, with a head of deep red hair in a crinkle, and the Leinster gray eye that could be droll as any clown's, or glacial, of a cold hate that would shock, and the face of him was browned to the sun, and unlined except between the eyes, a good big man, no doubt, and all of six foot in white shoes and socks, and white shirt and trousers, starched and pressed, never any different, never any other clothing or color, never any thought about him except cleanliness, whiteness, yes, a shining man.

There was deep blame to himself because they were not friendlier.

The boy was born within a day of Tomomi's first son, and the soul of himself was torn between the two, though Father Miklos was the only one to know it. Daniel had been born almost three years before of the warmest, most adorable heart, on a night of the full moon in Rio de Janeiro and all the world sang for him and his mother, and himself collected a band of musicians, and they danced through the city till the sun was up, and they piled on a tram, with the band on the roof, and sang themselves to breakfast down at the docks, and the stewards on the boats joined in and cooked at the quayside, and made coffee, and the police had to put them out to get any work done, and everybody was laughing.

It was the morning Tomomi Tomagatsu came out of the bank when himself was on the way in to get some money to pay the musicians.

Tomomi.

14 A granddaughter of the great man himself, about eighteen at the time, with the black hair piled high, and a kimono of blue satin and pearls, and the Great God Himself must have invented the morning to show her forth, not five foot of her, hair and all, from the feet like a doll's, and hands that seemed to have been whispered, and eyes of a smile that went through and through the heart of him, and a mouth ripe as the Virgin's own.

The mouth of Tomomi was in the mind of himself now, gentle, a wonder, complacent, abandoned, of a madness almost a drug.

"A father," she said, and bowed. "Everybody's so happy for you. We just sent our flowers to Fransisca. We shall wait to see her."

"Wait for me," he said. "I'll pay these boys. Come back with me, and you'll see her before anybody else."

They went back in the electric car, which moved so quietly he could hear the movement of her breasts against the kimono's satin while she breathed. She heard it too, and sat straighter, and looked at him, and they laughed. She laughed the smallest sound ever. Her eyes had a touch of the deep red cherry in them, but they were never brown. They were tender, nervous, unused to looking at men outside her own family, and then downcast in the Japanese tradition that old Tomagatsu insisted on, with all the formalities that divided the sexes. To ride in a car with a man however well known was a departure that made her breathless, never mind that her chaperon sat in front of the glass panel with the driver. Young women of Japanese families at that time had not begun to dress in the European style or to enter business, and Tomomi told him that she felt she was taking the first cold step in an unknown sea. She wanted to be an importer of textiles, but neither her father nor her grandfather would give her any help, and her mother and all the women refused to listen. They wanted her to marry well and create a family.

At the time, O'Dancy Enterprises were in first flourish, and himself knew the markets and the chief men inside and out. It was no trouble to scribble a couple of names on a card and tell her to write and, if she had any difficulty, to see him. Then they were at the house and everything was a dream of time and laughter in seeing Fransisca with a new son. But the Tomagatsu spirit was in Tomomi, never mind the appearance of nervousness. She opened an office down in Santos and went to live there with her chaperon and a nurse, and then she had a couple of girls working, and then a dozen more, and soon agents were coming from Japan to see only her, and it was no time until she had a business so large that her father took her into the Tomagatsu empire. From that moment, all the Tomagatsu women had the choice of dressing and living in any style they chose when they reached the age of eighteen, and of entering a university if they had the brains, or commerce, or of getting married.

It was some time before they met again. One noon, in Santos, on a hot day, and himself coming back from the Coffee Exchange after a brawling session, wet through, tired, but happy enough, he passed that first little shop. Amazed, himself stood there. It was prime outlet for retailers and the place was crowded, and the bales of stuff came out on the porters' heads, all with the double-T mark, and the buyers behind to count them into the waiting carts. Himself had to wait while a procession passed, and when he had the way, she was standing there, hands clasped in front of a flowered print, smiling, eyes down at tiny sandals, toes pointed in, but then they came up.

But in such a white blaze.

O, Tomomi.

"You are a thousand times welcome," she said. "So often I have seen you go by, but you never even look at me."

"I'll have to get my eyes attended to," he said. "I didn't even know you were ever here. I thought you had a small throne at the bank."

"This is where the business grows," she said. "We shall move next month to São Paulo, and this will be the import office. We've started our own mills. We shall soon be making more material than we bring in."

"So I've noticed," he said. "But I wasn't sure it was this company among all the others. You probably know I'm fifty per cent with your grandfather. I always had great confidence in your ability. And where else would we sell our cotton?"

"You will drink tea or coffee with me, please?" she invited. "I must be permitted to show gratitude to a partner."

"I never had greater pleasure in any business," himself said. "Specially when there's free tea and a comfortable place to sit down."

She went into a little garden lounge at the back of the place, all set about with rush mat walls, kept in a drip with water that cooled the air from hidden fans, and furnished in the Japanese style, with space, a low table, and cushions. A girl took his jacket and tie and shoes, and gave him a warm wet towel to dry the sweat, and a short cotton jacket and a pair of slippers. They sat and drank tea and talked business, and himself told her about Fransisca and the family. Paul had been born by then. Shaun was on the way, and himself was building in coffee and cotton and in city construction, and roads, and in development of rural estate, electricity, pipe lines, and factories of this and that, and the O'Dancy Development Bank was branching.

"They are calling you the emperor," she said. "I think I will too. Your flower is the chrysanthemum. I grow them for my pleasure. I have a new variety. I shall call it The O'Dancy."

"You'll not ask me if I like it, first?" he said. "What color is it?"

"Quite new," she said. "Dark red. A wine color. Very clear."

"Heady stuff," he said. "I'd like to see one."

"When they are ready I shall let you know," she said, and signed to the girl standing along the wall. "The master's shoes and jacket."

"Just started enjoying myself," he said.

"My buyers have been waiting for me for ten minutes," she said. "I have never been late before. I told them I was entertaining the emperor. They indulged me."

"You'll let me come again," he said, not a thought in him. "It's the coolest place on earth. And wonderful tea."

"It should be," she said. "It is O'Dancy, from your River Estate."

"I ought to feel proud," himself said, and kissed her hand, a delicacy without a jewel. "As it is, I'm only respectful. You've built a tremendous business in no time. Hasn't any man come along to put you in a house of your own?"

"Not yet," she said. "I have plenty to do here, for the moment. Please come in whenever you pass. If I'm not here, you'll always be served as though I were, I assure you. I shall give instructions. I ask only one favor?"

"Entirely your own," himself said.

"Don't bring anybody with you," she said. "Alone, or not at all. This is my room. I have invited you. Nobody else has ever been invited. Nobody else ever will."

That was part of the woman's lure. She was gentle and nervous, and smaller than most small women. But she spoke with something like male strength in that little voice. Nobody would misunderstand her, or if he did, she would put him right, there and then.

As she did Tomagatsu, her grandfather, to his face.

For many a month himself went into that cool, dark room, thankfully, and totted his accounts or even snoozed sometimes, grateful to be out of heat and noise. They rarely met, and then only for a moment, between her interviews with buyers. Strangely, it never struck him that he ought to build a cool office for himself. The company had always worked in the same shed, and they still did, and Fransisca had to insist on it before he saw sense. But then they built twenty floors and his office was like a futurist railroad station, and he hated it.

It was in the old shed, when everything had been moved out, that he met Tomomi one evening, with her accountant, to let them see if the place would suit them for a wharf warehouse, and of course it was exactly what they wanted in size, loading area, and nearness to the quay. The accountant went off to tell the agent, and Tomomi and he strolled through the evening's rose glow toward the office.

There were a couple of broken chairs and an empty filing cabinet, a lot of waste paper, and a square leather bed that had been in the little office since Grandfa Shaun's day, never used because few ever went in there.

"But you can't throw it away," Tomomi said, and sat down. "It is very well made."

"I thought of having it re-covered," he said. "Might do in the staff room."

"Let me buy it," she said. "I have the exact place for it. As it is. Cleaned and polished."

"It's yours," he said. "A gift."

She looked away from him, out through the door, at the sun's deepening rose-mauve on golden water.

"You made me a gift of freedom, and through me, all the women of my family, and we've influenced others," she said. "All I've given you is rest, sometimes, which makes me very happy, and a chrysanthemum. I would like to give you so much more. Japanese women still feel the kindly chains of the parental wish. We are not yet Brazilian, truly Brazilian. Not yet truly free, in the American sense of throwing off other memories, and doing what we would like to do. As others do."

"But you're doing me a lot too much honor, Tomomi," he said. "All I did was give you a couple of names. Your own name did a great deal more to help you. But it was your brains that got you where you are. Not me. I haven't done a hand's turn."

"You invested a great deal of capital," she said.

"That's right," he said. "In ships, railroads, rolling stock, telegraph, telephones, cotton, coffee, hides, and God knows what more. Too many pies for fingers. I've been too busy looking after myself to think about Tomomi."

"When the new telephones come, may I place my name on the list?" she asked. "I want one, personally. Not for the office. That will come later. For myself."

"You shall have Number Five," he said, and took out his notebook. "Grandam gets Number One. Fransisca, Number Two. Carvalhos Ramos, Number Three. Your grandfather, Number Four. You, Number Five."

"You won't have one?" she said.

"I'm the boss," he said. "I get five zeros. That's my number, forever. Will you have it installed at the apartment, here?"

"I've bought a house on the beach," she said. "I shall put it by my bed."

"The best place for conversation," he said. "You can look for it in about three months' time."

"Too long," she said.

Her eyes were closed, but the tears rolled, shone gold, and the black head went back, and back, and she raised the half-open mouth to the iron roof, and the great sob rang, rang, a terrible sound from so small a one, but no feeling was in her face and her hands were quiet flowers in her lap.

Himself knelt beside her, and put an arm about the warmth of her, and the head moved to his shoulder and she opened her eyes in the white blaze.

"I want a gift of you," she said. "Here. Not in months or days. Here. Now. You."

Himself was never the man for an argument. What surprised him was the strength of his feeling that he knew nothing about until she was naked under him and firmly virginal and taking the holy marvel in a rapturous movement of muscle within herself and not a movement of her outer body, and her eyes in unblinking white blaze a moment's edge from his own, and himself sapped, and weakening, and glorified in a new and marvelous way, and Christ's love retrieve the passing years, or bring again one kiss.

Tomomi.

"You're not holding your drinks as you did," Paul said, distantly enough. "Look, would you like to see the children? It's time for their meal. I like to bring them about me."

"My eyes run," himself said. "Not that I'm old. Memory's paid for in tears. Give me another drink, and I'll face the world. And your children. I wonder will God Almighty ever forgive me? I doubt it. I'll burn in the deep hell. I will. I deserve it. I'm resigned to it."

"I don't think you should have any more," Paul said.

"Be giving a man a Christ's drink for Christ's sake," himself said. "Do you not know the difference between drunk and not wanting to remember?"

Paul put his face close.

"Will you then come and meet the children?" he said. "They've been told you're here. Will you disappoint them?"

Himself raised his arms.

"Be cutting off my right hand, or left, or both," he said. "What would I be doing, disappointing a child, and them with my own mark in them?"

Paul laughed.

"They've that," he said. "Begod, you'll go in the books as a great sire."

"Here's to their Brazil," The O'Dancy toasted. "The finest country they'll ever know. If, that is, they ever know it better than a few of them alive at the moment."

"They will," Paul said. "I'm seeing to it. We've had some fine trips on your own bus lines. We never claimed the discount for knowing the owner."

"More fool you," The O'Dancy said. "That shows you're not a good Brazilian."

Paul turned on him.

"It shows I'm no bastard Euro," he said. "It's those Euro bastards who work off the tricks, and call it Brazilian. Bastards. Outside any law. And we haven't any. We only pretend."

"You're very sweeping," himself said.

"I'd like to be," Paul said. "By God, I would. There'd be a house cleaning, I'll tell you. I'd give every foreigner forty-eight hours to leave the country."

"You'd be living on air after the first twenty-four," The O'Dancy said. "You'd be ruined forever."

"My arse," Paul said. "Come on. The children are getting impatient."

They walked along the veranda, and through double doors into shadow of the huge room that went from one end of the house to the other, cool, with a sense of width and height, tiled in porcelain squares of designs in colors, with armchairs and reading lamps up one end, and the long refectory table down the other, a noble room, scented with blossom growing in pots, and the smoke from an open grill. A crowd of women and children in white clothes sat at the coffee tables, and plates made white circles, cutlery shone, and glasses. There were dozens of white shapes, but the faces and limbs were part of shadow.

"But, now, look, Great God," The O'Dancy said. "All these can't be your own?"

"Every one of them," Paul said at the side of himself. "Cleide, bring your youngest here."

Cleide was a big girl, big as Paul, glossy, black, as splendorous a woman as himself had ever seen. She wore a white dress and a number of starched petticoats, and a lilac handkerchief tied the stook of black hair so that it spilled over the top bind. She wore diamonds in her ears, on her fingers, and on the right wrist, and they flashed the prismatic reminder that no other stone so sings of itself. The baby had a paler skin, and the O'Dancy gray eyes, as numbing a clout as any himself had ever felt.

"What name are you giving this one?" he asked Cleide.

"Xerxes," she said, in a voice from the deep bones of herself. "That's Philomon. Sean. Theodorico. Jovina. Sandra. Andrade."

"Are you not about run out of something to call them?" himself asked.

"No," Paul said. "They're carefully named. They all have a birth chart. I'm not a bit worried about any of them. Their stars are bright and beautiful."

"You're a believer in stargazing, and such, is that it?" himself said. "What gives you the idea there's any substance to it?"

Paul smoothed the head of him with both hands, and looked at the crowd of his own making, and laughed a little.

"Oh well, now, it's an ancient enough practice," he said. "Atomic chemistry wasn't much a few years ago. It's still not much, but enough about it's known to see that it works. When we know a thing works sometimes, then we know it'll work every time when we know enough about it. That's us, in astrology. The effect of a turning world, generating a particular type of electricity, and as a consequence, the creation of specific fields of force at a particular moment. We might remember that our religion starts with stargazing, as you call it, when the Christ was found by the Magi. If they hadn't been sure of the stars and what they were told, would they have taken the trouble to make the journey with such gifts? Did you never think what might have happened if the stars had lied? Or if there hadn't been some wise men giving the science a little study before Christ was born? Would the little fellow have been known? Or suppose they got there, and only the animals were giving birth? Or suppose there was nothing at all? Or if The O'Dancy had been one of them, and he'd said to hell with it, I don't believe it? What then?"

"It's a question I've never put me mind to, yet," The O'Dancy said. "You didn't happen to find any Christs among any of these, did you?"

"Oh yes," Paul said, quietly as that. "They're all His brothers and sisters, are they not? They're all children of God. Like us, do you see?"

The O'Dancy looked at them all in their silence. Some of the mothers had never given himself a glance. Others he barely made out in the shadow. A few of them were touched with red light from the grill. A couple were outlined in sunlight rayed from the bamboo curtain. They sat with their children, silent.

"You've a rare assortment of women," himself said. "Are you looking for any more?"

"They know where I am," Paul said. "I believe they're rare enough. I've no other wives, or any side women. I have great joy of them. There's no man more thankful to God for many mercies."

"Are you not the biggest and blindest damned hypocrite that ever was?" himself asked. "This is against every principle. And your bone-idleness. And stargazing, for the Tears of Mary. If you weren't a son of mine, with a free roof and next to nothing to pay for food, could you fornicate with impunity? Who'd be footing the bill? What if everybody did this? Where in Christ's own blood would we be?"

"In Brazil," Paul said. "You're using that Euro mind of yours again. There's been no fornication here. There's been mating between two who needed to mate. No ceremony. We didn't require or permit that interference from anybody. The children are registered. That's all. There's been no divorce, that sham. I've never thrown a woman by. I've never denied a woman. I never forced a woman. I never took a woman because my name's O'Dancy and she's in my employ. I haven't done any of the things you've done all your life. I've lived here with the women who wanted to live with me. We've had children. This is not the half of them. The rest are at school. And I foot the bill. I've never used a cent of your money. Never would."

"But it costs money, by Satan's irons, and where's it coming from?" himself shouted.

Paul threw up his arms in The O'Dancy laughter—the ear thrummer, the ha-ha-ha-hawh-hawh—and all the women turned their eyes to him, and all the children gave him their faces, the dark faces, and small mouths of white teeth opened in laughter, and they all laughed the O'Dancy laugh—ha-ha-hahaha-hawh-hawh—the crusty tremolo, but the eyes caught the movement of light and they were all O'Dancy gray, all glittering, all Leinster gray, the eyes of himself, and the blood frozen to bleak rods within.

"I'll not use your oath," Paul said, and took out a handkerchief and put an arm about Cleide's shoulders, and her eyes in soft resplend upon him the whole time, and no doubt he was God, no doubt at all, because the woman would fight you for it, and Christ help you. "That name is the truest bad language in this house. Do you remember when Daniel made his duty, and him taken back to the Prime Father, may the wings of Him protect us?"

"Amen," The O'Dancy said. "I do."

"The saddest, blackest day of all," Paul said.

The O'Dancy put out a blind hand.

"Ah, Son," himself whispered. "Thank God on my knees to hear you say it. Sleep gentle on the Bosom, boy."

"Well," Paul said. "That day, young and unknowing, I came to the office. I was finished with school. They were trying to make a Euro out of me, and I'd have none of it."

"You had the idea then?" himself said.

"Born with it," Paul said. "Yourself had never been much in my favor. You could see only Daniel. And Hilariana."

"You're putting rusted thorns into the tripes of me, now," The O'Dancy said. "I don't know what was in me."

"Pride in another," Paul said. "One O'Dancy at a time, and nobody else lives."

"There'll be a candle burned for this," himself said. "I'm soul-sour about it."

"I waited in the office," Paul said. "I wanted to tell you I didn't want any more school. I wanted to come in the business."

"You did," The O'Dancy said.

"I did," Paul said. "Then that message went in. You were crying. Dan, Dan, my Daniel, you were saying. Have they taken you from me? And you threw that clock on your desk at me. I wanted to tell you. You cursed me."

"God's curse is on me," The O'Dancy said. "I don't remember."

"I went back and I got a little bag together, and I left," Paul said. "I stayed with Uncle Mihaul for a while. Then I found a place with Fazelli in the stables. You never knew. Then old Mr. Carvalhos Ramos got me a place with Hiroki's father."

"Hiroki," himself said. "That one. Son of old Inuye?"

"A marvelous man, he was," Paul said. "I learned everything from him. I was with him for twenty-odd years. And what did you know, or care?"

"You sent back my Christmas presents," himself said. "And birthday presents."

Paul looked, and his mother was warm.

"Your secretary sent them," he said. "What did you ever buy with your own thought? Daniel always did. And he always made it plain it came straight from yourself. You were thinking of me. But very busy. I never had a mother or a father. Only a brother. When he went, nobody. It was old Tomagatsu who led me to four other sisters. And three brothers. That's when I started to think. I became a real Brazilian then."

"You'd joined inspired company," himself said. "Tomomi lived, and believed."

"True," Paul said. "She was Brazilian, and meant to be, and was. Are you able to speak so coldly of her?"

"No, Christ's Death, not," The O'Dancy said. "Should I spill the salt in front of children?"

"Well, then," Paul said. "Should we let them eat a little?"

"Ah yes," himself said. "Would I be let come again? And take a couple on my knee and feed them, and make them laugh? It'd be a joy."

"Anytime," Paul said. "It's open house to any O'Dancy, near or far. You should see them with Hilariana. And Steb's lovely girl. That's a sweet pick. Koioko."

"I have to see her father," he said. "No later than today. I promised the boy. Why did you never choose one outside the color? Do you have a nice taste for it?"

"They are Indio, most of them, the root stock of the country," Paulo said. "Their people were here a world's age before Grandfa Leitrim. They're the true daughters. Cleide's an Ashanti Negress. You see that nose? But there's Tupi in her, and Moor, and Portuguese. She should have bred pale, but a good black one got there first. She never knew her father. Our children are all paler. Their children'll be paler still. There are Tupi and Caingang and Guaraní, here. Some pure, some a little mixed. But wonderful women. I say it. I know."

"I respect your opinion," The O'Dancy said. "How are they on the bed?"

"Attentive," Paul said, and walked to the door.

The O'Dancy wanted to wave good-by, but nobody, not one of them, was looking at him.

All the gray, glittering eyes had followed the father, gray eyes, the eyes of himself, thrown true from Grandfa Leitrim, and that one true to some other, long part of the soil itself, God love them all, and revere the earth that took to itself gray light and quick thought and with time reduced them to loam.

"The whole world's a tumbling tomb," The O'Dancy said. "Around we go, and we stand on the dead."

"That's about what it says in the Book," Paul said.

"Don't be getting off the subject," The O'Dancy said. "Where's my drink, and where are you getting the money from to buy it? Never mind about the others at school."

Paul went smiling into the room and waved his hands at shelves of red and brown and roan leather, gold-lettered books. Even if the man hated, or less than that, if he was contemptuous, or even mildly misliking, still, with it all, there was singular contentment in knowing that himself had the fathering. In remembering the nights with Fransisca, there was almost wonder, nearly joy, it might have been, perhaps a glorying, that a fine man, for all the noddiness in him, had taken life of her passion.

Himself had been merely stallion come home to a comfortable stall and a patient mare.

Tomomi called.

She said no word, made no request, never a demand.

She called, in the quiet spirit, in the quiescent hands, in the white blaze.

Perhaps Fransisca had known it or sensed it, but after the birth of this one, she was never the same, and himself ever wondered why, until that evening on the mountain all in the chime of the llama bells.

15 "You may never have known it, but old Mr. Inuye was one of the world's first practitioners of artificial insemination," Paul said. "I studied with him. When he died, I took his place. Hiroki's the senior partner. He deals with sales. I'm in charge of the laboratory."

The O'Dancy looked about the room at the books, most from the gold tabs, animal registers, and at photographs of prize cattle, a number of them belonging to himself, and long strings of blue, red, and yellow rosettes from shows himself knew nothing about.

"You don't mean to tell me you make a living out of the artificial stuff, and then come back here and throw your brains away," himself said. "Well, now, I'll tell you once and for all. I'm in absolute sympathy. There'll be no artificial nonsense wherever I am."

"Your herds have been built solely by artificial insemination," Paul said. "We use your beef animals to breed champions, naturally, for semen. And that's used with cattle that otherwise would either never mate, or go like a rattle of bones to the butcher, or breed a throw of no value. As it is, whether it's beef or dairy, you've got the best."

"And who allowed you access to my cattle?" The O'Dancy asked. "Was it Democritas?"

"The older Mr. Carvalhos Ramos, first," Paul said. "That was in old Mr. Inuye's time. I simply followed on."

"I don't know what to tell you," The O'Dancy said. "I can't deny you. But I can't accept what you say."

"Better look at your herd registers," Paul said, putting the drink down. "You'd best taste that, because there are less pleasant matters you have to be told about, that you'll also not accept. But there're done. The milk's spilled. You've got to decide."

"You're talking about this agreement you have with Hilariana and Steb to divide The Inheritance when I'm on top of the hill, there?" himself said. "I'll do what I can to stop it, be sure of that."

Paul wagged his head, and tck-tcked, and sat down, no man more a master.

"Nothing to do with it," he said. "And let me remind you, when you're up there, there's nothing you'll be able to do down here. That is, as you are now. If you've got sufficient strength to survive, you might be called back to help us. But you'd be a very different type. The purified O'Dancy'd be something to listen to. I'd do anything not to miss it."

"Are you now saying something about this spirit business?" The O'Dancy asked, and put the drink back on the table. "Listen to me. I'll have it up by the roots if I have to call the chief of police. I won't have it, I tell you. I won't."

"You should have talked to Grandam Xatina," Paul said. "And Grandam Aracý. And a few more. That's a hundred years gone by. And how many before them? And since? Isn't The House itself, both parts, a temple? Hasn't it always been?"

There was no doubt about what the man was saying.

Grandam Xatina's house, now the Women's House, and the older part, had always been places of curious sounds. As a boy, he had been either with The Tad or at school. As the future O'Dancy he had never been at a nurse's heels, and when The Mam and Tad died, old Mr. Carvalhos Ramos had himself out and away and only going back after graduation, but then there was his own suite that Grandfa Connor had built, off the main House. Himself could never remember going into the Women's House at all. There was no need. But in remembering it, now, there was ever a sniff of incense there, in the doorway on the stairs and at the main door in the patio, and shuttered windows, and deep shadow, and cane curtains in a squeak, and crones about the place somewhere, always in a singing whisper.

"Leave the women to themselves," Old Mr. Carvalhos Ramos told him. "Never interfere. They have their own way to live, and a man has his. Mãe Nueza is in charge. So let her be in charge. The only time you'll ever hear her name is when she needs more bed linen, or new carpets, or soap, and such things. That's not business for a man. The office will attend to it."

Fransisca had given up the Women's House at the beginning, and turned it into a sort of museum for the pieces she moved out of the main house to furnish in the style she wanted. From that time the Women's House was only for personal or chambermaids, and laundry and kitchen staff, and all the older women servants, and those on pension and not wishing to go home, and for young girls in training. Visiting nuns stayed often, and prayed in Grandam Xatina's chapel, though Father Miklos preferred his church, and never set foot in the smaller place, or could be persuaded even on a morning of pouring rain to take a service there and save the family wet feet.

"Out of one door, into the other?" he said. "You come to worship. Accept the necessary discipline. Come to church, as your fathers did. That's your time to consider the mistakes of the preceding week. The other place is nothing more than a sanctuary. An old woman's *prie-dieu.*"

In fact, it was far more. Grandfa Leitrim built it for the household when the jungle was only a few paces from the porch. Each grandam since had added statuary and gold until it must have been one of the most magnificent chapels in the country, though certainly, so far as the family was concerned, one of the least used.

Fransisca refused to go in after the first service, and Vanina, of course, had no religion except herself.

"I'd best start this from the beginning," Paul said. "I don't want to make too much of it. But you'll have to understand. So I'll go at it slowly. If there's any belief in you, be using it. If you've a prayer, you'll need it."

The O'Dancy held out the glass.

"D'you not think you ought to be filling this, first?" himself said. "On purely humane grounds? Even the surgeon puts you away before he cuts you. And what will you be doing, now, to me? That's so black in the face of you?"

Paul got up and took the glass, and went swift to the bottle.

"I'll do nothing but break your heart," he said. "If, of course, there's anything there."

"Having a tremendous one of your own, you doubt I've got any?" The O'Dancy said. "Look to yourself."

"You've shown little enough of it ever," Paul said, and came back with a fair one. "Be listening, then."

"Be keeping your orders to yourself," The O'Dancy said. "Talk."

There was nothing the man could say to cause himself any more surprise. The business of spiritism had been digested more or less, but for all that, there was no doubt in any part of the mind of himself about what to do. Detail by detail, starting first thing in the morning of a clean, wonderful day, himself intended to go through the record of every human employed or fathered on The Inheritance, and clear out those with any link to spiritism. Then through the herds and flocks, and in fact, everything with life or not, and the question of allowing that pesthole of a village to exist, and the plan for new roads and bridges, new electrical installations, and a decision on whether to run the electric line near the house with a private car for himself and the family, or put the line outside on the boundary and stick to cars, planes, and helicopters. Whether or not, it was strictly his intention to drop the plumb over everybody and everything. There could be only one master, and himself determined to show everybody which one.

"You see, you can't run a place like this without a woman," Paul said. "I used to think you could. But you can't. Nature'll beat you, to begin with. There are hundreds of women employed here that a man'd never see. Laundry, and sewing, and cleaning, and nursing kids, and in the dairy and cooking, and curing hides, and weaving, and making baskets and stuff, and looking after stores and tending school. Examine it, you'd be thunderstruck. You ought to pay off half of them. But you couldn't."

"Where would they go?" The O'Dancy said. "Their great-great-great-grandmothers did the same jobs. Why'd I sack them? Nonsense."

"Without a woman like The Grandam they get out of hand," Paul said. "Not out of hand so that a man'd ever see it. But out of hand the way a woman'd spot in a moment. Well, anyway. When The Grandam was alive, everything went well. When she and The Grandfa died, and she going the way she did, there were ceremonies going on for weeks. Then anniversaries. Every year a bigger feast. More people. From farther off. The place got famous."

"I never heard any of this," The O'Dancy said.

"Of course not," Paul said. "If ever you mixed with the maids, it was for one reason, and soon done."

"I never heard it better expressed," himself said.

"You'll perhaps find a place for flippancy a little later," Paul said. "When Uncle Mihaul came here, he found a wilderness. Of the spirit. There was nothing but this—worst—kind of spiritism."

"*Khimbanda,*" himself said.

"Don't, please, say the word anywhere, especially never in this house or near," Paul said, and put his hand down and touched the gray coil. "It's a horrible thought, and horribler consequences. Very well. Uncle Mihaul made up his mind, you see, to stay here and try to revive the Faith. Bring the sheep back to the fold."

"If I understood what you were talking about," The O'Dancy said. "Mihaul's been here almost since you were born. There's another doesn't know there's anything else in the world but the arse of him and a stool."

"You're wrong, but it matters nothing," Paul said. "Mihaul, the priest, set himself to cure the sickness here. Little he did in the first years. The rot was too far in. But old ones died off, and his influence gained, you see. The aura strengthened. He got great help from Grandfa Leitrim and Grandfa Cahir, and often from Grandfa Phineas. But he could never reach Grandam Xatina."

"You've had more of this than I have," The O'Dancy said, holding up his glass. "Do you mean he read their diaries, or thought about them, or some such?"

"No," Paul said. "They spoke to him."

The O'Dancy looked at the drink, and put it down and looked about the room. The gray coil moved a little, a blurred, sickening, anticlockwise motion, but the head stayed where it was.

"Paul," himself said. "The three of them were long cold at the time Mihaul came back here."

"They live in another world," Paul said. "The one we're going to. But if we have faith, and put ourselves in the way of it, and they wish, we can talk to them and take their advice."

"Which of us is drunk?" The O'Dancy asked.

Paul reached out and switched on the radio set.

"Would Grandfa Leitrim believe this?" he asked. "That's Australia."

The voice broke into the room so loud that the eardrums hurt, and then a squeak, and a North American was talking about fishing off the coast of somewhere.

"Australia to the United States in a moment," Paul said, and clicked a blessed silence. "What's between them and us? Air. We're told it's electricity. Waves. Any explanation'll do. The main thing is, it works. If they didn't hear it, who'd believe it? It's the same with Grandfa Leitrim. And Grandfa Cahir."

"You'll be recognizing the voices of them, of course," The O'Dancy said. "They were dead before you were born."

"You'd recognize Grandam Xatina's voice, wouldn't you?" Paul asked.

"I would," The O'Dancy said. "An empress among women. There might be one of her every century. Never two."

Himself saw the sun slipping pale slivers through the shutters, and all the furniture tacked with a point of silver, and the tiles flashing, and Grandam Xatina in the pink satin crinoline, sitting in the shadow of the great withe chair, and jewelry making a pebbled breast of fire, even in the Dark Room, her own room, with a nun humming at prayer in the chapel downstairs, and another in the corner, whispering in a ripple of beads.

"*Oapi*, if I were a young woman again," she was saying in the voice that sounded as though sieved through lace, "I'd live differently, *oapi*, yes, I would. Oh, I would, I'd live differently, yes."

"How, differently, Grandam?" himself asked, though he was not allowed.

"Oh, I'd not be held by any laws at all, not one," she said. "I'd do as I wanted. Nobody'd ever tell me yes, or no, or must, or will. I'd ride the horse. But I've let it carry me. I'd be nearer the Divine Spirit if I'd lived my own life. Now I'm near the grave, and no salvation near me. Unprepared in spirit or will. Spirit, your grandfa always said. Nothing without spirit. Without spirit, nothing. I should have run with a hundred. I never did. Now the spirit craves, but the clay's misshapen. If I were a young one now, I'd keep no law, or listen. I would not, or ever."

"You're talking a lot, my lady," Mãe Nueza said. "The reverend sisters will want to know what about."

"Tell them," Grandam Xatina said. "Tell them about the strength of a young ox driver. Tell them the way he leans."

"Arquimed is here, at the satin's scallops," Mãe Nueza said. "These are young ears."

"When there's hair in them, he'll remember," Grandam Xatina said. "Find The O'Dancy, handsome one. Go. There's no rest for the yearning mind. No sop for the spirit. Light a candle for me. Remember the light. There's nothing without spirit."

"Go, young one," Mãe Nueza said. "Tell The O'Dancy that my lady finds her words in the west wind. Remember your candle. In the box, by the door."

The Tad looked over the flame of the match while the candle took fire, gray eyes smiling a little, and sad.

"In the west wind, is it?" he said. "The woman has a way of putting it. Won't be long, then. And a deliverance, no doubt, poor relict."

"What's a relict, Tad?" himself asked.

"One that's left over, and nothing more to do," The Tad said, and lifted the candle. "Let's be setting this where it'll warm the prayers of us. And we'll think kindly of a woman in her beauty. Even if she was a black one, and I had no great love for her, she was a strong hand, and kindly to me. And I was all that stood between her own son and inheritance. Remember that, with her children's children. She was kind to me. I trust you. Be kind to them."

Paul pushed and pulled inside the lid, and closed, and sat down, fingers to forehead.

"Here's a tape," he said. "This was taken not long ago. When I asked for advice."

"Not what it may seem," Grandam Xatina said, strong, and gently herself. "Not at all. You are always wrong to have a strict opinion. The principle, what is the principle? What is the principle? Are you speaking of a habit? The habit brought down through the generations? Is this the principle? No, my son. We are so far apart in words. I am not always able to speak to you plainly. I must choose my words. You are used to a direct speech between bodies. And the habits of bodies. Make sure of this principle. Oh, my son, remember you are always wrong. It is earthly habit to cling. Cling. Ah, shellfish. But give more. Give more. It is love, my son."

Paul got up and lifted the lid, and stopped the whisper of the turntable.

"Was that the woman's voice?" he said. "I know it was. I've many a dozen recordings."

The O'Dancy tried to drink, and put the glass down, and clasped hands.

"Very well," he said. "There's no proof, and you can fake anything. But that was Grandam Xatina. I know it. How was it done?"

Somebody was coming singing along the veranda, and the song himself remembered singing as a child. Paul looked toward the door, half in a frown and smile, as though he expected it.

Cleide stood in the door, arms out, fingers moving, and her eyes were closed, and she sang a little without the words, but not in her own deep voice. A little voice, a child's, from the back of her throat.

"*Oapi, Pae,*" she sang. "Let us call Xangó. Let us call Xangó. O rose of gold, ah, golden rose, Maxumbembé, Maxumbembé, Orixá, ah, see Maxumbembé."

"But you forgot what I told you," Paul said, and stood in front of her. "Now Cleide. Listen to me. In the name of The Saintly Mother, wake, and take my hand, and kiss me, and go back to your children. Mother of prayer, strengthen my spirit. Release this daughter without harm. Pray for us, Holy Mother of God, that we may be faithful to the promises of the Lord Jesus. Amen. Cleide, now, my heart, wake. Wake, then. Look. It's myself. Paul."

Cleide shivered and opened her eyes, and saw her arms stretched out, and might have screamed, but Paul linked the fingers about his neck, took her waist in his hands, and pulled her tight to him.

"You see?" he said. "I told you to be careful. Silly girl. Give me a kiss, and go back to your boys and girls."

"Ah, O pure dreams of white, white water," Cleide said in her own voice, deep, seeming to shake the room. "I was looking over the table and I heard Grandam Xatina. She was next to me. She wore the Mary gown, and silver."

"Of course," Paul said. "She always does, to visit us. Bring some coffee for us, and you drink some."

She smiled at himself, and bent her knee, and went out, and her skirts were talking all down the corridor.

"A wonderful medium," Paul said. "But I prefer the children in bed, first."

"Would you mind if I told you it'd give me the Kerry Shakes to be living here?" The O'Dancy said. "The place is mad. The whole lot of you ought to be locked up."

All the children were laughing next door, and only a deaf one could deny the O'Dancy ha-ha-ha-hawh-hawh-hawhm and himself without any doubt, hearing the young voices, knowing it was the laughter of himself from the tender throat, and making no bones in mind that any one of them was his own through a true son, and the pride was roused in him.

"How, would you mind telling me, did you get that load out of yourself?" The O'Dancy asked, and nodded toward the young. "You must have been cocking half a dozen or more at the same time. Did you never do yourself some harm?"

Paul looked at the girl coming in with no sound except a rattling tray, and watched her put it down, and arrange the cutlery, and the jug of wine, and the glass, and bend a knee, and go out.

"Cleide's my wife," Paul said. "Cleide's the only wife I've had. The others all came to me of their own volition. Beyond the seed that impregnated, I've never touched them. They're all mater-familias by artificial insemination."

16 The O'Dancy was in a search of the mind of himself, but the plate of beef and mustard had a claim of its own.

"Had you any right to do such a thing?" himself asked. "Is there no law against this? There should be."

"They were all of age, all self-willed," Paul said. "They came to me. I never went looking for them. They wanted children, and decent quiet. They were sick of drunken fathers. They didn't want to be used, worn, deathly, before their time. As their mothers were. These are the sort of women who generally end in the roadway. In the public hospitals. Trailing an unnamed little creature or two, or three. Diseased, all of them. Product of natural union of course. Against a wall, or over a gate, or in an empty bus, or a rail truck, somewhere. These next door went into an operating room, and a physician saw they were protected. Here, they live. Happily."

"And they never call for a man?" himself said. "Aren't they unnatural?"

Paul sat farther back, and laughed into his hands.

"Never," he said. "There have been more than a hundred and eighty marriages here. The men know it's a better way of finding a woman. The child or two she's borne are part of their family. He's got to be a good man, and steady, or I won't have him anywhere near. The men are coming to me for a wife who's used to running a proper house. The woman makes up her mind whether to say yes, I'll marry, or no, I'll not. They meet here every week, the finding ones. Of those married, there's never been one gone wrong."

The O'Dancy listened while he chewed, and thought, while the glass upended the marvelous clear wine-red against a white shaft from the uncovered west window.

"Let's be asking the question uppermost," himself said. "In this case, who's the champion bull?"

"Never anyone except myself," Paul said. "Via the test tube and the refrigerator. I'm fit, mentally and physically. And I'm O'Dancy. That's important. The blood's clean. The seed throws clean."

"Great God," The O'Dancy said through a mouthful. "But, listen, how'd a man want a woman, so? Would he not want to marry one without the blemish?"

Paul got up, and went to the door.

"There's many a woman with the blemish that would make twenty of any man alive," he said. "Their instinct is to produce their kind. With or without the help of anybody. It's all in themselves. The instinct's generously hidden. Any male will do at the time. At any other time, he's what he is. Sometimes he corresponds. Then they're both of a mind. They become one flesh because they're of one mind. That's love. She could never see anybody else. He wouldn't give you a curse for another woman."

"You're talking like this out here," himself said. "In the city, or in any city, you'd be in court. Who'd listen to you?"

"The woman," Paul said. "She'd do more than listen. Women love, instinctually."

"For Christ's sake, you say that, knowing Vanina?" The O'Dancy said.

"I'm glad you've mentioned the name, for I won't," Paul said. "And isn't that why I wanted to talk to you? Poor benighted bastard you are, my own sire, too. God save us."

"Yes, very well, God save us," The O'Dancy said, and put down the bread and meat. "And now, talk, and be telling me, for I've the rarest mind of the one that partnered me to bring you out. Don't make me be asking was it worth it. But I'll wager that what was mine forty or more years ago was more beautiful, more delicate, yes, more woman, than anyone yourself ever knew."

Rain, the running silver bouncing the streaks of brilliant crystals across the lawn, all in a chatter and patter, setting the roses in a dance of drooping blossom, filling the paths with torrents halfway to the knee all in a skelter of petals, brimming and pouring from the stone plant baskets, cascading under the pergolas, teeming from the roof, spewing from the gutters, flinging blunt splashes against himself, almost blinded by sweet water that he drank easily as from a glass, with the clothes stuck heavy to his body, and his shoes out of shape, trying to find a way in, and the veranda closed by wire net.

And coming around the corner, under the falling scarlet of the poinsettia with the dark hair shining smooth to the head and flat down her back and the rain sliding diamonds, flashing jewels off the marvel of herself, walking with the hands cupped to catch a fill of water, and the hair of her thighs in frost of brilliants, Fransisca, nude, laughing.

But no surprise when she saw him, no sudden gesture, no attempt to run for leaves and make an apron. She, looking at him through the silver strokes, smiling with her eyes half closed, head up, and hands at her sides. For some reason, or none, there was no surprise in himself, but only an absolute will, sprung and grown then and there to marry her and nobody else, and neither of them ever having seen each other before the moment.

Himself went slow, pace by pace, and took both the hands of her, and kissed them, each, back and palm, and herself stood smiling, and no move.

"I am Arquimed Rohan O'Dancy Boys," he said, a whisper through the wash of rain. "Would you do me the honor of marrying me?"

"Yes," herself said, and there was never any more.

Seventeen, then, only daughter of Nestor Portenaves, a millionaire in coffee and lumber and one thing and another, so the union was not only popular but practical, for no doubt it helped, because her father died in that year, and everything came to Fransisca. But she was a clever one, too, and the only idea in her life was to make the country grow. It was just as simple as that. Her father owned a railroad. She insisted it should go farther. When the omnibus became less than a miracle, she wanted fleets of them. There were no roads. She wanted them built. Politicians had to be prodded. She bought a newspaper. Roads, buses, transport for merchandise, newspapers, advertising, radio, towns growing, construction, cement works, tile and brick factories, domestic utilities, banks, grocery and clothing stores, there was never an end to it.

Eleven o'clock at night was their own time, agreed between them at the beginning, on the very night of the honeymoon, when they were to be together for talking and knowing and loving. Every night at eleven for all the years, except in times when he was off somewhere, or she was on vacation with the children, there they were, in the big bed, she in a whole garment of perfume, himself close as a second pelt, sweating the same drop, in a way of thinking with her, speaking with her voice, she in the throat of himself, endeared, enloved beyond the edge of earth or any moon at all.

"You see," Paul said, looking out of the door. "It's not easy, this. Even though I hate you more than there's any hope of putting in words, I know I'm going to hurt you, and I hate that more."

"You hate me," himself said.

"I do," Paul said. "Everything, every rotten thing you represent. Hate."

"O, Son," The O'Dancy said. "Wait now. Between one moment and another, will you be waiting before you say you hate me?"

Afternoons in gold, and Fransisca hand in hand with himself, day after day, up above the snow line, living the wonderful hours of a little time by themselves, without children or servants or telephones, knowing they must go back to it all, and cherishing the moments away. The log shelter they slept in propped on a rock that looked over three valleys, and every morning the bantam cockerels roused them to see the sun rise in violet and lilac, and herself made the coffee on a twig fire in an old enamel pot on the stones over in the corner. A walk down the mountain to the hotel was enough exercise twice a day for meals, and the rest of the time they wandered about the mountaintop, watching tiny people working down in the rice fields, and strings of llamas carrying the copper ore, and Indios leading them gone to sleep standing up from chewing the coca. All down the other side of the mountain in steps and terraces, the coca bushes glinted the dark green leaves, and himself borrowed an Indio's lime stick, and rolled a leaf, and limed it, and gave it to Fransisca, and chewed one himself, but it did nothing for them except embitter their mouths. But the Indio rolled a handful, like hay, and limed it, and stuck it all in one side of his face till the cheek bulged, and he kicked the leading animal, and the bell woke the others, and they all got up grunting, and trotted, the gentle llamas, up the mountain path. Two days, from the mountaintop they watched the Indio, all the way down, across the valley and two rivers, and up the mountain on the other side, and the only times he stopped was to rest the llamas, and at sunset, he made a circle of them, and lit a small fire in the middle and sat there, either asleep or deadened with the coca.

Fransisca was not then thirty, of a loveliness that smote, though if she knew it there was never a sign or any show. She wore jewelry at night, sometimes, but in the day, only the earrings, the pearls himself gave her the day after they met in the garden, and the ring, the emerald, and the wedding ring. They were almost down in the hotel garden among the mountain shrubs she loved, and the lights came on, and a few people were strolling about the terrace, and a waiter pushed the bar trolley under the dew parasol and they could hear the bottles rattling.

"A kindly sound," himself said. "Should I mix an O'Dancy?"

"I believe we deserve one," she said. "I'm very, very hungry. I hope there's fish or poultry. Then I can drink champagne. So. An O'Dancy is the perfect complement."

He put one jigger each of Cordial Médoc, Triple Sec, and brandy in the shaker, poured in champagne almost to the brim, and gave it a gentle mix. Two glasses taken from the freezer, a careful pour until froth met the brim, and then himself put two fingers on the stand, and she had to bend down to drink without spilling any, but she always did, and while they were laughing, Amoru was calling him.

He remembered telling Tomomi about the place. Never had he thought she might go there. It was a night at the seaside house north of Rio, and no breeze, and heat that settled on their bodies like soaked sacking, and he spoke of snow and ice, and the ski runs and promised to take the family to Switzerland, and mentioned the mountains of Chile and Peru, and Andean peaks and the little cottages, and Indios asleep while they walked or stood, drunk or drugged on coca.

Amoru, his eldest daughter, first child of Tomomi, twelve years old, with her mother's beauty and the Leitrim eyes, and the red hair of himself waist-long, and none might ever mistake her for another's child when they stood together, that one, that precious and delightful one, looking at him over the shrubs, laughing surprise, and turning to call Tomomi.

"With your permission I shall have to introduce my daughter and her mother," himself said.

"You could hardly do anything else," Fransisca said. "A little late, isn't it?"

"It occurred to me that I ought to tell you," he said without once looking at her. "There never seemed a real opportunity."

"How many daughters are there?" Fransisca asked with no tone of temper.

"Three," he said. "And two sons, and one newborn."

"And their ages?" Fransisca said, politely interested, possibly.

"Twelve, ten, seven, five, three, I think, and four months," he said.

"A son," she whispered over the drink. "His name?"

"Atsuo Bohun," he said. "Daniel is older."

"You kept her all the time we pretended a life?" she said.

"We didn't pretend," he said. "It was true. And I never kept her. She's her own woman."

Fransisca had eyes about the color of the deep topaz and suddenly they were full, in a glitter, and she held out the glass for another.

"I knew I was going to deserve this," she said with no voice. "I didn't realize how much. Why don't you ask them over? We could at least dine together."

Himself filled the glasses, and drank to her, and bowed and went about the garden, but no Amoru. He called her, and called Tomomi up at the windows. Inside the hotel, he looked in the reading room, and the lobby, and the dining room, and in fair surprise he went to the reception desk.

"I'm looking for a mother and daughter," he said. "Tomagatsu. I just saw the daughter in the garden."

"Ah yes," the woman said. "They've gone to our other place on the plain. The lady thought the air wasn't suitable. A lot of people can't stand the height."

Himself saw the car turning the curve down below. There was no possible way of catching them. His own car was a fifteen-minute walk downhill to the garage.

Fransisca's second drink was untouched. The waiter told him Madame had gone in the hotel. Himself sat there looking at the valley and trying not to think. There would have to be an explanation ready for Amoru. Minutes going by and nothing settled, and a whole hour he sat, until the moon was almost up. He went in the hotel, and again he faced the woman and she looked at him almost as if he were someone else.

"But I thought you'd gone," she said. "Mrs. O'Dancy's left. More than half an hour ago."

"Left," he said. "Wait, now. O'Dancy. Was that what you were saying?"

"Mrs. O'Dancy paid your account and the driver's, and took the car keys and left," the woman said, and looked at him with her head on one side. "Surely?"

A run, and the breath in bloody rags up at the top there, in darkness, and no light inside, no wonder of the voice of her when he leaned against the wall and called. The night breeze, and a llama bell far away, and the thud of his heart.

Her clothes were gone. On the table a little heap of earrings, the emerald ring, and the wedding ring. No word, and no word for almost eighteen months, and yet Old Carvalhos Ramos had known where she was the whole time, never more than five minutes from the house, in the Convent of the Redeemer's Heart, and seeing Daniel and Paul and Shaun, and Belisaria and Kyrillia every day, and the children in silent consent with the mother and the nurses and governesses, ah, dear Jesus, that was the deep wound.

"You see," Paul said, a thunderclap of a voice out of the man. "The whole horror of this is your own sacred blindness. If ever you saw anybody else, if it was man, woman, or animal, it was all the same. Either there was pleasure for The O'Dancy, or not, and if not, to hell."

Tomomi in the Japanese house, down along the white beach, with everything outside Brazilian, and everything inside, even the toilet paper, of her own country. Asking himself, at the time, as he stood there, how he was able, how it became possible day after day to conduct himself as two separate men, well, he found it strange to consider, stranger to try to answer.

It was so simple.

Tomomi worked six days a week as hard as any of her employees. But she took a whole day off during any one week to read, or paint, or study flowers, or anything that danced in her mind at the time. Himself was never able to take a day off, and there were very few Sundays in his life when he was not at the office, or out at one of the plants. But on Tomomi's day off, and for an hour or two on Sundays, he ran down to the beach house, either for lunch or dinner, or just a drink, and it was always exactly like a visit to another part of the world, where his mind functioned differently, because his body was treated differently, and his spirit ever found refreshment in Tomomi's beauty, which was far more than of the body alone. She had no desire other than to live for himself. Their children were only part of her joy. The woman was joyous. The only time he ever saw her in tears was in an early morning, watching the chrysanthemum buds opening in the warming sun.

"Why would you cry?" himself asked her.

"The beauty fills me and it runs from my eyes," she said, with the dear weight of untied hair silken about his shoulders.

"Should we make some coffee and let it run out of our ears?" he said. "I've a great coffee hunger this time of the morning. Flowers are fine in their place. I don't believe they'd ever make me cry."

But they did, that small bouquet of white roses, the miniature roses grown by Tomomi, the only flowers on Fransisca's casket, that terrible day, yes, they made him cry.

"God dam the Nails of Christ," himself said to Old Carvalhos Ramos. "I'm getting a regular woman, here, crying my bloody eyes out, and I can't stop."

"Cry," the old one said, and a father's hand on the arm of himself. "Cry till you're dry. Cry for your sadness. Cry for a lovely woman. What else will cure you? What else will keep you sane? Drown your sorrow. Salt water's better than alcohol."

"Haven't touched a drop," himself said. "Not one. Or been near a bottle."

That was true, and curious. There was no wish in the world to drink. The body of himself seemed to have no weight. Moving about felt as if he might have been a ball of cotton. Food, even the thought of it, was nothing less than offense. Before that, he could drink his fair share with small effect, if any. But after, well, only two or three and he was mazed, often a babbling churl, and ever useless.

The days of his life had never seemed strange to him, or the way he lived, or anything he did, and nothing was ever inexcusably selfish except, of course, the matter of his conduct between Fransisca and Tomomi. Even there, he wondered what he should have done.

"I see nothing sacredly or even profanely blind about any selfishness of my own," himself said. "What's a man to do if a woman's thighs are wet for him? Turn his back? Tell himself to think pure thoughts? Run over his rosary a few times? Is that the way of it? Is there anything impure about a woman in love? Or about a child? Is your own impurity not in evidence with this houseful of sports? According to yourself, only one of those women ever felt the bounce of a man's balls. Is that pure? The only things sacredly blind about me is my cock, and cocks can't see. They do splendidly in the dark. Or should I be waltzing about in a white coat and a needle looking for a little light insemination? Purer, do you think, or less sacredly blind?"

Paul was looking at him with that half smile which came whole from disbelief.

"Sit down while I tell you," he said. "Now, listen. How many times have you been to the plant laboratory?"

"Twice, I believe," himself said. "Twice too many."

"You know her record, there," Paul said. "She's famous through the world. Not in your name. In Mother's. And you know why."

"I was drunk that day," himself said. "And if I'm not damn' careful, I'll be drunk today. But it's the day for it."

"Better keep a clear head for a while, anyway," Paul said. "You'll need it. You smashed the trophies and you smashed the girl's heart. Did she ever ask you why you did it?"

"Never," himself said. "She never did. The matter's never been raised between us. But it was some anniversary, or other, whatever it was, and the misery a gray morass in the soul of me, and I'd taken a lot of brandy. I walked into the Dark Room to see if there was a tantalus out. The place was full of flowers, and this line of cups and God knows what. On the very place where my Fransisca rested her beauty, and I ordered them never to dare to let anything be put there again. Very well, I fold my hands on it. I did, I went mad, and I smashed everything I could find. That was the way of it."

"Decorated in your honor," Paul said. "Everything done on the quiet for the great surprise."

"They got that, anyway," himself said.

"A thousand guests turned back," Paul said.

"They had a good lunch at the best place in the city," himself said. "Did I not apologize in person? And pay to replace the damage?"

"You couldn't replace what was broken in Hilariana," Paul said. "She crawled here. She wept here. A gibbering wraith, is what she was. You were ever the sun, moon and stars of her life, were you not?"

"That was when everything went wrong," himself said. "Whatever I did, or tried to do, she turned her back."

"Wrong," Paul said. "Quite wrong."

"Are you trying to tell me, and I know better?" himself shouted. "God be kind to Jesus, didn't I have to live in it?"

"It was going on long before that," Paul said. "You let Shaun and Belisaria and Kyrillia grow up without seeing you."

"I did," himself said. "If it was myself, I'd want never to see them while I live."

"They're Mother's children," Paul said. "How have you treated us? Any of us? What sort of father were you? What about the Jap's children?"

"My family by Tomoni are beautiful women this day, and solid good boys," himself said. "I did as much for them as I did for you. Educated them. Housed. Fed. Clothed. And even though you say I'm not, I tell you, I've been as good a father as most. Did I never put an arm around you? Or any of you, except Daniel? And Hilariana? I'd have been a hypocrite if I had. I never wanted to see any of you after that business of the convent. Miserable lot."

"They've all taken their prizes," Paul said. "There's only one of us not at the top. Stephen'll go up there. I'm sure of it. If it's only to spite you."

"Why would the boy want to spite me?" The O'Dancy said. "Have I ever mistreated him?"

"Mistreated his mother," Paul said.

"His mother's a bitch," himself said. "I never mistreated the woman. I dropped her for the used clout she was."

"She's scored a remarkable revenge," Paul said. "You remember old Mãe Nueza?

"I suppose as well as anybody," himself said. "Dead all these years? What of her?"

"She was always the general runabout for Hil-oh," Paul said. "She had Grandam Xatina's secrets, and Grandam Aracý's and there was little in this entire dominion she wasn't in, or knew most about. You never knew she was a marvelous medium?"

"O, Christ, there's this again," The O'Dancy said. "Will we never be shy of it?"

"That's up to you," Paul said, "Mãe Nueza taught Hilariana all she knew."

The O'Dancy flung his glass at the wall and Paul jumped away from the splinters.

"You've done enough, now," himself said. "Why did you choose today to tell me? Why could you not have been a decent brother? Why didn't you tell me when you knew?"

"I did," Paul said. "I knew last night. Well, I'd known she was interested in theosophy and spiritism and the Other Life, generally. But I'd thought she was too near the influence of Father Miklos to become anywhere near being an initiate."

"Initiate to what?" himself asked.

"*Khimbanda*," Paul said. "She's going to be installed as *iemanja* tonight. It should have happened last night. But. A couple of the adepts got hurt in a fight. It was put off."

"Wait," himself said. "Let's have this square. What is *khimbanda?* What's different from *macumba?* Where's *Umbanda* come in, or any of the other nonsense? I'm going out of this house, I swear before the Holy Bones of the Lord Christ, and I'll sweep the lot, root and branch. So let's be knowing what it is I've to deal with."

"Get Uncle Mihaul to tell you," Paul said. "It's something I don't want to discuss. But you may as well know I'm a member of *Umbanda* myself, and so are all my family. We appeal through the spirit. We believe with the true followers of Jesus Christ."

"You don't attend church, I know that," himself said. "What's your reason for depriving the children?"

"They're not deprived," Paul said. "But their heads aren't filled with nonsense. If they want to attend church when they're older, that's their business. It may surprise you that many of the *macumba* initiates attend the church and regard themselves as practicing Catholics. But it's a poison of the spirit. They seek the disembodied. Those who've passed on the other side. We commune only with the integrated."

"You're talking deep-sea twaddle," himself said. "But I think I know what you're getting at. It's what old Mãe Nueza got the hide of her tanned for, is it not? But she started again, after The Mam died, is that it?"

"She was in close thrall with the Grandam, right up to the day she died, about seven years ago," Paul said. "I've all the recordings here. She worked with us for a long time before I found out she was working with *macumba*, too. I put her out."

"You didn't tell me," himself said.

"I didn't think it was serious," Paul said. "You were in Paris at the time."

"*Khimbanda* is worst, would you say?" The O'Dancy asked. "What's different between that and the other two?"

"It's basest of magic," Paul said, watching the gray coil move, that blur of scales. "Magic, meaning a pretense of using the marvelous. Black, because it's the worst conjuration of all evil. It's of Satan. They worship Satan."

Paul bent and touched the serpent, and again the gray coil seemed to move, a sudden spasmic constriction, but the head was still, and the eyes were closed.

"You know," The O'Dancy said. "I believe you honestly believe what you're telling me. Do you believe in Satan?"

"As I believe in God," Paul said. "Without God, is there Satan?"

"Well," himself said. "Now be telling me. Where does this affect Hilariana?"

"A *candomblé* is the area of the drums, where these events take place," Paul said. "Hilariana created such a one here, but unknown to anybody. She wanted to be in touch with Mother. And Daniel. *Umbanda* and *macumba* were not strong enough. She started with *khimbanda* a long time ago. With Mãe Nueza. Then she brought down a lot of people from up north."

"By God, and they're working in that plant house," The O'Dancy whispered. "Did I not feel it on the skin of me? I'll have them out this very night, be sure of it."

"That's not all, by any means," Paul said. "Vanina began some years ago, I think, with Hilariana. Certainly, with Mãe Nueza. But she acted from hate. Hate for you, and I'm sure now, she'd made up her mind to revenge herself on you. Through Hilariana. She's no great moralist, that one. Sex for her is simply amusement. And sex is the broad base of *khimbanda*."

"How would she hurt the girl through sex?" The O'Dancy said. "Hilariana's never looked at a man."

"Naturally not," Paul said. "She was trained by Vanina from the time she was in school."

"Trained?" himself said. "Trained for what? She's about the most sexless woman in the firmament. The only man I ever saw her with was this one, lately. That's no bloody good anyway, if I know anything about men."

Paul turned his back.

"That's it," he said. "When she becomes *iemanja*, that will be her exclusive parish. The procuration, and induction, and seduction of girls and women, through the rites of *khimbanda*. Vanina made you a gift. A high priestess of the uropygium. Fair revenge, isn't it?"

17 Vanina and her women friends, well, yes, no doubt of it, there was the entire matter. Plain enough, now, what was never really plain before, and himself a truly blind one. During the time until their marriage there was never once when he found her alone. She needed people about her. She felt loneliness in the nature of pain. Those with her were always beauties of her own age, or younger, and she was ever an obliging one, taking somebody's daughter down to the sea, or to school in Europe, or presenting two or three debutantes at the seasons of the capitals, with all the dances and goings-on. That part of her life himself knew little about. She was daughter of a wealthy man, resident most of her life on the French Riviera, and so part of the swim wherever she went.

Himself floated in blue water off St. Tropez, watching life down below through a mask, and a power boat almost cut him in two. He watched it berth, and swam across, and walked along the beach to the two youngsters, watching their grins while himself was coming up, and they got no time to spar. They tried to fight, and one almost had the chance of braining himself with a boat hook, but he was unlucky. They were both knocked cold, and himself thrashed them with the fishing rod till it broke.

"Wonderful," Vanina said, behind there. "I wish you hadn't smashed the cane."

"Was it your own?" he asked her.

"No," she said. "I'd simply love to give them a few cuts myself."

"They're a bright pair of scabs, that's a fact," he said. "Did they do you some wrong?"

"No," she said. "I liked the way you were beating. I'd like to have that power."

"You like hurting people, is that it?" he said.

"What does it matter about hurting people?" she said. "I love the idea, the feel, what it does inside me. Why should I bother about what it does to others? You didn't."

"I punished them," he said, and looked at them, just beginning to open their eyes. "A little matter of compounding discourtesy with contempt. When a man starts showing his wrinkles, you know, this type of *caboclo* supposes him to be passé."

"*Caboclo?*" she said, and laughed. "Well, if they didn't know much before, they've learned a lesson or two now. Haven't we met?"

"Outside the Métro," he said. "Rue de Rivoli. Your niece and her friend were in the Marietta."

She clapped her hands together.

"Of course," she said. "Let's go out to the yacht immediately. And you're either Paulistano or Rio Grande do Sul. Yes?"

"Paulistano," he said. "Is that in the accent?"

She shook the head himself was already in love with.

"There's something strange I can't quite place," she said. "Or are you one of our 'underdeveloping' gringos?"

"I'm a developing Paulistano, and I'm sweating while the rest of you sit on your backsides," The O'Dancy said. "We're building a city while you people crawl about your village. I've just bought a railroad and a telephone system. Another type of airplane. Arranged for five thousand more people to come over and settle. Bought two ships. Milling equipment. Lighting for a new town. What have you done recently?"

"I bought most of Chanel and Balenciaga's collections, and some marvelous things from Schiaparelli," she said. "I refurnished my house in Paris. I found where I can get ass's milk to bathe in, but I prefer human milk, of course. And blood is really difficult, but I prefer it above anything. Heating it, I mean, it's a task. But when it's the right heat, it's got the most enchanting smell. And the texture. It's like being inside one's own body."

"Human blood," he said.

"Well, of course," she said. "One has to be careful, but most of my people look healthy enough. My doctor chose them personally. My name's Divininha Thuringen de Brosz. Everybody calls me Vanina. Let's take this boat. We'll send it back."

The two soft-roes were sitting up and wondering about things, but they made no complaint when himself helped her in, and while he started the engine and turned out they sat there. The yacht was the whitest in the bay and flying the flag of Panama.

"Something to do with taxes," she said. "I understand nothing about it. My mother's people look after everything. Have you lunched?"

"I'm not a luncher," he said. "A beef sandwich and a glass of wine, that's it."

"That's what you shall have," she said. "We'll go out on my terrace. I'll watch you eat a beef sandwich."

"You won't eat anything?" he asked.

"I'll eat a part of you," she said. "The part that's swelling in your little red shorts."

"Are you looking for youth in the wild, white ichor?" himself asked.

She laughed, and stretched the golden thighs, tightened the breasts against the cup of silk, shuddered, and looked at him in pink glaze of wide-open palest amber eyes.

"I can't wait to taste you," she said.

The yacht was larger than anything himself had owned, but there was no envy in him for those preferring a dance on water to a program ashore. Sea life had never appealed except on the liners, with plenty to do and a lot of people. The desire to float about, with twenty or more men doing nothing except run the ship and the kitchen, only to keep a few people properly to themselves seemed a disagreeable comedy. Divininha's mother had kept the vessel going to be out of the way of her husband, and Divininha kept it on because it was a way of taking her friends to other places, until friends and places palled, and then she went back to Rio de Janeiro or London or New York, or elsewhere, as she pleased. It seemed a normal enough life then, for a young woman with nothing much to do. Her friends were of her family, or her school and university, or of the worlds she frequented, or the riff-raff of the *boîtes* and night clubs. At any time of the day or night, when enough drink had run, the friends and hangers-on gave her delight in nude parties, and the practice of any, or all, the idling play of young men and women with time and energy in rich copartnership. Himself found no great amusement in the parties or what the people did. He could watch, cold, without the wish to ape or join. The body of a woman was his simple desire and Vanina's body was wholly that. She stood taller than himself, in heels a full head and shoulders taller, and she had those proportions elsewhere, except that her breasts were small but perfect, and her thighs were bones without weight, and she was always in the water, which showed in the muscle, and the sun beamed a body into coppery gold—ah, Creonice!—that betrayed the smile of an African grandmother a little way back.

A dedicated love of vice for its own sake and the absolute selfishness of her had been its own attraction to the streak of viciousness in himself, which he realized was ever there but not even latently dangerous. Himself was too much the master to act as slave, either in public or, for that matter, in private. Love gaming was all very well, but going into a woman—Creonice, God love you, and be rested, now!—was the only wonder, and staying with her, rampant, luminous, waiting for the holy passing of The Will.

They were on the terrace, and his sandwich and glass of wine were excellent, and the red shorts had been clawed at and almost torn off, and her hair covered him and she was in taste of the bud, and here came the launch full of gendarmes and the two soft-roes, in sticking plaster, with them.

"I'm glad I wasn't in happiest condition," she said, while he got his feet in, and buttoned himself. "If I'd had my suit off, I'd have ordered up-anchor and away. Then we'd have had an international incident, instead of a darling little personal one. Off you go to prison, and I'll wait for you."

"You won't be a witness for me?" he said.

"You've had twenty witnesses, my sweet," she said, and pressed a button, and a sun-blind panel slid up, and the group of people behind there all laughed, and shouted, and clapped hands while the officer beckoned. "I'm sorry you take such a very long time. But that was hors d'oeuvres, wasn't it? I hope I'm in optimum condition and appetite next time."

It took no time to deal with the police and lawyers, and to warn the two what would happen if they met again, yet they shook hands over a drink, anyway, and said it was no pain to be thrashed by a multimillionaire, and everything ended well enough, but the ship had gone when the cab got back to the quay. Himself forgot if it was weeks or months till they met again, and it was always the same. Same sort of life, same people, same drinks, same constant clacking of voices in half a dozen languages that she could slip in and out of in the same breath, and the same everlasting stereophonic plumbing of the crassest errors of pseudo-music, the same dreary misuse of keyboard, tube, and reed.

"You don't seem shocked," Paul said. "You haven't known about this, have you?"

"No, and I'm shocked, too, but now I see it, it doesn't seem as bad as it might be," himself said. "This girls-with-girls business is harmless enough if it's caught in time. What can a girl do to another? Tickle her? Nothing wrong there. If another didn't do it for them, they'd do it themselves, that kind. If they threw themselves about with men, there'd be a different story. But this *khimbanda*, now. I don't like it. Not that I'm any great believer in Satan. I remember getting the fright of my life when The Mam told me about him. But it wore off, I think. It's the idea of it going on here. I'll not have it, so don't be surprised at the way I'll deal with them. It's because I know what I'm going to do. That's why I'm not shocked. I can deal with it. I'm giving you and your *Umbanda*, and your houseful of odd spits until midnight tonight to get off The Inheritance. Did I say that plainly enough, or will I be saying it again?"

"You'll need our help to deal with Hilariana," Paul said. "I warn you. You don't know what's facing you."

"I'll need the help of none," The O'Dancy said. "I'll go through the place with fire. I'll burn it out."

"You'll have nobody left," Paul said.

"Then The Inheritance will be clean," The O'Dancy said. "That's what I'll have left. Cleanliness."

"It doesn't save Hilariana," Paul said. "On or off The Inheritance, she's damned."

"I'll be damned if she is, or will be," himself said. "I'm going to cure her this night. I'll put her to a man, by God I will, even if it's myself. No later than this very night. Is Chofi still tethered outside there?"

"Chofi died four years ago, which shows what you know about detail, here," Paul said. "His son's there, Shahbash. A better mount. Where are you riding?"

"Vanina's place," he said. "Remember. By midnight, be out."

18 Galloping across the short turf suited the mood of himself, especially since Shahbash was of the twenty-ninth generation of a famous Arab and direct issue of Rahman, with The Tetrarch in his veins, light of The Tad's eye, a link of rapping hoofs between himself and the land and the best of the family.

All the houses on The Inheritance were built about a square of garden rising in three shallow terraces, eight kilometers each side with the main O'Dancy house at the top in the middle, and everybody else about the edge in small forests of trees and shrubs. Nothing had been changed since the Grandfas' time. Himself had never permitted any. Vanina had built a new type of summer bungalow, but it was completely hidden. Fransisca's house was the same as Grandfa Leitrim's, on the outside, of logs, bamboo, and a rush roof. Inside, of course, it was of her time except for the old pieces she collected. There were many other houses about the place. Father Miklos had a house near the church. Democritas lived in Tomagatsu's old house. Hilariana lived in Grandam Aracý's house, though she had added and altered, always in accord with existing style. Belisaria had a small house himself had never been in that had once been a seed store. Kyrillia had a doll's house that had been Grandam Siobhan's wool-drying shed. Shaun lived in what had once been a stable. Daniel, a powerful thought of regret, now, but the wound was stitched and there were no instant tears but only the pulling of muscles in cruel urge for memory of a good boy, a laughing one, The O'Dancy in whom he saw himself, he, yes, he had lived in the old laundry, a place of great beams where the clothing hung, and long tables where the laundresses ironed and folded.

"This is mine," Daniel said those years ago, and he was fifteen or sixteen. "I'll have it done out."

"Very well," himself had said. "Would you want help to make the place livable?"

"No," he said. "I'll do it."

"You're The O'Dancy when I'm gone," himself said, and the pride in his throat. "Do as you will. Its yours. There's only one law."

"I know it," Daniel said, and put an arm about the shoulder of himself. "Never destroy, never change. Alter if you must."

"With great respect for those who went on," himself said. "That's it. Who'll make it right for you?"

"Well," Daniel said, and looking over the green. "A couple of chairs I saw in London. And some other things in Paris."

"In Hermès," himself said. "You're right. They'll fit here. And I also remember, do I not, the beautiful little Louise? But isn't she about ten years older than yourself? You'll bring her over, and she'll make a wonderful place for you, and she'll earn a fine commission. Will she be taking a baby back there?"

"She's bringing one here," Daniel said. "Will you let her stay?"

"Is it any of ours?" himself asked. "One of your own?"

"It must be," Daniel said. "She was whole when I broke her."

"Have you broken many?" himself asked.

"Enough to know whether it's right or not," Daniel said. "I'm not sure that I love her. But I'm not comfortable without her. If something happens to me, will you ever take care of her?"

"I will," The O'Dancy said. "No words. My hand on it. And what's to happen to you?"

Ever the memory of Leitrim gray eyes, o, sad, across the green.

"I don't know," the boy said. "I've a feeling. But I'm glad of this day. I've told you."

"Tell me what you will, it's the same," himself said. "When I'm gone, this is all your own. So be used to it. Now get up in the saddle and we'll gallop the megrims out of you."

So they did, ah yes, the square-cornered days, when a man knew himself linked in time by name and blood to another century, until His Majesty sent his regrets, and himself was left with not a soul in the world to care a damn whether it was life or death for The O'Dancy, or no life or death forever, and God blind them all. Himself gave a hellion's curse for the lot of them, whoever they were. A finger for them, and their mothers sharing.

Shaun, now, there had been a rare boy. True, and why not, he showed more of the blood of Grandam Aracý's Indio fathers, and a little more than a trace of Grandam Thebe's African strain, but he was ever a fine big fellow and a comedian from the moment he could bubble his milk. But that grandam, third wife of Grandfa Connor, had also left a touch of the shiftless in her blood, that came down the line to Shaun's father, a drunkard from birth, that died, bottle in hand, up there on Grandfa Leitrim's cross, and Fransisca took the children for her own, Belisaria, Kyrillia and Shaun, papers and all. Not that himself cared, since he ever regarded any fatherless on The Inheritance as his own to provide for. But it made a big difference in the children, for they looked to Fransisca as their own mother, but to himself never as anything more than a payer of bills.

Himself turned Shahbash on to the path, jumped the gate, and kneed to a halt on the grass patch in front of the veranda. It was a good house, long and low, well thatched, with flowers trailing, and shrubs in clumps.

The size of Shaun was a great surprise. He came out of the middle door in a pair of blue shorts, and the browned body reached almost to touch the black hair to the lintel.

"Well, great god of all the golden goats," he shouted. "If it isn't the old episcopalian himself, think of that. And how's the Communion wine tasting these days, you crusted sinner?"

"As well as it ever did," himself said. "And not so much of the 'old' for it's getting a little too true to be comfortable. You're not looking less than indecently healthy yourself."

"Well, I can still summon a generous thirst and that's the main thing," Shaun said. "Will you be having a little tipple?"

"It's not a drink I'm partial to," himself said. "What'll you offer me? Sugar cane?"

"That's all there is, and beer brewed in my own vat," Shaun said. "When I'm here, I live here, and I eat and drink here. Nothing imported, nothing brought in on tires or wings. In the place, and of it, that's the only way it is."

The room had been furnished with pieces made in the country, in red or richly dark woods, and all the chairs and couches were covered in polished oxide. Its atmosphere carried a weight of age

and a sense of being at home, without recourse to other Lares &
Penates, and even they, in a carved diaconicon that himself knew
had been Grandam Siobhan's, were in place on the south wall,
with an altar lamp's red glow in front.

"You live fairly," himself said, and sat in a comfortable chair.
"I just came from Paul's. There's trouble with Hilariana that'll be
put right in the next few hours. One question. Do you have anything to do with this *Umbanda,* or *macumba* or *khimbanda,* whatever?"

Shaun seemed not to have heard. He poured two measures of
sugar brandy, cut up two limes, half-filled two glasses with fine
sugar, pounded in the lime with a pestle, and poured the brandy
on the top. It was sweet, sour, livening, and icy. During the whole
time he said no word. Muscle moved in the smooth body of the
Indio under a brown skin darkened by time in the sun. The boy
had a good head of straight black hair, a small, fine nose, bright,
deep brown eyes with long lashes, the Indio lashes, and a mouthful
of white teeth that gave him the grin of a god, and hands that
might seem womanish, though in their time they had strangled
three men. He sat down with a cigarette and smiled, and lifted the
drink.

"The episcopal bishop padding about the see, is that it?" he said.
"*Auto-da-fé,* modern version? Most unrespected inquisitor, why
don't you leave perfectly harmless people alone? They only live for
a few years. For most of them it's a rotten existence. If they can find
something that amuses them, or gives them any small interest, why
would you want to interfere?"

"I'm not here to debate," The O'Dancy said. "I want a plain answer. Are you a believer in any of this poison?"

"I'm a great natural believer in all forms of poison," Shaun said.
"Isn't that what life's composed of? After all, it does kill in time,
doesn't it? Even a pope. How's your drink?"

"Very good indeed," himself said. "Surprisingly good. Do you take
a hand in any of these practices?"

"When have I ever taken a hand in any practices?" Shaun said.
"Dear old Mihaul, dear old Miklos, dear old whoever, and all the
incantatory stuff? It's all one. All designed to the same end. Bring
us into a gallimaufry. It's dying out, of course. Not quickly enough."

"I'm glad to hear that," The O'Dancy said. "Do you know anything about *khimbanda?*"

"Quite a lot," Shaun said. "Not exactly ex-cathedra. That's Mihaul's province."

"Does he have a lot to do with it?" himself asked.

"Ask him," Shaun said, drank, moved his cheeks over his teeth, and smoked the cigarette.

"I'm asking you," The O'Dancy said. "Because if you have, now or ever, you'll leave The Inheritance this night."

"No trouble at all, I assure you," Shaun said, and sipped again and moved his cheeks over his teeth. "I shall complete my baccalaureate as Brazil's Number One beachcomber, *cum laude.* The zenith, the pinnacle. I hope to call a world conference of beachcombers sometime next year. We'll hold it in competition with the Olympic Games."

"Do you do anything?" The O'Dancy asked. "Were you not trained as a lawyer?"

"Oh, that, yes," Shaun said. "No *samba.*"

"No what?" himself asked.

"No music, no rhythm, no life, no enjoyment," Shaun said. "I prefer beachcombing."

"On my money, you're entitled to," The O'Dancy said.

"That went a long time ago," Shaun said. "I lived with, and on, and off a couple of women for the past few years. I gave what Mother left me to Kyrillia."

"Then what are you spending?" The O'Dancy asked. "If you're using your name to run up debts, you're unfortunate. I'll not pay."

"Don't be such an episcopal bishop," Shaun said, and sipped, and moved his cheeks over his teeth. "When I need money, I sell land. By the time I die, I shan't have any."

"You're selling the land at Brasilia?" The O'Dancy said. "Why didn't you offer it to me?"

"Young Mr. Carvalhos Ramos always got first offer as Mother's lawyer," Shaun said. "He's got some very good prices, too. Why do you need any more land there? You own most of it."

"There's never too much to own," The O'Dancy said. "I put it to use."

"You'll be first to hang when the revolution comes," Shaun said, and sipped, and moved his cheeks over his teeth. "You and your gringo friends. To the rope. To the wall."

"You're of that gang, are you?" himself said. "I'm beginning to understand a little more."

"You understand nothing," Shaun said. "You never did. You're an episcopal bishop."

"You're drunk," The O'Dancy said.

"You oblige me," Shaun said. "I abhore sobriety. Unbecoming in a lover of life, don't you agree? Life, that's the self, and all comedy, steeped in alcohol. We don't know where we are, and we don't care. That's the condition known as karma. We're ready to exchange this personality for any other. That's my conception of a *samba*."

"If I was the cause of this, I'm sorry for it," The O'Dancy said. "I wish now I'd had more to do with you. A good leathering'd be the finest thing ever happened to you."

"Why do you episcopal bishops always talk in terms of punishment?" Shaun said.

"Why episcopal?" The O'Dancy said. "Why not catholic?"

"There aren't any," Shaun said. "Catholic bishops are all in the running for cardinal, and they're in the running for pope. Any Catholic bishop is pope-to-be-presumptive. Tri-crowned hierarch, receiver and giver of The Kiss. Beside that effulgence, what's an episcopal bishop? Simply a businessman once removed. No *samba*."

"You're what Grandfa Connor used to call a snaphaunce," The O'Dancy said. "Ready to take, give nothing back. What are you doing with your life? You're not even trying to pay back the debt of your birth. You cost a lot to bring into this world."

"No *samba*," Shaun said.

"You and your bloody *samba*," The O'Dancy said. "You're drunk on drums, some of you. It's because you were lifted into this world and given a conscience that you have a duty. Duty. That's the other half of conscience. Did you never know anything about it?"

Shaun stretched his legs and looked at the drink through the altar light.

"Only to myself," he said. "I know nothing about conscience. If you're talking about what's fondly called a sense of right and wrong. Nobody's yet told me what 'right' is. It always seems to be what's in the best interest of whoever's talking about it. Which may not be in my interest. So? No *samba.*"

"You deny the majority?" The O'Dancy said. "You're the last court of appeal? Everybody else is wrong?"

"I'm not worried about everybody else," Shaun said. "I'm worried about me."

"Anybody else can go to hell," himself said. "Isn't that it?"

"But why?" Shaun said. "They're already there."

"Cheap," The O'Dancy said. "Any money spent on your schooling was wasted. The school itself should be destroyed. For producing a monster like you without giving due notice you were free."

"Free?" Shaun said. "Do you know what you're talking about? You? You're a jailer. From birth. What's your vision of freedom? Anything that permits you complete liberty of action? But your 'freedom' may be my idea of incarceration. My idea of freedom you may think is slavery. Freedom, itself, is far beyond what we both mean. And that's the life for me. Not pat theory. No religion. No philosophy. There's no meaning, anyway. Nothing to offer. Death at the end? No *samba.*"

"If I hear the word again, I'll sling this at you," The O'Dancy said, and raised the glass.

"Sling it," Shaun said, and drank a little, and moved his cheeks over his teeth, and lay back, and smiled. "That might be a *samba.*"

"You'll not fight?" The O'Dancy said, hopeful as the next.

"What an episcopal bishop you are," Shaun said. "Of course not."

"I'd smash the hell out of you," The O'Dancy said.

"You're mentally and spiritually incapable of doing anything else," Shaun said, and drank, fingered his chest, moved his cheeks over his teeth, and looked out of the doorway. "Bankrupt, except in terms of national currency. Which you control, anyway."

"That I do not," The O'Dancy said.

"My dear Croesus, you forget I once was humblest clerk in your disgusting Enterprises," Shaun said. "I had enough law to be able to steal any poor man's money legally, enough to steal any rich man's, always providing I knew more thieves in high places than he did, and had the money to superbribe his bribes. I bring to your Croesian attention the affair of the O'Dancy mineral rights. Remember? Voegel fighting Trackmanner? I, the interpreter? Remember? Very smart young man. Absolute command of five languages, including, amazement of all amazements, his own dearly beloved *brasileiro*, together with a fair grounding in international law. The Americans should have won, but they didn't. They were puritan enough, imagine that, to refuse to pay flagrant bribes. So. *Deutschland über alles. Hoch.* That was a *samba.*"

"You disagreed, is that it?" The O'Dancy asked.

"No," Shaun said, and drank, and moved his cheeks over his teeth. "I became an apprentice. Not to sorcery, but to beachcombing. I shall remain beachcomber-extraordinary until the revolution."

"You think you'll be the boss, then?" himself said.

"No *samba*," Shaun said. "*Bossa nova*, perhaps."

"I'm interested in this talk about revolution," The O'Dancy said. "Where I am, I don't hear very much."

Shaun stretched further, laughing, mouth wide, at the ceiling, and Hilariana's silence was in him.

"That's a *samba*," he said. "You don't read newspapers? Or the reports from O'Dancy regents all over the country? You're not quite analphabetic, surely? I'm ready to believe a Neronian disregard for everybody but Pontifex Maximus Arquimed, himself. But even he must be aware of the signs and portents. Your personal haruspex, Young Carvalhos Ramos could tell you. He'll follow you to the wall on the day. He knows it. So. He'll defend you with any weapon. He may keep you alive, and ignorant, for a long time. Episcopal bishops die hard. They know they're going to hell. You'll go via the rope or the bullet. You'll be one of the first. And you'll deserve it. You worshiped a product of the industrial revolution in Europe. Wait till you have our revolution here. To get rid of it. And all you people who fill your coffers and do as you please."

"But aren't you also a product?" The O'Dancy asked. "I'm careless one way or the other. But here's a young fellow of good family and education talking like this?"

"It might surprise you how many more there are," Shaun said. "We're sick of sharing with gringos, and those who act like them. People like you. I'll be a beachcomber in my own country, and wait for the work worshipers to die. At least, the Christians had to wait for the death of pagans to supersede them in numbers, didn't they? We'll be patient."

"But the Christians made converts," himself said. "You shouldn't discount that we can too."

"They made converts by persuading the poor devils there was a place called heaven, and a loving God," Shaun said. "A pleasant tale, but there's no body in it. Except the One pegged up. Those who didn't agree were burned by the sons of a loving God. Hard luck. Isn't that what you're doing? Come work for me, and be my love at my price, or I'll starve you. Whatever I pay you, I'll take most back in one way or another, so that you'll never have enough to tell me you won't work. That's the classic form of slavery. That's arch slavery. Do as I say, or starve. Rebel, and I'll murder enough of you to put the fear of Christ in the others."

O, and yes, while the boy was talking, a morning in Puglia, and the street going uphill, and a shuffle of poor ones behind a red flag, with a trumpet and a clarinet or two, and a drum to beat the time for bare feet. Himself, in the green uniform, translating for the benefit of various animals, in and out of uniform, if not drunk on whisky, then on wine. A clash and clatter of thin brass beaten in front of dark, bony faces that reminded of the starving ones anywhere, Brazil as well, and in Italy everywhere at the time, and nobody giving a damn. And the uniformed one riding down toward them on a fair black gelding, nothing much, but an appearance of the brave, and the rider in clean khaki, and a black beret with the Polish eagle, and a whip. And riding into them, using the lash and cursing, and the drums all heels into a doorway, and the cymbals scattering, with the flag, down a byway and the rest in a pell and mell to be anywhere at all.

"No communists where I command," the brave one shouted, but in French, language of the first communists in the country of Liberty, Equality, and Brotherhood. "Get down, you bastards. I'll murder the lot of you."

"Yes," himself said. "I understand to some extent. But it's *khimbanda* I came to hear about."

"No *samba*," Shaun said. "If I talk to my mother, I'll curse her for choosing my father."

"I'm only sorry I was no father to you," The O'Dancy said. "But it's too late for that."

"That's partly what I mean," Shaun said. "It was miserable to know we had a father. But we never saw you. You never once spoke to me. Or to any of us. Adopted children? Why didn't you put us in an institution? At least we'd have had companions."

"What's this about talking to your mother?" himself asked.

"That's *khimbanda,*" Shaun said, and finished the drink, moved his cheeks over his teeth, and got up. "The other half?"

"Very well," himself said. "How would you talk to your mother?"

"Through a medium, naturally," Shaun said, cutting limes. "But I don't. Not because I don't like the idea, or even that I disbelieve. It's simply too much trouble. No *samba.*"

"Have you heard of anybody talking to her?" himself asked.

"Hil-oh has," Shaun said. "Always. The night you smashed all that stuff, we sat up, I think till daylight, talking to most of the family. They all said the same thing. Murder him. Clean the earth."

Himself watched the fellow pounding the limes into the sugar. Nothing suggested drunkenness, or anything out of the quiet norm. The talk was all of a level, no anger, no raised voice, no feeling except in the words, like whirling razors.

"Would it be taking you out of your way at all to tell me what it was?" The O'Dancy asked. "I'm of course interested here. And would it not have been kinder to tell me at the time?"

Shaun put down the pestle, and set his head back to laugh, but again, it was Hilariana's, with breath, but no sound.

"Kinder, that's a *samba,*" he said. "Who'd want to be kind to you? All, and I mean all, that stopped us murdering you, was old Mãe Bri-Bro. But that was when we cared enough about everything. Now, no *samba.*"

"Is it true that Satan's part of *khimbanda?*" himself asked.

"Part of everything, certainly the greater part of you," Shaun said. "You think you drag off to church to worship something you call God, don't you? You don't. You worship Satan. That's where Satan is. Always there. Trying to get back into heaven."

"Is this some of Mihaul's blather, for God's own sake?" The O'Dancy asked. "I never heard such talk."

"There's a lot more," Shaun said, and gave him the drink. "A slow, painful death to you."

"I probably deserve it," The O'Dancy said. "A quick painless return to sanity to you. It's high time. You and your Satan."

Shaun drank, moved his lips over his teeth, and pointed the glass at the south wall. The little altar lamp seemed to glow a larger, redder star. Stillness was part of the room, and the light fired all nearby, set a ruby in the Virgin's eyes, flushed the white robe, and put in roseate relief voluptuous members unseen till then, making her appear more nymph than Mother of God.

"That's there to keep him in good temper," he said. "It's his mother."

The O'Dancy stood and flung his drink, a small fireball spilling red gobs, and knocked the altar light swinging, and the holder fell through the open portals of the diaconicon and hit the figure in a crack of white shards clattering about the floor.

Shaun screamed, but in another voice, an old man's, not in health, and he seemed only half his size, hands out, knees half bent, feet dragging, abject in imploration, and he went toward the white bits and fell face down, a heavy fall that might have broken a few bones. Yet the voice of him was stronger and his fingers moved, gathering the pieces, but tenderly, by delicate touch. He seemed to writhe, and the muscle showed in back and shoulders, and he screamed high, full, and his hands came about his neck bent and twisted and his arms were doubled in a way himself had never seen, and as suddenly the muscles had gone and the body was smooth, and he got up, half-whispering, half-muttering, in another voice, a child's, in words only half-heard, but he was laughing and his eyes were like a drunkard's and saliva dripped on his chest.

"O, my father, my father," he gritted. "O, dominator. O, Father Exú, send out the Orixás. O, let us hear the slash and stab of my father's steel. Call the storms of *Khimbótes*. O, light the flames. O, break the Nailed Ones. Send the Thieves. Preserve Oxalá within the tomb. O, strengthen the voice of *iemanja*. Bring down the smoke of blessing. Save your faithful son, *dois-dois*."

The O'Dancy stood there, many words never heard, many sentences drowned in spittle that dripped in shining patterns over the floor while the creature picked up the pieces and started to build the figure within the little house. But if the voice belonged to lunacy, and the slavering mouth and starving eyes to hell, the hands were steady, quick, without error, and the figure was building from pieces of the base, upward, with tiny bits, large pieces, specks of white porcelain, and in moments, it seemed, the figure, from being in a thousand shattering, was whole again, and the eyes gleamed, and a whiff of incense was first faint, then strong, and the air shook in a storm of flies, black and iridescent, gathering about the light in a high-toned buzz drowning the invocation to a thin whisper.

A patter of feet behind and a shaking floor could only be Democritas Pereira, and he, a candle alight in one hand with a small censer rolling the thick, sweet smoke dangling from the little finger, and a plain wood crucifix in the other, passed, with never a look, through the cloud of flies and the kneeler beneath, and raised the cross, and swung the censer, and candle grease dipped white tears.

"In the name of the Father, the Son, and the Holy Ghost," he whispered. "Go. By the bell."

A bell clashed three times out on the veranda, echoing in the beams.

"By the book," Dem called.

Outside, somebody clapped a many-paged book shut.

"By the candle," Dem said. "In the name of the Father, the Son, and the Holy Ghost. In the name of St. Michael, Archangel Protector, in whom the Father confides the safekeeping of all souls, carnate and incarnate, I, humble servant, make appeal by divine prayer. In the holy flame of this candle, I command the fiends. Go."

He spat out the light in a cackling hiss.

In darkness, there was no sound. Air cleared of hum, and flies were still, unseen anywhere, and the room fell quiet in reddish light tipped with the white of candleshine. In a sprawl of strong limbs, taut in muscle, Shaun lay in front of the diaconicon. An arm moved, a leg, and ligament twitched, and he shuddered, raised himself, and knelt, breathing deep, coughing, swaying, and smiling he stood, and blinked, and Democritas passed, a massive shadow, and laid a hand on his shoulder.

"Well," he said. "Dear Master, you invite The Touch."

"Of course," Shaun said in the calmest, most ordinary manner, and apparently well back in the skin of him. "It's the way, and the life, that's all."

"What will happen, one day, when I'm not here?" Dem asked.

"Let's wait for the day," Shaun said.

The O'Dancy walked toward them.

"You appear to have forgotten I'm here," he said. "I've just seen a damned exhibition by a man I'd thought was in providence of a decent education. You acted as a slave."

"That's what I am," Shaun said. "A slave."

"Wait," Dem said, and crossed himself.

"You'll be giving me no orders," The O'Dancy said. "By what right do you appear here as a priest?"

"I was called, and sent," Dem said, and lifted the censer's lid in a warm puff of blue fragrance. "It's my mission."

"It won't be for long," The O'Dancy said. "I'm not taken in. If you think this has any effect, let me tell you now, you're mistaken. Dem, you've been a good one for many a year. You're due for a pension. It will be paid on the first of each month from this time on. There's plenty of transport. Order it, pack, and be off The Inheritance by midnight. Shaun, the same with you. Tomorrow, as ever I'm a man of the Christian God, I'll burn out both your houses and rid the place of the stink of you."

Dem toppled, and went slow to his knees, holding out his hands. "Dear Master," he said. "Don't send your Democritas away."

"I turn my back," The O'Dancy said, and went to the door. "Remember. By midnight. The pair of you."

Himself walked out to the cool garden, breathing the green sweet of cut grass, and untied Shahbash, raking his muzzle of bits of chew, and got up, grateful for the scent of a horse, and the feel of leather, and the little things of the life himself knew well enough that, if they had ever been enjoyed, now was the best moment.

Himself had nowhere to think or feel. There was nothing within grasp that might help. Remembering Grandam Xatina, and Grandam Aracý, and Grandam Thebes, and Grandam Siobhan, and Mãe Zuzu, and Mãe Nueza and a dozen others, well, yes, it was in the nature of a quietus, something more than a gag in the mouth, for they were all women of the family, and what they did had to be accepted.

But the spectacle of a fine, big fellow like Shaun in ruinous conflict with everything he had been taught was horrifying enough, though to see him in the act of cavorting beyond the bounds of lunacy, and another, supposedly a healthy one, Democritas, coming in there, and flapping books and ringing bells and blowing out candles, and intoning priestly dicta, ah well. Here was a different matter, and no warning anywhere. Himself was wondering who it could have been, flapping the book and ringing the bell, for there had been none to see on the way out. Himself turned Shahbash, and walked him behind the shrubs, and slid down, and made no more than a whispering way to the house.

Paul was on the veranda, Cleide sitting down there too, and weeping into hands flat over her face, and other women beside her telling their beads, all of them in white clothing. A white group, dark faces, arms, hands.

"Well," himself said, "what are all of you doing here? Why are you not on your way out, as I told you?"

"Have no fear," Paul said. "We're going. But we had work to do here, first. I warned you there'd be no peace for you. Do you now believe me?"

"I believe nothing I've seen or heard," The O'Dancy said. "Flame will cleanse it all, be sure."

"Will it also cleanse the ashes?" Paul asked. "Remember, you once had a fire here. Any idea why?"

"It's over," The O'Dancy said. "We long recovered. No interest."

Himself almost heard Shaun's "no *samba*," but Paul's face disbelieved. Cleide looked across the lawn. Her eyes still shone with tears, glittering, crystal, on round, beautiful Negro cheeks. The other women stood in white groups, twos and threes. Inside there, Democritas and Shaun were talking but not loud enough to be heard.

"Somebody once warned us never to cast pearls before swine, and I always thought it a little uncharitable," Paul said. "I begin to see that sometimes it can be just. You didn't remember, did you, that it was the night of Daniel's death?"

"Never speak of it," The O'Dancy said. "In your mouth, blasphemy."

"You were drunk, of course," Paul said. "Midnight Mass in the church for a dead O'Dancy. You insisted everybody stay with you. You insisted on lighting an altar candle for every year of his birth, and smaller ones for the odd months. Seven for his mother. Seven for the Grandfas. They added up to sixty-six. Sixty-six is the Mark. You never noticed when you put the pine tree in the barn, that for every one candle lit by you, there were ten more lit by others? You thought it a sign of love by those who'd loved Daniel? The great *candomblé* was held that night. That night, Hilariana went into trance for the first time. You lost your harvest? A small affair. You lost your daughter. Not only her. Shaun. A child. Belisaria. Your present wife."

"To hell," The O'Dancy said in deepest grief, tears in the run, and all the world a swum ruin. "Don't speak of my Daniel. I'm a lonely one, and no interest anywhere at all. Take your damned numbers and your candles and go into hell. Be out at midnight. I'll take flame to the lot of you. The morning will find us clean. Clean as Daniel, in glory these years, please God, and resting in the arms of Himself."

He turned about any way at all, and found Shahbash and jumped for the saddle, and off at standing gallop, a rare pattering, and the breeze drying his eyes though he was careless. It was true what Paul had said, no doubt of it. Everything the man had said was known, but, as it were, behind the eyes, or under the skin, or beneath the rose. Everything there, bell, book, or candle, saint or devil, was part of himself, as much a piece of upbringing as any tree about, but ever through the days disregarded as worthless. It seemed ridiculous that such old-crone nonsense should still carry weight in twentieth-century discussion.

But.

There was no more to be said.

It did.

19 Shahbash went across the cut grass full gallop. At eight points on The Inheritance square, Grandfa Shaun had set horse stands with four saddle horses ready day and night so that none might lack the legs for getting up to The House or anywhere at all.

Sire of Shahbash, Chofi had been sired by Tuli, by Ahmed, by Rafu, by Kai-Kai, by Glendale, by Honi Soit, and he a champion, sired by a champion of champions, Rahman, a great horse, and a fine friend of The Tad's. That was the first time himself had gone to Europe, and though the years were far, memory was ever bright, of London and Paris, and Venice, and a great bell in noon send of sounding music over the water, and a crusty loaf from a bakery, and The Tad cutting salami and making a splendid sandwich, and opening a bottle of wonderful chianti out there in the piazza, and the pair of them sitting on the cathedral steps, everybody else gone home to lunch, and themselves almost alone, and eating, and the pigeons gathering, one-eyed, talons up, ready for the crumbs.

"Remember these friendly ones," The Tad said, throwing a crust in a tumult of wings. "Whenever you eat, remember those waiting on what you leave. Remember the others, for there's nothing for them. Try to do something, every day, to put food in other mouths, money in other pockets, smiles on faces yourself'll never see. Try to earn your blessings. There's but one O'Dancy. Make him worth his salt. Cut a plain loaf now and again, and eat plain food, wherever you are. Taste what a poor man, poorer in goods than yourself, will eat. Eat it yourself, in gratitude that it's good, and see that you enjoy it. If you don't, or if you eat proud, there's a dirty name for you. Never be earning it."

Those sandwiches, and the long quiet walks with The Tad, himself remembered far more, in the detail, than all the banquets and

processions since. Bread came crusty to memory's teeth, even now.
A luncheon at a long table at Epsom, and cold salmon and cucum-
ber, and a thin white wine with fruit cut up in it, and The Tad
buying Rahman, and the man not believing the price offered,
and the check, written in a slam of book and pen, because nobody knew what a Brazilian was. The Tad was one of the first to
show the infidel where the true standard flew. Not one of them
they ever met knew that the green flag with a world in blue on a
golden lozenge was flag of the United States of Brazil.

"But darling," Graciella said, combing the long black hair in
their hotel. "There's only one United States, surely? It's a country."

"That is certainly correct," The Tad said, lying back on the
couch and eating pineapple squares floating in cognac, and himself getting one now and again, but watching the frosted back,
the whitest wonder, of Graciella. "But my country is also a unity
of states. We also have state's rights. Why don't they teach you
something at school?"

"I often wondered," Graciella said, and tied another braid. "I'm
going to take everything off in a minute. Do you think Arqui-
ologus ought to be here? Of course, I could find someone his size
or slightly older?"

"No," The Tad said, and got up, licking his fingers. "I don't want
him taken awhile. It'll do him no harm to see anyone as miraculous
as yourself, though."

Graciella dropped the voile dressing gown and stood, and himself remembered a whiteness, and a black tuft, and The Tad
kissing her shoulder, and pulling down there, and her, bending
inward and laughing.

"My God," she said. "You're ruining a minor. I wish you'd let me
get someone for him. It'd be such fun."

"No," The Tad said. "His mother'd never forgive me. And anyway, he's not in age. But the sight of you'll do him no harm. Never.
A lovely woman never yet hurt any man, at all."

"Darling, you're so sweet," Graciella said. "I don't know what
I'll do when you go back."

"I'll leave you well tended," The Tad said. "You'll never have to
run with another. Let's say. Unless your middle gets the better of
you."

Well, yes, all in a gallop across the lower level. A turn up the Connor path, built of stone, and Shahbash dropped his gallop and, wise one, trotted in the lawn to the right of the flower beds, up to the house of Kyrillis, another one that himself had never been in, that was dark, and nobody near, and himself was saddened because, well, suddenly, there was a will to see the fellow. But while Shahbash turned his white head came a thought of Graciella, naked those years ago, looking at himself as if he were a man. Oh yes, it was plain enough now, but she taught the value of black pearls on a white body. The same, anyway, as Bruxa taught the value of pink pearls on a black body.

"Christ, if you've got to have another woman, why do you, must you, is it so utterly necessary to pick a black?" Fransisca screamed. "I'll find women for you. I'll buy them. I'll throw them at you. But not Negroes. I won't have something in me that's tittilated some slavish horror. I won't."

"There's a slave and a Negro in me," The O'Dancy said. "There's many an Indio. D'you think I don't know it? Or feel it? If there's no Negro in you, be Christ, I ought to find one and cross you. Never speak of horror. Or else speak of yourself. A Negro woman is glorious in her right. If she finds glory in me, I'll thank God."

"You should have married one," Fransisca screamed. "Why did you foul me?"

"I never fouled you," himself said. "If I'd known you were blind, do you think I'd have come anywhere near you?"

Fransisca, that blind one, and utterly beloved, screaming and stamping and trying to find him to claw.

"But girl," he said. "You can't see. You've never seen. What do you know of a Negro?"

"It's what I'm told," she said. "It's a thing that crawls. It's the terror of the cockroach. Or the winging thing that bites."

"Pass the dear hands over your own dearness," himself said. "Feel, only beauty. Is there anything there of any winging thing, except an angel? Or something that crawls? Has it any common spell with a cockroach? Tell me, now. Be telling me. Girl. Fransisca. Tell me."

"No," she said. "I'm me."

"Then so is any black one," himself said. "Or gold, or coffee, or any color at all, that you've never seen. Who tells you these things?"

"Would you expect me to say?" she said, so quietly.

"I love every living moment of you in any shape or color at all," himself said. "Tell you what I'll do. I'll find a girl. Nobly and purely black. Herself. With as much right on earth as either of us. As much property as any Negro in the country. She's an O'Dancy. Down the line. I'll have her here. I'll have the clothes off her. Pass your hands. Then tell me where's the difference."

That was Lua, daughter of Uncle Drehan, black, the pure blue-black, marvelous, the sweetest woman out of chains, with a laugh, and a voice that would stand the hairs, and so much in the heart of her that a half of the world was her own only if she smiled.

"Pass your hands," himself said to Fransisca. "Tell me what you find."

"This could never be black," Fransisca, own love, and all delight, said.

"Now tell me," himself said. "How would you be telling black from white?"

"What color am I?" Fransisca said.

"The color of one of Grandfa Shaun's peaches," himself said. "Now be telling me. What color is that?"

"Will I ever know?" Fransisca said.

"I'll be bringing the peach," himself said. "Then for what good it'll do, you can run the difference between it and yourself. There's little except in size."

But if it did any good or not, there was nothing to be got from Fransisca's smile, and she said nothing, but Lua was with her from then till the time she got married, and then Turquinha took her place, as black and bigger, and a better protector, because Tomomi had trained her, not at the beach house, but in the city. Not long after, Lua's mother came to see him in frayed white linens and rope-soled slippers, hair in a cloth and a pipe in poke from her apron pocket. She had the cream in her from her father's side, but the darker tone began above her bosom and he knew that the mark would be a saddle to the waist or farther down.

"Master," she said. "Lua's husband wants to leave her."

"They only just got married," he said.

"He found Lua with child," she said.

"So?" he said.

"So," she said. "The child is yours. He also says you had your way in front of your wife."

"To prove to her that a black woman is no different from a white," he said. "Tell him not to be a fool. If the child is a boy, I'll double the wedding gift."

"A black woman has no value?" she said.

"If it's a girl, and she's black, a true Negro, ten times," himself said.

"An O'Dancy child is never black," she said. "A little milk, or much, in the coffee. The O'Dancy rice makes a fair pudding. But a dark one has no value?"

"If she's fairer than Lua, five times," The O'Dancy said. "Tell her to let me know when she mothers."

"Her man will let you know," she said. "He swears by the Thorns he will clean his knife in you."

"Many have sworn so," he said. "Tell him I have a bullet that requires to be cleaned. If he will provide the carcass, I shall be grateful."

But the man had sworn by the Thorns, and he kept his promise on the night he flew from the doorway in a howl of the northeast wind, and only a steady aim stopped him, turned the wrist, broke the elbow, and he fell, screaming until a kick in the mouth silenced him.

"I won't charge you," himself said in the hospital at the bedside. "Everybody has a use on this earth. Lua was very useful, not only to me, to my wife. She brought you a house, and money, and a different life, didn't she?"

"I want her, entire, without another's foal," the man said, staring at the ceiling.

"Wait till the foal trots," himself said. "We'll find another stable."

Laughter stretched the bruised lips.

"That, yes," the man said. "I feared I would kill them both."

"If you love her so much, I'll have the child taken immediately," himself said.

"Better," the man said. "I can go home, and she's mine."

Kyrillia took the boy, and called him Kyrillis, after herself and a friend of the family's, a Russian of noble line. She insisted on the

K in the spelling, though in Portuguese the K does not exist. Nothing would shake her, even as a child, a fair-haired, beautiful, long-legged heart-warmer she was, and grown a beauty since, with a business head on her that Tomomi saw first, and put her in the city office to learn a little, and then himself had her sent to a fashion house in Paris. A couple of years there, between Rome and London, and she was away to New York to learn about the garment business, and after that there was no holding her. The double K was known all over the continent with the double T, and the Tomagatsu-O'Dancy dress and textiles business was the only one where the O'Dancy name took second place. Tomomi saw to it.

"Would you not let me buy the whole thing out?" himself begged her.

She laughed at him, and gave him a black cherry on a stick.

"No," she said. "Tomagatsu-O'Dancy. It is the first time the women have beaten the men. Your mouth is black with cherry juice. I love you."

Any attempt of his own to alter the balance ended blessedly on the mat, where the strength and grinding muscles of Tomomi and the darleen tenderness of the woman had ever ended everything.

Shahbash went by himself to the house of Belisaria, because he knew where the feed was, and lights were on, and music spreading through the leafage, and flowers in bloom, and fountains spraying, and dogs baying a great chorale. Given his head, Shahbash went quietly around to the stables, and Turú came out to take him. Himself walked through the garden, and the fishponds, to the back of the house, but the dogs, unseen, told everything, and Belisaria came out on the veranda to whistle at them, and saw himself, and opened her arms, opened her mouth, herself in checkered trousers, gold sandals, and nothing above, and a marvelous woman with a pair to worship.

"The old wreck himself," she said. "Heaven above, how many years? I've just been looking for a blouse. You don't mind a little discreet shamelessness, do you, darling? You know how we look, now, don't you? Or is it only below the navel? Sweet, what have you been doing? You look simply too."

"It's how I feel," himself said, and walked with her, into a room that set him on two feet, with no word.

Tomomi, certainly, was there in Japanese pieces and pictures, but there was more. A lot of French paint was hanging, and sculpture made odd shapes, and furnishings, sometimes of Egypt, and then of now.

"A room I'd like for myself," he said.

"Take it," she said. "A little gift."

"It's an O'Dancy I'm hearing," himself said.

"Please God you never hear another from this throat," she said, over at the bar. "You look awful, and you shouldn't. Poor sweet, what would you like to drink? You look as though a real Whalebone Straitjacket might set you right."

"Be mixing me one of Grandfa Connor's own Whalebone Straitjackets, then, and know you're the only human creature I've met this day," himself said. "Why are you here? Kyrillia's away."

"She's here," Belisaria said, lifting down the bottles. "She's rather worried. Too much to stay at her own place. Her servants left her. So did mine, except the men. Darling, what's this about Paul and everybody leaving? I mean, that's simply too. Isn't it? Wish I'd been corked as tightly as this."

She had the glory of her mother in her pelt. Other Nordics, yes, white and beautiful, but in Belisaria another fall of snow, a further glist of crystal, ah yes, Graciella, that white one.

She poured white rum on ice, shook in Angostura, waved the mixer, and filled up with champagne.

"Lots of lead in the pencil, darling," she toasted. "Plastic refills where not. What?"

"I was never worried till lately," himself said.

"Darling, that's simply," she said. "Do come and practice on me whenever. There are far too few men, do you think?"

"Something's been happening," himself said. "Men going off with men. Girls with girls."

"It's too," Belisaria said. "Kyrillia's been really quite demanding all the afternoon."

"But, dear Christ," himself said. "Is she not your sister?"

"I suppose she is, in a way," Belisaria said on the other side of the bar, and dibbling the nipple of her right breast with a lazy forefinger. "But does that matter, really? It's the moment, isn't it?

There isn't anything except the moment, is there? Honestly, is there?"

If there was one law, or one principle, or one commandment for everybody else, and one for The O'Dancy, or if the same law, and commandment and principle were in being for everybody including The O'Dancy, that was a fine one to try to decide in the moment. If a woman was a woman and had control of her need and her body, and wanted the man she wanted, if he was begger-man or anybody else, there was no reason to deny her the wish or the act. Himself had never denied. There was no good argument why a woman should be less than a man in any moment of decision. Herself, it was, and herself to say. Whether it was another woman seemed to amount to the same thing. It was for her to say.

But there were other matters to be thought about.

Fingering a slither of warmth, well, yes, they were moments, the riches of memory, but whether pleasure was only in the other body, or partly of it and partly of the mind inside, or if it was only of himself, within himself, an expression of the vice, if vice it was, to be condemned only in others, that, for the moment, himself could not quite decide.

"Not sure," himself said. "After I've drunk this, I'll be less sure, so let's postpone the discussion. What do you know of *Umbanda, macumba,* and *khimbanda?*"

Belisaria, she, crossed herself before the words were well in the air.

"Enough to want nothing to do with it," she said, suddenly frightened, looking smaller, peaked. "Kyrillia came here babbling, simply babbling, about visitations. I don't know what happened. She ran in screaming she's seen the Devil. I gave her a pill. It's this awful day. I hate it. Hated it as a child."

"Why did you come back here?" himself asked.

"We've always come back for Easter," she said. "They all expect it. Vanina sent us the most pathetic invitations. So we decided we'd come here yesterday. I wish I'd flown to New York. Oh, now look. You can help me. I need about a hundred and fifty thousand dollars. The *boutique* I'm opening. Fifth Avenue on Fifty-first. London and Paris are doing really well, but restocking gobbles up the cash. If I buy with cruzeiros I lose my profit. Well, almost. Would you take a mortgage on the stock up there? I've got some property, too, if it's not enough. I know what bank managers are. Say you will, darling?"

"It's yours," he said. "I'll tell the office. Don't worry about a mortgage. If I can't take your word, I'll take nothing. When will you pay back?"

"Three months, or before," she said. "Easily. I can't get enough stones to supply. Amethyst and garnet, they're scarce, or the workmen go on strike, or something. All the others, I could sell ten times the quantity. Can't get the stuff. That's what's wrong with us. We create a market, then we can't supply."

"Not true," himself said. "We create a market, but on low wages. Did you ever try raising the wages to tempt a man to work?"

"Wouldn't do any good," she said, sitting beside him. "My own people in the Taparinga mine? They take a month's wages and we don't see them for the next couple of weeks. Pay them more? They'd be away longer."

"I want to know more about this *khimbanda* business," himself said. "I'll discuss labor or anything else at the office. But I'll have this *khimbanda* blight off The Inheritance."

"I don't blame you in the slightest," she said, and the fright was back in her eyes. "I won't have another woman here unless she's absolutely clean. Soap-and-water clean. Body-and-soul clean. Tomomi's daughter's finding me some Japanese girls. Life's impossible. There's even cannibalism."

"There's what?" himself said.

"Cannibalism," she said. "Eating children."

"I'll never believe it," The O'Dancy said, and put the drink down, and stood. "Why would you say such a horrible thing?"

"Because it's true," she said, and got up. "Come with me."

20 She took a jacket off a chair and went through the room to the passage dividing the house, walled in Japanese silks, with mats and low tables, bringing a piercing thought of Tomomi, and into a bedroom, all of The Inheritance, with the dark furniture of Grandfa Phineas' time.

Kyrillia lay on the blue sheets, nude, deep in sleep. The tan of her back and legs showed the shape of her sun suit and made her bottom absurdly white. Belisaria gave her a gentle slap, pulled the sheet over her, and went through the other door, to the second bedroom, again in the Grandfa Phineas era, with a lamp burning before a fine wood carving of a Madonna.

"You don't take much notice of Her, but you keep a light on," The O'Dancy said.

"I take a great deal of notice," Belisaria said. "I do, honestly. She's enormous comfort to wake up to. And we need all the help She can give us. Look here."

She went into the room on the other side, a smaller bedroom, and out to a veranda. In the far corner, boxes and baskets were heaped with colored clothing, of bright greens, reds, blues, and a pile of dead flowers, fruits, and, again, raw and cooked meat in scraps, blackening, in the rot.

"Why in the name of God would you put this here?" The O'Dancy said. "Have you gone mad?"

"It's there till Paul comes for it," she said. "I won't touch it."

"But who brought it here?" The O'Dancy said.

"They must have had a *candomblé* here," she said. "We rarely use this part. It's too dark. When I got here, I went around the house to see if the maids had been keeping their hands in cold cream. I found this. I screamed the place down."

The O'Dancy used a parasol to turn the things over. The remains of a lamb, a goat, five chickens, and two small, half-mutilated carcasses that might have been human all piled in a heap with their friends, the flies.

"Monkeys," himself said, and relieved.

"Look again," Belisaria said. "I've seen monkeys too, you know. Those are two newborn babies, and they've been murdered."

"Why didn't you telephone me?" The O'Dancy asked.

"I telephoned Paul, immediately," she said. "He said he was seeing you, then he'd be over. What can you do about it?"

"I'll get hold of dear Democritas, first," The O'Dancy said. "Then I'll call the chief of police."

"Oh, my God," Belisaria said. "That settles it. Police, inquiries, fuss, nonsense. I'm off. I'll fly tomorrow morning. How can you find out whose children these were?"

"Monkeys," The O'Dancy said. "I'll find out who put this stuff here, and they'll be off The Inheritance within the night. I'll lay a level million."

They went back, but Kyrillia still slept in the same position, and The O'Dancy lifted the hand and found the arm heavy, and put it down.

"Have her brought up to The House," himself said. "She can't be left here if you're going. That's no sound sleep. That's drugs."

"Of course," Belisaria said. "We've all drugged for years. Dear Vanina's influence."

The O'Dancy threw up his arms from hopelessness and walked out to the foyer.

"Once, we were a responsible family, or I thought we were, or most of us," himself said. "As good as most, at any rate. Will you tell me the cause of taking drugs? Are you not to be cured?"

"Not if we don't want it," Belisaria said. "Drugs are fun."

"Ah, nonsense," The O'Dancy said. "A marvelous girl like yourself?"

"It's not what *you* want, darling," Belisaria said. "It's what we want. Why are you so suddenly solicitous? It's most unlike you. Did you ever give us five minutes' thought before this? Are you afraid we might bring you a little publicity? At long last?"

"Never came into my head," The O'Dancy said. "But I'm sorry, very sorry I didn't think a little more. For all of you. I was angry."

"Angry for all these years?" Belisaria said, in the moment, very much like Hilariana. "We tried and tried to see you. You never would."

"I was terribly angry at the deceit of you," The O'Dancy said. "If I think of it now, I'm still angry."

"Children aren't deceitful," Belisaria said. "It's what they're made to be. Ask Bri-Bro. Ask her to tell you."

"I never had two words with the woman," The O'Dancy said. "I don't much care for the type."

"Most capable," Belisaria said. "She's been wonderful for all of us. And Hilariana. You must admit she's turned out a marvelous girl. Not me, darling."

"Nothing too wrong with you, but I still don't like her," The O'Dancy said. "What's this about you tried to see me?"

"Oh, now, Tad, Mãe sent her to see you on at least three occasions, that I know of, personally," Belisaria said. "I was there, in that damned little cell they put her in. We had to describe the wonderful carvings and furniture. We were simply awash with tears."

"And what the devil for?" The O'Dancy shouted. "She wouldn't come out of the place."

"You wouldn't let her come out," Belisaria said, and tears ready. "You ask Bri-Bro what you told her. Stay there, and rot, didn't you tell her? Do you think I'd ever forget it?"

For the first time in all the years, himself found not only no word of any language adequate but not even one so much as available.

"It's not a bit of use staring at me," Belisaria said. "What's done's done. Thank God I had a business head. I've managed to do fairly well. But I can tell you, there were moments when I'd have loved a Tad to go to, and tell my heartbreaks to. I always seemed to have such a lot."

"Darleen Bel," himself said. "Understand this. Never once did that woman come near me. Not once. Never did I say such a thing. Never would I. Every time I tried to see Fransisca—and may she adorn the Throne with the beauty of herself—I was refused by the mother superior, or some such. Did any of you ever try to see me?"

"What can children do?" Belisaria said, but a new, clearer eye was in her. "Listen to me, Tad. I know very well you're not a liar."

"You're telling the plain truth," himself said. "Not because I can't tell a lie. But it's not worth the damn' trouble. Especially in this matter."

"Then something's been miserably wrong all this time, all these years?" Belisaria said, tears in fall, and no move to stop them. "Great God in mercy, how can that have been?"

"I'm going, now, to have a word with Madame Briault," himself said. "If you want to come up, do. If you find her strangled, you'll know where to look for the most satisfied murderer you'll ever meet."

"I can't leave Kyrillia yet, but the moment Paul comes, I'll hop in the car," she said. "Would you like to take it?"

"I can ride quicker," himself said. "I'm no revengeful man. Let me kiss you, now, and be knowing that from here out, I'm your true Tad. Better tell Paul. And when Kyrillia wakes up, let her know. Will you stay?"

"I'll stay," she said, and kissed him.

"Thank you," The O'Dancy said. "Suddenly I love all of you very much."

He went out, a little blind, and around the house, to the stable. Turú and Gil were at the rail. Shahbash had his muzzle in a bucket.

"When was there a *candomblé* here?" he asked them quietly.

"The night before last," Turú said. "Master, my wife was sent away. But she had no part. I swear it."

"Everything will be settled with justice," himself said. "What part did either of you take?"

"None," Gil said. "Master, strike me down. None of us here have sniffed the smoke. We are of The House family. Father Miklos is our priest. What do we need with the black spirits?"

"Who was here?" The O'Dancy asked them, from the saddle. "Name them."

"We had gone to The House to meet the Lady Belisaria," Turú said. "I saw nothing. My wife saw nothing. But in the morning, the dogs were trying to get at the meat. Then the Lady Belisaria cursed at us, and sent our wives away. What shall we do without women? Our lives have always been here."

"What do you know of *khimbanda,* and *macumba,* and *Umbanda?*" himself asked.

Their eyes slid to each other under the hatbrims.

"We are of *Umbanda,*" Turú said, down at the ground. "We seek the nobler spirits."

"You'll seek them beyond this inheritance," The O'Dancy said. "Pack your goods. Be out by midnight. Democritas will send transport."

Turú fell on his knees, hands clasped, weeping, a small boy.

"But dear Master, should a man be punished for his belief?" he said. "We are of the Church. We attend the church. But we are of *Umbanda* by belief, also. Was I not initiated by your own grandam, the Lady Aracý? And most of us? Gil, here, at the same time. We are fifty years with *Umbanda.* Have we harmed you, Master? We've kept harm away from you. Till lately. Now the strangers come."

"Which strangers?" The O'Dancy asked. "By what permission?"

"Ah, Master, *eheu,*" Gil sighed, and the man was hopeless. "If we must talk to save our families, then still you will find reason to curse us. The Lady Hilariana brought in the strangers."

"They were at Mouras Bentos last night," The O'Dancy said.

Both men nodded.

"The Lady Hilariana is responsible for this filth, here?" The O'Dancy asked.

Turú nodded, and pointed toward Brother Mihaul's house.

"There is their greatest enemy," he said. "They put up an altar beyond the walls of his house while he was in church. We tore it down. They built an altar in his garden. We destroyed it. While we were out, there was a *candomblé* here. We came back too late, and we knew nothing till I saw the dogs."

"How did you know there was an altar built there?" The O'Dancy asked.

"We heard the drums," Gil said.

"Who'd dare beat drums on The Inheritance?" The O'Dancy said.

Gil shrugged.

"Wherever they please," he said. "Perhaps they know when you are not here."

"There's a lot been going on that I know nothing about," The O'Dancy said, and turned Shahbash. "But I will, depend on it. As to yourselves, wait for tomorrow. I must decide."

"God defend you, Master," Gil said.

"I am no man's master," The O'Dancy said, and gave Shahbash the knee.

But he was, and himself knew it, starting the jump over the hibiscus, and gathering for the higher jump over the stone wall, and in mid-clear, a thought of Tomomi, in the pink Kimono, coming out and facing Tomagatsu in black ceremonial dress and ready to kill.

Listening to them, in the strange staccato language, lovely when Tomomi whispered her love poetry to himself, which he never understood, which she never translated, which at other times sounded like a clack of machinery, and wondering at the quickness of their speech.

"What is it?" himself asked, breaking over them. "I apologize, deeply, for interrupting, but is this anything I ought to know about? For if not, I'll wait in another room."

"My daughter is a cheap woman, and a mother of nobody, without name or family," Tomagatsu said in the Portuguese taught to him by Professor Riskind.

"Your daughter is my dearest love," himself said, a cold man, and equally ready to break or kill. "Her children are mine. They are O'Dancy. They will inherit from me. They are my charge. They have name and family. I say so."

Tomagatsu put his hands, folded, in the groin and bowed.

"I hear the voice of your father, and grandfather, and great-grandfather," he said at the floor. "This may be well at this time. It is not well for me. Tomomi should be married. She should have her life with other women of her family. I should be proud to bring her to my table. I should be honored to receive the kiss of my grandchildren. But she is hidden. They are hidden. Their father is spoken about behind the hand. She is spoken about with a grimace. The children were squeezed into this life, as feces.

What name is this, O'Dancy? On which paper? They are Tomagatsu. But they have no name."

"They have my name," himself said. "It is enough."

"It is not enough," Tomagatsu said. "It is nothing."

"You are too old a man to take a glove in the face," The O'Dancy
said. "Send one of your sons in your place."

"For many years I have commanded my sons not to kill you,"
Tomagatsu said at the mats. "I should kill you. But I remember
your fathers."

"You forget me," Tomomi said. "I am not Japanese. I am *brasileira*.
My children are *brasileiras*. Of this nation, none other."

"This man has a wife by Brazilian law," Tomagatsu said. "Who
are you?"

"I am a woman," Tomomi said, and bowed, in her wonderful,
graceful way. "My name is Tomomi. I have two beautiful
daughters. I have another, climbing the unknown mountain inside me. I shall give life to more, because each time I love more.
Not a name. Or property. Or law. I love a man. And a country
whose people decree that a man shall live as he chooses, and the
children of the union are citizens. This is Brazil, of our time. In
which other country could you have become a millionaire?"

"We speak of principle," Tomagatsu said. "His fathers were men
of principle."

"Where it interferes between a man and a woman it is no longer
a principle," Tomomi said. "The principle is, I love. Life follows."

"You are no longer part of my family," Tomagatsu said.

"I was not a part of your family from the beginning," Tomomi
said. "You are of Nippon. I am *brasileira*."

"You are nothing," Tomagatsu shouted. "Remember what I tell
you. Nothing. A day will come, and you will die. I shall die.
This one, The O'Dancy, will die. My children will control Brazil.
We have the principle. We have the discipline. We have the
brains. You? You have no more than your love? A geisha without
a house? No price? Nothing."

"Leave my house," Tomomi said. "From this day you are nobody. From this day I change my name. I am no longer Tomagatsu. I am O'Dancy. Leave this house, and I shall order the maid to
sweep where you trod, and swill down the paving outside."

Tomagatsu shouted at her in Japanese, but she was looking at himself.

"This silly old man," she said. "Silly, because he lives where he was born. But his work has been here. Old, because he never learned. Those who never learn grow old. He was a man. Now? A log, ready for the fire."

Tomagatsu had understood perfectly.

Brazilian sun had burned the lines in his face, and the tight muscle of his body had strengthened in Brazilian jungle. Most of his years were Brazilian, but his thoughts had never been more than Nipponese. In silk, sashed and capped, hand on sword hilt, he yet seemed naked, deprived of dignity.

He drew in his breath, and bowed deeply.

"I leave your house," he said.

"When you die, I shall cover you with chrysanthemums," she said.

"You speak as a foreigner," Tomagatsu said.

"We never met," she said.

Tomagatsu sucked in the long breath again, and bowed again, and walked out, and the maid saw his face, and slapped a hand over her mouth and shrank against the wall.

Over the dulled rap of Shahbash's gallop in short grass, another sound pierced the wind rush, of somebody shouting, chanting. A touch of the rein brought the horse still. The shouts seemed to come from a group of trees where a grotto had been built by Grandam Siobhan, a fine marble lych, and a Madonna from twelfth-century Spain, with seats on each side, and fountains to cool the air. Shahbash turned his head and went off in a smooth canter, taking the rise without strain, and a hand pat on the neck brought a snort, perhaps of pleasure, but he never broke the long stride until he reached the shadow of the trees. Himself slid down, and tied the reins about a low branch, and walked toward the grotto. They were boys' voices shouting, dozens of them, though nobody was permitted in the grotto at any time except members of the family, and twice a year, on the days of birth and death, a procession for remembrance Mass.

Trees cleared at the edge of a semicircle of flowering shrubs about the fountains. In the hollow around the lych about thirty shouting, dancing boys were flinging stones, cans, fruit, and the ground was littered.

The Madonna had been taken out of place and lay on the left-hand seat.

The O'Dancy screamed at them, not words, not curses, not blasphemy, but only the anger that was in him, inchoate, immeasurable, and they ran, and himself stood gaping.

Judas Iscariot hung in effigy under the lych roof, life size, in a white bloodstained robe, and a red wig and beard, long and unkempt, and glass eyes, horridly gray, horridly red hair and shining gray eyes, a terrifying caricature of Arquimed Rohan O'Dancy Boys, himself, and in a squat upon his shoulders, in scarlet and black, Satan, holding trident and irons, spear, sponge, and crown of thorns.

A stithe of rotting meat was in the place and the stench of putrifying fruit, and over all a stealth of incense from a row of tin lids along the plinth, full of ash, match ends, and cigar butts.

The O'Dancy felt the rot gather within himself.

Red hair in stream about the shoulders of the Thing that stared gray, glassy eyes brought sickness, first, and a weakness of the legs and sight. Without anger, and without thought for damage, himself took matches, in fives, applied the flame to the robe, to the feet of Iscariot, to the toes of Satan, and watched the fire take hold of the straw and cotton stuffing.

"My turn, now," himself whispered up at hell's master. "Your turn later. Be trying to do as well."

Flame breathed hard in black smoke, curled about the mouth, destroying the *risus*, blistering the nose, and the eyes seemed to live a moment in laughter, but the glass cracked, snapped, and the sockets were empty. The rope broke, and the mass showered down in sparks and fire.

The Madonna was too heavy to lift upright.

"No word have I," himself said, on his knees beside her. "Tonight we shall clean, and refurbish, and pray cleanliness forevermore. This I promise, a sinner, but determined. So help me, the Lord Jesus and all angels. Amen."

He crossed himself, and kissed his fingers, smelling the smoke on them, and looked at the burning pile. Nothing was left except flame, sparks, black ash, and the trident head, the arrows, and the crown of thorns twisted from barbed wire. He turned his back, and went up the rise to Shahbash, and mounted him, and took heart and pleasure in the instant thunder of a well-bred gallop.

"Remember this," The Tad said, that time, after he thrashed Chagas for leaving a horse tied up for three days without space to crop. "If a smile has no result, then take the whip. But if you use the whip, take care of the knife. And if not the knife, then fire, or poison in the herds. Remember Christ. He took the whip to the money-changers, but nobody, not even Christ, uses the whip with impunity. The money-changers got behind the priests, and they used patience, and perhaps many a greased palm, and Christ was crucified. There was a great money-changers' banquet that night. Always remember, you can treat people with a smile, or with the whip. If it's the whip, be warned."

The grandson of Chagas had been among the crowd of boys. Shahbash made nothing of the hedge about the house, and trotted almost to the door. The father helped with the milch herd for The House, and the mother was laundress, good people of many generations in the same place. Himself clapped hands, and a daughter came to the door, a little one, in a short dress, barefoot, with a white bow.

"Well," The O'Dancy said. "Aren't you the image, then, of Clené?"

The child nodded.

"Then come," himself said. "Be giving me the hand to kiss."

She gave the hand, he kissed, and she looked at the place, and up at him.

"Where's your father and mother?" himself asked.

"Pae has gone to the house of the Twelve Apostles," the child said. "The Mãe is with Mãe Filomena at The House."

"And where's your brother, Fernando?" himself asked.

"Stoning Judas," she said.

"Oh," himself said. "Why would he be doing that?"

"He is the devil's brother," she said. "He brought the wickedness of money into us."

"Wickedness of money," himself said. "Is money, truly, wicked?"

"It is truly wicked," she said. "It is wicked to have money."

"And who told you that?" himself asked.

"The saintly mother," she said.

"And who is this saintly one?" The O'Dancy asked.

"The Lady Hilariana," the child said.

"Tell your father I was on a visit," himself said, and went toward Shahbash. "You'll grow up a beautiful woman. I see it in your eyes. Just like your mother. Tell her that, will you? Tell her I kiss her hand."

"You didn't kiss my hand," she said, and held it out. "You didn't say good-by."

"Oh no, and I did not, now, think of that," himself said, and went back, and kissed the hand, and again she looked at the place. "Will you always be asking for what you want?"

She nodded.

"You'll do well," he said, and went back to Shahbash. "Tell your *pae* to see me about a school for you."

Shahbash had no need to be told where to go. The horse stand was near, and he knew he had done his share. Rapping across the grass toward the trees in rise, himself heard the helicopter and wondered if Steb was flying, or who, on such a day, and nodded in thought of Hilariana, and her talk of superstition. But if *macumba* and *khimbanda* had any basis, then she must, too, indulge in the superstitions with little room to accuse others.

The mind of himself was steady enough, for reason that in the soul of himself was held the strict intention to burn out, word and detail, superstition or not, the Devil and all black thought to the contrary, down to the ash, and sift all to the cleanly winds.

In that, and only in that, himself was tranquil unto the opening of the Gates.

21 Brother Mihaul's house was over on the least used side of the living area, beyond the kitchen garden and the river. It had been a store shed for tobacco, and he had walled it, and added a veranda, but no more. Himself had been there three times in his life, the first with The Tad to watch the crop dried, the second with Brother Mihaul to give him permission to live there, and the third to approve the alteration. It seemed to himself that they had met no more than a dozen times in their lives, and then not for more than thirty minutes or so, if that. The man was indeed a recluse. He shunned any company. Even though he wore the monkish habit, he had never taken a service or entered any church and never under any circumstances would he meet Father Miklos, though the holy man had tried often enough in earlier days to arrange it. What the reason was himself had never bothered to find out. Every man had to live his own life as he wanted, and only he was responsible for his soul, and if he ignored or declined earthly succor, then he had nothing to say at the Gates. But then nobody had the right to say anything this side of them, not even a brother.

The bridge had been strengthened with adzed beams, and a stone supporting wall curved along the banks of the river, both an agreeable addition himself had known nothing about. A garden, of flowers and shrubs in quiet tend and full of bloom, went all the way to the house and well beyond, and the fragrance of tobacco fell sweet. There had never been a garden or grass there. It had been a rutted, muddy, sandy space for the wagons. From the size of the trees it seemed that Brother Mihaul must have begun planting a full twenty years before, and that was surprising, for himself had thought the fellow lived as an anchorite in the midst of an arid patch, with dust in rise from every puff, and the heat beating in through a holed rush roof, mosquitoes ever in whine about his ears, and nothing to his feet except the bare, broken boards.

The house was truly, magnificently Grandfa Phineas, with a wide stone path all around—"Will I not go dry of foot into my own house, then? Oh yes, but I will!"—and a road going away toward the track to the mountains. There were no windows, but an outer wall had been added and the roof widened to cover the space. It arrayed itself, long, low, a deep, baked brown with probably the best thatch on The Inheritance in a fine surround of shrubs and trees, a place to be proud of, clearly the home of a man of substance with careful thought for his property.

Shahbash trotted down to the horse stand, and Uvald' came running his old flapping feet.

"Is the Brother Mihaul at the house?" himself asked.

Uvald' took off his hat, and looked about as if a knife had clipped an ear.

"The meeting is held," he said in a bare whisper, finger to lips.

"To hell with the meeting," himself shouted in the Other Language. "I've a meeting of my own with him."

Uvald' stared, licked his lips, and mumbled.

"Where was the altar Turú and Gil found, here?" The O'Dancy asked quietly, dismounting.

Uvald' pointed to a nearby part of the wall.

"The *candomblé* was there, but we burned and buried everything," he whispered. "There was another over in the front. We burned and buried that. Laurisdes and Felix are here all night. But they won't come again. They know what to expect."

"They?" The O'Dancy said. "Who are they?"

"Sons and daughters of Satan," Uvald' said, and stuck his right thumb between the first and second fingers, and raised the fist to ward the Evil Eye.

"Their names," The O'Dancy said.

"If we knew, we would set the cross upon them," Uvald' said.

"What's the whisper for?" The O'Dancy asked.

Uvald' looked toward the house.

"The meeting," he said.

"What sort of meeting?" The O'Dancy shouted. "Has the man ordered no visitors? How many are in there?"

"There are many of us, Master," Uvald' said. "It is a tent of *Umbanda*."

The O'Dancy took off his hat, and stood in marvel, looking at the house.

"Well, well, now, just think of that," himself said. "Caught them all, with the meat in their teeth, at long, long, last, have I not? Ride over to Democritas Pereira. Tell him to bring a truck, pump and gas tank over here, immediately. We'll see what to do with a tent."

Uvald' shook his head, a man in misery.

"Democritas Pereira is here," he said, lifting his chin at the house.

"Aristotle Souza," himself said, naming the second overseer.

"Here," Uvald' said.

"Plinio and Trancred," The O'Dancy said, naming the two third men.

"Here," Uvald' said, to the brows in misery. "Master, everybody is here."

"Are you here as a lookout?" himself asked. "Why are you not inside?"

"I am here to make the cocks crow," Uvald' whispered.

The O'Dancy stared at him, but the mouth of himself refused to say the words. The house seemed quiet. The flowers bloomed. Trees were green and still. The sun was warm, bees flew, and there was silvery talk from the river.

"I've a feeling I'm going mad," himself said, almost as quietly as Uvald'. "That's what it is, you see? It's not good to feel so. Have you not a boy you could send for Father Miklos?"

Uvald' raised his chin again.

"The sacred father is here," he said.

The O'Dancy stared at him for many moments until the dark cloudy eyes looked down, and then, by strong will, himself turned and walked away, toward the side and the nearest door. In quiet air there was sudden, faint sound of shouting and beating of gongs and drums. The door pushed open, into a laundry, of hanging sheets, and an electric washer and dryer, and the smell of soap. Through the other door into an ironing room, and hanging lines filled with white clothing. There was no other color except white.

The door swung into the kitchen, with a big gas stove, white cupboards, shelves in glass, stainless steel about the place, freezers in white, all white rafters, tiles, doors in and out. Himself went through the In door, to a dining room in mirrors and gold panels with Florentine frescoes, a long refectory table, twenty chairs in crimson velvet, and bowls of white orchids on the sideboard, on the table, and on the service stand at the window.

"Well, Brother Mihaul," himself said aloud. "You live fairly, and thank God."

The swinging door on the other side opened, and José, brother of Democritas, put his head in, and set his finger to his lips, stared big eyes, and rolled them toward his left shoulder in warning.

Himself took the short one by the forelock and pulled him into the room, and went through the door, and let it swing behind there, looking at a foyer, with wide doors and windows both sides out to covered veranda gardens, furnished with Guaraní rugs, pottery, sheared and polished oxhide chairs and couches, and a wall filled with icons of all sizes, in silver, gold, ivory. In a glance himself saw where a great deal of O'Dancy profit had gone. Yet there was odd pride, and no small pleasure, that money in whatever amount had at least been spent for beauty in a rare craft.

The shouting and drumming and gonging flew up again, but nearer, and a voice shouted, and then was silence.

The O'Dancy tiptoed across to the door on the extreme right, which looked less important than the double door in the middle, and tried the handle with great care. It turned. He looked behind, and saw José looking at himself with hands at prayer. The door opened without sound, and himself went through, to a corridor, with a cloakroom's overflow of racks of clothing and hats, and a lavatory at the end clearly marked, for men, with a bas-relief *toga virilis* in gold. At the end, a door, and when himself opened it, a heavy leather curtain, first, and a red velvet curtain a yard in front, and in the darkness between, when the leather fell in place behind, knowledge came that many eyes waited, many bodies warmed, many people were beyond.

"We have paid everything to the correct amount," a voice said. "What we exchange among ourselves is not subject to tax."

"Read the law," another, sterner voice said.

"That law is not for us," the first voice said. "The laws of Rome we obey. The laws of all others are for those who wish to obey."

Shouts, drumming and gonging flew up again, and stopped in a moment.

Himself realized that the voices spoke a form of Latin far nobler than any he had ever been taught, strangely abridged but authoritative, and the cold feeling came into himself that he listened to speech of times long gone.

But the stern voice was Democritas', and himself would have sworn the man had not a word of any language except the *brasileiro*, ever spoken in generous periods taught to him by Father Miklos though always in the accent of the farm.

Voices talked again, but in a language that at first himself thought might be German, and was not, and when the fourth voice, drier, more remote, spoke at length, he guessed at Hebrew, and knew himself to be correct, for that voice undoubtedly was Efram's, and one of the others could only be Paul.

Slowly under careful hands, the curtains parted just far enough to give himself a view beyond.

Faint light showed the heads of those sitting on the floor.

To the left, all darkness except the white shine of many eyes in small movement. To the right, at the end of the room, a dozen or more men in white clothing under a cone of white light seemed to be asleep in chairs about a long table on a platform. On one side, Brother Mihaul, in white habit, sat in a chair, staring, head on fist, at the table. On the other, Father Miklos sat alone, with the crucifix upheld on his knee.

"Resume," Democritas said in that strangely stern voice, so unlike his own.

"The coins were made of wood by one Simon, a carpenter, also in arrest," a sleeping man said, on the left, and himself saw Alcides Ribeiro, chief accountant in the coffee warehouse and the steadiest man in the whole concern. "Those coins used to exchange the commerce of the sea had a fish carved in them. Those used in commerce of oil, a lamp of one wick. Those used for grain, a wheat sheaf. Those for leather, a bull's head. For wine, an amphora. For offerings, a dove. For cloth, a distaff. I produce the coins in evidence. On the reverse side, it will be seen that all of them are carved with the star of David. There is no mention of the emperor, and none of the majesty of Herod, or any mark of respect for the Sanhedrin, or for the priestly office, either within the temple or outside. In short, this is a device to cheat the Roman law, the Judean court, and all Hebrews under those twin jurisdictions, whether one or the other, by depriving the common purse of this part of the coinage, and the accrual of its value, which would serve to lighten the burden on those now paying these onerous taxes in the coinage of Rome. The followers of the Baptized use these coins among themselves in the exchange of goods. Since their wants are simple, these coins serve their purpose. Oil can be exchanged for fish, and if the value of the oil exceeds that of the fish, so many coins preserve the bargain. If clothing is exchanged against wine, then these coins redress a balance on either side. In this manner, many thousands of bargains are being struck every day, with great loss to the common purse. But the tax is fixed, and it must be paid. Those sums toward its payment, which ought to be available, are lost because of this commerce in mere tallies of wood that cost nothing, and have no value. The mischief of the tax falls, then, upon those honest men who use the coin of Rome, or of the majesty Herod, which can be exchanged for Roman coin. These, of the Baptized, cheat the common purse. Those who cheat the common purse are thieves. Thieves are crucified. I ask for death, by crucifixion, for this self-confessed close friend of the Baptized, Iscariot, surnamed Judas, sometime of Galilee."

An arm in front went up, and the room dinned in shouts, drumming and gonging.

The arm fell, and with it silence.

"It is no crime to use other coin by Roman law," another sleeper said. "All coin is free. Only tax must be paid in Roman coin. That is the law. If it were criminal to use other coin, then the changers of money commit how many crimes every day?"

"But this use of a wooden tally," Alcides said, with a lolling head, and still asleep. "These cannot be coins. Coins have a value. These have none. They cannot be changed at the tables."

"But did you not just say they are being changed where they are acceptable?" Paul's voice said, and him at the end of the table, with saliva dripping from a flaccid mouth. "And these wooden coins must have a value, or would they be accepted? The test of worth is acceptance. The test of value is what can be got in exchange. These coins pass both tests. I see no harm in this. The territory has been in healthy trade for the past half year. Far better than in former years. Am I to suppose this to be due to the use of these wooden coins? Is more trade being done because of them? More bargains struck? Answer me this."

Some of the sleepers moved, and Democritas mumbled, and Efram sat straighter, speaking the sonorous Hebrew. Felipe da Silva, a coffee grader, and no better man, replied, too, in Hebrew, though he had never finished in elementary school and never moved from the warehouse after the day he started work.

"Come," Paul said. "The question of coins is finished. What other charge is made against this man?"

"He incites these Baptized to rebellion," Alcides Ribeiro said, but in deep sleep, or so it seemed. "The streets are filled with them. The branches of palm, their sign of acclamation, covers every way to the temple."

"There are no rebellious thoughts among the Baptized," Altino Dantas, the transport controller, said. "They came to greet the Master. They brought palm fronds to carpet the streets against the dust. We have ten commandments from our Father, and one from the Son, and these preclude any thought of rebellion, or any feeling except those of faith, and hope of salvation in our Father, the Lord God."

"It is a god we do not recognize, and a son of a carpenter, no more, and these do not give commandments, which are in the sole province of the emperor," Democritas said.

Up went the arm in front, and the drums, gongs, and shouts filled the place, but no sleeper moved.

Down went the arm, and the room was still.

"Which commandment is this, from the carpenter?" Paul asked, and snored.

"He commanded that we love our neighbors as ourselves," Altino said.

"Proceed," Paul said. "In my judgment, that is not a commandment, but adjuration to a sect."

"But Lord Governor," Democritas said in the strange voice. "It has already been stated that he is called King of Judea."

"Many give others any name they please," Paul said. "To be named, so, is not the prerogative only of carpenters. You and your Sanhedrin, Caiaphas, do you not pretend yourselves to be arbiters of Judea, lords of the ark, and guardians of the 'chosen' people? Do you not set yourselves against the true glory of Mars, our beloved protector?"

"Mars, we believe to be the Latin name for the Lord God, and therefore we believe in part," Efram, called Caiaphas, said.

"That part is where I have the liveliest interest," Paul said. "Let us hear where we diverge."

"This matter of the Baptized," Efram said with greater power. "Who is this to take our time?"

"Agreed," Paul said. "Judas Iscariot is on trial. We shall revert to the question of the other part, later. But I thought both were sides of a problem. Very well. Did Iscariot order these coins to be made?"

"Nobody orders except the Master," the sleeper said, and it could only be Shaun, awake, open-eyed, and staring, but a stare not of his own eyes, which were brown, but enormous opals of fire that from movement among the seated made them cringe. "He is our Lord and governor. He is Son of God. He is the Baptized. He is the light, the way, and the truth."

"Wait," Paul said. "It seems that these are fanatic, and led into other ways. This Baptized should answer to the charge."

"But I provided the evidence," Shaun said. "I told them to put me before the Lord Pilate. Find that I am innocent, and all my brethren in the Baptized, and see the strength of Roman law. I gave them the coins."

"I see no harm in them," Paul said. "I see no great harm in you, or in what you have done."

"But, Lord Proconsul, if this one goes back to his fellows, surely they will riot in the moment," Efram said. "We have done our best to warn Your Excellency. We can do no more."

"The streets are filled with a noisy crowd," Democritas said. "If we have to use the flat of our swords, we shall hurt a few."

"That thought controls a rabble," Paul said.

"Let the Baptized stand trial," Efram said. "He ordered the making of these coins, which ignore the illustrious Caesar, and question Your Excellency's authority."

The arm went up, and the din of shouting, drumming, gonging began again, and ended when the arm went down.

"Let my clerk consider that," Paul said.

"Perhaps, Lord Governor, it should be pointed out that the Baptized is even now returned under escort of the Ensign Fabricius Lycurgas, Praetorian, of the Legion of Tiberius," another sleeper said, Moacyr Amancio, in the bagging warehouse, never a day at school and never off The Inheritance. "The majesty Herod questioned him in the matter of this claim to Judea. It was found void."

"Take them both to your temple, and there try them," Paul said. "This Iscariot, I absolve."

"We could not offend our precincts," Efram said, cold, dry, remote. "How can they be tried at the temple? They are not of our faith. But is it to be told to the Lord Caesar that mere carpenters issue coins in defiance of all authority? Shall every man issue his own coins? Is the law to be flouted by any vagabond? Is the Lord Caesar to be held so lightly?"

"No harm is done," Paul said. "What you do among yourselves is of no importance."

"But the tax is upon all, and not upon some," Efram said with no change of tone, head back, asleep. "All men are held to pay just tribute to Rome. If some, by device, escape that tribute, and thrust more of the burden on others more honorable, is this just? Does the law condone this? Might the Lord Caesar concur?"

"Release this Iscariot," Paul said. "Retain the coins as evidence. Bring the carpenter before me."

"He is innocent," Iscariot shouted, writhing in the chair.

"Remove him," Democritas said. "If you cause any contention among your kind outside, be sure that Praetorian blades bite. Lord Proconsul, if there are casualties among us by reason of civil unrest, then this, too, must be explained in the report to the Lord Caesar. A riot can be prevented by example. That crowd is ready to destroy the city. Are we to permit them to shout that a carpenter is King, not merely of Judea, but also of Rome?"

"Shouting does no harm," Paul said. "If they wish to believe this carpenter is a god, very well. It would amuse me if you believed it, Colonel."

"I believe only in my Praetorians and quiet streets," Democritas said. "I will order this man brought here on a charge of inciting to riot. The evidence is in our ears at this moment."

Up went the arm and the seated crowd scrambled up, and the din of shouting, gonging, and drumming reverberated for moments, until the arm went down.

In silence, Shaun wept.

"Ah, Christ Jesus, what have I done?" he moaned, turned, struggled in the chair. "Ah, Petrus, Petrus, help me, now, help me."

"There is no help for the stupid," Petrus said. "They are self-cursed, and accursèd of all men."

A chorale of screams that became an ear-piercing cockcrow brought the crowd to cover their heads. The men at the table moved, seemingly about to waken. Brother Mihaul got up, and went to each in turn, and laid a hand on a head, a shoulder, and looked down at them, smiling, until he was sure each knew where he was, and passed to the next.

The people sitting down raised a hymn, with heavy rhythm of tambourines, and almost immediately the men at the table began stretching, rubbing their eyes, blowing noses, bending their arms, yawning, so many sleepers coming out of a measureless dream.

The O'Dancy opened the curtains, and pushed, without pardon, through the crowd, toward Brother Mihaul.

"What in the name of Christ is this, going on here?" himself said. "Is every mother's son of you insane, or something? Father Miklos, what are you doing here?"

"A moment, now," Brother Mihaul said, shorter, it seemed, grayer of eye, sharper of speech. "Remember where you are. A word too many, and I'll have you flung in the river."

"The hell you will, be Christ," The O'Dancy said.

"But that's the very way of it, do you see?" Brother Mihaul said. "In Christ, I will, for you're nothing but a money-changer."

"Your blaspheming doesn't become your habit," The O'Dancy said.

"I was never blaspheming," Brother Mihaul said. "I was explaining in your own terms, what you might expect if you step one ell beyond a clearly defined line. This is not your property. You haven't a syllable to say. Now, then, what are you doing here without permission?"

"I've all the permission I need," The O'Dancy said. "You know bloody well I have. If it's a legal match, I'll win. Be looking about, now, and tell me, what is this?"

"It's whatever you think it is," Brother Mihaul said. "Be wasting your breath on somebody else for a few minutes. I've work to do."

He went off, toward the men grouped about the table, and himself turned to Father Miklos.

"Perhaps yourself'll explain," he said. "What are you here for?"

Father Miklos was never more himself. Serene the man stood, calm of eye and hand.

"I believe, to observe a small miracle," he said. "And not for the first time."

"Are you not ashamed to adorn yourself with that crucifix and say what you just said?" The O'Dancy said. "Is it not time I had a word with the bishop about your age, and the state of your mind?"

"The facts are known in all the relevant places," Father Miklos said. "I shall be retiring after this year's harvest. I shall devote myself to this work. I judge it to be as important as any I might do in the small time left to me."

"I regret I ever lived to hear you say it," The O'Dancy said. "What devil's work are you consigned to?"

"Let us sit down," Father Miklos said, and went to his chair, and signed to João to pull up another.

"I'll be damned if I want to," The O'Dancy said.

"Then be damned," Brother Mihaul shouted from the end of the table. "For if you don't change your ways, and that soon, you're damned anyway, and the only way you'll ever have of joining the decency of creation will be when you come back here to plead for our help. Be remembering it, now, and listen to a wise one."

"I'm taken by the throat," The O'Dancy said. "I don't know what to think, or where to turn."

"Then sit down," Father Miklos said. "Let me tell you, without detail. As, let me remind you, on other occasions."

22 Where the leaves whispered, and hidden women mourned, and time was idle in a sad moment infinitely long, Creonice passed, smiling, stretching out the nipples of her breasts between tender pecks of finger and thumb, eyes up, tongue in flutter, a sheened, candlelit coppery-chocolate wonder of limbs and glowing thighs, resting on a hip, bending a knee, on the other hip, bending the other knee, moving side to side, pulsing momentarily in the beat of the *catareté*. Engulfed, silent at wild eyes, and the secret woman-laughter, immersed in sweat warmth, and ever afraid of a body far stronger than his own in wild contortion that left him breathless and nerveless, there, himself knew, the root of vice began, feeling triumphed, thought faltered, and all, from that instant, became a struggle between a wish to return to the darkness and savage whispers and a will to conform to all that himself knew to be correct, that was planted in him, and not to be throttled.

Fransisca—and all white flowers, now, perfume her name—had never been a Creonice, and had never understood that need of his, if himself ever knew what need it was. But it was never in that one, of lying together in scientific exploration of the body, a passing of moments in tactile exercise of marital privilege, no, there could never be any more in that, to himself, than infantile squander of the marvel, the only marvel, the passing of the Seed, an Adam in glorious company of Eve.

Small play, acquaintance rights, husbandly fondling, all alike were emotional horror, born of the known and cold. That market place of want had not obtruded until Rhoda, a semicolon in the flow of days, took himself by the hand, and she a few years older, with a pretense of schooling outside the country, and bound to show her difference, her maturity, her superiority, by conduct she considered other than bucolic, and worrying his trouser front, and

slopping her kisses until he ripped the clothing off her body entire,
and spat between her breasts, and left her.

"But darling," Fransisca said. "What do I do wrong?"

"Nothing," himself said. "Everything you do is perfect. According to the book. The doctor. All the old women's advice. Perfect.
You've a body with a hole. You respond. That's perfect. But a man
doesn't get hard with that sort of perfection. At least, I don't. I'm
soft. I'm what Old Mr. Carvalhos Ramos used to call 'that dangling
thing.'"

"But darling, why?" Fransisca said. "Don't you love me?"

"More than anything alone," himself said.

"Why do you say 'alone'?" she asked.

"Because there's nobody else," himself said.

But there were always knowledge of Tomomi. She reigned, a
fall of blossom in the mind. Sudden thought of her, and the staff
in himself strengthened, and whether conference or luncheon or
dinner engagement, whatever, he went out to the car, and took the
turns down to Santos, a gay madman, and sounded the small whistle outside the wall of the beach house, their own signal, and she
always pressed the button to open the gate, always, through all the
years, the gate opened, and he passed through, and the gates
closed behind, and he rested his back upon them until she came,
and bowed deep, and took his hand and invited him into the house.
At first, he ripped off his clothes, and ripped off her kimono, and
carried her in, to the floor of the first room. But little by little she
taught him her own way, and she first took off his shoes, and put
on slippers, and took off his jacket, and undid his tie, and took off
his shirt, and undershirt, though by then he would have the kimono
off her, and the next hour on the floor. Yet the day came that she
undressed him entire, and led him to the bath, and stewed him,
with a firepot underneath to keep the water hot, and took him out,
to a couple of women masseuses, and they made him feel every
muscle in his body for the first time in his life, and then she took
him, limp as a horsetail, from a freezing shower, and he was more
of the male than he had ever known, and from that time he let her
dictate what was to happen in her house. Delight was in their
dinners, on cushions at the low table, of so many dishes that he
never more than tasted, and she shaking the beautiful head, in sor-

row, never in scold, and leading him, an invalid of the table, out, to the bedroom, a mattress on the floor that felt like a dawn cirrus, and taking her revenge, while he tried to withstand the chaos, and she laughing, and moving the muscles of herself within, but only a fraction, and enough, and himself crying out and dying in the moment, and herself waiting almost until the male spark was cool, and herself dying, in the garment of black hair and the wonder of her Nipponese kiss, that dry, drowning, and reviving miracle of the lips and soul.

"Don't dare touch me," Fransisca said clearly, in the darkness. "I heard you."

"It took a long time, but I'm here," himself said, out of breath with the climb. "I've come to take you away."

"You'll never take me," she said. "I am novice. I shall take vows."

"You'll hell," himself said. "You're my wife. Come now, let's be out of it."

"I'll scream," she said, but she had never moved since he was in through the window.

"Scream," himself said. "You'll come with me. I've walked the front of this place often enough. Get up."

"Never," she said, and lay there.

All anger passed where the leaves whispered, and the hidden women mourned. That cold stripping of institutional linen, the pull at thin bedclothes, and the lying-on of a body faintly warm under the cold shell that had no fragrance he remembered, but only the stale shudder of the unbathed, the unending Adamesque ritual, the cold, infructuous kiss, the utter wrench of glory foregone, and stillness between the two.

"Have you finished?" Fransisca said loudly, as at a telephone. "I never know what you're attempting. It really is ridiculous. Do leave me alone. I've told you. I want to take vows."

"Take your vows," he said, and raised himself, a deathly weight. "I'd advise a bath, first."

Fransisca, ever, yes, impeccably herself, screamed and struck, screamed and screamed and struck, and the door was opened and he stood in white light, and women shrieked, and gave him time to go through the window, and off, on the ladder, holding there, while the firemen wheeled him down, sobbing the tears and not one drop of water in himself. The dry sob, that one, of the male, that hurts, and leaves the inner scars that never heal.

So, Hilariana, born of that cold, that frozen night, in silent writhe of laughter.

"But how could you dare?" Old Mr. Carvalhos Ramos said, pale, trembling, within a week of death, if anybody had known. "A house of nuns? Nuns. But a nun? Consider this."

"My wife was in there," himself said. "Now let her stay."

"Not there," Old Mr. Carvalhos Ramos said. "Here is the order. Your wife is committed."

"Committed," himself said. "What's that?"

"She is committed to the state mental institution," Old Mr. Carvalhos Ramos said. "Now, with your friends, and mine, we shall get her out, and put her in a more comfortable surrounding. I fear she is quite mental. She injured a number of the nuns. She had to be restrained. The doctor ordered her removal. That's why I'm here."

No need to beg or argue. The order was signed, and himself and Father Miklos went to the place, that annex to purgatory, where men and women went naked, slept on stairways, in corridors on top of each other, but without the will to be men or women, but only bodies in search of sleep and the touch of another being, and twenty doctors attending ten thousand, and a thousand dying each week. Fransisca, beautiful still, shining the unknowing smile, yes, in that stench of the unwanted, smiling, leaning in a corner, making no attempt to resist, and two strong girls lifting her, and a comet's arc of drivelers straggling behind, touching their coats, plucking at their sleeves in hopeless plea to be taken too, away, and out to the air, to the clean, clear miracle of a wholesome breath in silence and sunlight.

"How can it be permitted?" The O'Dancy said, himself trembling. "How in the love of Christ can they allow it?"

"They," Father Miklos said, but laughing. "Why should it always be 'they'? Is it never you? What will you do? Subscribe? Is that enough?"

"They ought to have doctors, nurses, attendants," himself said. "Wait till I get back."

"How many doctors will make a career there?" Father Miklos said. "Would you? How much would you pay them? How many nurses? How much does a woman want for that type of work? You ask, you demand that others do this work you wouldn't dream of doing. It's always somebody else, isn't it?"

"Civic duty," himself said. "Why would you laugh?"

"Don't disgust me," Father Miklos said. "Is this the humbug I detect, at last?"

"Bedamned," The O'Dancy said. "There must be a way to help."

"The usual way, by charity of the Church?" Father Miklos said, seriously enough. "A sisterhood in charge? That's been the solution in most cases, hasn't it? Holy women. But there are too few. Elsewhere, poor homes give aggregate of the devoted. Here, there are very few houses not rich in love, at least. Girls marry early. Only a few join the sisterhood. It's not a career. There's no money."

"Is it only money, then?" The O'Dancy said.

"Pay enough, you'll have all the help you want," Father Miklos said. "Of, of course, a certain kind. Those who love money do not seek the Church."

"But those who have the money support the Church," The O'Dancy said. "Is that it? Without us, what would you do?"

"Spend more time at prayer," Father Miklos said. "I believe we do too little in these days."

Down at the beach house, in the years, the children were coming into flower, the evening hours were the dear times, and a procession of little girls, each a little shorter than the next, coming into the room to bow, and present the day's work, kneeling, a sumptuous half-circle of beauty about himself, Oto-O-San, and their mam, Oka-A-San, kneeling in the shadowed corner with the tea, and the small, white porcelain jugs of *sake*, and the warm, damp hand towels in tight rolls, and the voices chanting poetry, sometimes translated by Tomomi, oftener not, for himself loved the sound, the pure music, and words only gave a shape, never the emotion.

"Shall the children go to the Christian Church?" Tomomi asked one night, in blue shadow, and the chrysanthemums a gray, mauve, and crimson glory massed behind her. "I have nothing to teach them, except what I was taught. It will never do for their time and the future. Should they be Christians?"

"Well, Tomomi, my beautiful," himself said, at loss. "I suppose they should. They ought to have some knowledge of Grace. What makes you doubt?"

"I don't doubt," Tomomi said. "I don't doubt, at all, that the Christian way is good. The thoughts are good. But the Christians themselves, those I meet, should my children grow like them? Is it the Christian teaching that makes them what they are?"

"What are they?" he said, and fearing what she might say. "We are made a gift of the Knowledge. If we use it or not, is that the fault of the Church? The priests try hard enough. How about you Buddhists?"

"I think we do better with what we have," Tomomi said. "But this Brazil is not a Buddhist country. The spiritual climate of all countries depends upon the first men. Those who made the history. Buddha waits, patiently, for all men to think with him. He has the time. Christ says, 'Come unto me.' It isn't tomorrow, or some other time. It's urgent. It's now. It's *brasileiro*. Brazil is now. And in the future. You agree? Shouldn't they join the Church?"

"Of course," himself said, miserable, for no thought of it had ever entered the rusted iron grille of his mind. "I'm deeply ashamed. I should have been first to suggest it."

"Little girls have to be thought about," she said, as near to admonition as she ever went—and a garden of her own chrysanthemums, now, in thought of all the opulent savor—bow your head, and be clearing your eyes—of that one woman, the dedicated, Tomomi, the glory—"Little boys are not so important, there. They take care of themselves, later. But little girls grow to be women. A woman needs faith. In something."

"I failed you," he said.

"Of all men, you have been most faithful," Tomomi said, and laid the lovely head on his shoulder. "I was determined to be *brasileira*. Any man could have taken me. I wanted only children born on this soil. When I saw you, I said, That is the man. I waited. Such a long time. When you noticed me, I danced. So. We have seven children. Even the sun isn't happier than I."

"So you trapped me," himself said. "I should have known I dealt with a witch."

"I am a witch of the *no*," Tomomi said. "I take off my mask, and I am who? Me."

"Thank God for years of beauty and memory," himself said. "I'll send Father Miklos to catechize the children. Boys as well. Men have need of the Faith."

"Ask him to talk to their mother, as well," she said. "I would give my blood to be of their Faith."

"From the moment I first touched my eyes to your own, from the moment God's vision gave me the privilege, have you ever been of any other?" himself said in passion. "Do you not think I asked for prayers to be said for you, these years?"

"You must tell me where," she said.

"Where you refused to go," himself said. "The Inheritance."

"My children may go," she said. "I, not. I am not the woman. Therefore, I will not be a visitor."

Think now, think well.

Days in Europe with Daniel, that should have been glorious copy of those in the years before with The Tad, and were not, but only a consistent disappointment, an acrid lesson, especially that day in Venice, and the shop himself remembered so well, closed, and the two of them walking along without a look for each other in the slimy smell of small canals that each of them knew would never have been allowed, smell or slime, at home, to find a bakery, but never the same bread as before, and walking farther to find the ham, and olives, and salami, and farther for tomatoes and lettuce, and a flask of chianti, and borrowing a knife to cut the bread, the stale bread, and the man behind the counter with the face of a thin hen, and whiskers growing about the beak and in the wattles of him, laughing because the cork broke in the bottle.

"Why is it so funny?" himself asked. "Does a rotten cork remind you of anybody in your family? Or is it any advertisement for anything else you sell?"

"It's you tourists," the man said loudly, and everybody listening. "You come here, you buy a sandwich and a Coca-Cola. You sleep on the piazza. What is this? Tourism? Stay at home. Eat your sandwiches there. A flask of chianti? You make a lamp of the bottle. You Americans, you weaken my gut."

"If there were more of us, you'd disintegrate faster through your telephonic arse," himself said, and threw the loaf at the whiskery face, and the bottle just missed, but the wine and the pieces of glass showered on him. "Never again will I be here, either in spirit or in the flesh."

"Could we not go home?" Daniel said, out in the air, the canal air that stank of sewage. "Is there anything here?"

"Only the bones of yesterday," himself said. "It was here I heard 'La Gigolette.' But there are so many fiddlers in so many cafés cheek by jowl, you can't even hear yourself drinking the muck they call coffee. It's the world of tourism. To hell with it. We'll go to Paris and get you a girl."

Daniel—was ever a finer first one, but never, God Almighty be holding him close, now—he, yes, he, well cured of Europe, and every hand out, every tongue a dog's in the hang for cash, no courtesy, no thanks, he, by his own wit, God love him, he found his own girl. A beauty from out of the ground, clean-grown, a darleen, no less. Himself gave her no attention except a hand and a bow, and filled Daniel's pocket, and told the porter to send a man to watch them, and God help everybody if anything happened wrong. Nothing ever did. Daniel, ah, now, wait, dry your tears, that good one, gay as a twopenny button, coming back next day with this girl twice as big as himself, and still shy, though if she looked at him, a dynamo ran to shake the floor.

"What would you want to do with this one?" himself asked, after almost two weeks. "Is she coming back with us?"

"She's going to somewhere in the East," Daniel said. "She's teaching, and she can't break the contract. But after I've finished my examinations, I've promised I'll go there."

"And herself'll teach you a little more," The O'Dancy said.

"I've been teaching her," Daniel said.

"And am I permitted to know where you were taught?" The O'Dancy asked.

"At The Inheritance," Daniel said in small surprise. "In the main coffee shed. There are so many girls. Much more beautiful. More life. Life? Animation. I had to teach this one what to open. She thought we entered through the navel."

"A French girl?" himself said. "Impossible."

Daniel shook the dark red head.

"That's where she put me," he said. "Now, I've another girl. Ah, different. While you were downstairs buying the diaries, remember? Very well. We were in the little room. Could I take her on my own?"

"She's yours," himself said. "I'll order a table at Maxim's. Could I not meet her? Drop in, let's say, after dinner. Ten minutes, no more."

"I'll be expecting you," Daniel said—ah, listen to The O'Dancy, now, the one that never was, all angels lighten his way—"but don't be giving her your look, now, will you? She's rather more delicate."

Yes, to hear the boy talk, nothing wrong with the heart of him. Careful of a woman, that was Lesson Number One. And that fine one, Frenchly fine, beside him at the table, and looking appealingly at himself as if asking forgiveness for misusing a pair of short trousers, she, the innocent, unknowing, in mid-bite of a young minotaur.

Daniel, killed in action, and Lys, killed by a bomb a few weeks later, and himself with one thought, working the months to find that daughter, the little one, the red-haired, gray-eyed one, without knowing who himself ever was, yet held out her arms and himself taking her, and no word from any, out of that crèche and into the car, and so, forever, part of himself.

Serena.

23 Himself awoke in the quiet room looking at the long table, and the single white light. Father Miklos had left his chair.

There was tiredness, and hunger, and certainly thirst for companionship.

"You've had a fine little nap," Brother Mihaul said, and looking down, kindlier, far, than he had ever been. "Our Miklos has gone off to take a service. It's time for us to talk. Will you listen? It was never my own wish to be less than the best of brothers. When you've heard me out, you'll possibly agree. Are you listening?"

"I am," he said. "But a little something in a glass'd never come amiss."

"The very mixture I just asked for, would you believe that," Brother Mihaul said in great admiration. "Tea."

"Tea, my cosmic sphincter," The O'Dancy said.

Brother Mihaul folded in on the lap of him, it seemed, and the tonsure came down in a tremor.

"I finished joking," he said, showing the laughter. "Now, be drinking your whisky, and I'll tell you what's in marvelous train, here."

"Is this the *khimbanda* everybody's talking about?" The O'Dancy said, and took up the glass. "That's what I want to know. I've sworn to burn it out. And as soon as I drink this, that's what I'll do."

"And there'll be many to help," Brother Mihaul said. "This, that we're doing, is a further spiritual reach we call *Umbanda*. We work with the highest, the ultimate form of the 'white' spirit, not the black. *Macumba* is a way of using the evil in all of us. Elementally, it's sexual. It calls out the lower form of the spirit. *Khimbanda* is far worse. It's worship of Satan for Satan's sake, for love of evil, and that's all. It's a horror that began in the dark time. It's not confined to this country. The priests found it here in the fifteenth century. They proselytized the Indios, first, and then the African slaves.

Christian, Indio, and African made a fine mixture. Or so the saintly slaveowners thought. They made their slaves go to church, worship God, the Christ, the Holy Ghost, and the Virgin Mary, and all the saints, every last one. So the Indio and the African became Christian. It saved them a flogging. It also gave them an opportunity of worshiping their own gods on the sly. They translated their gods into ours. They borrowed Church ritual, the altar, candles, flowers, ornaments, incense. After a couple of generations, they had their own priests. And they had priestesses. That was part of the African fetish, which had a female coadjutor, and they were helped by the plantation owners' wives. When the men were away, and there were no priests, the women took the service. They were saintly women, of course. Bringing the spirit of love to the dear slaves. Am I clear so far?"

"You said just now it's a horror," The O'Dancy said. "Would you explain why?"

"In two words, and I don't want to waste any time on it," Brother Mihaul said, and the small gray eyes of him sharp and serious. "The worship of Satan produces a satanic soul. They recognize all those not given to God. They work on them, though the victim may never be aware of it. They are the Khimbótes. The followers of Satan. And I speak of them as I speak of practicing churchmen. They exist. They believe. They practice. They have power. Never be doubting it. Where they are, the rest of us are in peril. I mean that."

There was no doubt in the mind of himself, at all. There was nothing particularly new in what Brother Mihaul had said, either. It was the manner of saying it. The man was changed beyond all recognition, not in looks, but in attitude. There was none of the old bitterness, brusqueness, rudeness.

The man was gentle.

"I'll accept it," himself said. "I see no reason not to. But what's this you were doing when I came in here?"

Brother Mihaul nodded, and Felipe brought in a silver service of tea on a folding table, and put it beside the chair.

"You see, Arquimed, I've had almost fifty years of experience with a particular type of research into the movement of the human spirit," Brother Mihaul said, and poured the tea. "It's the spirit I was interested in, nothing else. I knew in the beginning, instinctively, that somebody had to find out how this *macumba,* which is peculiarly Brazilan, could be turned into a religion pointed up, instead of down. Here you have a nation that's rotted, virtually rotted, in its lower elements, by the blackest form of magic. It doesn't matter what brains or ability there are on top. If the lower levels are rotten, what's to happen? That's why I left the Order. To come here, study, analyze, research. Produce a form of worship that might satisfy ordinary people. You may ask why the Church doesn't satisfy them. Or why the other denominations aren't good enough. It's simple. There's a spiritual restlessness in our people. It's the outcome of white and Indio and black souls and bodies intermixed. Europe, South America, Africa, intermarried. The children, the generations, of those unions. It's not to be put aside by denial of its existence, or by a few patronizing words, or by contempt. Too many are guilty of trying to ignore it. Invariably, they are quasi-Europeans. But there's a knowledge of the spirit world that's part of our Brazilian blood. Tens of thousands of us are born to be mediums. There's no room in the Church or in any chapel. No allowance is made for us. The Church forbids. The chapels ignore. What do we do? We go to *macumba.* I prefer we go to *Umbanda.* That's a form of spiritism that evolved from the love of God. What we're doing here is direct result of my work and many another's. We're materializing the souls, or the spirits, of those gone. We begin to hear the words they spoke during the period before they died. That is, before they left the earth."

"You believe it," The O'Dancy said.

"Implicitly," Brother Mihaul said, and drank tea. "I've been in control every step of the way. When it became evident what was happening, I called on Father Miklos. I believe he'll join us in a few months. Of course, there's no more adamantine enemy of *macumba,* and the other, than that one. He waged war on five grandams, and how many aunts? He lost, of course. He had to. You can indeed fight Satan with holy water. But you've to find him, first."

"Don't tell me the grandams were worshipers of Satan," himself said.

"Next thing to it," Brother Mihaul said, in mid-pour and looking up. "Did they not give every opportunity, in their hopeless ignorance, to the growth of it? What were they doing? Trying to get into speech with their husbands, primarily. And who was medium for three of them? Mãe Nueza. As nescient an old biddy as you'd meet in a month of Sundays. She told them any tale. Had everything lavished on her. So others started copying her to take a little of the gilt. Your own nurse, remember what happened? The other girl put a curse on her in trance. So the old girl slit her any way at all. Then the control medium, the girl's brother, went out for her with a blade. They never found him, did they?"

"The Tad probably took good care of that," himself said. "Look, then. I'm not sure what you mean by a medium. Why are all of us not mediums?"

Brother Mihaul put the cup down and laughed a fine O'Dancy ha-ha-hawh-hawh.

"Oh, now, wait a moment, here," he said. "Are you not as fine a medium as any of us? If ever you gave yourself the preparation."

"Me?" The O'Dancy said. "A medium? As I've a hope of Christ's blessing, never."

"It's only because you are, that you've any hope at all," Brother Mihaul said, all laughter gone. "You never used your gift. The talent's in fallow ground. But it's there. Anyone with a knowledge of good and evil and aware of the difference between the two, and strong in belief, can become a medium. We're all spirits, are we not? Or why do we speak of the Holy Ghost? Giving up the ghost? These are not simply playful words. Do you imagine that the millions practicing spiritism in this country, alone, are all mentally deficient? Or charlatans? Or self-deluders? Or self-hypnotized? Or a mixture of all of them? Are we all no more than self-deceived? Or criminal lunatics?"

"I've never met enough of you," The O'Dancy said. "And I've no great wish."

"Strange," Brother Mihaul said, and filled Grandam Aracý's teapot. "Here you've controlled the place, The Inheritance, all these years. You've always known about *macumba*. There isn't a man or woman among us who wasn't born into it, into the deepest knowledge of it, what's more. Now, consider. When was there ever a thief found? Nobody dare steal even a grain of wheat under direst temptation. Why? They knew they'd be named in the moment."

"What about the two from Mouras Bentos?" himself asked. "They could have died. That would have been murder. And how were they brought here? Who invited them?"

"That's quite another pair of chicken," Brother Mihaul said, taking a fork to the lemon slices. "I was coming to it. Let's finish about what's being done here, first. How long were you outside?"

"A few minutes, no more," The O'Dancy said. "You've altered this place. I felicitate you. You're living differently to the way I ever thought. I'm glad. It sets a fine example. I haven't been much of a one."

"Now I'll argue with you about that," Brother Mihaul said with some of his old aspirity. "You've been a wonderful example of a man minding his own business. It was always a cold night-fear of my own that you'd come down here one of these days, full of zeal and the Creature, and start trying to encourage me. You never did, and I thank our Father in heaven. For if you'd known about these things before, you'd have destroyed them. I know it. But if you had, you see, I'd have had to start all over again elsewhere. As it is, I've had the time, through these years, to instruct these people, or the majority of them. And I've found the way, now, to destroy both *macumba* and *khimbanda*. *Umbanda's* the potent force, and those who worship in that form can only grow in the spirit until, gradually, the restlessness leaves them, and they can, or their children one day will, go wholly to God and the Church, without artifice. At the same time, I'm not sure of it. I believe even Mother Church will find something to her benefit in this. It's a prayerful hope. A man must live 'for' something, not merely 'by.' That's in the scheme, of course."

Was the place Caserta, or wherever it was, that upside-down catacomb and tomb of the Spirit, and himself in a room, frozen, and lighting a fire in a bucket, and some fellow running in and telling him to put it out in case of fire, and the floor of tile and the walls of stone, and himself telling the busybody to go to hell, anyway, and busybody coming back with a gent all ribboned above the left teat, a prize cow, doubtless. Well, yes, remembering the orders given in a small voice, or else clear out, and go back to

Naples, and I shall send your general officer commanding a report, that was about how it was. No trouble about it at all, and himself telling the prize cow to go to hell, and leaving the fire burning, and collecting all the paper on the desk and pushing it anyhow into a bag, and leaving everything else, and going down those stairs, whistling for the first time since himself put foot in the hole.

In the jeep, dear tool of free men, turning that corner over the rail crossing, and seeing her under the trees, waiting, a beautiful major, no less, and himself pulling up and saluting, and she saluting, and in her eyes, the bluest, clearest blue and quiet home of smiles, a question about his uniform, and she getting in and showing that leg, think dearly, if it was never a kiss for the eyes, and she introducing herself, would you not be knowing it, Penelope, no less, and himself falling in love with the sound, every syllable, and telling her so and she laughing, and suddenly the day in a shine, no longer that cold, muddy-road, bare-branch gray of Italian winter, but even a degree or so above zero, and was it sunny or not, no matter, for the sun was in a lovely woman's heart and she warmed the world, and a whole sward of violets in dearest bloom in thought of her, now.

"If it's all the same to your honor's self, I'm a colonel of the Eireann inconceivables," himself said.

"Have the Irish declared war?" she said, and hands up, together, under the chin of her. "How marvelous."

"I see no marvel in it," himself said. "Have we ever been not at war? When's there been peace between us and anybody? We hate the sinful world."

"Which regiment did you say you were?" she asked.

"The inconceivables," himself said. "Nothing born of optimism. We're out of a dried egg."

"But are you infantry, cavalry, artillery, or what?" she asked.

"A little of each," himself said. "Nothing too much. We're great believers in taking things as they come."

"You sound like the forty thieves," she said. "Ali Baba was always a great favorite of mine."

"Ali FitzOcham Baba," himself said. "Let's be having the thing right, now. One of the Kilkenny Babas. He was the regiment's first colonel. We have his insignia. Forty empty pots. It's always been an aggravation. Empty pots and whistling women, nothing worse can happen."

"Show me your identity card, will you, please?" she said, and out with her own.

Nothing for it, because there was plenty of traffic and all she had to do was make a sign.

"Colonel Arquimed Rohan O'Dancy Boys," she read, and laughed the wide one, the happy one. "United States of Brazil. Isn't that awfully strange? I was hoping to meet somebody in the Brazilian Army. I had a friend at school. She was Brazilian. Her father was Japanese."

"She lived in São Paulo," himself said instanter. "Ten thousand lire, I'll tell you her name."

"I haven't got ten thousand," she said. "I'll bet you ten."

"I'll take a kiss rather than ten times ten thousand," The O'Dancy said.

"On," she said. "What's her name?"

"Soyaki Tomagatsu," himself said.

"Magician," she said, and laughed. "Of course it was. Do you really know her?"

"And her great-grandfather, the finest man ever born, and she as dear a girl as I could ever dream," himself said. "And a head on her. A physician. You're with the medical corps, then?"

"No," she said. "I went mad, and got into something else. Where is Soyaki?"

"She's up in a place called Campinas," himself said. "Last time I heard, she'd two children, both boys. But she keeps the clinic going. Are you married?"

"I was," she said, looking in front. "My husband was killed last year."

The falter in the voice. Drive straight to the front, a little faster, a little more relaxed, but for Christ's sake, now, be warned, no word of sympathy. Between himself and herself, only Daniel, and the boy was another born for His Majesty to regret to inform, but, yes, there were others equally dear. That was a small surprise, anyway. Himself had never given a thought to others' tears.

"Would it be, do you suppose, a good idea to stop for lunch?" himself said after a long time. "I know a place off the road, here."

"If it's any tiny degree different from those rations," she said. "Even at the club it tastes the same. Chalky bread, and glung."

"I promise you considerable difference," himself said. "To begin with, it's in the finest tradition of the Neapolitan kitchen. There's no better."

Mama Guaraglione was around the back of the house, with the ducklings at her skirt ends, hanging up the wash.

"Do you never do anything except scrub and cook?" himself called. "Here's a princess I've brought. What's in the pan for us, now?"

She raised the hands, well, brown claws, yes, and held her face, brown too, lined with the deep, regular wrinkles of those whose time has been of the fields under the sun with sweat for ointment, and she smiled the light of ancient eyes and perfect white teeth, whiter because of the amber skin, and sang his name, and lifted one side of her skirt a fraction, and came toward him in the tarantella, and they danced a couple of steps, and she bent her old bones, laughing. They had a lunch of dish after dish, and the wine as usual, and himself brought the coffee from the jeep, with a box of tinned goods.

"Stolen rations?" Penelope said, tunic off, tie off, hair down, chin on hands. "I wish I'd known."

"I don't steal," The O'Dancy said. "These are my rations for a week. I save them for her, and she cooks for me."

"How did you find this?" Penelope asked. "Everybody else is so lucky. They fall into things."

"This was our bivouac area off the ship," himself said. "I had a headquarters here. I've others farther up. My country places. I've an apartment in Naples. Be having no curious notions. I buy what I want."

"How fortunate you are," she said. "Have you been in action?"

"I have," The O'Dancy said. "I'm a little aged for it. It's a young man's business."

"Where were you?" she asked.

"On top of a mountain farther north," himself said. "I'll let you into a secret. Our greatest enemy isn't the German, though he's bad enough. It's ice, and snow, and a freezing wind. A *brasileiro's* fathered by the sun. Take away the sun, and heat, and he'll die of pneumonia. That's what happened. We left half a brigade up there."

"Should you tell me that?" Penelope said. "How do you know who I am?"

"Who gives a Christ-damn who you are," himself said. "Not I. You're a woman. That's enough."

"It's not by any means enough," she said. "We're fighting a war. People are dying while we sit here."

"It makes no difference to what's a man and what's a woman," himself said. "Because a lot of pin-brained politicians shove millions into shooting each other, is that any good reason why I must become somebody else? Think like somebody else? To hell, if there's any war to be fought, we ought to fight it as ourselves. I'll tell you this. You closemouthed people give away more information by what you don't say than any loose-mouthed from chatter. You, for example. You're in chemical warfare. Why surprised? It's in that identity thing you've got there. If you know what you're looking for. You've had a rough time for the past couple of weeks and you've got a week's leave, or more, or you wouldn't have that bag and the haversack. If you were going away or up the line, you'd have a lot more. Wouldn't you? What do you suppose they'll do without you? A whole week without Penelope? Will any of us survive?"

"All right, Sherlock, you're near enough," she said, and drank the wine. "This is very good. But people are still dying. And we're sitting here."

"And pleasantly enough," himself said. "Let's talk more about living than dying. We'll die, anyway. Those who've died are saved dying later. One kind of death instead of another. Death anyway. So? Live."

"You don't believe in everlasting life?" she asked while himself was opening another bottle. "It's difficult to know what we'd do with ourselves. Living's bad enough. Isn't it?"

"Don't confuse your own conception of life with everybody else's," himself said. "I think you're a little tired. You've had a great deal to contend with. Some of us get knocked about to such an extent we stop feeling. We stop using our senses. We function on commands. Somebody issues an order. We obey. Like machinery. We know what to do. We do nothing for ourselves. It's more comfortable. It's a horrible state of mind. It's subhuman. Next stop, the psychiatric ward. That's why it's full. People stopped thinking for themselves. They stopped living for the time being. They exist."

"That's right," she said. "That's how I feel. The more one knows the more one realizes what disgusting brutes we are."

"I'd never think it of yourself," The O'Dancy said.

"I'm part of it, and hating it," she said. "Misuse of brains and vitality at one end, sheer horror at the other."

"You'd not be talking about Acquapendente, would you?" himself asked. "We got there just after."

"Where's that?" she asked.

"It's a village up the road," himself said. "The French put in the *Goumiers Maroc*. It's an Arab lot. The Germans left. The *Goums* went into this village and raped everybody. Men, women, and children. All ages. Anyway at all, and more than once. If you'd seen those people, I can tell you, you'd accept all that falls with absolute equanimity. Not because their bodies were grossly mishandled. Their minds were assaulted. Dignity, pride, decency, the smaller sensibilities, gone. An entire village of scores of families deprived of spiritual, mental, or physical substance. Mothers handled in front of sons. Sisters before brothers. Fathers before daughters. Sons before their mothers. Babies. How will they live together in the years to come?"

"Don't, please," she said, and turned, upsetting the glass. "There. Now, what's Mama G going to think?"

"Be sitting quietly, and she'll take care of it," himself said. "Would you care to go to the opera tonight?"

"I'd simply love to," she said, and the blue eyes smiling again. "I hope it's *Madame Butterfly*. That was the last opera I heard with Soyaki. A dozen of us went from school. She thought it ridiculous. We adored it."

"Japanese, they're all the realists of all realists," himself said. "And the greatest poets of all. That's strange. Some languages, they make a shape in the mind with a shape of words. The Japanese work in the spirit, gentle and beautiful and tender as a mass of sweet peas. Did you ever push the nose of yourself into a bowlful? That's it. Are there any words, at all? There are not. Then, be kneeling to God and giving thanks."

"I don't want to go on a church parade tomorrow, but I'd love to go to church," she said. "I feel empty. I'd love to fill up."

"Are you Catholic or pagan, or what else are you?" himself asked.

"I don't know," she said. "I'm anything that'll give peace. I used to go to confession. But I stopped. Army chaplains are such nothings."

"Now, I'm your man," himself said. "Tell you what. I don't know of any church in Naples or near here that'll rest the heart of you. The one I know is distant. Where will you stay?"

"I suppose," she said, but slowly, "Where I usually do. That I hate. That barracks."

"Mama G will give you a plain, whitewashed bedroom and a bath of hot water, here," himself said. "We'll rise at four-thirty. There'll be coffee, hot rolls, bacon and eggs at five. At five-thirty, we'll be on the road. About four hours to get there. The most useful service in the world in the world's loveliest church. You know why? They've nobody to appeal to except Almighty God. Everybody's passed them by. Nobody gives orders. Nobody tells anybody what to do. No church politics. No clerical maneuvering. Simply priests in exercise of a sacred calling. And about a dozen people. Those who didn't lose their faith."

"Where is it?" she asked.

"Find out when we get there," himself said. "Will you sleep here?"

"Yes," she said.

"Then you'll be at the opera tonight, and in church tomorrow," himself said. "Get your baggage out, have a bath, lie down. Mama G'll call you at five."

She stretched her arms wide, and ruffled her hair.

"It's rather nice to be jollied about by a man, again," she said, and got up, and walked out.

But it was ballet, not opera, and he got a box almost on the stage, and she sat through *The Enchanted Toyshop*, enchanted her own beautiful self, and when they came out in a clumping horde of khaki uniforms, she wanted nothing except to go back to Mama G's. They did, but off the main road, out of the traffic, along the quiet lanes under the trees, through the vineyards, to Papa Tomaso, and him still open, with bits of cotton alight in little pots of oil, and the place filled with the faces of olden Rome, and playing *truco*, and dominoes, and gambling fortunes in wooden toothpicks, not a cigarette among all of them, not a cup of coffee, not a glass of beer, wine, or anything else. Welcome for an emperor himself got, too, and bringing out the cartons of cigarettes, and a dozen vermouth, and a couple of brandy, and his own bottle of whisky appearing, a small marvel, saved from the last time.

"There's my conception of honesty and decent friendship," himself said to her. "Did the man know I was coming back? He did not. But the bottle's put by. He said if it was fifty years, it'd still be put by. These people are starving. They haven't a smoke. Or a drink. Nothing to cushion the aches of living."

"They shouldn't have started the war," she said.

"Oh, now, wait a little," The O'Dancy said. "What did these ever start except a family, and the spring seed? Wars aren't born here. Go to that office in Rome. And the other sty, in Berlin. These poor ones, they have the small riches of their lives torn away from them. Mama G lost her husband and two sons. Cattle, sheep, livestock, farm tools, everything. We rebuilt the house for her. She was living in a cave at the back, there. What, do you think, except the Virgin's own tears, would ever console her?"

"But she's so cheerful," Penelope said.

"Oh yes," himself said. "She's cheerful, and God love her every moment."

She was still up and cheerful when they got back, and himself put the pocket alarm on for four-thirty, but late as it was, Penelope put an iron on the hob, and cleared the table to press a uniform. The alarm and the owls woke him, and he found his own uniform on a hanger, looking brighter than it had for some time, and his boots polished. Penelope came down in shirt sleeves, pillow-plump about the eyes, and beautiful, and Mama G kissed her before she got in the jeep, and said she blessed the house. Off, through the side roads, away from military traffic, through villages in ruins, and towns half destroyed, and past farm houses staring from hollow windows, and over the bulldozed tracks through barrage areas, among wrecked vineyards, and splintered orchards, hour after hour, and possibly fifty people seen on the way, old women, old men, sometimes a child.

"The country's deserted," Penelope said. "What on earth will they do?"

"What Italians have always done," himself said. "They'll work."

They came out of the trees and joined the road going up the hill, crowned by the black and white cathedral among the olives in groves, all in a float on cypress against a blue sky and ruffs of white cloud, and no sign of life in the place until they were into the narrow streets, and through the archways, and a few men recognizing himself and bowing, and following along to the great doors. They went in, and he sprinkled the holy water on himself, and on her, and they sat down in front near the altar. She was long on her knees, and himself looked at the ciborium, up at the dome, at the simple ornaments, and the choir of monks sang a magnificent Te Deum. The service was in Latin, with only a few people from the city in the place, but the choir left rich memory in the vault. Afterward he drove to a vineyard, and took out a cloth, and the food Mama G had packed, and a fine bottle of white wine one of the men had given him, and they ate and said no word, in the green vine's shade all jeweled about in the clustrous grape, a fine, long white, and a small, amazingly sweet black, and wild flowers about, and he made a crown of them, and set it over the brows of her, and she lay back, and turned over, and drowned, then, in the bitter, O, the bitter tears.

Himself walked off, downhill, and sat on a slab and smoked a few cigarettes, but what thoughts they are at those times are always in one ear and never a thing coming out anywhere at all. She was still in a quiver when he went back, and he helped her on with her jacket, and set her tie straight, and put the hat on with the badge between her eyes, and the tears were still in fall, and there were wild-flower petals in her hair, and he left them for beauty, and a touch of God, and grief.

Halfway he stopped and lit a fire, and made coffee, and a few women gathered, and they all had a drink, but Penelope stayed in the jeep and a little boy climbed up in her lap, and she put her arms about him and they shared the mug. When he drove off the women blew kisses and waved them out of sight.

"Why didn't you give them the coffee?" she asked.

"There wasn't enough to share," himself said. "If I'd tried to, they might have had a cat fight after we'd gone. Hungry people are no great respecters of the person. I've seen it happen. They got a tin of beef, instead."

"Another week's ration," she said.

"That's right," The O'Dancy said. "I've a month's rations for four aboard here. The other three are dead."

If himself had ever hoped to swallow his tongue, then it was, for the tears started again, but then she took an enormous breath that broke on a half sob, and instantly she sat straight, and wiped her eyes, and was herself, and beautiful.

"I've never cried like that," she said. "Thank heaven I met you. That wonderful ballet last night, and that glorious cathedral today. And such a wonderful day altogether. And Mama G, I love that room. And it's a copper bath. She polishes it. I've been a wretched nuisance. I'm ashamed."

"You're nothing of the kind," The O'Dancy said. "You needed every living moment of it. A stiff upper lip's all right in its way. If ever it breaks, it might take the heart and soul, as well. You've nothing to feel shame about. You're a fine woman. There's none happier than myself that we met."

"I'm glad we did," she said. "I'd quite intended to kill myself today. Or tomorrow."

Himself stopped the jeep in the quiet lane, and birds were still at song.

"Give me the gun," The O'Dancy said. "Don't be arguing. I felt it when I held your jacket."

She reached inside, and took out the heavy little brute, and its warmth lay in his hand for a moment, and he threw it far into the brier.

"There are lots of other ways," she said.

"Don't be thinking of them," himself said. "Remember. There are prayers for you, too."

She put her arms about him, and kissed him, but he kept his hands on the wheel, for he knew himself.

"Hadn't kissed anyone for years," she said, and sat back. "It seemed time."

"Will you be doing that again when we get to Mama G's?" himself asked.

She looked away, smiling, and nodded.

Next morning, when he took her in a cup of tea, she was sitting knees-to-chin in the copper bath, and her grace in a puddle of light from a window high up in the wall, and the gleam of her whiteness in clear, greenish water ringed about by shining red copper on black-and-white tiles ever held the heart of himself, and the tea was getting cold while he kissed her breasts, and he had to go down for another.

"Darling, this is better, it really is, than being dead," she whispered. "It is all for something, isn't it? If it's only for this?"

"What else is it for, then?" himself whispered to her. "It all begins with this, does it not? Without this, and what comes of it, is there anything?"

Ten days later, and himself waiting those hours at the café down there by the palace, and no sign of herself, supposedly coming in for a couple of hours' shopping. Back to Mama G's hoping, but nothing except Mama G's surprise. Back to the café, and the man he had left there telling him that no woman officer had stopped, or passed by. Around all the clubs and messes, and nobody that looked like her, and a rat gnawing at the heart of himself. Back to Mama G's, and again, only the soft sorrow of ancient eyes and praying hands. A night's vigil brought nothing except the first song of a bird while the morning star was yet gold. Into the jeep and out to Caserta, and the place more a tomb with more prison stench with every pace into it.

"Ah yes, sir," the woman clerk said, at the telephone, and startled.

She put the telephone down, and looked at himself, and at the pencil she held.

"She died at three o'clock yesterday," she said. "Some sort of fever, they said. I'm terribly sorry."

"Fever," The O'Dancy said. "When will the funeral be?"

"It was last night," she said.

He found the place, and he got a marble cutter from Naples, and together they planned a fair distyle, with an amphora, and he paid a woman in the village to keep the flowers fresh, week by week, and, when there were none, to dress perennials by the bunch so that never should thought of her be less than green and beautiful.

"This won't be allowed," an officer said while the masons were putting the slabs together. "It's a military cemetery. She'll be sent home, you know."

"Until she is, here's where she'll be," The O'Dancy said. "If any bastard-son-of-a-whore so much as sets a finger near, I'll kill him. I don't speak a tremendously good English, but are we anywhere in near distance of understanding each other?"

"I get the substance," the officer said.

"That's all we have a need for," himself said. "You can put the regimental insignia down here at the foot. Up there will only be her own name. Penelope. That's music enough to founder the world, and beauty to light us all forever."

"You loved her," the man said.

"I did," The O'Dancy said, and wept, bloody fool, and the man put a hand on his shoulder, and left. A good fellow, and himself found out where he was and sent him a case of the best.

So.

Penelope.

24 Brother Mihaul spoke at the telephone out there as if to Tokyo without any line at all, in his own not inconsiderable church-filling bellow.

"They want you at The House," he said, with his head around the doorway. "A matter of great moment, doubtless. Four of them, and Mr. Carvalhos Ramos. Now, there's a prize beauty."

"Don't be insulting the best legal brain in the country," himself said.

"The most accomplished pharisee of the epoch," Brother Mihaul said. "An egregious example in any language. A thief. How did such a father produce such a son?"

"Wasn't the father," himself said. "It was circumstance. In a system of thieves, you must be a better, or the best, thief. He's the best. That's why he's my lawyer."

"I wonder will there ever be a finer pair," Brother Mihaul said. "Now will I be letting you know the rest of what's going on here, or have you had enough?"

"The two supposed to be corpses," The O'Dancy said. "Hilariana's prepared to swear both were door-knocker dead. I spoke to one a couple of hours ago. Alive and half kicking. The other's supposed to be in equally good health. I never knew there was any rising from the dead in *macumba*. Is there?"

Brother Mihaul sighed at the teapot, nodded the gray head, and looked up at the golden star of David on the wall to the left of the altar.

"We'll have to go back to the beginning, here," he said. "The greatest physical influence in the *macumba* rite is African. There's not much doubt about it. There's a traditional coming-to-life on the African West Coast to this day. The spiritist influence is far more Indio, of this continent. Inca, Aztec, Guaraní, and all the subpeople have a lot in common, though they're not by any means the same, and they shouldn't be confused. But their manner of worship, in essence, was spiritist, and it's plain there was a trance condition. *Macumba's* an African part of speech that signifies that little scratching instrument they use to generate a particular rhythm."

He walked over to the wall and took a conch off a rack of other instruments, and a short length of swordfish bill, and drew the edge over the serrated lip of the shell in a snore, louder or softer as he applied pressure. Behind the curtain, a bass drum picked up a contrarhythm, and a tenor drum, and a lighter drum rippled a cross-beat.

"*Atabaques*," he said, and drew the curtain, showing Eloy's stare behind a long drum, and Uvald' behind a smaller, and Orestes with the smallest between his knees. The rhythms were not new, effect was not new, but for all that, never mind that the men were known, and The Inheritance lay beyond the door, and Brother Mihaul was nearest kin to himself, a chill was starting in the hackles.

"I'd never put up with much of it," himself said.

"There's too much Indio in you, not to mention the African," Brother Mihaul said, and pulled the curtain. "Grandam Xatina was almost pure Ashanti. You can't go much higher than that. I feel it, of course. That's what brought me into this. Instinct, intuition, call it anything. Well, then, where the *atabaques* are, and there are always three, the big one, the smaller, and the little one, that's the place of the *candomblé*. That rhythm helps to bring on the trance condition. In the lighter state, there are ceremonial dances for men and women. The male dancer must always express himself physically. The chief spirits are believed to choose a champion among them, and they arm themselves with blades between the toes. Well, of course, their feet are almost like hands. They're extremely prehensile, and there they go, dancing in circles and jumps around each other in a great looping of arms and legs, powerful and quick as healthy men can be, and they often die of bloodlet before anybody's noticed they're hurt. The one who cuts the others most, or the one, let's say, left standing up, that's the champion, and he's supposed to have the most powerful spirit looking after him. Everybody heaps him with gifts until he meets somebody better. The two last night were victims. They met a champion in Julião."

"Julião, my God," The O'Dancy said. "Don't tell me he's a *macumba* fellow?"

"One of the worst," Brother Mihaul said. "He's gone. He'll never come back here."

"Dead," The O'Dancy said.

"Dead to *khimbanda* forevermore," Brother Mihaul said. "We put the cross on him, and the holy water, and he's off and away, free of the devil and all his works, all praise, now, and Light about us."

The O'Dancy stood.

"You're making me nervous," himself said. "I can't take it in. Knives between the toes? I've seen the dance. I never saw any knives. That's Bahia nonsense."

"Julião is from The Inheritance, and his father, and many a father before him," Brother Mihaul said. "He didn't use a knife. He had razor blades between his toes. We had to put poor Glicerio back very carefully, I can tell you. His tripes were all over the floor."

"You doctored him," The O'Dancy said.

"Paul was there before me," Brother Mihaul said. "He put the cure to him. In trance."

His eyes never flickered under scrutiny. They stared back, gray, untroubled, smiling.

"But you believe it," The O'Dancy said. "There's no doubt in the mind of yourself? You're saying what you know to be a fact?"

"I was present, and many another," Brother Mihaul said. "You have Hilariana for witness. You saw the man. What more?"

"If I were to dare to say men were raised from the dead, what'd happen to me?" himself said.

"Well, what?" Brother Mihaul asked, and enjoying himself. "It's been done many a time before. When was the last time you saw a doctor on the place?"

"We'll soon have a good one in the family," himself said. "He'll put a few of you quacks where you'll do no more damage."

"You're speaking of Stephen, of course," Brother Mihaul said, and a whole wreathing of smiles about the head of him. "I believe he's the only pride I have. He'll be a supreme surgeon. To say nothing of a wonderful physician. The boy's dedicated. He's as I was, and the Lord God be praised."

"You?" The O'Dancy said. "You gave him a lesson or two in Latin, and what else?"

Brother Mihaul laughed, the true O'Dancy guffaw, and a bright world of honest delight was in it.

"Oh, Arquimed, don't you know he's the greatest medium of us all?" he said. "Brought up into it, here. Entered into his first trance at about six years of age. Raced through school. Look at his university status. But he'll dedicate himself to our people, you see. He'll not choose the way of wealth. It's too simple. He's chosen the Shepherd's crook. Not the other kind."

The O'Dancy stood, and passed dry hands over the beard, and heard it, yes, almost with relief.

"I'll have a word with the boy in the light of this," himself said. "Have you put a spell on that defenseless head with your nonsense?"

"Spells are in your own vocabulary, along with witches, and elves, and all the dear little fairies and wills-o'-the-wisps," Brother Mihaul said. "That's a well-trained, healthy brain. He'll devote himself to physical well-being as I devoted myself to the spiritual. Between the two, and what's going on among the believers, we'll pray to achieve the health Almighty God meant for all of us."

"You can't annoy me," The O'Dancy said. "I've iron in the soul of myself. I've sworn to burn this poison out. Burn it out I will."

"You'll be prevented," Brother Mihaul said, serious and cold, and leaning back in the chair. "Remember what I tell you. One way or the other, in conformance with the will of God, you'll be prevented. There's been too much work here. Too many souls saved."

"Saved?" The O'Dancy said. "To be burned in hell?"

"That will be decided by their Judge," Brother Mihaul said. "You'll grovel before the same Eye with us all. In that day there'll be no hiding anything or 'saving' anybody. We've had all the proof we need in this room. We know a little about the Judgment."

"You've heard the Judgment here?" himself said. "Am I to believe in your sanity?"

"What does it matter what you believe?" Brother Mihaul said. "Does it matter what overgrown children believe? They've time to learn. There are some to teach them. Time and intelligence are on our side. Only a little while ago the airplane was a dream. Today, people are off to the moon. And I tell you, at that table, we've heard the testimony of some of the souls, judged, and passed on for work in our own world, and others. You, for example, heard the passage of words at the trial of Iscariot. There's no proof, and therefore no validity. Yet. But it'll come."

"You taught them Latin, of course, to give it a semblance," The O'Dancy said. "It just struck me."

"Then let it strike you again, as it struck me, like a thousand times ten thousand flaming thunderbolts, no less," Brother Mihaul said. "None of them speaks a word of any language except his own, and that one not very well. Not one's a scholar. Paul and Stephen, I except. But that's not a Latin I know. Or that I ever heard, except here. Those are the spoken words of two thousand years ago. They're coming back to us through the simple, cleanly spirits of those men. And their women. Tonight we meet again. With the blessing of Almighty God, we shall pray to hear the trial of the Lord Jesus Christ, and to be present at the Crucifixion. What have you to say to that?"

"I thought I knew, and I thought I'd heard, every phase in the corrosion of blasphemy," The O'Dancy said, "I find I have, indeed, been a child. You only make me the more determined to burn the place out of the ground. Don't be holding any meeting here tonight. Be warned, now. I'm going to burn the place out of existence. Telephone Democritas Pereira for transport and any help you need. Save those icons out there. I'd never want to destroy marvels of handiwork."

Brother Mihaul's smile disturbed by the clear light in the gray eyes, leaning back there, dressing the white pleats of the habit over his knees.

"There was ever only the handiwork of one, and himself in trance, and taking instruction," he said. "In the past few years. Myself."

"But I'll never believe it," The O'Dancy said.

"Painted there, with many a thousand in witness, by now," Brother Mihaul said, looking at the table. "Myself, that could barely draw my breath, painted, and carved, as you say, marvels. But without a single recollection. It's not in me. It was put in me, though. I'm not moving from here. If you wish to burn, then burn me with it. You're blood brother to those who burned the books at Alexandria. To those who crucified. To all those humbugs who profess to believe. Burners of witches. Hangmen and stranglers. Crudest manifestation of the worst in the human spirit. The sort we deal with. As we shall one day have to deal with you."

"Somebody else'll be giving the orders," The O'Dancy said. "At the moment, here, it's myself, and I'm telling you now, be out at midnight. The day's not ended, and a cruel one it's been, but I'll have the place cleansed and purified in time for the Rising of the Man."

"Why should you be caring about the Rising, sententious, impoverished humbug you are?" Brother Mihaul said, but pleasantly. "Did you never pass through the eye of a needle? A dedicated pilgrim along the way of fornication. How many bastards have you?"

"None," The O'Dancy said. "My children are all citizens and all well looked after. I've added to the country's riches. That's more than you've ever done."

"I never so misused myself," Brother Mihaul said. "If we hadn't relatives on the Bench and other places, you'd have been in prison many a time. The country's uncivilized, or you'd be behind the bars on how many counts of rape?"

"Never raped a woman in my life," The O'Dancy said. "Not worth the trouble."

"Is making a mother out of a fourteen-year-old anything else but rape?" Brother Mihaul said. "You've done it many a time. The little one, Ahatubai, is this moment in labor. Give thanks you're The O'Dancy. You'd have been dead these months."

"Ahatubai?" himself said. "Do I remember her?"

"How should you, among so many?" Brother Mihaul said. "She's daughter of Alcides. He was at point of swearing to kill you, but we prevailed. He resigned himself. Young Carvalhos Ramos signed the documents."

"I'd never heard of it," himself said. "I'll have a word with him. I'm miserable about it. I am. Miserable."

"Miserable," Brother Mihaul said in a whisper, part of the confessional. "To have the grace. Miserable? And what about Ahatubai? Should she not be in a transport of all delight? And her poor mother? And the father, breaking his heart? The beauty she was, the little one, Ahatubai."

That was it, the night of the argument, down at the cane mill, and the bullocks turning the crushing wheel, and through the groans and squeaks, the sugar spouting silver down in the vat, and Alcides coming along with a tray of glasses and a bottle of sugar brandy from the last fermentation, and Simão Tomagatsu pouring the *sake* he brewed at the rice farm, and all of them comparing glass for glass, and deciding they preferred beer. It was a fine night to laugh, for the rice yield was the greatest ever, and the price was highest, and the sugar cane was sold before it was cut, more than himself had ever planted before, and at half any previous cost because of the new tractors. Max Uberlander drank with them, come to bid for the cotton, and Lars Widttebolt, the tractor factory director, brought the new assembly-line plans for himself to see, and there were others, and Professor Riskind, in his nineties, but clearer in the head than many a sprig.

"If the men in government could forget, for a moment, this sterile mother they call their country, and bring in a quarter of a million schooled Europeans to counterbalance the African dead weight here, then in two generations Brazil could be with the earth's leaders," the Professor said. "As it is, the African and the Indio must always be the most important political influence. They have the numbers. They are free to vote as they wish. If they feel they want to work, very well, they work. If not, not. But no country 'grows' in that manner. No country lives. It exists. In doubt. Inquietude. Uncertainty. There is no brain. No dominant mentality, except that of the most impressionable uneducated. Never mind how many professional men are employed and no matter what they do, that weight of ignorance will destroy them. It is simply a matter of time. The Armed Services will restrain the indisciplined up to a point. But when the economy of the country comes under the power of the politically misinformed, then the Armed Services will be seen for what they are. Excrescences on the body politic. Useless. An empty threat. They'll kill some, wound others. But the very workmen they kill and wound are those who paid in sweat to buy the rifles and grenades that killed them. And the wages and pensions of their murderers. But then, work stops. Bankruptcy supervenes. First private. Then public. And finally, national. So? No money to pay the Armed Services? Then? No Armed Services."

"Without the threat of armed intervention, what could happen in this country?" Lars Widttebolt asked. "Anarchy? I prefer the Armed Services."

"You will have anarchy in any event," Professor Riskind said. "With few exceptions, not enough to disprove, much less to prove a rule, your students are below any standard elsewhere. Many of them can bribe an examiner into a pass. Because many a professor earns less than a mechanic, far less than a secretary. There are many professors, of course, who cannot be bribed. Politically, how long do they last?"

"You are unnecessarily bitter, sir," Max Uberlander said. "We must make allowances. The young men here seem to me as healthily capable as any others anywhere else. I have some very good boys working for me."

"I have taught 'some' very good boys," Professor Riskind said. "The majority were hopeless. What they call here playboys. Nothing but the toys of their fathers."

"Toys," Lars Widttebolt said.

"Little toys," Professor Riskind said, and looked at him over the pince-nez. "Papa says, Ah, my son, you shall have an easier life than myself. Here's a car. Here's money. Go anywhere you choose. Enjoy your young days. I was never able to. I will enjoy life through you. Go to the university. Pass your examinations. Or I will bribe your professors. So? Yes, so. So, Brazil dies. You don't expect growth or new ideas from that type of dry-nursed cretin, do you?"

"I'm a little appalled," Max Uberlander said. "My sons, certainly, are not that type. Which examiner can be bribed? You slander the profession. Every man or woman in the serious business of teaching is maligned. I think you are misinformed, sir."

Professor Riskind took the pince-nez off the end of his nose, and closed his eyes. He looked for a moment like a small, bald pekinese.

"My bladder protests," he said. "Where is the men's room?"

"Unless you care to walk half a mile, it's behind the nearest bush," himself said. "Our fathers knew nothing about porcelain troughs, chains, or anything else of the kind, at all. They let it go, wherever it was. There wasn't anything else, do you see? Same as this place."

"I choose the hibiscus," Professor Riskind said. "The disposal of sewage is a European invention. It still isn't understood in the greater part of this country. But it's the mental and social sewage I'm most concerned with. Spiritually, we might just as well discuss so many artifacts. Pardon me."

He raised himself out of the chair, and walked, almost lopsidedly, leaning on the heavy stick, toward the hibiscus.

"A very forbidding man," Lars Widttebolt said. "On general lines, I think he may be right. I don't think we've got enough young ones to take on where we leave off. I don't see it in any of my sons. I may be wrong."

"But why did we come here?" Max Uberlander said, and opened his hands on his knees. "We wanted to make something? We had the European urge? Make money? I acknowledge it. I wanted to. I did. But my children never heard me say that. They grew up naturally. Aren't they interested in things that interest me? I wasn't interested in the things my father was interested in. Why should I be angry with my children? Aren't they as clever as I am? Pity. But do they laugh, and sing, and enjoy their lives? Ah yes. Then? I have no quarrel. They have a better life than I did. I shall die happily. I heard my children laugh. My father never heard me laugh. He didn't live long enough."

"Sentimental rubbish, dear sir," Professor Riskind called between whisperous bursts on the other side of the hibiscus. "I regret that another duty does not, for the moment, permit an appearance. Your father didn't live long enough? Neither did mine. The war of 1870 made me an orphan. My mother, whom I never knew, ate a rat. From hunger. My father died in the advance of the German Army. Neither was French. But it was fashionable to serve the French cause. It was supposed to be the most civilized nation on earth. It was not. It was merely the most genteel. More easily copied, swallowed, enjoyed. And enjoyment is the most difficult state to define, after happiness. I acknowledge I have been happier here, in Brazil, for the past forty or more years than, possibly, I could have been elsewhere. That is because, first of all, I had time to read, and to choose what I would read, and when, and where, and how, and nobody ever tried to prevent me. Imagine that. I taught. Nobody ever told me what to teach. Consider. I have had some thousands of pupils. In my opinion, the best of the earth. Of course. They were my pupils. Never did I have a failure. Fail at one examination? Then work for the next, and pass. Naturally, with a bribe."

"You were never bribed, of course," Lars Widttebolt said.

"But I was," Professor Riskind said. "The O'Dancy, himself, tried to bribe me. And failed. And why? Because Mr. Carvalhos Ramos paid me so much more. Nobody could bribe me. That doesn't say that I didn't bribe others. How did The O'Dancy pass in modern history? A bribe. In mathematics? A bribe. In literature? A bribe. For the rest, considering, he did very well. That was many years ago. But it could also be done today. It is certainly being done. There is nothing that cannot be bought. Money is the key. Is it wrong? Immoral? Is there a criterion? Does the country need one? The people themselves don't seem to think so. And we don't care what others think. We live. We grow. We flourish. God is a *brasileiro*. Isn't it so?"

Lars Widttebolt bent over the copper pan, trying to coax another *nogueira* nut to burn, but the match flared, and he flipped his fingers.

"In the name of sanity," he said. "Why don't you modernize this place? No electric light, running water, lavatories? Dirt roads, everybody like a redskin with dust? Lighting nuts to see who we are?"

"If it's not to your satisfaction, get in your car," The O'Dancy said. "The Inheritance is almost what it was nearly two hundred years ago. It won't be changed in my time. There's electric light in some of the houses. There's a bit of stone paving in the parkway. Most of us have a bathroom. A kitchen. But that's all. Go back to your factory. I prefer this."

"I think I'd agree," Max Uberlander said. "There's so little of the country that isn't exactly like everywhere else. Telephone poles, advertising signs, street lights, all the ugly errors of progress-that-isn't, and too few signs of growth. The best we've got is the architecture. Brasilia's going to be magnificent. It'll probably be the world's most magnificent city, unless the landowners get off the leash and build those damned piles of boxes."

"Won't be enough people wanting to live there for many a year to come," The O'Dancy said. "I've got a house there. But I've never lived there yet. I use the hotel."

"No servants?" Lars Widttebolt said. "It's a problem."

"It's not the servants," The O'Dancy said. "It's a new city. Nobody there. It's an uncommon quiet place at night. No wonder they can't get the women to stay. Will they ever?"

"In the old days the women stayed where they were put," Max Uberlander said. "Now, they do as they please."

"Some," The O'Dancy said. "Not all. This place is just as lonely. Most of the women are here since they were born. You understand the difference? A city woman might find herself lonely. What is lonely? Not enough inside the skin and bone of yourself? Need somebody else? Others? Streets? Lights? It's not a new disease. Radio's done a lot for it. Television's doing a fine therapeutic job in the town. They're just as lonely, there. We'll have it here, soon enough. Can you go anywhere without that damned noise? They're even walking about with a little box jammed to their ears. But there's too much empty space in this country to ignore the real problem. That's fear of loneliness. Fear of distance. And the quiet nights."

"Well, here again, now, see here," Lars Widttebolt said, and the pale blue eyes in a glint from the flame of *nogueira,* and long, fair hair lofting in a gentle breath. "I was a salesman for thirty years all over this country. How many thousands of men do I know with their own farms, and their wives and children, and lonelier than this?"

"Compared to the millions, what percentage?" Max Uberlander asked. "I wouldn't live anywhere except the city. And I don't blame others. To such a problem, I have no answer. Obviously, everybody cannot live in a town. Perhaps this is the mark of the foreigner. He or she must live in a town."

"Specifically, not," Lars Widttebolt said. "Most of the families I know came out here in the past thirty years. Brazilian, that's purely Brazilian families, principally landowners, they generally live in the towns or cities. For a few months each year, at any rate.

Wealthier, they travel. We can't afford to. We're foreigners. I don't want to, anyway."

"They'll always call us foreigners," Professor Riskind said, turning the stool with little taps of his stick. "Fifty years in this country, naturalized almost forty, but I'm still a foreigner. Three generations from now, your children will still be foreigners. To some. Africans, of course, are never foreigners. Indios, never. Afro-Indio, they're the blue blood. Portuguese extraction, with a touch of African and Indio, they're the aristocracy. So they think. And they call the rest of us foreigners."

"You think foreigner, that's why," The O'Dancy said. "I've got Irish, and African, and Portuguese, and Indio of many peoples in me. But I'm a foreigner to most. My name's foreign. It's not Portuguese or Indio. So? Is anybody worried? I'm not."

"You've got a curious accent," Max Uberlander said. "If you'll allow me."

"No more curious than any of ours," Professor Riskind said. "Certainly no more curious than millions of the so-called 'true' sons up and down the country. Listen to them up in Bahia. Or in Rio de Janeiro. Or down in the south. It's not the same language. But there must be foreigners. The simple must have their shield, the righteous prop. It preserves in them a sense of 'being' somebody. They are, so they think, *brasileiro*. They comfort themselves in their shiftlessness by proclaiming their 'oneness' with Brazil, their indifference to all outside influence. It excuses their indolence. Brazil swallows all, they say. But without the foreigner there would be nothing to swallow except hungry people, a few millionaires, and flies. What is truly foreign, of course, is the concept of work."

"Ah, but I've got many good men on my payroll," Lars Widttebolt said. "They work hard. Brazilians, all of them."

"Sometimes," Max Uberlander said. "I'll bet their fathers were Italian or German or Scandinavian. Or Japanese. Or North American. That's all I've got working for me."

"You're as bad as any of the people you call indolent," The O'Dancy said. "They have their defense, you have yours. They're contemptuous of you. You're disdainful of them. But old Mother Brazil knocks both your heads together. I agree with Professor

Riskind. As a former snotty-nosed pupil. We could do with a quarter of a million young technical fellows. Wed the girls that are here, settle down, work, produce, create an export surplus. Bring in a hundred thousand trained farmers. Give them the land and tools free for ten years. We'd be well up there in that time. We've a tremendous potential market in Russia and China. But we'd rather talk politics than markets. Dare mention doing business with China or Russia, you're a communist. Whether you're conservative or communist, does it matter? This country'll never be conservative, that's certain. And we'll never be communists, either. It's a cold-weather product. For a couple of hours during the day we wave a fan, or sleep. So? No communism."

"Many don't have that opinion," Max Uberlander said. "By law, a communist state could certainly be voted into power."

Professor Riskind laughed, and put his chin on his stick, and closed his eyes.

"Simão has been very quiet," he said. "What do you think, Simão? Born here, great-grandson of a famous man. Dear former, brilliant pupil of mine, what's your opinion?"

Simão had the look of his great-grandfather, but his spectacles flashed the light of the burning fat.

"We are in the growing period," he said gently, in the tight smile of small, white teeth. "Every country feels the pain of growth. Some men become rich. Others are envious. Able men are not envious. They have no time to think of others. They must do what they have to do. The incapable are envious. Envy leads to hate. There is a great deal of hate in this country. When I was in Japan two years ago, they told me how they hated Americans because they were in occupation. But they copied everything American. It is the strongest influence. Now the Americans have gone, and everybody wishes they were back. There was more money. If all the foreigners left Brazil, it would be the same. Those who were left would wish them back. Foreigners built Brazil her cities. Foreigners put the country on wheels. Built the roads, railroads, airlines. Foreigners found the oil fields, built the pipe lines and tankers. Foreigners created the majority of its industries. Foreigners people the cities, staff the factories, earn wages, create an economy. What is a Brazilian? For-eigners feed Brazilians. When I did my military service, I was never called by my name. I was called hey, you, Jap. Or Nippo. But those who called me that were often two generations behind me in naturalization. Should I have told them? Or made a complaint? Kick the wind. My great-grandsons will not be foreigners. They will be Brazilians. I shall be patient."

"And make money," Max Uberlander said.

"All I can, whenever I can, in whatever type of commerce," Simão said with smiling certainty. "It is my duty to direct myself, first. After that, to direct others. For this I was born, and educated, and trained. It is also my pleasure."

"Are you a happy man, Simão?" The O'Dancy asked. "You're what? Thirty?"

"Thirty-two, sir," Simão said, and bowed, even seated, and think of his great-grandfather, now, with a sheaf of golden lilies in the name of him and safe in the Light, forever. "I have no clear concept of the word. I would rather live the Japanese life. But I must live as a Brazilian. I must deal in business in the Brazilian manner. Very well. I deal. I have no regrets."

"But are you happy or contented?" The O'Dancy said. "To be without regrets, that's the emptiest way to live. You've sterilized yourself? You've swallowed a mental analgesic?"

"No, sir," Simão said, and made the slight bow again, deferentially. "I have my way to live. It pleases me."

"After all, that's true of myself, too," Max Uberlander said, and smoothed a hand over his tureen. "Come to think of it, I've put up with a lot simply to please myself. Now, possibly, that's the secret. To please ourselves, we let others please themselves? Is that it? It's an easy way to live, surely?"

"You don't have to worry about morals," himself said. "Your own or anybody's. Just be kind to appearances, that's all. That's about it. If it's anything very bad, or if it's birth or death, then you go to church, and hope. That's if you have anything in the heart of yourself for church. Church, after all, that's discipline."

"I'm not a Catholic," Max Uberlander said. "We've been Lutherans a long time."

"And are they not disciplinarians?" himself asked.

"Ah yes," Max Uberlander said. "Very strict. But there aren't many here."

The O'Dancy got up and stretched, and walked out to the limits
of the light, and beyond, to the dark path going down to the cane
press. Almost three times older than himself the place must have
been, and perhaps even older, for Grandfa Leitrim had lived in
The House for many a year before setting the bounds, and others
had been there before him, for it was a daughter of them he had
married, down there in the cane mill, and he cut two hearts and
their initials on the center post, and flowers had been put there
fresh by the day ever since.

Himself tried not to remember an impatience with the talk.
Every time two or three were gathered together, there was the
plaint in the midst of them. Always, never mind what, the shortcomings of Brazil, the venality of her people, the incompetence of
her ministers, the idleness, the stupidity, the everything-else, came
up for discussion by experts, and ended in the same way, in the air.
Always the shortcomings.

Rarely the blessings.

So often himself had wanted to rave at them. But as host, no.

"Never spit in a man's drink, or tread on a woman's skirt," The
Tad said that time. "If you're at home and rendering hospitality,
then let your guests do the arguing. For the time being, you share
the firmament with God Almighty. You'll listen, but you'll never
open your mouth. You'll agree, you'll encourage, you'll see the
glasses are filled. Apart from that, your duty is to make time itself
a pleasure."

Alcides had left the truck down at the stairway. Luiz came out of
the kitchen with a cup and saucer and a coffeepot, and went
down the steps, calling. Somebody moved in the back of the truck,
and Luiz poured a cup, and they laughed, and he went back, up
the steps, and into the kitchen, and the door slammed.

Only for the walk, himself went down the worn stones, considering, once again, the sweat in carting the hundreds of thousands of
slabs from the mountains, twenty to the ox-cart, two oxen to the
load, five days there, seven days back. Hundreds of men must have
spent their entire lives loading and walking, and unloading, and the
example was ever in the eyes of himself whenever laziness took him
by the lids. Somebody was looking at him from the back of the
truck.

"Well, and who's here?" himself called.

"My *pae* is Alcides Ribeiro," the clear, small voice said. "I'm waiting for him."

"Is there any reason to sit out here?" himself asked. "Would you not like a little to eat?"

"Thank you, I'll wait till we get home," she said.

"You might have some time to wait," himself said. "He's casting his books with the accountant. That's a long business. Come. Let me take you to the dining room. I'll tell him where you are."

"He'll be very angry," she said, still in the darkness of the truck. "I'm not supposed to be here. But I was coming from the bus."

"I'll talk to your pae," himself interrupted. "Sitting in a truck, indeed. Be doing me the pleasure. Accompany me to the dining room."

She stood, and came to the tailboard, in moonlight, and the blue glow of shadow in a dark skin, though lighter than her father's and small features, black hair wound in a bun on top with a ringlet of flowers, and a smile of white teeth, and held out her arms, and he took her about the waist. She lifted her knees to clear the edge, putting her weight on his shoulders, and he held the slightness, and lowered her, and she let her legs hang, and her arms were rigid for the moment, and while she slid against himself, slowly, he felt the woman, and she stood close, with no attempt to step away.

"You're the pae of Serena," she said, almost in a whisper.

"Yes," himself said. "Anything wrong about it?"

"No, nothing wrong," she said quickly, defensively. "But you're not her real pae, are you? You're her Grandpae, but she calls you pae."

"That's right," himself said. "What difference does that make?"

Her eyes were enormous, and, in appeal, consuming.

"I wish I could have everything I wanted," she said, and the teeth gleamed. "She does as she pleases, and she's only a year older than I am. Nobody ever says a word to her. But I stayed out after the school party and pae whipped me. Only twenty minutes. A cut for each minute."

"You're afraid of your pae," himself said.

"I hate him," she said quietly, amply. "I have a friend. We're going to Rio."

"A man," himself said.

"A girl," she said, and laughed. "We can type and we'll work in an office. We'll soon find places. But we'll stay out as long as we like."

"Supposing I tell your pae what you're thinking of doing?" himself said.

"You wouldn't," she whispered, and put her arms about him. "Please. No. Promise me."

"Then you'll promise me not to run away," himself said. "That's a warning. How much longer do you have at school?"

"Until examinations," she said, downcast. "I hate it."

"You hate," himself said. "Is there anything you love?"

"I love you," she said, up at him.

"Listen, now, this is nonsense," himself said, and took her by the hand. "Come. We're off to get a little to eat."

"Why doesn't anybody believe what I say?" she whispered, but on the edge of a scream, and stamped her foot in a spurt of dust. "Why is it nonsense? Is it because I'm only the daughter of a book-keeper? If my name was Serena Daniella Lys O'Dancy Boys, would you listen? She has everything. She can stay out. She has a car. A motorboat. Her picture's always in the magazines. Because she has a Grandpae? Because she has money? Why can't I?"

The O'Dancy looked down at her. At first she stared, but then she smiled. There was no bravado in her, but a clear kind of courage.

"I'll tell you how it is, here," himself said. "We're all born at a particular time and place, and we've all certain work to do, and it's a matter of faith."

She shook her head a wider and wider wag, and put up her hands to save the bun.

"No," she said. "I don't believe any of that. We make ourselves. Nobody else does. We do. And if we're born with money, it's easy. If we're not, it's difficult. The rest is simply a story. We're taking that, now. A matter of faith? I wrote an essay on it. Faith is what makes you believe a brick wall's a straw mattress. Walk through it, and discover your mistake."

"You have no faith?" himself said, walking a step or two up, and wondering what to say. "That's a calamity, is it not? Do you not go to church?"

"We must," she said. "I hate it. It's idolatry. Everywhere you look, an idol. And the priest talks about them as if they were real. Why should they teach one thing in school and another in church?"

"I don't know what they teach you," The O'Dancy said. "But I think it's a pity a bright one like yourself must think in such a manner."

"Haven't you talked to Serena?" she asked.

"About these matters, no," himself said. "Do you go to the same school?"

"I used to," she said. "But Pae couldn't afford the fee. We still write, sometimes. But our lives are different. She knows I'm poor."

"Nothing poor about you except the way you think," himself said.

"You say that because you're rich," she said. "If you weren't, you'd agree with me. What could you do if you were poor? What work could you do? You couldn't even keep the books, like Pae. Could you?"

"Perhaps," himself said. "You're a cheeky one, are you not?"

"Why am I cheeky?" she said. "Shouldn't I say what I think? Why do we go to school? Isn't that where we learn to speak? Then shouldn't we?"

"I suppose you should," himself said. "But it's a strange way to be talking for one of your age."

"Pae says that," she said, and stood still on the stair, looking at himself with the truly enormous eyes. "Is it necessary always to consider what age we are before we speak? Should I say, Very well, I'm nineteen, now I can speak of this and that? Or, I'm sixteen, so I can't discuss that and the other? But we know about many things. Why shouldn't we talk about them? They have to be lived through. Then when I'm twenty-three? Will that be the time?"

"A cheeky one," himself said. "You'll speak of things best when you understand them. We all know 'of' a lot of things we don't altogether understand, so it's better to keep silent. Isn't it?"

"How are you going to know or learn if you keep silent?" she asked.

"Looking and listening, and reading all you may," himself said.

"I've read everything," she said with fine impatience. "And books cost too much. We haven't the money. The library's too far. Serena gets in her car, of course."

"Envious of Serena," himself said.

"Well, who isn't?" she said. "All of us are."

"A remarkably unhealthy state," himself said. "Her presence there's not been a good influence, it seems to me. Would you like to go back to the academy?"

"Pae was too poor to pay for me," she said with a turn of the head. "No. Besides, what's the use? When I finish I'll still be poor. Like Pae."

"I don't know why your pae's so poor," himself said. "He earns well."

"Four brothers to go through school and university," she said. "The girl suffers. Always. He says it's not worth the risk of spending money, and then I get married. I shan't get married. I'll work. And I'll have all the men I want."

"Why do you think of men?" he said. "Isn't it more sensible to be thinking of getting married, and having a home of your own? I mean, when you're older?"

"If you weren't so old, you wouldn't talk like that," she said.

"You're being needlessly offensive," himself said. "I shan't believe you were taught to be rude at school or at home."

"It's true, isn't it?" she said, and looked at him.

Down where the leaves whispered and women mourned, the face of himself was held for that small moment in light that showed the grin. The scent of the girl's hair, the way she turned her chin to smile from the side—ah, Creonice, how shall the long-dead be blamed?—but the challenge was a hint in darkness, and the hands of himself were on her, and the blouse buttons came undone, one by one, and himself threw it over her shoulders.

"You'll have all the men you want," he said. "Am I one?"

"If you don't tell Pae," she said.

"I won't tell him," himself said. "You won't, will you?"

She shook the dark head.

The blouse fluttered to the floor. In deep shadow of the cane press himself saw little of her except soft light on the points of blunt breasts. Hooks made the unmistakable diminutive screech of disengagement. The skirt, part of darkness, fell, and Eve stood, in bluish glow of outline, munificent.

"Will you change Pae's truck for a car?" she whispered. "Then I can use it. If you tell him."

"I'll tell Democritas Pereira," The O'Dancy said. "What else is there you'd like?"

"Oh, I don't know, lots of things," she said, and slipped the white brief and in a couple of graceful dance steps, moved the hips and let it fall. "I can't have a motorboat. There's nowhere to keep it."

"Well, now," himself said. "Supposing I send your pae a membership to the club? You can do all the boating you want."

She put her arms about him.

"I love you," she said. "You are the first. The only one. 'A prince of riches,' they call you."

But there was never any doubt of shame in the mind of himself, and remembrance held the curse of misery, even if all was done that himself could think of, and she was helped to live as she wanted. Democritas was told to see about the car, and the membership, and to find out if Alcides wanted to keep her at the academy. Himself left for Japan, with Tomomi and the family a couple of days later, and in that time forgot. Long after, he heard her name.

Ahatubai.

"Miserable," himself said. "But she's had a better life these past months than she'd have had otherwise. I saw to it."

"Oh, listen to this, now," Brother Mihaul tremoloed, and held up his hands. "The thief spends stolen money more fondly than its owner, is that it? Was there ever a more benighted hypocrite? Ruining a child, and furnishing excuses? If there's anything to burn, why not set fire to yourself?"

"I'll doubtless have my turn," himself said. "I'll deserve it. But you be out by midnight. There'll be a cleansing tomorrow."

"I can think of no better place to burn than here," Brother Mihaul said, and sat back comfortably. "Let my ashes blow, too."

"Then they'll blow twice," The O'Dancy said. "Once here, and once again down there."

"No such place," Brother Mihaul said. "You'll have to serve a little time with us to find out what you're talking about. You're in for a few smart surprises."

"Fill your slaves with it," The O'Dancy said. "I'm of the Church."

"That's right," Brother Mihaul said, tranquil, that was what the man was. "Go back to your church, and especially the one at The House. Pay it a little visit. Go downstairs to the oratory. Have a good look around. I promise you a marvel. Look in the sacristy as a special duty. You never heard of a woman priest in the Church, did you?"

"What nonsense are you talking?" The O'Dancy said. "Do you dare suggest there's a sacrilege? What woman priest?"

"A friend of Hilariana's," Brother Mihaul said. "Introduced, I understand, by the person you 'married,' and her doxy."

"Ah well, now, here's the third time this day that one's come into the sun," The O'Dancy said. "Madame Briault? The years she's lived here, and how many times have I seen or heard her? What's she to do with it? And if you knew, why would you not tell me?"

"Without any proof?" Brother Mihaul said, and turned a priest's face, strait, and the pale eyes, deadly, and so calm. "There's a ceremony due to go on there, I don't know when. It should have been in another place last night, but we found them out and set the cross on them."

"At Mouras Bentos," himself said. Was that meat and stuff theirs, or yours?"

"Satan's," Brother Mihaul said, and lifted the crucifix. "His followers are here. That Briault woman introduced the peer of them all. A notorious creature. Own handmaiden to the devil. Beware her presence."

"If it was goose flesh you'd be giving me, you're out a few miles, I'll tell you that," The O'Dancy said. "What's this one's name?"

"I don't know what she prefers to call herself," Brother Mihaul said, and raised the crucifix a little higher. "Here, at The House, they call her mother Iemanja."

"Iemanja," The O'Dancy said. "Isn't that what they're going to call Hilariana, with her nonsense?"

"That's what the woman's here for," Brother Mihaul said. "If you permit any such crime, I don't know what you deserve."

"I'll not deserve much," The O'Dancy said. "I'm going from here to put a stop to that, first, and the rest will follow. Iemanja, is that it?"

"That's it," Brother Mihaul said. "They also, I'm told, call her Maexsa."

"Maexsa?" The O'Dancy said in no voice. "But I know the woman. I drank with her. Yes. I did. No later than this night just gone."

Brother Mihaul crouched back in the chair, and the lower teeth bit into the lip.

"Arquimed, Arquimed, now God save us, The Touch is upon you," he whispered, and in a wide fling of his arm, reached into a bowl and dipped the sprinkler. "All you do is cursed. All you say is perverted. All you think is betrayed."

He splashed the water into the face of himself, to the left hand, and the right.

"In the name of the Father, the Son, and the Holy Ghost," he prayed, and raised the crucifix. "Protect Thy son, Arquimed. Cast Thy Light about him. Suffer that he may walk among the fiends without harm, without fear, without temptation. Amen."

"Maexsa," The O'Dancy said, and the itch of water running down his face. "Well. No wonder I'd have paid anything."

25 In stretch gallop across the pasture to the Long Steps, The O'Dancy knew himself held to make immediate decisions in matters half known, or shammed lifelong, or impatiently cast aside, matters of concern to ex-slaves and their children, of possible or known interest to senior women of the family, but never of remotest moment to any of the men.

In a dry mouth, himself knew, and the soul of himself spoke true, that Brother Mihaul had the right of it.

There was utter need to bring simple people back to the Faith.

First thought that seemed to blaze, flame, fry, in stark infuriation, enveloped Hilariana in all entirety. Himself wondered how they could have been driven so far apart, once so warmly, gloriously close. The nights in Paris after her study, and weekends outside, and picnics along the shore south of Rio de Janeiro, and hunting trips up in the mountains beyond The Inheritance, all of them, so many of them, remembered to the detail. A thin-legged girl, with two long plaits that seemed to drop down into black stockings, watching an enormous jaguar, and lowering her rifle, and the jaguar rumbling and turning away, and padding off, each pad a single pound that seemed to shake the earth.

"Why did you not shoot?" himself asked. "He'd have been kind to your toes beside the bed, would he not?"

"He didn't try to hurt me," she said. "Why should I hurt him?"

"You'll never be a hunter," himself said.

"I'll have better dreams," she said. "He had such lovely eyes."

"Your own moithered him," The O'Dancy said. "It's as well, because here myself was stood, and unloaded."

"You were perfectly safe," she said. "If he'd come on, I'd have shot him."

The innocent self-confidence of that time was at odds with his impression of the grown woman that morning. A quality was gone, certainly the quality of goodness, which once had shone from her as a light, that particular quality of the eye, which told plainly that here was one of no harm to any living thing anywhere.

It was gone. Hilariana was no longer the self of the daughter, guarded momently in memory of her mother, treasured, adored. Lady professor, scientist, lecturer, director of how many companies, and head of a famous laboratory though she might be, some delicate part of herself was no longer there. She was not feminine. She was merely a woman, told apart from a male by her shape.

But there was instant freeze in thought that Vanina, too, was certainly woman, but far from feminine.

Bruxa was black, but a woman. Stand within a yard of her, and the senses would burn warning that the Female was near. Look at her, and know that a man might drown in the massive sweet of her thighs. Beside any thought of her, the warmth, the eyes, Hilariana was merest furniture. But not always had it been so. In Paris she was ever the small empress of beauty itself. The knee-length red hair, the deep red, deeper than henna, was the only love of Giraud, the hairdresser at the hotel. No assistant's comb ever touched her. The crown of his professional life, he called it, put up for the first time on the night of her seventeenth birthday with a small tiara of diamonds, and she in white silk and her mother's emeralds, and Giraud standing beside himself, and the tears in a run down the man's face.

"It is something to have served beauty all my life," he said. "But now I know that tonight I retire. I was becoming a little weary. And after this, where would I find time or temper for the heads that come to me? Split, burned, dried, cut by shoemakers, I'm to re-dress them after this? No more. This is the most beautiful woman I have ever seen. A child, yes, but veritably a woman. Believe me, I know."

The man might have been talking for the money's sake, and flattery comes easy to masters of the comb. Yet that appointment was not included in his account, and when he was asked, he told the secretary that his services were a gift on that night, the night, as he had said, of his retirement.

Even at Maxim's, that hen pit of beautiful women, she stopped the talk for unforgettable moments, when a lid coming off a dish held the clash of Assyrian cymbals, and heads turned, and a woman with white hair raised the lorgnette and said, but loudly, without rancor, "*Adorable!*" and the men murmured accord.

At the Tran-Tran, and the Bul-Bul, and the Double Six on Boule Miche, she was queen of small courts, but her favor was not for one, or for any, but equally for all, and she whirled in, sipped coffee, and whirled out, and everybody groaned to see her go. Except the girls.

"Isn't there one man you like more than any other?" himself had asked her one night, and wished he never had. "Isn't there one among all your student friends?"

"There's only one," she said quietly. "You know his name."

"Not still?" himself said. "Hiroki?"

She nodded.

"Nobody else," she said. "Everyone else is paper."

Remembrance of Tomomi, and all chrysanthemums adorn her memory, was enough, for there too the word of one woman and one man had been from one moment long ago, until death.

"If you feel the same when you graduate, we'll find out where he is," The O'Dancy said. "You'll be old enough, and you'll have seen something of the world. Have you any idea where I'd find the boy?"

"None," she said. "And I'm not even faintly interested."

"You just told me there was only one," himself said. "Now, you're not interested? What's this? The Irish coming out in you?"

"I told you I'm not interested," she said in French, which seemed to make each word, in itself, a further intrusion into the luxury of boredom. "I have other things to do."

"You might tell me about them," himself said, suddenly chilled by a tone he had never heard before. "I'd like to know what I'm to prepare for."

"My certificate of maturity," she said. "I shall need it for my graduation."

"What you mean is fairly clear," The O'Dancy said. "Once I sign it, I no longer have any control over you. By law. Is that your meaning?"

"Precisely," she said, and stood. "I'm going home. I'm tired."

Himself got a peck on the chin, and she stopped a cab, and that was all.

"You've got some kind of a little monster, there," Hilljohn, his London manager, said, a silent witness until then. "Very beautiful, true. But inclined to ride an extremely high horse."

"She was trained so," himself said. "And you're not employed to criticize."

"I'm not employed," Hilljohn said, and got up. "I don't like to see the man I work for treated like a third-class servant by a little piece of nonsense who ought really to have gone across his knee. I've had a most pleasant time. Sorry to leave like this. Good night to you, sir."

There went the best man on the pay list, and they felt the loss for many a year in competition with the company that snapped him up on the following morning.

"A shame," Hilariana said when she was told. "I liked his accent."

"He didn't appreciate your manner," himself said.

"It's been a man's world till now," she said. "We've been door mats, concubines, unpaid drudges, helpmeets. There've been far too few real women in the world of action. I intend to be one."

"Oh," himself said, "I didn't know you nourished the ambition."

"Why do you think I came here?" she asked, with the braided red hair gleaming in pale Parisian lamplight. "After this, I'll go to London. Then India. They're doing wonderful things with plants in Calcutta. Then to the United States. Then Russia. Then home."

"Why leave Russia to the last?" himself asked. "Is it not dangerous, anyway?"

"Because I want to compare everything else," she said. "And why dangerous? Those I've met here seem to be as civilized as anyone else."

"Are you sure you want to be away so long?" himself said. "All on your own?"

"I must," she said, and the gray eyes gone silver, now. "I'm homesick. I love my Brazil. But it's a task. I have a duty. I can wait."

"Be giving me both your hands and I'll kiss them," himself said. "One for me, and one for our Brazil. So."

Himself dismounted at the horse stand below the Long Steps,

surprised that Didimo was not on duty. Whistles brought only an echo. Saddle and bridle went on the rack, and the horse trotted out to crop happily enough. The Long Steps had been built by Grandfa Phineas and planted by Grandfa Connor, a splendid thought to both. They went up from the flat, in wide ramps of twenty blocks, to the garden on the summit, and on to The House. Given the lungs and legs, they led a quicker way than going around, either on horse or even by car.

Himself remembered the hundreds of times he must have gone up and down, and a day when Grandam Siobhan refused to go a step farther, and the men had to come down with Grandam Xatina's sedan chair and carry her up.

"That's it, now," she said, getting in and wrapping the skirts under her knees. "I always wanted to sit in this thing but I could never find the blessed excuse. Right, glory's the day, and off you go."

But almost at the top one of the poles cracked, and only the tremendous strength of Epaminondas saved the box from falling over the edge into one of the fishponds, and Grandam Siobhan had to be pulled out by her laced boots, skirts anywhere at all, and a crushed hat about her ears, and she hit the roof a crack with her parasol.

"Take that for the curse on you, devil's own box, you are," she said. "'Pamin', you get three months' extra pay, and you'll come with us to Rio."

Himself never forgot the wilderness of 'Pamin's smile, for the man knew that there he would marry with Zulmira, Grandam Siobhan's laundrymaid. They did, and had a family of eleven children, all alive, though they both had been in rest for many a year, and all good thought to them.

There were never any lights anywhere on the stairway.

At the top, an electrical system lit the garden and the swimming pools. That glow shone pinkish against the clouds, but there was some other light, yellowish, about halfway up, and he hurried in case there might be fire in the shrubs that could burn perhaps unseen to the top where stands of old trees were so much tinder.

The lungs of himself brought the breath in a boil, and his legs

had done too much sitting at desks and in cars. Over the rise of
the fifth block, himself stood stock-still.

Three candles were alight in a careful triangle about a rough
cone of paste, perhaps a mix of mandioca or flour and water, and
at the base two cigars had been crossed, one over the other with
the uppermost pointing up the stairway. On a short stick at the
tip of the triangle, a plucked chicken hung by the neck on red
ribbon.

Himself of cold rage stamped out the candles, kicked away the
cigars, scraped the paste off the stair, and threw the fresh-killed
chicken over the shrubs in a black, neck-and-legs arc, down into
the pasture, and wished the owls, rats, and ants well of it.

The sign told all that a *candomblé* was being held, and since
the cigar pointed toward The House, that was where, and it seemed
that others were expected to use the stairway.

Anger went in laughter, thinking of the fine crimp there was
about to be put in all their nonsense, poor twisted children, no
more than that.

At the stair top, all the garden lights showed fairway to The
House, but a hum turned into a great shouting and laughter over
at the swimming pool. Himself stood for moments in wonder, taking
breaths easily, but finding anger in the rise, for in a lifetime there
had never been any such behavior in Holy Week, especially on
that day, and in the mouth of himself was taste of abomination.

A slow stroll across the lawn, through the herb garden, and
along Grandam Atheria's rose walk, and quietly, without claim to
attention, himself stood at the end of the cabaña, looking across
the pool crowded with at least a couple of hundred youngsters in
the shortest trunks and least bikinis of all experience. Everybody
seemed to be drinking, and Serena, in a pink swimming suit, with
the deep red plait tapping the backs of her knees went along to the
bar with a tray of glasses, and behind the counter, Kyrillis pulled
out corks and poured with the briskness of a professional barman.
Serena held a glass to the light, and polished, rapt.

A truly lovely girl, not yet all the woman she promised, a little
slender, a little gentle and innocent in the glance, still in softest
virgin blush that cannot be contrived or hid, so plainly daughter of

her father, and yet with her mam's sapphire tinting the gray, the palest Leinster gray, of her O'Dancy eye.

Past seventeen now, heiress to the millions himself had set aside, and living for recent months an entirely private life all her own, or so she thought, for the men employed to protect her wherever she went were under strictest orders never to show themselves except when they might be needed.

A fine student, her professors reported, with special interest in the arts, ancient history, and economics. But she was never the companion Hilariana had been, perhaps because customs had changed a little and himself lived more in the city, traveled more, and she and her governess were rarely in the same place, and in any event, during the school years they saw each other only during vacations, or when, with a hunger for something of his own, he went to the school for an hour or so to stroll the garden with her.

But they were a generation removed, and talk was difficult. Their ideas about music and painting, for only two examples, were at opposite ends of the logos. She had a passion for the art of her time, which himself respected, though he loathed the "art." Music had been basis of their first, brief because he left, quarrel.

"I can't stand Bach and Mozart and that stuff," she said. "It's like having a foot bony in a grave."

"Without them, you'd be the poorer this day," himself said. "They taught the rudiments of technique, to begin with. They explored the realms, and brought back the riches."

"That's right," she said. "And like everything else that's served its purpose they ought to be in a museum. It simply makes me shiver. Old, and dribbly. Brrr-rr."

"Like myself," The O'Dancy said, and stood. "You'll learn as you grow older."

"Not about that," she said with her father's decision. "I haven't a moment's sympathy. Tonic scales and nimble fingers, and that's all. Doesn't cling."

A stroll through the shadows gave a long view of the cabaña floor. A meal had been served, and waiters were clearing, and the two in the bar were filling trays with drinks, and young fellows ran in and took them away to groups on the lawn with guitars in chord and voices in harmony.

A long moment himself wished for those years again, and sighed it far away.

The party must have had plenty to drink, for the bottles lay in dozens beyond the bar and cases were thrown anyhow. Lights in the pool were green, in the cabaña red and mauve, and beyond, in the garden pale blue and pink, and yellow under the trees, among the shrubs and in the flower beds. Young men and women, in the least they could wear without being nude, lay about in any shape, prone to upright and all between, with constant movement in all the noise they could make, everybody outshouting a neighbor, and dozens singing in chorus, with drums of chairs, iron tables, plates and glasses, and the pool rippling heads in flashing, splashing water, and bodies diving in, climbing out, jumping in, crawling out, and a samba procession led by a trumpet and drums in a thump and chant toward The House.

"Well, then," The O'Dancy said, putting an elbow on the bar. "How are they liking my whisky?"

Serena almost dropped the glass, looked at the roof, and touched her lips with the tip of her tongue.

"Taddles," she said, in a whisper. "They told us you were away."

"That was all the encouragement you needed?" himself said.

"Hi," Kyrillis said, only that, and only one look, and going on pouring soda.

A big, dark-haired, sunburned fellow, with the features of his father and not quite the O'Dancy gray in a hard, glistening, altogether not to be trusted pair of eyes that made himself aware, despondently, that here was another one, grown up on his own and no father to put a steadying boot behind him, or talk to, or be with.

"Where's Hilariana," himself asked.

"Here, somewhere," Serena said, and put a glass in front of himself.

"No," The O'Dancy said. "I'll go in. I want a bath and a shave."

"You can do with it," Kyrillis said.

"I don't need any telling," The O'Dancy said. "Whose idea was this party?"

"Mine, Taddles," Serena said quietly, and himself warmed to her honesty. "You see, there're the underwater championships tomorrow, and the Aleluia Ball, so I invited everybody up to celebrate closing of term, first, and get primed for the dance, you see?"

"Primed?" himself said. "Are any of these going to be driving back?"

"Oh, nobody drove," she said at her beguilingly temptressest. "I brought them out by plane."

"Plane," himself said. "How many?"

"Three," she said. "Two full, and a few over. Do you mind? Terribly? Hilariana told me it would be all right."

"Of course it's all right," himself said. "Nothing at all wrong with it. At any other time. But did you not remember the tradition of The House? On this day? Covered windows. Sealed doors. Silence. Did you not?"

"Oh, Taddles, isn't it time to stop all that?" she said. "Shouldn't we? Surely we're past the Middle Ages?"

"Time to kill the sacred cows," Kyrillis said, but not in the Other Language.

"Those who speak of sacred cows have no conception of what's sacred, to begin with," The O'Dancy said, cold, loud, deliberate, in the Other Language. "A miserable, unhandy lot, themselves polluted, and profaning every other thing around or about. And no cows of their own, either."

"I'm a dependant, is that it?" Kyrillis said in the Other Language, and banging the bottle down. "Why don't you say what you mean? I ought to keep my mouth shut? The great O'Dancy speaks?"

"You're a blather-mouthed, unwholesome pipsqueak, that's what I mean," The O'Dancy said. "Did you hear me? You've the look about you that you're not worth your salt."

Kyrillis put the glass down. There was no fight in the fellow. The eyes were no longer hard or glistening. Wretchedness was there, and the worry of one not yet a man for all he was well past the estate.

"All right," he said. "I'd murder anybody else. But. You're correct. So."

The heart of himself went out to the boy, for he was little else.

"You've the same name as your father," The O'Dancy said, quietly enough, over the noise beyond. "It's not the type of talk myself'd want to be hearing from a man of the family. Tell me, now. Why would you say that? Did I put the fly in a deep pool?"

Serena came from behind the bar, and ran, arms wide, and put them about himself.

"Taddles," she whispered, close. "He's not as bad as you think. He's really not. And he's looked after me."

"You needed taking care of, then?" himself whispered.

The smile in the one lustrous eye himself could see was enough of an answer.

"I'm sorry about the party," she whispered. "If you're angry?"

"Angry, not," himself said. "But there's care for tradition. Do you think your own father, the finest man ever born, would dream of it? Do you think it right in his daughter? It's a day of misfortune and terror, till midnight, and Judas is forgiven, and led back. That's the belief of The House. What others believe is small interest to any here."

"Led back?" she said, leaning away, surprised. "Was Judas forgiven?"

"Well, darleen, use the topknot, who but sinners are ever forgiven?" The O'Dancy said. "Have you never listened to what you say in catechism? Did the man not have the kiss of the Lord Christ upon him? Was the rope not about his neck but he put it there? Did he not jump to his death, himself willingly, and only to end the hurt in the soul of him? Why would he not be forgiven? Is it such a terrible hard Heart we pray to?"

"I wish I could believe like that," Serena said, and loosed her arms, and stood off. "It sounds, so, well, what? Unintelligent, sometimes."

"Oh," himself said. "Generations of the unintelligent, is that it? The O'Dancy, finest flower. His son, a witless one. Father of yourself. The Inheritance? Fruit of the unintelligent. Your own life, the expenses, to say no more, paid for by whom? The unintelligent? Everything you are, or have, or are going to have, every mortal penny, any blade of grass or leaf of cane, and every mouthful you eat, or have eaten, or will eat, all, part of the unintelligent?"

"Well, if you're going to argue like that," Serena said.

"I'm not arguing," The O'Dancy said, a lamb. "I'm not even discussing. I'm asking questions. I'm a poor foolish one. I've been Unintelligent all my life, and my fathers before me, and after me, my son. All of the Unintelligent. So be kind, and tell me out of the goodness of the darleen heart of yourself, what should a poor Unintelligent one do? Hang himself? This is the very day for it."

Serena came in a different way, a woman's comforting way, and put her arms about himself and kissed.

"It's not a bit what I meant," she said. "I'm sorry. Deeply sorry. Was Daddy really a religious man? This is hardly the place to ask, though."

Daniel, in the lace surplice made in The House by all the women, and them fighting to get their crochet needles in even for a couple of stitches before being pushed out, and the scarlet cassock made by Grandam Siobhan her own self, him, then, serving Father Miklos in the chapel, ringing the bells in the wrong place the first couple of times, and all the women shaking with laughter until Grandam Siobhan's murderous eye caught them at it, and yes, a morning when the boy went through the service perfection's own self, and Father Miklos saying they had a born priest in the family.

"Not overreligious," himself said. "But he knew his duty."

"I can't see that religion has much to do with duty," Serena said. "Duty's a social affair, isn't it? Self-discipline, and so forth. Religion's purely a personal matter, surely?"

"That's right, very personal," himself said. "Any O'Dancy ought to provide an example. Of faith, and discipline, and duty. There's no worse example than myself. But I know what I must do. I was trained to it. Blind and careless I've been, that's the fact. But I'm old enough now to know my errors. And regret them. And try to put them right. That's where religion comes in. It tells me where I'm wrong. Better, what's proper to do."

Kyrillis shook his head, laughing, looking along the pool.

"They won't believe what I'm going to tell them," he said. "Do I believe it? Is it a gadget to get by? Could I use it? The plain word is hypocrisy? Or self-delusion?"

"That'll depend on whose mind you're using," The O'Dancy said.

"I doubt your own will do. To put yourself in the discussion at all, what's your own faith or belief?"

"Just myself," Kyrillis said. "Everything I know, anything I've learned, that you've paid for, of course, tells me it's pure fantasy. Politics on a slightly higher level. Get everybody to accept an existence, in or out of misery, on promise of something better after death? It worked all right a little way back. Not today. They opened a few schools."

"Wasted a lot of money on some of you," The O'Dancy said. "Is there nobody learning an A B C without losing faith?"

"Oh, there are some," Serena said. "But it's a sort of observance."

"Or bourgeois get-together," Kyrillis said. "Nests of praying mantes."

"Be grateful there's somebody to pray for you," The O'Dancy said. "It wouldn't surprise me to know it's been cause of your salvation. So far, anyway."

"But salvation's a gift, isn't it?" Kyrillis said, and laughing. "All you have to do is pray, and confess, and believe, whatever that means, and the Gates are wide open. Your harp's the second on the left, sir. Watch the cherubs. They pinch."

Serena shook the deep red head and the plaits swung.

"No," she said. "I don't like that, Kyr. People do have a belief. It ought to be treated with reverence, I think. Even though I don't really sympathize."

"Right enough," The O'Dancy said. "But he's wrong. There's no guarantee of any harps. Never mind how you pray, or confess. It's by what you do. And what you don't do. It has to be earned. It's by your works down here. That's how you'll be judged. Our courts here are a small copy of the court elsewhere. That's where you'll know if you're to have salvation."

Kyrillis looked down at his feet, shook his head, laughed, picked up the glass, and looked at Serena.

"It's almost unbelievable," he said. "I almost don't believe who's talking. Priests are paid for it. It's their business. They're incapable of anything else. But him, for Christ's sake."

"Father Miklos was here before I was born," The O'Dancy said. "He's never had a cent in wages. Not a cent. Food and vesture.

Church expenses. Nothing for himself. And you told us the reason. For Christ's sake."

"No, look, this gives me the gleet," Kyrillis said, turning to the door, lifting a tray of filled glasses. "'Nena, bring the ice."

"You're begging me to fling you out," The O'Dancy said. "But I'm a steady one. I'll make no move till you graduate. Then we'll see where you are."

Serena leaned against himself. The girl trembled. Kyrillis stopped there in the doorway, back to them.

"He knows," he said. "That's why he's here."

"Oh, Kyr," Serena whispered. "Kyr."

"Come on, now," The O'Dancy said. "What's worth tears? And what is it I'm supposed to know?"

Serena stood away, and himself put an arm about her. She had been a child when last himself had seen her in sniff and sob. But this was a woman's distress and the blade slipped deeper in.

"I was sent down," Kyrillis said without a move. "I won't graduate. You see? Won't. Can't."

"Why?" The O'Dancy asked.

All three of them still, Serena with a hand on the shoulder of himself, and resting her forehead, and the sound of teardrops falling on the sleeve, and a guitar party coming closer and somebody beating a booming rhythm on an oil barrel.

"They found cocaine in his room," Serena said. "Three girls were taken to the hospital. All the rest to the police station. Mr. Carvalhos Ramos kept it quiet."

"You weren't there?" The O'Dancy said.

"No," Serena said.

"For that reason I'll help him," The O'Dancy said. "Kyrillis, what help do you need?"

"Money," he said in the beaten voice. "The hook's in. I want it. I want the stuff."

The tray fell, glass scattered, and the man was animal, showing his teeth, staring the hard glisten of eyes not O'Dancy gray.

"I'll murder for it," he said.

"Kyr," Serena whispered. "Please, Taddles, help him."

"Why didn't *you?*" Kyrillis screamed across the bar at her. "Millionairess, isn't that what they call you? Anything you want. Bodyguards. Bodyguards? Without me, you'd be the biggest whore of the lot. Wouldn't you? Next stop, the stuff."

"No," she whispered. "Never."

"Anybody want you to?" himself asked. "Anybody offer you drugs?"

"Ha, Christ," Kyrillis said, shaking his fists, bubbles at the mouth. "Offer? I begged her but she wouldn't. She can get what she wants. Where everybody gets it. She's always got it. But she won't give."

"Not poor Vanina," Serena shouted at him. "It's not. You know it's not. She's done everything for you. How dare you say it's Vanina?"

"Right," himself said. "Tell me, now. Who is it?"

"Bri-Bro," Serena said, and raised herself. "What could possibly happen here without her?"

"Years, I never knew the woman was any but scuttling for The House," himself said. "Here, she's become an importance, is that it?"

"Well," Serena said, and paused, looking at Kyrillis. "Kyr. Please don't cry again. Not here. Please. I can't bear it."

"Let's hear the reason," The O'Dancy said. "Why should the man cry?"

"I want the stuff," Kyrillis whispered, leaning across the bar, and the mouth pulling down and a shiny stare, and the hands of him shaking, trying to flatten the curls. "I've got to have it. I've got to. You hear?"

"Tell you what I'll do," The O'Dancy said. "Come with me to Dr. Gonçalves. Put yourself in his charge. If you'll take the treatment, there's nothing I won't do for you."

"Treatment," Kyrillis screamed. "Treatment? There's only one."

He chased the words out of the bar, across the splintered glass, and ran through the crowd along the pool.

"He'll try to see Vanina again," Serena said. "He'll get the same answer. From Bri-Bro."

"Stay with your friends," himself said. "I'll go up there."

"Do come back," Serena said. "I'd love to introduce you. To your guests."

"I'll lose a little dirt, first," himself said. "Have you no Japanese at the university?"

"Oh, lots," she said. "Why?"

"There isn't a single one here," himself said.

"Well," she said. "They were invited. Honestly. Everybody. But I think they help their families. They're not terribly good mixers."

"Writing on the wall," himself said.

She regaled himself with the softest kiss, and as he walked across the garden, a thought was in mind of Lys, her mam, Frenchwoman, and if there was not a talent they all seemed to be born with and to hand on, of a secret tenderness, if that was it, in dealing with a man, that all others seemed to lack.

A thought of Tomomi argued. Flowers, in memory of Fransisca crushed cool scent.

There was no great worry in himself, or any sense of urgency about anything at all, because what was to be done was about to be done, and after that, everything would settle down in peace and decency once again. Two words to Madame Briault, and an order for a year's salary, and the car, and that was settled. A few men to rope Kyrillis and take him in to the clinic, and the boy would be under treatment that very night. Every problem had its own simple solution.

Hilariana was reserved for special inquiry, and so was *Umbanda* and the other nonsense, which perhaps was part of her own particular caught-upness. Himself made wide margins for a girl brought up on The Inheritance. A girl was subject to God knows how many different types of women, whether nursemaids, laundry-maids, chambermaids, or personal maids. There were so many minds. So many skirts. Under every skirt, an entry. Each entry, a mind. Each mind another way to think. To feel. To speak.

A thought, now, a blunted spear, the sudden, heavy wound, of a little one, younger than Serena, as lovely in her way, sweating, beading silver at the brow in labor to bring out an O'Dancy.

Now, at the moment, she breathed in travail. And the night lay about, silent, and himself walked, yes, in comfort.

Watching the cabaña lights greening grass underfoot in velvet glow all the way to the rise, himself wondered if there was any real difference between the Indio llama drivers, dulled and blank with coca, knowing only what they had to do and where they were going, and The O'Dancy, dulled and blank with something else, was it the power inherent in a name, or the use of money, or whatever it was, that permitted so selfish a form of living with so little feeling or interest for others, even for those of the family. They were only so many in a troop of llamas, and himself an Indio, stupid with drugs, living the long, lit hours either comatose, or unthinking, or anyhow unendingly regardless except for the moment and what was in it for his will, his pleasure.

"Bedamned but I'll say it," himself said, strictly to himself. "A snaphaunce is what I am, beChrist, and what I've ever been. Take everything, give nothing. Business, yes, a deal here and there, a buying, never a selling of property. Roads into avenues, into boulevards, and villages growing into cities, into a metropolitan wen. Very well. And more than a half of it your own, land, buildings, rights, rents forever. And what else? Those of your own, each one a responsibility, blood relation or relative by duty and service gone whole or part to the Devil. And yourself not far behind."

But while himself thought of the words, passing under the rhododendron heavy in white blossom, there, in front, a plucked fowl hung by the neck in light of three candles about a cone of paste, and the cigar pointed toward The House in whiffle of smoke.

Himself kicked out the candles, scraped the paste off the path, trod out the cigar, and picked up the chicken by the ribbon. Any sort of feeling seemed to have left brain, body, spirit, even the self of himself, the one himself talked to, that one felt nothing, not anger, not impatience, not sorrow, not anything except a coldness, in and out, as if ice packed blue about the brain.

But himself knew the feeling to be hard ground for doing murder with no mark on the conscience, no pang in the bowel, graceless, beyond appeal.

Voices were soft from the pool and only faintly the singing laced the breeze. Silence was about The House, a vital quietness, of birds at roost, and blossom folding, and leaves curled to the night. The fine thatch of the main building shone in star glow, and the massive bulk of oiled boards, hewn logs, and tree-trunk supports sent out welcome in the fragrance of noble timber. The garden door slid without sound, and himself shut and locked it. Only the

main door lights were on, about fifty meters distant in the middle
of The House, but himself had walked the paths since boyhood,
and there was no pause in the way, along the curving stones of
Grandam Atheria's small plant garden, all in a breath of night
flowers, and raising a hand, as ever, to white parakeets perched
in darkness, and green and gold quetzals shining now and then,
and the flame breasts of toucan, and here and there, the bibulous
twittering of budgerigars, naturally, for of all the thousands of
birds at rest, only they must talk, long branches of them all in a
nuzzle.

Tiradentes, his wolfhound, sniffed the wire mesh, waiting to
give greeting. Himself whispered, and the dog sat, watching the
chicken being tied to the door handle. Instead of entering The
House, himself went across to the Women's House, kept as in
Grandam Aracý's young day with cut flowers in all the shrines
up the stairway to the main portico, and giant flowering plants to
the ceiling inside. Grandam Siobhan's "devil's box" still rested a
little awry over in the corner, and old Mama Toti should have been
sitting in it, as she ever had as doorkeeper, general guide, and
gossip. But her blanket was folded on the seat, and seat and
blanket were cold to the touch, so she was at least thirty minutes
gone, and that was against all custom and strictest order.

Somebody should have been in her place.

Up on the top-floor landing, the corridor was quiet. There were
no lights. Downstairs again, himself went through to the Glass
Room, where Grandam Piratiua, second wife of Grandfa Phineas,
had put in walls and a ceiling of Venetian glass and thousands of
pieces shone in hidden lights and the place glowed like a grotto.

There was no sniff of a recent meal. The table shone the familiar
rosewood gold. Forty-two chairs sat stiff as ever in dull red leather.
Venice and Murano sang in the open throats of a thousand
goblets.

Nothing had been changed since a day, long before himself was
born, when Grandam Jurema had bought the table from a viceroy
of Dom Pedro, though the name, title, and pride had passed long
since. The flooring had been parqueted by Puxe, and the chairs
came from an Italian carpenter in Curitiba, nameless, except in
his work of more than a hundred years before.

Himself stood there, savoring decent quiet, and realized, as water floods into space enough, that those gone before, the grandfas and grandams, The Tad and The Mam, had lived a better, richer life than himself, and had thought, had sought, had bought their wish and made it so, down to his day.

For the first time himself began to know that others had dreamed, and then had taken time and trouble to bring their wishes into being.

Yet even while manual beauty was building about them, in the years the chairs had been filled with people of O'Dancy blood, all, now, in dust, still the worship of other gods had been celebrated about them, whether they knew it or not, and the civilization they presumed to enjoy was delusion, a merest lacquer. The earth underfoot, the root of the family, was in threat of damnation, though himself had escaped the knowledge, perhaps because of Professor Riskind and Old Mr. Carvalhos Ramos, or because The Tad had died when he did, and every gentle thought to the frothing mouth of him, and forgive The O'Dancy, boys, altogether now, yes, forgive The O'Dancy, boys.

Strange, though, if damnation it was, then, thinking of The Inheritance, little harm had come of it, at any rate, in the time himself had lived, and nothing arose in mind to point a fault or any great disaster in the lifetime of any before himself. The death of Connor by accident, and The Tad by others' blades, and The Mam by razor, and Daniel in act of war, and Lys in the bombing, and Fransisca by typhus, and who else, great God in mercy, but sufficient, victims possibly of the vague chances of life, or in any event helpless offerings to the absolute certainty of death, and not to be affected, whether in love of the Trinity or in worship of any other group of supposedly powerful unknowns. The unknown God the Greeks had worshiped, the One whom St. Paul had made known to them, had done nothing to save either him or his Master from death by crucifixion. The Christ exhorted sons to turn against fathers—"Of course," Professor Riskind said, "and why not if the fathers, demonstrably, by the passing of time and the changing of habit and custom are seen to be wrong?"—and the Virgin had fled into Egypt rather than trust in the power of the Lord God to save His Son and herself. Yes, there were questions, and faith

could crumble, and poor, faithful-at-heart Turú was right in pleading that a man ought not to be penalized for belief or punished for
his faith. But which was the true belief or what the right faith was
splendid conundrum.

Serena, that loveliness, had no belief anywhere, so she said,
and herself a product of years with the nuns. Hilariana, that angel
of other times, was become nearer devil than anything with wings,
so it was told.

Hilariana, daughter of Satan, and Serena, without faith.

Incredible.

But himself knew the look, the voice. Hard character supported
the words. She was too young to be argued with. She knew
better. Serena, that one, did not Believe. And the question became enormous in mind, thinking of the crowd down at the pool,
undergraduates of the university, and how many might kneel in
the light of the Faith, and how many from superstition that, if they
did not, then disaster, even so far as failure in final examination,
would be their lot. With such, there was no future to be told.
They would consult themselves. Lip service would come in lieu
of duty. Duty, discipline, words, no more, stupidities practiced
in other times, when the old people obeyed their masters, and
masters made the law, masters set the pace, because only masters
had been to the university, and only in the university were knowledge, power, authority. A few, perhaps, would kneel when life
taught the lessons of death, sickness, and misfortune. But the
radiant heart, the believing spirit, the faithful one, was no longer
rule but rarest exception. No longer did the family go by habit to
church, no longer did Father Miklos enter The House as one of
the family, no further did the holy days interrupt the working
week, month, year. Judas' Day, yes, because it was in the tradition
of The House, but not because it was the day before the Nailing
of Christ, day of Betrayal, Cockcrow, and Remorse.

There was no general belief in the Lord Jesus as Son of God,
or in hope of Salvation after earthly life, or in the Grace of the
Savior.

Unintelligent, said Serena, herself little princess of Augusta
Street, patroness of ice-cream and sherbet bars in company of
scores of others dressed and made-up in the same manner with

barely a match stalk to choose between any of them, and lately, by report, entering places not so innocent for disc and guitar parties, where she brooded with the others, listening to rhythm and drinking alcohol while the young fellows tried their hands. Her body-guards reported her white-and-gold convertible outside a dozen such places night after night, for she was a wise one, and the crowded floor was always safest, though all the proprietors had been warned to take good care of her, or take what came.

Silence was in the Women's House almost with force enough to hurt the ears. A chair kicked by mistake had the sound of a falling wall. Everything in the kitchen was put away, white, shining. All the coffee filters were hanging, dry, so the women must have been out since early morning. Through the Glass Room, himself took a crystal, and went downstairs to the Dark Room, thinking of Grandfa Phineas coming back that night and finding his second wife with a man, and throwing a chair at the lamp, and going at it in the darkness, and breaking the man's spine across the firedogs, and cracking her neck in his fingers, and ordering the windows nailed up evermore and the door sealed, and the room's remaining so till Grandam Atheria's time, and she opening the door while Grandfa Shaun was away, and the skeletons still there, and having them boxed and buried beside the fireplace, and the windows and the door staying open, and herself ever sitting there, for it was the only cool room in the house.

The tantalus should have been on the sideboard, but there was nothing out, and the chest was locked. The crystal shone there, dry, looking foolish. In the corner, a light burned over Grandam Aracy's *prie-dieu*. The Madonna on top wore the dark cloth for Holy Week. A thought of Brother Mihaul, and himself went to the door of the oratory. A smell of incense not long smoked lay on the stair, heavier toward the foot, but if the women had been out since the morning, then somebody without right must have fired a censer not more than a couple of hours before.

The oratory was dark except for a candle at the door behind the altar, and the red lamp over Grandfa Leitrim's chapel. There was no size to the place and fifty people could fill it choking. But it was paneled in jacaranda, red-and-black-figured timber in gentle shine from generations of polish, all carved so many years before in pilasters, and bunches of grapes, flowers, and fruit, a gift of some of the slaves freed by Grandfa Phineas long before the proclamation of the Princess Isabel. The grandams, each of them, had her own seat, Grandfa Leitrim's five, and three not counted, and Grandfa Phineas, eight and four not counted, seven of Grandfa Shaun's and five not counted, three, and four not counted for Grandfa Connor, and only one of The Tad's, though there had been others himself had known if The Mam had not.

Himself stood there, thinking of the men and their women. "There's a lot of bow and scrape hereabouts," The Tad said, that time in Paris. "A lot of people calling themselves this and that. They can do it while they've the money to pay for it. Take away the money, and they're none more than those on the street. We've more to uphold us at The Inheritance. That's because everybody knows who they are. They can't be paid to be somebody else. You mean, president, senator, deputy? Ah yes. But they're still the same man. They're paid to use their ability for their country. They remain themselves. These others are what? Rag dolls. They'll rot apart, never fear. But I shall stay The O'Dancy because the first Grandfa cleared ground, and so did the second and third and fourth, and so will I, and so will you. We employ hundreds, and our work feeds hundreds of thousands, and for that reason men take off their hats. But there's no scraping. It's the United States of Brazil. Courtesy, by nature. Servility's a curse."

So much forgotten of what The Tad had said, but then, each seat for many a long year had rested a body perhaps two or three times during the week and certainly twice on Sunday, but of all the life they had lived and the children born and the million acts of their waking time, and the trillion words of their speech, not a sound was left or any sign, except in The Inheritance it- self, and a bridge in memory of somebody or a path or a garden, a stairway shrine, or a seat in the oratory.

The altar was bare except for the covered crucifix, and all the statues in unlighted niches along the paneling were covered in black cloth, except a life-size of Mary, in the corner near the sacristy, bought by Grandam Aracý from Rome, wearing the purple velvet cover made by Grandam Rachael.

A crawl started in the neck of himself. A little streak of light was reflected under the gold lace edge. Only candlelight had lit the corner since himself could remember. Candlelight was white.

Not red.

The place was silent. Incense held in the air.

By fair effort himself left the back seats and walked down, past the front seats, and stood before the statue. Red light shone thin under the fall of velvet.

The door to the sacristy was open. Himself walked in, and stood, looking at curtains neatly drawn over choir dress, piles of hymnals, and a censer on the table.

The censer was still warm to the fingers.

But in the far corner, Mary the Virgin lay hidden except for the praying hands among a heap of colored linens.

Almost without strength and with no name in memory, The O'Dancy called on his blood, and turned, a pace at a time, in silence, to reach the doorway, out to the space of the oratory, and turned again, and looked up at the covered statue. The red light seemed to spark.

In a leap he tore at the velvet, and it fell on him and he fought to pull the folds away, smelling the dust, and looked up.

Satan crouched.

Light shone on scarlet legs, torso, grinning head, eyes glinting, hands in bony clutch of hammer and nails and a crown of thorns, and the iron tools of the *candomblé*.

The O'Dancy tapped a leg, and it clashed.

Himself turned about and went back to the sacristy and along to the cleaner's cupboard. The heavy hammer for the water pipes hung with three smaller, and he unhooked all four, and swung the heaviest, back to the oratory, and stood off a couple of yards taking good aim at the head, and threw the weight with all the strength in himself and for a moment the steel flashed against the staring eyes. The hollow shape fell in clay clatter except for the legs below the knee. A tap with the smaller hammer broke legs and feet off the pedestal.

To the altar, and himself flicked off the cover from what should have been the crucifix.

A phallus, replete to the hirsute detail, shattered under one hammer blow.

All around himself went, yes, in a waltz of thorough cold enjoyment, stripping the covers off the statues in the niches, each an exemplar of some personage to do with the *candomblé*, each in strict turn flicking in bits under one crack of the hammer, black, brown, coffee, white women, black, brown, coffee, white men, nude or in robes, on horseback, in boats, on stools, on couches, in chairs, in caress of themselves, or others, in attitudes that graced ability but cursed belief.

Running sweat and half blind, himself looked at the shambles, and spat, and turned to the stair, but sound of dogs in whimper brought him still. The doors upstairs were shut. Tiradentes was outside. But the whimpering was near, prolonged. On tiptoe he ran to the sacristy. The whimpering was louder. Just beyond the cleaning cupboard, a small room usually served as a breviary and dressing space for nuns.

The key was not in the door, and not on the hook. The whimpering was loud inside.

Again to the cupboard, and the iron rake that cleaned the stoves came cold to the hand.

The point in the door, and a heave, and the old latch lock broke, and the door swung quietly.

Three candles in a triangle lit the small room, and the carcasses of goats and chickens, throats cut, bloodying the floor, and white mattresses, and women lying naked, seven of them, asleep, though some groaned and whimpered, and when the whimpering was loud they turned and seemed to struggle, and lapsed in quiet breath.

All of them were shaven bald to the polished skull, and blood had been spilled over them, and all of them were spotted in daubs of red and white paint, on head, face, and body. All of them bled slightly from small wounds in the top of the head, in the upper arms, in both breasts, near the navel, both sides of the pubes, both thighs, calves, and ankles. Four were dark, one coffee, and two white. Two of the dark women he knew as unmarried daughters of men in the warehouses. Two were strangers. The coffee-tint was daughter of a laundress. The one white woman was known to himself, but without hair there was no placing her at that moment.

The second, moving and turning could only be Hilariana sleeping, shaven, bloodied, spotted red and white over the body with the dried blood in narrow runs from small wounds.

The O'Dancy went out to the oratory, shut and locked the heavy door, trod over the clay bits to the main door, locked it, and walked upstairs, both keys a weight in his pocket, into the Dark Room and to the telephone, and dialed.

"Mihaul," himself said, loud and cheerful. "Would you come over here? I was just in, visiting the sacristy."

"Were you now?" the voice said carefully, too. "You'll be needing a few devoted women and a pail or two of water, then?"

"I will," The O'Dancy said. "Keep the men out. All of them."

"They've your permission to enter, and to do all that's to be done?" Brother Mihaul said with more confidence. "We'll have no misunderstanding or second thoughts about this now, will we?"

"None," The O'Dancy said. "Clean the place out. I'm calling the doctor."

"Leave it for the moment," Brother Mihaul said. "Don't call anybody. I'm going over for Father Miklos. I'll be there in a little. Those people called again. The ones waiting for you. Was Hilariana there?"

"She was," The O'Dancy said. "With six others, asleep."

"Excellent," Brother Mihaul said. "We're in spendid time. Be rested, now. All's well everywhere. We're held safe."

"God love you," The O'Dancy said, and put down the telephone, and leaned against the wall.

26 The O'Dancy went in a stroll, no more, feeling the sweat cool, letting breath come easy, across the end of Grandam Atheria's garden, through the roses, taking strength from what was his own and untouched, and into The House by the main door. Two cars waited, and lights were on at the heliport behind the trees. Januario hurried out of the pantry hooking the collar of the white coat, and Rui came behind.

"Whisky," The O'Dancy said, and Rui turned and ran. "Where are these people waiting?"

"In the Leitrim room," Januario said. "I told Mr. Carvalhos Ramos the Younger you were inspecting the coffee."

"You did well," The O'Dancy said. "So I can see them like this without apology. But I'll have one drink first. If it's not the best I ever had, it'll come near enough. Anything happened here today?"

"Nothing, Master," Januario said, and helped off with the jacket, and held out the other. "A quiet day. Only those four visitors with Mr. Carvalhos Ramos the Younger. They came two hours ago. They had dinner. When should I serve you?"

"When I ask," The O'Dancy said. "The Lady Hilariana. Have you seen her?"

"This morning, with friends," Januario said. "They went in the Women's House. After that, I don't know."

"I wonder does anybody," The O'Dancy said. "Come on, Rui. Pour it out."

All three watched the Creature drop splendid gold. Everything stopped for those moments, of gurgling, and the sneeze of soda water, and the fine cheer of the tray when Rui turned it to present the tumbler.

The O'Dancy lifted it in toast to Grandfa Leitrim's bust in wood on the stairway.

"I doubt you know what's gone on since you began," himself said, up there. "But here's one'll finish a lot of it. I promise."

Himself drank long, the grateful length, the cold heartener, and the warmth after that first moment, and the world coming to life here and there, and a better look about things.

"Well, then," himself said, and smiled at both, and Rui touched the gray hair with a forefinger, and laughed. "Is either of you mixed up in this *Umbanda* business?"

Both straightened, and the smiles and laughter passed and Januario looked sideways at Rui, and down at the tray.

"We are of *Umbanda*, Master," he said softly, with small hesitation.

"Was it not the Lady Xatina that took you in?" himself asked.

"The Lady Hilariana," Januario said. "By the Lady Fransisca."

The O'Dancy raised the tumbler.

"Will I hit you with this?" himself said. "What, the Lady Fransisca? When did she have any knowledge at all, or anything like it?"

"Master," Januario said, and prayed his hands. "When the Lady Fransisca came back from the hospital. That time."

That time, yes, of screams and then silence. And screams and silence. Smiles for a little, and grimaces after. Drugs, and doctors, and a drove of nurses. That time, of screams and then, for weeks, silence, and smiles again.

"Very well," The O'Dancy said. "That time. What of it?"

"Mãe Nueza made the cure," Januario said. "She brought the Lady Fransisca into her life again. Her own life. Not another's. She spoke with her own voice. She knew her own people. Mãe Nueza brought her from the darkness and the weight of other spirits."

"It was Dr. Gonçalves," himself said.

Januario shook his head.

Truth was there, inarguable, and the world shook with the head.

"Darling," Fransisca said that evening, and was ever more surprise or delight to hear the quiet voice of her. "You know, something's been very worrying. I've had the most awful dreams."

"Now, you're not to say one other single word," himself said, sitting on the bed and holding the blessed hands. "You've had a little trouble. But it's all over. Do you feel well?"

"Wonderfully well," Fransisca said. "But there's just one more thing. I'd like Mãe Nueza with me, instead of outside the door.

Could she go in to São Paulo and get herself some dresses and things? Then she'll feel more comfortable."

"She can go in tomorrow," himself said. "Is there anything else?"

"You might give her a little present from me," Fransisca said. "She's been wonderful. She's telling everybody the baby'll be a girl. Would you like that?"

"Marvelous," himself said. "We'll call her Fransisca, after her beautiful mam."

"No," she said, and held his hands tightly. "I'd like another name. Hilariana."

"Where'd you get that one from?" he asked. "I like it. Hilariana."

"Oh," she said. "Well, it came to me."

"When she comes to us, that's what it'll be," himself said. "Hilariana."

Perhaps many things, and if the old one had been with her, there might have been no typhus infection, no open window, no death, no homecoming in the casket, a shining shape, and the dear face of herself unmarked, unlined, framed by a leaden coif.

Himself held out the tumbler.

"Another, smaller," he said. "Tell me, now. Januario, we were almost born together. Rui, you're not far behind. I ever thought the pair of you good men. No nonsense. What do you find in this *Umbanda?* Where's it different from what you can get in the Church? What brought you to it?"

"When Mãe Nueza took the devils from the Lady Fransisca, Master," Junuario said. "She told us she could. She did. Then the Lady Fransisca became *Umbandista*. And the Lady Hilariana. First, we joined the meetings."

"Where?" himself asked.

"In the Silver Room," Januario said, lifting his eyes above. "Then, after, we became of *Umbanda*."

"How'd you do that?" The O'Dancy asked. "Sign a paper?"

Januario smiled.

"We entered trance," he said.

The O'Dancy drank.

Januario, plain-spoken, direct, as honest a man as any ever met, spoke with no sign of embarrassment and with much of the authority of Brother Mihaul.

"How'd you get into the trance?" himself asked. "Did somebody help you?"

"The saintly father guided us," Januario said. "We were there with the others. Week after week. Two or three nights. Then we had Faith. We believed. Then the Spirit entered us."

"Two or three nights a week?" himself asked. "Why not all the time?"

"We are only men," Januario said. "We aren't strong enough to carry them. They know when it's enough. They leave. But they are with us in safeguard all the time."

"Very well," himself said. "What good's it do you?"

"We are strengthened to help others," Januario said. "We are strengthened in ourselves."

"What of *macumba* and *khimbanda?*" himself asked.

Rui shook his head, and held up the fist with the thumb between the index and second fingers.

"*Macumba* is for dirty children," he said. "The other is for the unclean."

"You've seen none of it here?" himself asked.

Januario looked the honest eyes, but the glaze in them told that he would die rather than speak.

"Among others, it is here," he said. "Among us, no, Master. Never."

Himself put the tumbler on the tray.

"I've seen terrible things," he said. "It was never in the mind of myself they could exist here. They'll be put right. But I need help."

"It's here," Januario said, and raised his arms. "The help's all around us. Ask, and the help comes. Not always as we want it. This world was not made for us alone."

"Save your sermons," The O'Dancy said, and walked up the stairs, and in passing put a fist on the shoulder of Grandfa Leitrim the way The Tad ever did.

The corridor along from the stair had been a hayloft and seed store. All the grandams had their portraits along the inner wall with the grandfas and sons opposite. Carpet took sound from his steps, and he walked into the Leitrim room with the noise of a ghost.

Arruda Lopez Amaral sat with his feet on the mantel reading

a typed report and smoking a cigar. Nelson Barrosa Trocolli smoked a pipe and played patience in the window seat. Teodoro de Abreu Anchieta played chess with Lycurgo Cunha Pimental, and a fifth man, unknown, swung his knee in the armchair, looking at disaster.

"I was told there were only five," himself said, and the voice a thunderclap under the raftered ceiling. "Where's Young Carvalhos Ramos?"

All of them jumped. Lycurgo knocked the table over.

"Never mind it," The O'Dancy said. "Welcome. I hope you've had all you needed. How about something to end the drought? It's been terrible all day in this part of the country. What brings you here, and who've you brought as a guest, and why didn't they see him downstairs?"

"We're here on business," Teodoro said. "We've just met this gentleman. Ulisses is visiting the lady of The O'Dancy."

"Redan Vasconcelos," the young man said, and bowed. "I'm honored, sir. I was asked in by Pupi. Aristedes? A friend of your daughter's, sir? We had a strange, um, well, an adventure, certainly. My car was damaged, but your mechanics are looking at it. You see, I wanted to get back to São Paulo tonight. My daughter's having a birthday party."

He looked at the others as if they knew, and shrugged, looking down at the carpet.

"If your daughter has a birthday, then you ought to be there, is that it?" The O'Dancy asked.

Vasconcelos nodded.

"I promised I'd be there," he said.

"Then you'll be there," The O'Dancy said. "Touch that bell at your side, be so kind. What was this adventure you had? Was it on The Inheritance?"

The young man had more color in his face, and he straightened his tie, shook himself into the dark suit, passed a hand over a lot of black hair, and pinched the upper lip in a rasp of mustache.

"Wasn't far away," he said, uncertain again. "We'd been down to a *macumba* procession. At the river. I don't take much interest in that sort of business. Never did. But this one, well, there was a lot of singing and dancing, and people going in the river, and throwing flowers in, and all that."

His hands went back to the tie and he pulled at the knot and fumbled a little with the collar, but he still looked down at the mat.

"What were people going in the river for?" The O'Dancy asked, making a fine show of nothing. "What sort of people? Where was this on the river, by the way? Was it on The Inheritance, did you say?"

"Oh yes, sir," Vasconcelos said, with the smile he might have given an alarm clock in full batter, open-eyed and a higher pitch in his voice. "It was near the O'Dancy Foundation. Down that steep part."

"I know where you mean," himself said. "Daniel's Flight."

"The stair, that's it," Vasconcelos said, and snapped his fingers. "There must have been hundreds. They looked drunk. But they were just in a trance, so Pupi was saying."

"Would you mind using his other name?" The O'Dancy said. "If you'd be so kind. Was my daughter in any of this?"

The young man looked at the others, and down at the mat, and felt in his jacket pockets.

"Perhaps I oughtn't to have mentioned it," he said. "Anyway, it was afterward it happened. We couldn't get back the way we came. Too many people. So we left Miss O'Dancy Boys there, and came back here because Aristedes left some things. Then we ran into those spiders. I never saw anything like it. Big as plates. Bigger. Luckily we had the windows shut. They were jumping up."

Januario fidgeted with his gloves to catch an eye.

"Serve something to drink," The O'Dancy said. "We need it. Very well. Spiders. What then?"

"Well," Vasconcelos said. "Luckily I've done some night driving. I watched the way the trees had been cut on either side of the road and steered between. Couldn't see the road for hundreds of meters. I don't know how long. The sound of going over them."

"They're big things," The O'Dancy said. "What caused the accident?"

"No accident," Vasconcelos said, and laughed. "I simply drove all hell's blast and skidded on a corner and hit a tree. But not too hard. Broke the windshield. Bumped Aristedes' head. But we were still running, and I got here. Those spiders, I tell you, I wouldn't believe how they could jump. And their eyes. Like small diamonds. Millions of them."

"Didn't know you had that sort of thing out here," Nelson said. "Thought it was all cleared away?"

"There's plenty," The O'Dancy said. "And everything else, too. Take a ten-minute walk toward the hills, there."

"No, thanks," Arruda said, and lifted the glass Januario had poured. "Spiders and snakes. God defend us."

"Amen," Teodoro said. "Doesn't Butantã want them? They were advertising for reptiles the other day."

"They're always out here," himself said. "They've a free hand to catch snakes, insects, anything they like. I'm like you. Snakes, and that, I'm too much of Adam. Not enough of the saintly Patrick. And no Bruce for spiders, either."

"Black hair all over the car," Vasconcelos said. "And that smell. I don't believe I'll ever get it out of my clothes. I'll burn these."

"Where's what's-the-fellow's name?" The O'Dancy asked. "Is he in the house?"

"I think so," Vasconcelos said. "We came in near the airfield."

"The side door," The O'Dancy said. "How long were you between leaving Daniel's Flight and getting here?"

Vasconcelos looked at the mat.

"We didn't come straight here," he said, and looked at the others, and up, at himself. "I don't want to speak about it. I wish I hadn't had anything to do with it."

"You're whetting appetites, here," The O'Dancy said. "Between Daniel's Flight and here, where did you go? Am I not entitled to know?"

"We were at the O'Dancy Foundation," Vasconcelos said. "There was a service of some sort there. I don't want to say any more, sir."

"You're entitled not," The O'Dancy said. "Supposing you go with Januario, and get ready for the flight. Take you about an hour to São Paulo. Your car will be there tomorrow, wherever you say. May I ask, what's your profession?"

"I'm a chemist," Vasconcelos said. "On my own. Fairly small. Insecticides. I've been supplying the Foundation. I do hope, sir, I shan't lose business because of this?"

"Not at all," The O'Dancy said. "And you certainly won't lose business on your daughter's birthday. Do you have anything to deal with black widows?"

"Several things," Vasconcelos said. "But it's difficult. It needs experiment."

"Drop everything else," The O'Dancy said. "Start work on it. I'll underwrite you. Any amount. Where did you last see my daughter? What time?"

"About three hours ago," Vasconcelos said. "At the Foundation."

He was still looking at the mat. The right hand went up toward the tie and seemed to forget where it should go and dropped in a tired swing of the forearm.

"She has long red hair, in case you don't remember," The O'Dancy said.

Vasconcelos shook his head.

"There was a ceremony of some kind and women were having their hair cut off," he said. "That's partly why we came here. I hope I'm not making a great inconvenience?"

"Not at all," The O'Dancy said. "Januario, attended the gentleman's comfort. Inform Mr. Carvalhos Ramos I'm here."

"This way, sir," Januario said, and wheeled the buffet to the fireplace, and led to the door.

The O'Dancy sat down.

Quiet was in the place, not only the usual utter quiet of that part of The House, but an added silent thunder of four men waiting to present their minds in matters they thought important.

"Very well," The O'Dancy said. "What's so serious you'd be here instead of in Brasilia?"

Lycurgo looked at Arruda and, on the nod, became spokesman.

"Sir," he said. "We are up against a rock."

Ah, but the rock was reached in the cutting of Hilariana's hair. There was no further to go, no distance to think, no reason to live. What was in the human mind to permit such an enormity, there, truly, was the rock, awful, insurmountable.

"Be telling us," The O'Dancy said. "I doubt your rock's more than a pebble."

Nelson pulled a face at the pipe, but it deserved more.

"Agrarian reform," he said. "That's not a pebble. The country could split apart on it."

"Don't believe it," himself said.

"Popular feeling's clamoring for it," Lycurgo said, and looked at Arruda. "Isn't it?"

"Popular feeling," himself said. "A medium breeze, you'd never hear it."

"We mean, the syndicates and unions will fight for it, and they've got the power," Lycurgo said.

"They're not getting it from their members," The O'Dancy said. "They've got a few newspapers misprinting for them. A caucus of politicians trying to cadge votes on it, and plenty of them in the pockets of the real estate crooks. Agrarian reform's a fine-sounding piece of bait. I've had the wind of it all my life. Now, you tell me, what exactly is agrarian reform?"

"It's a device to help the country into socialism," Arruda said. "Once it's passed, it opens the door to everything else."

"That's words," The O'Dancy said. "Let's have it right. What is agrarian reform? I know all about the few of us owning so much per cent of the land and the rest owning nothing. The poor are always with us. Very well. You're going to put it right. How?"

Nelson shook his big head and pushed the spectacles farther up his nose.

"That's not what we've come for, sir," he said. "We haven't anything against agrarian reform provided it's equitably legislated. There's no idea of taking over private property."

"Yet," The O'Dancy said. "Bring in any law on agrarian reform, and how long'll you have rights of private property? The very laws you make to protect the people getting property under the reform will be used against private property owners. You can't have two sets of laws."

"No, sir," Lycurgo said. "We're not immediately worried about passage of the law. What we're worried about are the elections. The big vote will go to the man advocating agrarian reform in those states where free land has appeal. You said let's have it right? Very well. You must come out strongly for agrarian reform. You must be the champion."

The others nodded. An air of relief blew over all of them.

Lycurgo looked down at the hands stuck between his knees. He owned coffee and cotton estates, bars and cinemas in many towns and villages, area franchises with breweries and soft-drink factories, a transport company, a healthy official family of five, and healthy unofficial families uncounted. His law practice merged accountancy and tax matters, and many foreign companies retained him whether for business or diplomatic reasons, because he knew where most of the skeletons rattled and which baffle would keep them quiet and for how long. But he had always been a good hard worker, up from nowhere, with a sharp intelligence that seemed to know exactly how far to go, and that was his rarest gift. Nelson had much more of the same type of property, but his father had been wealthy and so his education was altogether superior and so were his principles, even if they never prevented his cheating a friend and excusing himself by saying that others handled the deal. Yet, though he was not always to be trusted, he was inestimably useful because he knew most of the thousands in law, banking, and broking, and his forecasts, whether of market trends in or out of the country, or of prevailing opinion on any political issue, were invariably and sometimes shockingly accurate. Arruda had always been a proprietor of estates up and down the country, heir of father, grandfathers, and grandmothers. His indifference to commerce was only a little less in degree than the open contempt he showed for the moneymakers, and to find him in such company was surprise in itself. Teodoro, tall, reserved, looked more of a diplomatist than cattleman and race-horse owner, though his shares in many industries made him a multimillionaire without moving out of the saddle room where most of his business was done. Beside him, Lycurgo sat awkwardly on one side like a fattish bull terrier, pulling down the top lip with the lower, nicotinic teeth.

Obviously, Young Carvalhos Ramos had brought them together, oil, acid, milk, and water for a purpose.

Lycurgo represented the youngish, self-made man, the real fighters with everything to lose if certain political bastions gave way. Nelson was there because of all he knew. Arruda, because he cared nothing except for his country, and Teodoro, possibly, because there were so many like him, without political belief or affiliation, unmoved by any issue, convinced that, as life had gone on before, so it would in future and the less done to interfere, the better.

"There's not a foreigner among you," The O'Dancy said. "But the idea you're putting up is foreign, and not a bit of good to us, and you'll have to alter the Constitution to put it through. The Shah of Iran gave out a lot of land. Is that the example? Italians have had some given them. Is that where you got the idea? Mexicans have become proprietors of bits and pieces. Of what? Who became God Almighty by giving them the titles? The Cubans have had slices. Are they happier? What's your idea of agrarian reform? Beautiful sounding. What is it?"

"Ulisses ought to be here," Teodoro said. "He explained it better than anybody."

"No reason why not," The O'Dancy said. "His father was the greatest advocate of his time. I wish to God that devotion to duty had come down. This is best proof it didn't. Agrarian reform, me? Never."

Theodoro looked at Lycurgo.

"You should have kept quiet till Ulisses came," he said. "I thought you'd do better than that."

"I haven't started," Lycurgo said. "That's how I took it, first of all. Till I'd thought about it. No, sir. It's not just giving people land. What we're worried about is the votes. Something's got to be done to retain our seats. And it's not a bit of good arguing with the voters in the rural sections. They'll fill the urns for agrarian reform. It's the new coming of Christ, that's what it represents. They can see a house of their own, their own land, a few cows, and comfort for the rest of their lives. That's where the voters'll go. That's why we have to be the reformers of all reformers. Offer them more, say it oftener and louder than anybody else."

Januario knocked, and held the door open for Young Carvalhos Ramos.

"Ah, sir," he said, coming in, arms outstretched. "We really are most ashamed to disturb you. You look extremely well."

"That's the whisky," The O'Dancy said, and shook a hard, dry hand. "What's going on upstairs?"

"I merely waited there," Young Carvalhos Ramos said. "I didn't see anybody. Lot of noise. Anyway, there's far more here to discuss."

"Just a moment," The O'Dancy said. "Were you invited up there, and you waited and nobody came to see you?"

"An elderly woman came along when I went up and asked me

to wait a few minutes," Young Carvalhos Ramos said. "She didn't come back."

"Madame Briault," The O'Dancy said.

"I never met her, so I don't know," Young Carvalhos Ramos said, and looked at his watch. "Thirty-eight minutes. That's how long I was up there. This Madame Briault, I've signed checks for her for years. The companion?"

"Possibly," The O'Dancy said. "Sign another for twelve months' pay, and another for five years' severance. A ticket to wherever she wishes to go. She leaves tonight. Make it so, and let me know through Januario when it's done. Gentlemen, excuse me, but nobody of the name of Carvalhos Ramos is kept waiting in this house."

Himself went out to the corridor. Rui waited on the stairs and stood aside.

"Find Madame Briault," himself said. "I'll be in the Silver Room."

"The Silver Room is full," Rui said. "The door is locked."

"Open it," The O'Dancy said.

"Master, I have no key," Rui said. "Only Mãe Bro has keys anywhere."

"Dear Mãe Bro," The O'Dancy said. "Tell Madame Briault I am going to the Coffee Room. She will be there immediately. Tell Zilda I want to see her without delay."

"Zilda, Master," Rui said, staring. "Zilda's been gone more than six months. Sent home."

"Who attends the Lady Divininha?" himself asked.

"In the place of Zilda, there is Aura," Rui said. "She went home for the day. With the Lady Divininha, there are friends from São Paulo."

"When did these friends arrive?" himself asked.

"Before noon," Rui said. "They came in the airplane with Master Kyrillis."

"Get on the telephone and find him," The O'Dancy said. "I am looking at my watch. Find Madame Briault, and bring her here. By the hair if necessary."

Rui bent at the waist, and closed the door.

27 The Coffee Room was ever the place of business, and the walls were glassed with charts of the world's waters, signed by the captains of two-, three-, four-masters and steamships, most of them, from the black star in the lower right-hand corner, gone down with all hands.

"But, darling," Vanina said that afternoon. "Why do you keep such a horror? It's a cemetery."

"Brazil, yes, and America, was born in sail," himself told her. "In white grace, and the breath of God, we came alive. If ever we forget it, God forgive us. The room stays. Those charts are the proclamation of nameless men. Each was a hero. He purposely sailed for the unknown. That was us, till we became known. Then we started putting on medals. It became easy to get here. So the easy boys came here. To hell with them. The Coffee Room stays as it is."

So.

The room had never changed since the time of The Tad, and there was doubt if in his time he had ever allowed the slightest alteration from the time of Grandfa Connor, and he left everything alone because Grandfa Shaun was still alive, a terrible man with an eye for change.

"Now, what the hell is that?" he shouted at the new fan throwing a blessing of cool air. "What's this? Am I to break every bone I ever had falling over it?"

"If you'll be keeping your respectable self over on this side, you'll have all the benefit and no catastrophies," Grandfa Connor said. "Don't be wandering about."

"Never hear a word you say," Grandfa Shaun shouted, and took the long white beard in fingers and thumb, and dandled it up and down. "You don't think I got this walking behind a horse, do you? Is it to be blown every way in the world and not a syllable anywhere? Am I to catch a deathly fever sitting in a wind, and not a spawlpane to give a Creator's damn one way or the other? That I'm not, begod. My house, that's what it is, and many a good year in me yet, and out with that. Out with it. To hell and the hotbed of all damnation."

"Get it put on a rack tomorrow," Grandfa Connor told The Tad. "Poor old thing can't see above the waistline. He's going to the tomb. When he feels it pulling down the temperature, he'll put up with it."

But the man never did.

"Shut the windows," he bawled. "Get curtains across the doors the way my own tad and mam ever did. A wind's blowing knives out of the end of hell and every blade, b'Christ, finding me. Four walls and a roof about us, and the blizzard on us the way it would be in the pasture. If pasture's what you want, for Christ's sake be out there. Leave me in me own house, in calm and peace."

"You'll die of a tubercle, that's what it's going to be," Grandfa Connor shouted. "You'll perish of rotten air and worms."

"Rotten air and worms, is it?" Grandfa Shaun screamed in a sacred passion and banging his cane. "Wherever yourself is, was there ever a sweet breath? And if worms are in question, did you look in a glass lately? Be off. Be out. Get gone. And take your Houlihan's shebasset with you."

Nobody ever found out what a Houlihan's shebasset was, exactly, but a day came when himself asked Grandfa Shaun, out in the herb garden, and the old one looking the ringed gray of fading eyes, and the smile in them almost an alarm.

"Grandfa Leitrim knew," the old one said. "The Tad once told me, but I forgot what all of it was. It was to do with the Little Men. There's a lot think they live in bogs. They're gullible. For what would anybody be doing in a bog, except getting drowned? Look at our own bogs, here. Well, these Little Men, d'you see, they go about looking for trouble. But they try to cure it. So they create a shebasset. It's a thing you can be tripping over and dislocating every last knuckle of your arse on. That's the ordinary ones. Ah, but the Houlihan's own shebasset, now. There was a masterpiece."

Those were his last days, and he insisted on wearing the clothes of his young time, those woven by the Grandam Alzira and her women, the smocked and embroidered white shirts and trousers, the jackets of a million stitches in colored patience, and the leather hat with the laces, and top boots jingling the great silver spurs that told of him all over The House.

"Cuchulain, there was the golden one," Grandfa Shaun said. "But his flag-bearer Houlihan, that was the laughing friend. Never a black thought in the man, never a shadow in the mind of him, never a bad word or rumor of misdeed. Ah, but he fell asleep, and he dreamed, and out of the goodness of himself he engineered a terrorous structure, now, of ends and spikes and thorns and such, that if yourself ever got in, well, then, God knows if you'd ever be out, what with getting caught here, and spiked there, and poked a bit and scratched, and cut, and chopped, and savaged, till a man'd just find a space, and lay his length, and look God the Father in the ball of His eye, yes, the way I'll be doing any day at all, and saying, 'You see what's happened here? Thy will be done.' So the Houlihan was wakened by Cuchulain, ah, the golden one, and the question was asked, for why the hell is the house shaking on us, and yourself asleep and the bedclothes kicked down to the other end of b'Christ? But the Little Men knew all about it, and they wheeled the shebasset out of the Houlihan's waking mind, and left the man innocent the way he ever was, and himself laughing. From the moment when the time has to be, the Little Men wheel out Houlihan's own shebasset. You'd never be out of it. The way it is with myself. Do they think I don't know one when I see one? Am I not looking for it every moment of the day? The very moment I see it, by God's own grace, won't I be knowing it? And no sound from myself. Not one. Myself'll know it."

"The old gentleman's out in the west wind," The Tad said. "Leave be. The Lord God's tending him. When he's needed, he'll be taken."

"What would he be taken for?" himself asked.

"Well, they'll possibly be needing a hand on a new fence about Paradise," The Tad said. "Or a word or two about coffee. Maybe. In these things, a man never knows. Some live a long life and they never seem to do much. Others are taken young, and most they ever wanted to do, never done. Don't be wearing your mind on it. Thankless stuff is what it is."

But if The Grandfa shouted about the place at times like a four-year-old, and rattled his spurs when he knew he should not, and generally behaved so that all his small world knew very well he was still alive, yet the man had served a working life of almost a full century, had fenced The Inheritance in its entirety on horse or on foot with ax and machete, and every harvest was gift of his duty, and any cent in the bank, any bean in the bag, direct result of his young years sweated out in the jungle, instead of wastreled in a chair with the shaded comfort of The House about himself and all the women he could wish. The man had no statue except in the green granite cross on the hill, and a plaque in church, and the trees he planted about the garden. But memory of Grandfa Shaun was in every mind in the family, and in everybody's at work, and the day never passed without some thought of him, some pleasant tale told among one or other, and surely no man can be forgotten when the small tales of his time are metal for splendid moments, ever repeated down the generations, and Serena, five ages away, with her own favorite tales of the man and her children and grandchildren waiting to hear them more than once, or could any man trail that length of brilliance and yet have lived for nothing, or need stone carved in his likeness to be remembered, yes, and greatly loved.

Himself wondered then, in the light of shaded lamps and the glitter of glass from all the charts, and the deep red of paneled walls, if that O'Dancy called Arquimed would also be brought to instant life in moments so far out of his own time, and if that was not another secret of the life everlasting, and key to a dictum that where two or three are gathered together there am I in the midst of you.

Rui stood in the doorway.

"I left a message for Mãe Bro, Master," he said. "I think she is with the others in the Silver Room. But nobody hears me."

Those doors hid an iron sheet in both, put in when Grandfa Phineas kept the coinage in the great closet. Only dynamite would open them, and the room itself had walls of timber balks, a double ceiling and double floors, and never a sound came out.

"How many are in there?" himself asked.

"They came in through the side and up the balcony stair," Rui said, at the floor.

"How many are in there's what I was asking," himself said, quietly, though.

"There was food for a hundred," Rui said. "We served it in the garden. Before the Lady Serena came."

"But nothing went on here today?" The O'Dancy said. "Isn't that what you told me?"

"A usual day of no happening," Rui said, at the floor.

"Who cooked for them and the other?" himself asked.

"Mãe Lurdes and her daughters, and Mãe Aparecida and her daughters, and Mãe Ostelina," Rui said. "The men prepared the meat and the fires."

"They came up here and into the Silver Room by the balcony stair," himself said. "Who invited them in?"

"The Lady Divininha," Rui said.

"She's in there now?" The O'Dancy said.

Rui nodded, at the floor.

"Where's Madame Briault in this?" himself asked. "What's she doing?"

"Helping the Lady Divininha," Rui said.

"To do what?" The O'Dancy said. "What are they all doing in there?"

Rui put his hands together.

"It's a *candomblé*, Master," he said.

"I had to ask," himself said. "You'd never tell me?"

"Better you should know nothing," Rui said, suddenly straight, and loud. "These are of the Closed Road. Should we bring down The Touch upon the whole house?"

"What is this Touch, for the love of all men?" The O'Dancy shouted. "D'you know what you're talking about, any of you? What's The Touch?"

Rui held up the right fist with the thumb between the first and second fingers, second time in fifty remembered years the man had shown any sign out of the ordinary and a shock in itself.

"The caress of the scarlet Dove," he said. "Daughter of Satan, mistress of the Closed Road. The road to salvation."

"A sensible fellow like yourself believes all that," The O'Dancy said.

"I believe, Master," Rui said. "I believe The House is in danger.

We believe. All of us of the White. Here, in the Silver Room a *candomblé?* Who could believe it?"

"The signs were outside," The O'Dancy said. "They pointed here."

"You touched them?" Rui said, and went back toward the door.

"I not only touched them," himself said. "I destroyed them."

Rui turned to look down the corridor, and put a hand on the jamb to swing himself out, and half-bowed, and ran.

"Ah, but, sir, I'm sorry to keep you waiting," the crumbly voice breathed.

Madame Briault rustled the stiff silks of a flowered peignoir and made a two-inch curtsy, and held onto the towel around her hair. Himself had not remembered her so short or so stout. Her face glistened with cream, pocked in the skin, and a width of cheeks, and the features all squeezed in the middle, low, thick brows, deep lines in the forehead, eyes with the tiny glitter of elderberries, a globule of nose, a small mouth of thick lips, four separate chins, and a smile of slightly twisted headstones warily turned half-face toward himself.

Anxiety pumped where she stood.

"Would you be seated, please," himself said. "I want to talk to you."

She seemed only to turn her bottom to the side and rest on the edge of Grandam Auriluci's chair, carved out of a tree root, with heads of men capped with silver and silver-horned beasts, smoothed by time into dear friends.

"Belisaria told me you carried messages between myself and my wife, that is, the Lady Fransisca," himself said. "Be telling me, then. When was that?"

"Messages?" she said a whisper. "Oh. I can't remember."

"Try, then," himself said. "Did you ever say I had told her to stay in that place with her drunkard's bastards?"

Madame Briault put both hands to her face and the elderberries became a little larger.

"Ah," she whispered. "Ah, sir. When did you say such a thing to me?"

"That's what we're here to decide," himself said. "Do you remember any meeting at all between ourselves at the time?"

Madame Briault looked away and pinched the side of her mouth until the lips were full cushions.

"Sir, you must remember that you were often not yourself, and many things, perhaps, escaped your attention," she said calmly, with the sudden, serious preoccupation of a superior nurse. "It was a time of great anxiety. For everybody. You must forgive me, but we all feared your violence."

"Nothing violent about it," himself said. "I wanted what was of my name."

Madame Briault nodded at the long rows of Grandam Orbellia's jade and crystal figurines.

"The Lady Fransisca felt so helpless," she said, in a stare. "You know she hated being blind?"

"If there's any extraneous information I happen to require, it'll be asked for," himself said. "What I'm wanting to know now, is when we had any conversation at that time."

"But, sir, who could remember after all these years?" she said, almost a prayer, nearly on her knees. "All I remember is that you were not always yourself. And we very often were so frightened we had the night watchmen inside the house."

"It's not denied I was drunk," himself said. "But I've a fair memory. Did I ever tell you to tell the Lady Fransisca to stay in that place with her drunkard's bastards? Answer that, first."

She moved about in the chair, looking here and there.

"I believe you did," she said. "And you also instructed me to look after the children's schooling."

"One at a time," himself said. "Where did this occur?"

"In the waiting room of the convent," she said.

"You're sure," himself said.

"Perfectly sure," she said, and sat up and turned the elderberries directly to him. "Just after the, well, the episode."

Himself nodded.

"You know, of course, that on the following day I left the country and wasn't back here even for the funeral of Mr. Carvalhos Ramos, the best friend I ever had," The O'Dancy said. "How could we meet?"

"Then it was before," she said, and the tears began. "I don't know. I don't remember when. But it did happen. You can't say I haven't done all I possibly could. I've given my life to this family. I'm very proud of being even a small part of it. I served your dear Lady Fransisca heart and soul. I served her children. They ran to me. They're a credit to this house. Dare I say they're a credit, also, to me? And I've served the Lady Divininha all these years. Everything's been difficult, but never mind. Some of us don't expect a carpet of roses, no? But a word now and then, even a small word? Might we not expect even so much? Never one coin of increase in wages. Not one. And have I ever asked? Not even on pain of death. Never. Others, also, have their pride, sir. I have mine."

Thinking of her, thinner, in blue linen, was it, and a flat black straw, coming in with Old Mr. Carvalhos Ramos, and presenting references from somebody or other, and a clerk in the next office howling with a finger squashed in a file drawer, and she showing a fine black silk calf going through the door and taking charge till the doctor came, though by that time the injury was bandaged and she was one of the staff.

"Don't do anything about that little French pudding," Divininha said that evening, not long after they arrived the first time. "She's an excellent needlewoman, and a splendid short cook, and she's wonderful with the children and odd jobs. You can leave her to me."

"Short cook, that's herself, or does she cook stubby portions?" himself asked.

"A short cook, wonderflood, is somebody who can whip up anything in two minutes," Divininha said. "Some can. They're very few. I can't. Did you ever try her *vatapá?*"

"I never did," himself said. "Does she put it on a plate?"

Divininha pulled a lobe and laughed.

"You're impossible," she said.

Vatapá, now, that sumptuous mixture of rice and saffron and shrimp.

"Are you still the cook you used to be?" he asked. "How long is it you made a *vatapá?*"

She sniffed, and smiled.

"Oh, it must be years," she said. "I haven't cooked at all. Far too much to do. The children, and things."

"But the children have been out of your way for a long while," himself said. "You had no dealing with Serena. Wasn't Kyrillis the last?"

She looked at him, and nodded, many times, deliberately, and turned away.

"I knew that's why you wanted to see me," she said, and the voice was crumblier than ever, and yet there was a hardness. "He's disgraced his name. I told him. He wouldn't listen."

"You mean," himself said, taking time, "what, then, getting sent down from the university?"

She looked about at himself in real surprise.

"Sent down?" she said. "He shot two men in a taxi. Yes. Last night."

"God in heaven," himself said. "Who told you this?"

"He told us," she said. "The Lady Divininha wanted him to go to the police. But the Lady Hilariana seemed to think you could do something."

"The boy wanted drugs," himself said. "Do you supply him?"

"The doctor allows the Lady Divininha a certain small quantity," she said. "Sometimes when he was beyond reason she let him have enough to settle his tremor. But not as a rule. He made a nuisance of himself tonight. I shall tell you something. He is very dangerous. He'll say anything, do anything to get what he wants."

"I'll deal with him," The O'Dancy said. "Do the police have any information about this taxi affair?"

She looked at the ceiling and sent a short breath down her nose.

"Police," she said. "Pay enough, what information will they ever have?"

"We'll see," himself said. "Well, then. Do you know anything of this *Umbanda* business? Ever hear of it?"

She appeared to shake herself and had to be quick to hold the towel from slipping all the way off. The hair was braided over both ears and the plaits piled on either side of a parting in mid-scalp, like a couple of bird nests with a deep space between them. She bound the towel tighter and sat up.

"Sir, I know sufficient after all these years," she said. "We are completely safe upstairs, of course. I permit none of it, not the mention, nor the sound, and I won't have any women connected with it in the suite. Even for the laundry."

"Glad to hear it," he said. "Did you ever hear of the Lady Hilariana's connection with anything of the sort?"

Madame Briault laughed the crumbly little laugh, and sat more comfortably.

"She's had to deal with it, certainly," she said, a little breathless. "But anything to do with it? Ah, no. Nothing. Nothing at all. I should know. After all, I know her from the cradle. A woman of great intellect, no? Profound culture. What could she possibly have to do with such a stupidity? *Umbanda?* Worship of slaves by spiritual slaves? Ah, no. Certainly not my Hilariana. And after all, hasn't she far more to do?"

"Possibly," himself said. "But we seem to have our share of it here. Wouldn't you say?"

Madame Briault showed two more chins, and the elderberries seemed larger than the whites.

"But, sir, without control, what do these people do?" she said, in the most pitying whisper. "Imagine, that Pereira man, Democritas?—yes, that one. And his wife. Both of them. *Umbanda.* Everybody else? Naturally. He's the overseer. And he's not the only one near to you, sir."

"My brother," himself said.

"And others," she said. "I have my place. I say nothing."

"You never felt like retiring on pension, and going home?" himself said. "I remember that house of your parents down there, near Angoulême, was it not?"

That early summer with Hilariana, taking Madame Briault down there as a great treat for a few weeks with her family, the day of sun, and the garden in crowd of flowers and herbs, and vegetables under dozens of rows of glass bells, and hollyhocks of any color rising in warmth without a stirring breath, sweet as from between the vernal breasts of Maia herself, in splendor. A funny old house of wide doors and low ceilings, and silent people in washed clothing that carried the smell of the laundry, and a marvelous soup in the kitchen, and luncheon under the trees, and a little barrel of *calvados* to take back with them to Paris. A strange place for dear Bri-Bro, the worldly one, to be born in, and telling Hilariana she was never comfortable a moment until she was on her way back to the city.

Madame Briault stared at him, and breathed once.

"You don't think I could go back there after all these years?" she asked in a higher voice, without the crumble. "I've got nobody there. Everyone's dead. Besides, how could I live there? What's there? I haven't got a house. Where would I live?"

"With your pension, that's for you to decide," himself said. "I want no words with you. You've served The House very well, I suppose. But your explanations don't satisfy me. Go up, now. Get any help you need. Be out of The House before midnight tonight."

"Tonight?" she said, and stood slowly. "Tonight? You mean, this night?"

"This one," himself said. "Tonight. Not tomorrow. Mr. Carvalhos Ramos has your checks. Tell him where your monthly pension checks should be sent. That's all."

"That's all?" she said in unbelief. "You must be mad. Who's going to take care of Vanina?"

"The Lady Divininha can look after herself if there's no other woman about the place," himself said. "Be off, now."

"But you don't know what you're saying," she said, and the smile seemed to have an extraordinary light behind it. "Who'll look after things as I have?"

"We're very thankful for your help," The O'Dancy said. "Go, please."

"Your wife's a drug invalid," she said, bright and crumbly. "Who'll take care of her?"

"I didn't know that," himself said. "I'll find out about it."

"There's a lot you don't know," she said, hand on hip, wagging the toweled head, turning the rustling barrel here and there. "If I go, if you send me out, a lot of people are going to know a great deal more than ever you've known. You thought it was drink? Never. You think she never had men here? But, dear sir, of course she did. And women."

"Go, please," himself said, but the knees were too weak, too shaky to stand at that moment.

"This Kyrillis," she said, and laughed, a high, crumbly sound that choked, and she swallowed. "The adopted son of Kyrillia? Adopted? He's her own natural son. Born when she was sixteen. The father? You don't know?"

"I don't believe a word you say," himself said. "Get gone."

"Ask her," Madame Briault said. "Wasn't I the midwife and nurse and everything else? You don't know what you owe me. Perhaps his father will pay me?"

"Ask him," himself said. "I've no interest."

"Mr. Carvalhos Ramos will enjoy defending his son, no?" she said, moving the hips in rustling silk. "I'll take more than checks. More than any pension. A plague comes closer every moment you skulk there. O'Dancy? We shall discover what this name means. Go up to your wife. Dear Vanina. She's with a man. Did you know? A friend of Hilariana's? Did you think? My dear sir. What use has your daughter for any man? Or your wife for any male when I'm there to console her?"

"If I get out of this chair, I shall kill you," he said.

She made a wide, strong movement of legs and arms and the peignoir slipped aside for a moment. She wore ankle boots of black leather, but her legs were in scarlet hose. In the quick move of hands to close the skirt, the bosom opened enough to show scarlet below the neck. Her smile had changed. The woman seemed to grow as she stood there. The extraordinary light in the face was not some trick of vision. The smile was losing its wariness. In those seconds the hands were claws, the face became a livid bare-tooth terror and breath snarled in her throat.

"Christ help us, woman," The O'Dancy said. "You're insane."

"Exú points," she whispered, pointing at himself and sweeping the arm all about. "Iemanja wakes. We shall worship the Father of the Closed Road. The Dove will bring you the Kiss. The Kiss, of Three Nails."

"To hell," he shouted. "To hell with you."

She spat, and flung herself about and the peignoir flew in a rustle and the figure was scarlet, nude, and she ran.

The O'Dancy wondered if he was dreaming as in those times, so often, when the self tried to struggle into being and other weight kept the eyes shut and the body stayed still, and the mind pleaded against the knife in the spine.

Januario looked around the doorway. The man was frightened nearly to tears.

"Master," he said.

The O'Dancy took strength from another's fear.

"We're dealing with something out of our competence," himself said, and tried to smile. "That poor woman's unbalanced. Call the doctor, first. Then get every man and woman out of bed, or wherever they are, and into The House. Understand? Anybody who doesn't appear can leave The Inheritance. I'll have the place, roof to cellar, scrubbed and polished clean before morning. We'll be ready for Father Miklos and the holy water. Then they can all take three days off. Understand?"

Januario nodded.

"But there are still others, Master," he said, uncertain, eyes on the move. "Nobody will come while they are here."

A door shut quietly, solidly, farther down the corridor.

"The Silver Room," Januario said. "They're still in there."

The O'Dancy walked out, down to the double doors, and tried the handles.

"Master," Januario whispered, in the doorway of Grandam Xatina's room. "This is why. Here's full sign."

He pointed a white-gloved finger inside, but he made no move to enter.

Himself pushed open the closed leaf, and stood a moment, and walked in.

Grandam Xatina had lived most of her married life between her patio, her bedroom, this room, and the Dark Room, and this room had ever been known as her own, and nobody tried to make any smallest alteration, for every piece had been chosen by herself, and each had its history, and all sat together in small, lit glory. Eighteen when she became third wife of Grandfa Shaun, pure Tupi on both sides, of flashing grace and sharp sense, the glorious heart of her chose what she wanted in the galleries and salons of Europe, as she said, with love. Strange that a girl of no background beyond the thatch-roofed house, still out there in the foothills, little knowledge of the world except what Grandfa Shaun had taught her, could travel about in cities and towns without a word of any language except her own, and simply point and pay and without question possess a prize of its kind. It was told that Grandam Xatina's room held the best collection of Greek and Roman furniture, ceramics, and paintings in the world. She bought at a time when there were few agents and no laws against the export of art, and her money was gold, which spoke loudest.

But instead of the Pompeian murals, the walls were hung with scarlet mats and ropes of red flowers. Each chair, table, statue draped a scarlet cloth. Under the bay window, tables made three sides of a square with red velvet banquettes all around on the outside, but the napery was black. Fruit piled in epergnes, jellies and molds were scarlet in light of scarlet candles, and powder had been pinched to a cone in three goat-legged stands making a triangle in the space.

In the corner, where Grandam Xatina kept her sewing table out of sight of the door and draft, as himself expected, a huge statue of Satan crouched between two naked "doves." The likeness made it certain that the thing had been made especially to represent himself, and except for the beard and mustache certainly it was no bad copy, though the phallus in fine erection was ever a flattery. The fire irons made splendid weapons. One swing with the shovel reduced the thing to a heap of fire-clay shards. The scarlet "doves" were glass-eyed, smilingly horrid contortions of full-breasted women, with both hands between their thighs, and a smash for each showered the floor with pieces. Each phallus between the dishes on the table shattered under the flat of the shovel, and the three-legged incense burners toppled at a kick.

The buffet table shone red in light of small red lamps. The dishes were all red, jellies or meats in red aspic, and wine glowed red in glass amphorae.

The O'Dancy stood for a moment to get a breath.

"Who arranged this?" himself whispered, though a shout was meant.

"The Mãe Bro," Januario said in the doorway.

"Has it happened before?" himself asked.

"Many times, Master," Januario said.

"You never told me," himself said. "You knew what I'd do."

"If others called me a mad one?" Januario said. "If this was not here, could I tell you?"

"But what in the name of God is it?" The O'Dancy said. "What is it for?"

"*Khimbanda*," Januario said, and crossed himself, kissed his fingers, and held up the fist with the thumb between first and second fingers. "It is the Feast of the Closed Road."

"What's this stuff they eat?" himself asked.

"Jellies of lamb's blood, chicken's blood, calf's blood," Januario said. "They say there are jellies from the blood of babies. Meats. Pastes."

"Which mother would permit it?" himself asked. "How could it be done?"

Januario nodded at his hands.

"Many mothers are not married," he said. "They can be paid. Many children are not wanted. They can be bought. At any age. A good meal. A pill of coca. Leave the remains for the rats. Who says a word? Who listens?"

The O'Dancy looked at the man, but doubt was not in himself. The whispers, the stories of a lifetime came back, a wave, unbelievable to the waking mind, instinctually accepted, disregarded, relegated in a time of tall buildings, lit streets, radio sets, and cars.

"Give me a hand, here," himself said, and took an end of the buffet cloth. "Fold it over, and pull it on the floor."

The long black cloth swung up under power, and fell in a smash of glass. All three tables in turn were stripped of cloth and substance. The wall hangings came down in a pull, flowers fell, draped chairs and statues were cleared, and all the candles and lamps were carefully blown out.

The O'Dancy switched on the room's lights. White statuary gleamed steady notes of beauty at tranquil rest in time.

"Find Tavares," himself said. "Tell him to put out a suit. I want a bath and shave. Father Miklos will soon be here. He can deal with the rest of it."

"The gentlemen downstairs, Master?" Januario said.

"They've waited this while, so they won't deny me a moment or two," The O'Dancy said. "Serve them all they need. Open the Connor champagne. I'll drink a glass. Did that fellow Vasconcelos get off?"

"He went, Master," Januario said. "The young man, Kyrillis, looked for the Lady Divininha. I told him she was not to be disturbed. He called me many names."

"Tell Moacyr and Gilberto," The O'Dancy said. "They'll need

ropes. Find the young Kyrillis, bind him, if necessary. Put him in the Jeep. Take him to the Gonçalves Clinic. Leave him there. See me when they return. Understand?"

Januario bowed and left, and himself went out and looked at the closed doors of the Silver Room, and hesitated, and resolved to let Father Miklos deal with it, and turned along to the elevator. The grille closed soft, and himself went up in relief and a feeling of coming home.

Tavares was at the telephone when the gate opened, and he made a click of tongue against cheek, and put the receiver down, and motioned with his hands to the dressing room. The man was deaf-mute, but he made himself known by clicks down the receiver, and listened for taps in reply, that was two taps to tell him The O'Dancy was arriving, three that himself was not, four to finish for the day, and five to come down for instructions. Otherwise the man spent his life in the suite and everything shone.

If he could read lips or not himself never knew, never tried to find out, but treated him as any other about the place, which seemed to suit everybody.

"A dark suit, black shoes, white shirt, blue tie," himself said. "How have you been?"

Tavares clicked, bent his head, took the jacket and threw it in the linen basket, and went in to turn the bath taps.

As a matter of small luxury, himself went into the study and swung out a panel that ever held a bottle since the moment Fransisca had decreed it should. A small one sufficed and a mouthful, surprisingly, was enough. Himself had no wish to drink. Beneath the feet, a sabbatha was going on, contravening all tradition of The House, dreadful accusation of carelessness and irresponsibility enmiring many members of the family and their servants, any thought of it hollowing reminder of a fall from grace.

A look at himself in the glass, short whitish hair in disorder, shadowed eyes, dragged-down mouth, lined unshaved cheeks, was enough.

"Cobwebs are over yourself, O'Dancy," himself said aloud, and raised the glass. "Promise a cleansing, and start with your own filth first. Mind and body. Leave the soul till last. Your own knows little enough about itself. Evidently. *Deus me Libere.*"

The small gold key fitted the panel to Fransisca's room, and, holding the crystal, himself went in ever with the feeling as if to something more than any cold cathedral, more than any crutch-hung shrine, more than to the throne of Death and Judgment, for here was tenderest memory and dearness of a woman, and love itself, long gone, long grieved, long needed, and God put hands warm, now, about the heart of her.

28 Fransisca's sitting room was place of her womanliness that he went into with a sense of home-coming, almost expecting to see her walking never with any pause or doubt, for wherever chair, table, or other piece was put, she never mistook her distance, and she once said she felt everything between her eyes, and got angry only when she had to deny she felt deprived in being unable to see.

"Feeling's enough," she said that evening. "I use the language I've learned. A word is a shape. It's like a bird, a solid something that flies, and yet in my hands it's warm and frightened, and it must eat, and that long wing has so many feathers, and each feather is all little hairs on a quill. Isn't that a word? Isn't a word like that? So many things in one?"

"You don't feel an operation's going to be any use?" himself asked. "There's a man thinks you'd have a chance."

"No," she said. "I prefer me as I am."

"God love you every moment," himself said. "So do I."

Floor, walls, ceiling, and everything else was white, and the long north window always gave enough light for him to make a way. Fransisca chose everything by touch, and so there were some curious groupings and odd pairings, but she was happy, and that was enough. There was none of the recognized masters of furniture. She liked to sit in a chair for comfort of the bones, and at a table to eat and drink and talk. Each chair was firm accommodation for the backside and spine, and the tables deferred to the height of her elbows. A table he once brought her as a present from Tomomi never got a moment's discussion after she clipped her shin on the edge.

"Outside with it," she said. "It's cut my stocking."

"I'd like to cut my throat," himself said. "I didn't see you near it soon enough. It's a lovely piece of work."

"My leg has a bruise," she said. "I won't have it. Whatever it is. Outside."

So.

Tomomi's hesitant peace offering or attempt to be known or desire to introduce herself, whichever it was, went for nothing and a wound in the heart, and so did the prize chrysanthemums.

"They smell like undusted furniture," Fransisca said. "Outside, please."

"Darling mine, let me tell you, now," himself begged. "These are the flowers of gods and emperors."

"Make a present of them," she said. "Gods and emperors haven't any noses. Outside, please."

Outside.

Fransisca's dictum. She had a small world of small things that she could touch, or hear, or smell, but a far greater world of ideas, thoughts, notions. On her desk was the last day's work she ever did, and the last wax record she made, which himself often put on for a few sentences only to hear her voice. All her clothes were in the wardrobes, locked in glass as she had left them.

"For heaven's sake, Taddles, give them away," Hilariana said, and so impatiently. "It's simply morbid. Plenty of girls here would love those dresses. Especially the underwear. They're all completely out of fashion but a good dressmaker could make a lot of our women very happy. Why don't you simply give them away?"

Himself could hardly tell her, especially after that tone, that every now and again there were great surcease and a feeling of being able to live again, just to go in there, in the darkness, and open one or other of the wardrobes, and take an armful of that emptiness, and sniff the distant sweet of perfume, and imagine her as she had been when the stuff was still warm from her beauty, yes, and leave the silent salt upon them that none ever saw.

"But how could you say you love me, and yet have an entire family by that Japanese?" Fransisca said. "Must I always wait, and know that you're with her? Am I so ugly, or cold? Or tired? Are you horrified because I'm blind? Many people are."

"No, my heart, no," himself said. "Don't I pray I could tell myself?"

"Is it a temptation?" she said. "Is it of the eye? That you wish to take her beauty? Like the thief Father Miklos read about? 'If your eye offend you, pluck it out'? Is that the sense?"

"Not that," himself said from a deep pit of helpless sadness. "Tomomi has her beauty. But it's of the soul, too. Of the spirit. Of the woman, herself. If you met her, you'd know what I meant."

"No," she said. "We shan't meet. You make me know what the word 'hate' means. I hate her."

"You don't," himself said. "What you hate is what you feel for her."

"I refuse to talk about her any more," Fransisca said, and held up the hand, flat. "Enough."

So.

But the argument was ever in himself. It seemed impossible or incredible, or what?—that a man could love two women, two families, equally—and regard them all in some part of himself as one, without division or any difference in the quality of feeling. Against law, against constituted society, against advice that a man should live with one, even against his own best sense, against the voice in confessional.

The mating with Tomomi had been glorious accident, once experienced never again to be questioned, and she became part of life that himself had rather not lived unless in her partial but most beautiful and tender company.

"You must live with your own woman," she said. "We can never marry. I am not Christian. I couldn't change. I prefer, not marriage, but simply my own life. I have my work. I have known you. I asked you without words. Were you cruel to me? Or contemptuous? To marry, that's like a machine. The machine turns, and now two are one. Not for me. We are always two. You and me. That's how I think of us. You and me. A woman wiped the feet of your Christ with her hair. It was a long time ago. But you know her, don't you? And how many times have I wiped your forehead with my hair? Shan't I live too? Are the feet more important than the head? I think the head is pleasanter, don't you?"

How not to love so dear, so silly, ah yes, so wise a wonderful woman, ever herself, ever the surprise.

"The maids are gone," she said, on the rainy afternoon when she opened the gate in a blue kimono and on her head, the most enormous white satin bow he ever saw, that made her seem even smaller. "I told them to come at five o'clock because I want to be in the office at six. They said it was too early. I told them to go. People must work when their work is useful."

"It's a big house," himself said. "A lot to do."

"I shall not have a maid for six months," she said. "When I am too fat, I shall look for a maid. Not before."

"You can't run that business and be a housemaid," himself said. "Let me get you a couple of trustworthy girls."

"I can run that business and keep my house clean," she said, and brought his slippers. "I do not want simply a housemaid or a cook. Or any maid or servant. I want a woman who loves a house. Who makes my house her own. I don't want someone who wants work. I don't want someone who lends her time for wages. I don't want time. I have enough. I want a desire for order. A woman who desires order."

"The moon is so far away," himself said.

"But near enough," Tomomi said. "I shall find her."

She found her in Elvira, from Santa Catarina, a big girl, with the African not far away in an athlete's body and the calves of a cyclist, and a contempt for men, at least, so she, over the years, said. But a night came and police white helmets were at the door and the lady Tomomi O'Dancy was asked to accompany them to the mortuary, and there lay Elvira, and two men, all three caught in *flagrante delicto* and killed by a third lover, a suicide.

"Never pay attention to what people say," Tomomi said. "See what they do. Poor girl. She had great pain, great hunger. If she crossed her thighs, she dripped. She needed many men. So. She feared them. She spoke against them. She turned the contempt she felt for herself and her appetite into a hate for them. But, you see?"

"When did you see her drip?" himself asked.

She leaned back on her knees, covering her face.

"I should be more careful," she said. "But we have a cabaña on the beach. She always wore a swimming costume. It is a light garment. Do you wish to know any more? Because I shall tell you only one small word. No."

"Did she have a child?" he asked. "With three of them, she'd be lucky, not."

"Five, that we know, and she never told me," Tomomi said. "Poor girl. Those visits to her mother, that's when they were born. They'll be attended to. She was a good woman. Too much a woman. Too good a woman. She was always at church. Her conscience ground its teeth at her appetite. She thought her feeling was wicked. If she had less conscience, she would have had an easier life, many more lovers. In that way, appetite is satisfied and the years are happy."

"What of your own appetite?" himself asked.

"I was fortunate," she said. "I have my training. My religion. My work. And you."

"And what, without?" himself said.

"Perhaps a brain would save me," she said. "Perhaps. Without the brain? In a night club. A *boîte*. Or a bordello. No? Live once, live well, die young. Very good."

"That's the selfish outlook," himself said. "There's work to be done, too. And the best work's done when the appetite's calm. That's in later years, surely?"

"How do we know?" she said. "My grandfather was an old, old man. But five of his sons died before they were forty. They were the best brains. The hardest workers. My father was a wonderful man. He died too young? Very well. But he created enough in his few years. The work still goes on. How do we know? Tell me."

"Not in words," himself said. "I've no brain. Myself's a thinking will. With a projection."

"And a little more acumen than many," she said, and lay back, slowly, uncurling her legs, which himself ever remembered as the whitest, most graceful shift of beauty, for Tomomi had the slim length, thigh to toe tip, and she wore flower garlands about her ankles, and about her thighs a ribbon strung with roses that came away at a pull.

Fransisca wore only her perfume, and came toward him gleaming, and held her arms wide, and wrapped him, and that was her love and her trust.

"Why did you leave me?" himself asked her on the night of getting home from the hotel. "Could you not have told me straight it was all ruined for you? Couldn't you have told the woman to scribble a line? And why leave your jewelry?"

"I was sick," she said. "I simply wanted to get away. That's all."

"I'm leaving these things on the dressing table," himself said, and the rings and bits rattled on the glass top. "I'd give everything for it not to have happened. I wanted you to meet years ago."

"Enough," she said. "I was sick. I had to come away. Now I'm better. But I won't meet her. I won't."

"Very well," he said. "No more."

Ah yes, too simple, though nobody guessed at banked fires, except perhaps Democritas, but now, with later knowledge he might have known from somebody near her, perhaps even from herself.

"Master," he said that afternoon, and shook the handkerchief out of his waistband and held it in the right hand.

"Well," himself said, and waited, for the handkerchief out of crease was signal that Democritas was disturbed.

"I approach with maximum caution," Democritas said. "Not without many hours of thought. Prudence dictates at least so much. The Lady Fransisca has the intention of penetrating further into the Church?"

"Further?" himself said. "She's never out of the oratory, or the chapel. How could she go further?"

"If she became holy woman," Democritas said.

"A wife and mother doesn't become holy woman," himself said, and still felt cold down the back. "Where do you hear this?"

"Woman talk," Democritas said. "Ephemia told me. She's heard stories. But she was frightened to tell me."

"Why wouldn't Father Miklos tell me?" himself said.

"Perhaps the holy father would be the last to hear," Democritas said.

True, there were many nights that himself went in to her, and found her before the *prie-dieu*, and waited and waited and it seemed since she knew he was there that she stayed on her knees until he left.

"Why not let us pray together?" he asked her.

"My prayers are my own," she said. "Why should I share them? How much to you, and how much to your Jap, and others?"

"That's no good way to pray," himself said. "Or if you pray, it might be rather to move that hate off your shoulders. How can you feel so, and yet pray?"

"How can you feel so, and talk of 'moving' hate?" she said. "Isn't it because you hate me that you go to your Jap?"

"No," himself said, the sound itself a great stone, now, opening a tomb or closing it was all the same. "Is that why you don't want me near you?"

"Supposing I took some other man, and had children," she said. "Supposing I took a Jap?"

"I suppose, in fairness, I'd submit," himself said. "But not here. You'd find somewhere else. Or I would. And I'd never share you."

"Why should I share you?" she said. "Enough."

But then Father Miklos waited at the Long Steps down on the paving in front of the water-lily pond, in the white soutane, hands behind, looking at the pads of leaf in burst of white, and blue, and lilac buds.

"There's something to be decided, now, that won't wait the night," he said. "The mother superior of the Convent of the Redeemer's Heart has sent a messenger. Your wife has applied for admission. Possibly a six-week retirement. Your permission is sought."

"Six-week retirement," himself said. "What for?"

Father Miklos looked at the water lilies. A few short white hairs brightened the sunburned skull above the nimbus, and his eyes looked tired.

"It's a good way to find out what's in the mind," he said. "She hasn't been at all herself. I think she's doing too much among the people, here. Listening to too many problems. Involving herself emotionally. Spiritually. Perhaps the dear girl would like to free herself of thoughts."

"Anything that'll bring peace to her," himself said. "Let her enter. Would I be allowed to see her?"

"It might require a little diplomacy," Father Miklos said, happier. "Let us work to bring her back here the old, wonderful laughing heart we remember. That, first. Other things after. Yes?"

But she was never afterward anybody himself had ever known. If that suffering over the years was worth the joy of Tomomi during the same time, himself was unsure. If Fransisca, as she ever had been, were offered all beauty and laughter, in place of knowing Tomomi, himself failed in the heart to think of the answer.

Tomomi, yes, and the others held their appeal against all argument or any accusation of spiritual or moral damage or disregard of the social code. Appetite, indulgence, enjoyment, yes, lust, that was the master and there was never the will to deny, for the word itself, and what it meant, seemed too strong a term for the gentle things himself did, and in any case when the feeling was strong there was little enough patience to listen.

Tavares stood in the door and sent his shadow down the room, tapping three times. The bath was ready.

Whether in that covering of light a balance in vision was disturbed, or if the eyes of himself were more used to whiteness, or whatever it may have been, but a tall shadow darkened the corner. Fransisca's *prei-dieu* had always been there, a low desk with a prayer book in Braille, and a diaconicon below. But nothing above.

"Tavares," The O'Dancy said, loud as his throat would let. "What's that in the corner?"

The man must have heard in some way, for he clicked and shook his head violently.

The O'Dancy got out of the chair by pushing himself, and went around the furniture, touching familiar pieces almost with pleasure, expecting to find another Satan in staring grin. But the high gold crown of a life-size Negro Madonna appeared out of darkness, hands in blessing of all women in travail, even in shadow glowing the blue of her cloak and the golden orphrey, soothing the mind with the benign grace of her smile.

"Who put this here?" himself said. "Who'd dare bring this in here? Was there a blessing by Father Miklos? Who was in here?"

Tavares held up his hands, pointed at something in the study, crossed off twenty-six fingers, closed his fist and held it up in strengthy sign of the male, pulled his hair and made the motion of a curl, stuck both forefingers in his ears, took one away to hold a stethoscope to his lungs, pointed to the Madonna, and jabbed the finger at himself, and it was plain as if he had shouted the name.

"Stephen," himself said. "Estevão?"

Tavares might have nodded his head off.

"Put there for a good reason," himself said. "Very well. I'll not be hasty. She's more beautiful than I'd thought. I'll have a word with him. He shouldn't have come in here without permission."

Tavares shook that head, clicking a Geiger count, pointing the forefinger directly into his own chest.

"You brought it in?" himself said.

Tavares pointed into the study again, and The O'Dancy went out, looking at Steb's photograph on the desk.

"Steb brought it in," himself said. "You miserable heathen, isn't that what I was saying?"

Tavares pointed at the photograph and made a sign of prayer, pointed into his chest, wrung his praying hands, and pointed toward the Madonna.

"You asked Stephen, and he brought it in here," himself said.

Tavares laughed, almost danced, crossed himself, and kissed his fingers.

"Not such a heathen, either," himself said. "Very well. Why did you ask Stephen? Why Stephen? Why the African Madonna?"

Tavares showed a small ivory crucifix, and stuck his thumb between first and second fingers and held up the right fist.

"To protect you," himself said. "Against what?"

Tavares shook his head slowly, pointed to himself, and made the sign of the cross with the crucifix.

"Protecting me?" himself said. "All right. Very thoughtful of you. But against what?"

Tavares put both forefinger knuckles to his forehead and the fingers stuck out as horns, and he crouched, staring, grinning, and slapped himself upright, clicking, and held up the crucifix.

"Very well," himself said. "You're talking about this *khimbanda* business."

Tavares dashed his hand into the water jug and splashed about, click-click-clicking, and held up the crucifix.

"Very well, it won't be mentioned," himself said. "And are you of this *Umbanda?*"

Tavares put his hands together, and bowed.

"I'm very fortunate," himself said. "Fortunate you're not the other sort. Right. Bring me a drink, and I'll be taking a quick shower. Ask Januario to find Estevão. Get hold of Democritas

Pereira. I want Madame Briault out of The House tonight. Understand?"

Tavares clicked, smiled, moved as if he might have danced, and went out clicking.

Himself went through the study, lined with O'Dancy records compiled over two hundred years, and alight with mementos left by the family, and all his own, brought from here and there, every one a memory and prized, though not everything was worth a second look.

"What on earth do you want a string of champagne corks gathering dust for?" Vanina asked. "Why don't you throw them away? And all this other rubbish."

"You'll be good enough to leave everything the way it is," himself said. "Those corks, if you must know, came out of bottles I drank with Fransisca on our honeymoon. All the other 'rubbish,' as you call it, brings a dear memory."

"Some beautiful things here, darling," Vanina said. "But it's spoiled by this utter junk."

"There's plenty of junk in every life," himself said. "You're not rid of it by hiding anything. My junk joins up with the other parts. Leave it all alone, and whole."

"Then I won't bother with it," Vanina said, and walked out. "I won't touch anything in this entire damned museum. All grandfas and grandams, and don't touch this, and don't move that. I'll build a place of my own."

"Do that," himself called. "But don't forget. Not one brick on another till I've seen the plans and approved the site."

"You've got to be the great I AM, haven't you?" she screamed, out on the stairhead. "The place stinks like an outhouse, anyway."

"Build your own," himself said, and shut the door.

The bedroom had never been altered since Grandam Aracý went out that morning to die in the garden. White walls, blue curtains and white breeze nets, two white rugs of foxes caught in the hen run by Grandfa Shaun, a large bed with slender carved posts in applewood, blue cover, white valances, a semicircular table on either side, on the left with the figure of St. John the Baptist, on the right with Mary Magdalen, and in the corner, a *prie-dieu* with an ivory crucifix, a Bible, and the lamp that had never gone out since Grandfa Phineas struck flint and tinder a hundred and fifty years before, and as in his day, perhaps, the same reflections from candlelight on the flooring of polished blocks.

"For God's sake, can't we have electric light?" Vanina said. "I like to read in bed."

"Nothing more restful than candles," himself said.

"I'll have to sleep somewhere else," she said. "This is nothing more than a lying-in-state. Only we're not embalmed. But you might just as well be."

The O'Dancy lay back on the pillows and laughed at the plain white ceiling.

"Case of corpse calling cadaver listless," himself said. "Bring me something with a pulse, and I'll show you."

"Two can play that game," she said, and flung off the bedclothes. "Don't trouble yourself about me in future."

"All right," himself said. "But don't let me find you with anybody else. I'll kill the pair of you."

"I know you Indio-Negroes," she said from the doorway. "You'll get no opportunity. And I won't divorce, or sue for it. And I hope I live another thousand years."

"That'll be the dry millennium," himself said, and turned over.

It was a heavy door, and the slam might have taken out a wall or two.

The bathroom had been The Tad's and not much had been altered, except that Fransisca found an Aphrodite in Beirut and said it felt like her, and always poured warm, soapy water over it, and in that long time, day after day, morning and night the figure had become a golden color, lovely to see, always a heartbreak to touch in memory of another beauty, but that one vital with laughter. White marble walls and floor were set with bas-relief tiles in alabaster brought from Naples by Grandam Jacyndra, all alive with men and women of two thousand years before, in the public baths, in the market place and strolling the town. Water spouted in constant hot or cold pour from the open maws of gold carp into a Roman bath found by Grandam Tiridín. The Japanese tub and all the cut-glass bottles that Tomomi had sent from the beach house were intimate part of himself, but with the smell of fresh water and generations of soap, they were all bolsters of confidence, proof that The Inheritance was still in being, setting the will firm to keep it so.

The shower took no time to freeze into mid-brain and isolate some idea of himself as a small, shivering speck that might have died without a dry towel to bring warmth, making way for a feeling that life was worth while and ought to be prosecuted, even with anger, to ensure at least some general move in the direction of Christian ethics, if not a mass application on all levels, though in asking himself what he meant by Christian ethics, there was certain small surprise to find nothing in his head. While the razor went about cheeks and chin he tossed the question. There was little doubt anywhere that precisely what it meant lay in the mind of himself, though for some reason words were not ready. Faint noise of guitars and voices outside were reminder that, whether or not, at least a couple of hundred hebephrenics would be a long way from any desire to conform, and those at the meeting down in the Silver Room would be even further. If it was epicureanism himself meant, or hedonism, he acknowledged uncertainty, because his own share of pleasure had been large enough, though Christian ethics had always ruled except where women were concerned, though there again, women, too, could live ethically and still give themselves to pleasure when they chose. Nobody could have lived closer to Christian ethics than Tomomi, and in fact not a single woman he had ever known came readily to mind whose life had gone very far from the Christian standard, if that meant doing unto others as they would have others do, or loving their neighbors, or keeping most of the Ten Commandments and regretting lapses in the rest and asking forgiveness.

"Yes, but you see, it's not that," Professor Riskind said, with the panama on the back of his head and a book on his knee, and twisting his finger in the folds of the black bow. "It's a question of seeking a state of grace leading to salvation. That's what produces conduct which becomes known as Christian. Just behaving yourself within the law and conforming to certain local standards doesn't make you one, whatever you say. A Christian is a believer. He believes in the Way, the Light, and the Truth, you see, and he lives it. Doing what you know to be wrong and then going to confession, and attending Mass, and merely acting remorse is only a peculiar type of dishonesty. Outwardly of the devout. Inwardly a hypocrite. If you look at Russia, for example, even the communists, who call themselves atheists, still live a remarkably 'Christian' sort of life. They keep all the Commandments. They murder people sometimes. A great many people. But how many do we murder in this country? We allow people to die of hunger and disease and the effects of miserable poverty. It can all be cured by law. Where's the legislation? Where are the Christians? Filling their pockets, naturally. God is a Brazilian. Isn't that what we say?"

The afternoons of lectures in the heat and Sergio coming in every twenty minutes or so with small cups of coffee were among the pleasanter, more fruitful periods himself could remember. Certainly, the professors had one by one and often in a group dropped into his mind the combined knowledge and experience of all their years, and the same system himself had used both with Daniel and Stephen. Paul was never on the scholar's side. He was always in the stables and cow barns, and since natural talent directs the true male, the work a boy picks without guidance ought to be held sacrosant, and himself saw to it that nothing was put in his way. Perhaps that was one reason why Paul had never been close, though it was no excuse for allowing the child to grow into the man without even knowing as much about him as the merest schoolmaster.

That type of neglect, himself knew, was root of the disgrace in the oratory, the meeting in the Silver Room, the behavior of Madame Briault, and any number of other matters that had to be dealt with before morning, and the thought recurred, and he took strength from it, that the placid state of his mind was possible only because he knew what strict means were at hand to cleanse, and to maintain what had ever been the decent way of The House, so far, at any rate, as The O'Dancy men were concerned.

Fresh linen and a light suit brought a feeling almost of omnipotence. While he poured another small one to take himself happy into the elevator, Tavares used the clothesbrush, and a cloth for the shoes, neither needed, yet Sergio had done it for The Tad, and all had to be done as Sergio had taught.

"Listen to me," himself said. "The sisters, are they still cleaning the oratory and the chapel? Mãe Isis, and Palmyde and Felicia. Or have they been changed?"

Tavares shook his head and pointed down toward the servants' houses.

"Good," himself said. "I'm glad something's still the same. Tell anybody who wants to know that's where I've gone."

29 The O'Dancy went down in the elevator to the basement, and listened, before he opened the door, to silence that gladdened, and went out in the wheaty air of the store shed, and across the threshing floor, along the passage, into the oil-and-friction smell of the powerhouse, and out through the lattice. The night had no sound, or any light, and on that side of The House, no windows were lit. Through the rock garden and over the little bridge, with stars white in the ponds, and all the shrubs grown tall in his lifetime, black and still, and the sky a deep blue he remembered, and air cool on the face, the same, yes, as on the night Tomomi died, dear Christ have an arm strong about her, and everything in life a gray desperation.

Different from the time Fransisca went.

Life stopped then.

But nothing stopped when Tomomi died. Everything went on. His sons took on the business without any halt. Two of them never even flew back for the funeral. Two of the daughters stayed where they were. Amoru and Tomika and Satsuco had their arms about him. The other sons and their wives held a service for themselves.

"Now they are grown I can't raise my eyes," Tomomi said. "I should have thought more, I suppose. It didn't occur to me. But we never think of others, do we? Or of the years coming? But they come so quickly. Yesterday, babies. Today, young men. Frowning. Cheated. Name, but no status. Power, yes. Tomagatsu or O'Dancy, the names have power. But not respect. So. No love for their mother. No respect."

"Contempt for their father?" himself asked. "To hell with them."

"Don't say it," Tomomi said, and the hand himself still felt, soft on his cheek. "A thought like that does damage."

"Let it," himself said. "They were given life. A chance to live.

Better than many. Each is healthy. Has a brain. A business to fall
into. Why? Their mother created it. For them. They're dissatisfied?
Tell them to find something else. But they won't. You know why?
Their mother's name is Tomagatsu. Their father's name is O'Dancy.
If they use the brains they were given they'll be princes of the
land. They know it. Nameless or not, in or out of marriage.
Marriage? But, Christ, they're not Christians. Who's their God?"

"In this society, after all, you must have a name," Tomomi said.

"Society, my arse, what name?" himself said. "What society? The
counts and hangers-on? How long do they last without money?
What keeps them there except money?"

"Very well," Tomomi said. "But you were born of a marriage.
You speak from a high point. My children were born in love. Anybody could have been their father."

"No, now, wait a minute," himself said. "Don't make me angry
with you. Anybody could not have been their father. Or I mistook
their mother. Anybody could not have given them their eyes, their
hair, the other marks. Anybody could not. It was myself."

"But who are you?" Tomomi said. "My lover."

"The world was created by lovers," himself said. "I'd rather
myself your lover I ever was than your husband."

"We should have practiced control," Tomomi said. "I was selfish.
I could have prevented all of them."

"And what?" The O'Dancy said. "Where's the difference between
you and anything else on the bed?"

"But the scientists are in agreement," Tomomi said. "There are
too many mouths. Not enough food. Everybody will starve. If I'd
done my part, there'd be those fewer discontented mouths. Wouldn't
there?"

Himself looked at her. She sat cross-legged on the cushion, elbows
on knees, forefingers pushing up the corners of her eyes. She was
not much younger than himself, but she looked, in her maroon
silk, and the piled hair, and the white, satin-petal skin, perhaps
going on thirty, though it was never possible to tell.

"Would the scientists not find in the goodness of their hearts
a reasonable excuse to cut their throats?" himself said. "To hell
with the bloody scientists. There's always some bloody Jeremiah.
I'd rather have loved you these years than save the world. That's

the difference between me and Christ, if you like. It's why I'm condemned for a sinner. I'll burn. Very well. But I've known you. It's worth it."

She sat forward and wrapped her arms about the knees of himself.

"Now, I hear," she said. "That's all I wanted. You've been a wonderful husband. No woman could have been happier. But you don't respect the scientists? That's strange. I thought you had a special reverence for men who devote their lives to the hidden things?"

"Am I not a bit of a scientist, then?" himself said. "If I had another life, would I not devote it altogether to what you've got hidden? Ah, to hell. How are you to tell what's to be born and what's to go down the drain? If everybody practices, what's love? Another drink? It's the thought of what's to come of it that makes of love a lyric. To some, it's terror. Let them wear rubber. Rubber and studs and pills. And naked bodies and kisses. Kiss the wondrous breasts. Let it go. It's all right. She's got a fine rubber cap. Scientists?"

"They are thinking about food," she said, and the strange white blaze up at him.

"Don't be annoying me," himself said. "Who the hell is interested? Let them find the way to grow more food, then. And leave the world to instinct, and to lovers. To hell with scientists. They've ever been proven wrong."

If it was the next day or not long after, and Dr. Gonçalves' secretary telephoning from the hospital to say that Tomomi was there, nothing serious, but she would like to see him, and himself gaveling a board meeting closed, and going up there, and Dr. Gonçalves coming out on the steps to greet him, arms wide, and that stone face, and white hair all ends in the breeze, and the terrifying shrug.

"I'm deeply sorry," he said. "Nothing more we could do."

The policeman came up the steps and said the car had to be moved.

A man came out with a hose and started swilling, and smiled to be excused.

Wash of water, nothing still, going, moving, passing.

The clock struck whatever hour it was, though not in the time of Tomomi.

A family, father carrying a black baby in frills, mother laughing carrying another, and two little ones going down the steps one at a time, and the evening darker, showing the thin moon in rise, though not and never for Tomomi.

Nothing stopped.

"Profoundly sorry," Dr. Gonçalves said. "She was under treatment for some months. I wouldn't advise your seeing her. For the moment."

Which moment. There was never one. Nothing stopped.

So.

The beach house went to Amoru, and the rest they settled among themselves. The bath, that old red-brick bath where himself had boiled for half his life, and the toilet-water bottles, and the *sake* jugs came to The Inheritance.

"What's that thing?" Vanina said when she saw it, dried-out and red, in the white bathroom.

"It's the resting place of a fond lover," himself said. "They'll bury me in it. With a magnum of champagne and a red chrysanthemum."

"The sooner the better," Vanina said. "You'll make a wonderful toast."

When Fransisca was taken, and garlands enfold her, there was Tomomi, and solace of a kind. But when Tomomi went, there was nobody, and nothing any longer moved in life except the Creature, which deadened for a time and then maddened, and loneliness became lunacy, and it had to stop. Dr. Gonçalves said, and no drink for three months, and himself in the clinic for all that time, and coming out like a new one, except for weakness in the knees, and no patience, and small capacity for any drink at all.

"Would I not be better dead?" himself asked.

"Go back on three bottles a night," Dr. Gonçalves said, "In two months or less, I'll sign your burial certificate."

"I'll not be giving you the pleasure," himself said. "Table water and fruit juice, that's the sentence. I'll pray for the will to keep off the other."

Himself was satisfied that no great distress came from pushing the bottle away, though a drink or two made a difference at a cattle show to close a bargain, or at the races to hail a victory, or at the birth of somebody's child, or in memory of a friend, yes, there were many little events not to be celebrated in water, or juice of one sort or another.

The night before was one example, for there was no way of taking in three good men to supervise the transport of a fine buy of champion calves and not to offer them a drink, or refuse to drink with them. After church, they went in the bar near the stockyard where they had left the truck, that was clear enough in the mind, and then down to the garage to get new batteries, then the bottles of acid, and some tools for the tractor workshop, and everybody going out to the storeroom and coming back loaded, and then checking the stores lists, and everything going in the truck, and João doing an unusually fine job of roping it all down.

Then it was time for one drink before going home.

"A helicopter reposes up at the airfield," Dem said. "It would permit a far more comfortable journey than this."

"Remember what night it is," himself said. "Anniversary of the Three Denials. This truck's as safe as we'll find. I've been to church and had my blessing. No flying for me tonight, and I'll not stir foot tomorrow. Let's go to Giuseppe's for a good drink."

"One of us should stay with the truck," Dem said. "A thief'd find his fortune here."

"Very well," himself said. "Toss for it. Then when we've had a drink, we'll toss again, and the loser comes back here and lets the other come up. Then two of us toss, and one goes down to relieve the other. Then the two left behind toss to see who does the last relief. That way, at least three of us get four drinks. Or should we work it with algebra?"

As it happened, nobody knew how many drinks there were, for they seemed to be tossing coins all night, and himself in the chair, and one face going and another coming, until all four were met together, tearful and boisterous, in that place with all the red light behind the bar, and the musicians only black shapes against the red, and red walls, and seashells and nets.

And Maexsa.

Crossing the outer garden, and stone paving shining in the stars, coming into the rose arbors, and faint scent, and hit in the heart to think of Fransisca, now rest the dear head, and a memory of Maexsa that, drunk or not, came to him in moments of luminous clarity. Himself had been near enough to women to know that she was careless, and the hair of her was unwashed, smelling of smoke and the city's soot. All the perfume in creation covered nothing. If the hair was unwashed there was reason to doubt a soaped body. Yet a madness had begun at some time, of the type that takes a man's mind and makes of him a Romeo or a murderer. Himself chose somewhere near the Romeo, though there was no basis for it. She was no beauty. Legs, yes. Legs himself had ever loved, tall, or slim, or muscular, or bony, or thick, nothing mattered so they were legs of a woman, two warm lanes of loveliness leading to an entrance ever a joy. Silk drawers, yes, but if all hands were busy as his own, and every night, silk drawers she would need of the weight she had chosen, and the frills about the thighs, too, enemies, no less, of the probing finger.

How they got in the place, there was a mystery, except that once they went out of Giuseppe's to get Dem from his turn at guarding the truck, but in going back, they missed a street, or it was too far, or João was crying for a horse that died, and then they were drinking champagne in Maexsa's and there was no need to move, and the girls were undressing each other, and nobody taking any notice until the fight started and Maexsa waving that machete, a razor, that cut through fish net in a whisper.

One drink to go home, and the loss of millions to pay for it.

There was no proof that anybody had led them there. It might have been that a couple of the girls had invited them in. What was half clear was that somewhere a friend of Vanina's had managed to take the attention of himself, and again that morning had got in the way at the fire, and there was far more than chance in it, for that woman, at the moment, was in the Silver Room. If any of them were right, with talk of The Touch, and water splashing, and thumbs in fists, then she might have set a spell, or such, or a curse, though if himself was too old to care, there was experience enough in the head never to deny the could-have-been.

The hedges had thickened in the years, but the dogs started

barking, and Mãe Isis came out and stood white in the gap, and saved himself a shout.

"Ah, Master," the old one said, hands on his sleeve, leading him in the darkness, and light white in a snapping switch from the room beyond. "We heard you. Palmyde guessed right. She knew by your step. What shall we make for you?"

"Nothing, Mãe, nothing," himself said, and cursing the neglect of kindly ones loved by The Mam and Tad and Fransisca. "I came to speak of the oratory. You still clean the place? And the church?"

"Every day," Mãe Isis said, pointing a finger. "But yesterday and today we were not permitted to go in. I told Father Miklos we won't go in again until he's taken the cross to both of them."

Mãe Palmyde and Mãe Felicia, a few years younger than Mãe Isis, curtsied in the door, and shook hands, laughing and chattering, not a clear word among them, but happy to see him, and tears silvering in glaring light, and a chair set, and coffee water going on the gas ring, and a cake coming on the table, and Mãe Palmyde bringing out the bottle of cane alcohol and four glass thimbles.

"Wait, now," himself said. "Have any of you anything to do with *Umbanda?*"

Mãe Isis shook her head. The other two stood still, staring as only Africans stare, the wide eye that never blinks, and the pupil in the middle of the white, and not a move.

"We are of the Church," she said, and crossed herself, and the other two crossed themselves, and nodded agreement.

"What's your opinion of it?" himself asked.

"Good people," she said. "They do a lot of good."

"Have you thought of joining?" himself asked.

"We clean the church and the oratory," Mãe Felicia said. "How could we join *Umbanda?* Father Miklos would send us to everlasting fire."

"And we would lose the work," Mãe Isis said. "Our mothers and grandmothers would curse us. Did they work all their lives for careless daughters to lose their places? We aren't young women. We have our responsibility."

The three bustled about, setting cups and saucers, bringing the filter, the coffee, and the spoons kept in a drawer. Each wore an embroidered white linen dress, half-sleeved, high-necked, long in the skirt, tied at the waist, and a white cloth covered their heads. Aged they were, but with barely a line in any round-cheeked face, and the mouths in repose seemed to have been carved by a jeweler, so full in the lip, smoothed, defined at the edges, in laughing, a frame for whitely healthy teeth without space or any profit for the dentist. All their working lives the three had done nothing except follow their mothers in caring for the church, and Father Miklos' house, and the oratory and the little rooms. For so many years, not another thought except their families.

"A moment here," The O'Dancy said. "Why would your mothers curse you? If Father Miklos has the cross over you and the Virgin's light is ever about you, why should any curse of the dead affect you?"

Mãe Isis was eldest. The other two watched her, Mãe Palmyde looking up from the blue light of the gas ring, Mãe Felicia still bending over the table setting out the plates, both still, and Mãe Isis looking up at a plaster statue of the Christ in benediction above the door.

"Our pae was grandson of the Lady Aracý," she said, eyes in white flash. "Mãe told us to be careful how we used our lives. The Lady Aracý had great power. With the White Side. We know it."

"Mary Mother slip a hand under your chins, for I'd never do a moment's harm to you," himself said. "Listen, then. If it were not for Father Miklos, and a thought you might lose your jobs, would you be in this *Umbanda?*"

The three may have moved their eyes at each other, but it might have been the light, one bare bulb hanging from the rafters, pulled over by a piece of string dangling pennants and small flags from the corner.

Mãe Isis moved the arms crossed over her waist and the hands fell to her sides.

"Yes," she said, and the other two nodded, and quietly went on with what they were doing, as if ease, at last, was in the air.

"Why were you waiting here, dressed, tonight?" himself asked.

"Young Djalma's riding out warning everybody to be up at The

House," Mãe Isis said. "We were going. But we wouldn't go in. Unless Father Miklos tells us."

"He'll be there," himself said. "Now be honest. Why should you join *Umbanda*?"

Mãe Isis raised the long bony hands and let them fall.

"Master," she said helplessly, and looked at the other two. "Well?"

"We know it in ourselves," Mãe Felicia said quickly, staring across the table. "I hear the voices. I feel them all about. Better to join them, be with them. But we turn our backs."

"We are of the Church," Mãe Isis said, and crossed herself. "The reverend father condemns them. There are penalties. Life in purgatory. Besides, we are daughters of a grandson of the Lady Aracý."

"Don't be saying anything for my benefit," himself said. "Where are your husbands?"

Mãe Felicia smoothed the tablecloth, and her eyes stared white in shadow with the bulb overhead.

Mãe Palmyde stirred the coffee.

"All right," himself said. "I'll tell you. They're at the House of the Twelve Apostles."

Mãe Isis sighed, eyes shut, and laughed, clasping her hands.

"Ah, Master, but you knew all the time," she said. "Why should we hide anything from The O'Dancy, son of a son of a son of the Lady Xatina, of the Lady Aracý, of the Lady Auriluci, of the Lady Tiridín, and all of them on the White Side? Why did we hear your step tonight? Why did we know it was you, and no sound, and nobody to tell us?"

They were laughing quietly and nodding, and again there was feeling of peace in the place.

"If your husbands are of this *Umbanda*, why aren't you?" himself asked. "Come on, now. I want the right explanation. What about your children? Have you not eighteen between the three of you?"

Mãe Isis poured the cane alcohol, Mãe Palmyde spooned the coffee through the filter, and Mãe Felicia measured the slices of cake. They all looked alike, three big women in white, apparently deaf, but from the set of their heads, each waiting for the other.

"They're grown, Master," Mãe Isis said. "Out of the house, most of them. Their own families."

"But all of *Umbanda*," himself said, soft, not to distress them. Mãe Isis nodded.

"Most," she said, and offered a glass thimble. "It's the oldest on The Inheritance. No harm will come to you. Our prayers are in it."

"My prayers for you," himself said, and drank a mild, sweetish fire. "Very good. Now, gather yourselves. What's in *Umbanda* for you? What do you have to do? What's different between *Umbanda* and the Church?"

"In church we pray," Mãe Isis said. "We have the Virgin Mother, and the Son, and the Father of us all, and Father Miklos makes the way clear. But in *Umbanda,* we are more a part."

"Explain it," himself said. "How are you more a part?"

"The messengers come into us," Mãe Felicia said. "They come into our bodies. They work through us on earth."

"We become mediums," Mãe Palmyde said. "We cure the ills of the earth. Why should we be sent to purgatory? The white messengers, the spirits, aren't they also of the Father? He created all things."

"Have you spoken to Father Miklos about this?" himself asked.

The three looked surprise at each other, and they turned away in a whisk of skirts, laughing.

"Not to be mentioned," Mãe Isis said. "Not one word. For him, *Umbanda* is part of the devil. The Church, yes, believes in the Devil. *Umbandistas* don't. Or in hell."

"How can you go to church and not believe in hell or the Devil?" himself asked, and took a cup of coffee from Mãe Palmyde. "If you believe in God, then you must believe in the Devil."

Mãe Palmyde shook her head, and took the cake plate from Mãe Felicia.

"There are spirits dispossessed," she said. "They live in space. But they wait to enter the thoughtless. Bad thoughts, weakness in the mind, that's like a hole in the wall. They enter. In that way, we have thieves and murderers, and fights, quarrels, thefts. Bad thoughts, that's an evil spirit. Temptation, that's an evil spirit working in them. Prayer, that's for one, for the world. That's the Church. But the White Ones, of *Umbanda*, they go out to meet them, not on their knees, not in words alone, but they offer their bodies. Take me, enter, Holy One, use me to purify the world, the dark world, the wicked, the vicious world, use me to raise up the dispossessed, to bring them into peace, into the all-consoling peace of love. This is made with chipped coconut and banana paste and angelica and honey. It's the recipe of your own mãe."

The O'Dancy laughed at an offer made without change of pace or tone, and took a slice, and bit, finding a taste forgotten from childhood.

"Very, very good," himself said. "You could do worse than send me up a small one every week. But listen to me. If you're not now of *Umbanda,* how is it you know so much and speak so well of it?"

The three stared, Mãe Palmyde with a piece of cake almost in her mouth, Mãe Felicia with the coffeepot almost in pour, Mãe Isis with a thimble held out to Mãe Felicia. The three, black against white linen, blue wash walls behind, and an oleograph of Jesus of the Sacred Heart on the far wall, a calendar beside the bedroom door, a white cupboard, a white-clothed table, a few square-backed chairs, three lives of words and thoughts and work with bucket and brush and furniture polish, and knowledge of all the children, the rage and blaze of passion, the lyric moments of conception, the pains of birth, the worries and angers, the thousands of meals, and how many friends and acquaintances, and detailed pattering of the family and The House, and every other family and house in and around, all caught up, held, twisted, whirling in a moment, with knowledge of good and evil and God and the Devil and the love of the Virgin Mother and forgiveness in the Son, and not a letter of the alphabet between them.

But in that quiet air, it was not lost that Mãe Palmyde had spoken with the certainty, the peace, and the schooled knowledge of the dedicated.

"We are more than people who live and die," Mãe Felicia said, and poured coffee. "We are with the White. We work against the powers."

"What of *khimbanda?*" himself asked Mãe Isis.

The three looked at him, and the right arm of each was behind her back, and he knew the fist would be closed with the thumb between first and second fingers to ward evil and prevent its passage through their bodies.

"We know," Mãe Isis said. "We won't go in The House. Not till Father Miklos has been in."

"You mean Brother Mihaul," himself said, and stood. "I'm glad I came down. You've a great deal of work to do in the oratory. Now. Look at me."

The big eyes came up at himself, but slowly, the eyes of good, and gentle, and frightened women.

"Lift up your hearts, for I love the three of you and all in your families," The O'Dancy said. "Be enjoying your lives quietly now, and tell me. What of Hilariana?"

The break was in the voice, never meant, cursed in the moment, gulped, regretted.

Mãe Isis put an elbow on the table and rested the bridge of her nose on the fist and closed her eyes, and Mãe Palmyde slid her arms over the table and lay her head down, turned away, and Mãe Felicia leaned against the wall and the flat of her hand covered her eyes.

"Not her fault," Mãe Palmyde said. "Taken against her will."

"Tell me," himself said. "When? How?"

"The old one, Mãe Nueza," Mãe Isis said. "She was a medium. Of the Black. They spoke through her mouth. Used her bones. Hilariana was a baby."

"How in the Name would I ever know it?" himself said, almost seeing the years of whispered instruction, and the eyes of Hilariana, the child. "Who could guess? Who'd believe?"

"Ah," Mãe Isis said. "Nobody would believe. Nobody. But we knew. Who would tell you? Everybody afraid to go near. Everybody afraid of The Touch. A curse in life."

"What is this Touch?" himself asked.

"A gathering of the Black beside and behind," Mãe Isis said, and raised a hand to the Christ over the door. "They use you. You think you do as you want? No. As they want. You think you don't believe this or that? Of course. They don't want you to. They tell you what to believe and what not to believe, and what to do and what not to do. You think it is you? No. It is them. That is The Touch."

"Are you able to see it?" himself asked. "Would you say I was cursed?"

All three were still.

Mãe Palmyde turned her head, but her arms stayed over the table.

"Many, many years you walked with The Touch and we knew it but how should we tell you?" she said. "What would you say?"

"Lot of things sound foolish," Mãe Felicia said. "Ask one of them Indios from the interior, never been to church, never heard a priest, what he's doing kneeling down and getting up, and he'll tell you it's all foolish. How do you make people believe?"

"They believe when they see," Mãe Isis said. "That's all. Tell a man there's food on the table. That table got nothing on it? He won't believe you. Put something on the table, he'll sit down. Don't have to say another word."

"You believe what you see," The O'Dancy said. "You 'see' the White?"

All three nodded.

"They're more beautiful than us," Mãe Felicia said. "I'll be happy to go. Happy to come again and do good."

"But this Indio from the interior?" The O'Dancy said. "How do you get him to be baptized, first of all? There's got to be a lot of 'belief' there. Hasn't there?"

All three were still.

Mãe Isis shook her head.

"Like children," she said. "Children don't believe. They're told what to do. What's right. What's wrong. They do wrong? They get punished. They grow up knowing. It's no 'belief.' They do what they always did. These from the interior, they're the same. They come in the Church, they get clothes, they get food. So. They believe."

"What shall I do with Hilariana?" himself asked.

The three turned to each other, brows up, as if the question was unusual proof of failure to grasp the obvious.

"Well, Master, now you know, now you can cure," Mãe Isis said, and the other two nodded. "You must know, first. Father Miklos doesn't know. And what could he say to her? She doesn't go to church. But the saintly father, he knows. With your help, and ours, all of us, she's going to come back. The Touch passes with the blessing."

"Help me, now, Brother Mihaul," himself said, and stood. "Be ready. The House and every last thing in it must be cleansed before the morning."

The three nodded, and not a line of doubt in any face.

"We should thank you for visiting us poor ones," Mãe Isis said. "The cake will go to The House this day every week. But will Mãe Narcissa allow it to be served?"

"Mãe Narcissa will take care of her kitchen," The O'Dancy said. "Januario will serve the cake to me. And I should have come here long ago. And everywhere else. Is there anything you want? Anything that would make your lives happier?"

Mãe Isis folded her hands under her chin.

"At the same time the Lady Hilariana is blessed, the Lady Divininha should also go under the cross," she said. "She has been led. She is a good woman."

"A good woman," himself said, and tried to look at the words. All three nodded.

"Madame Briault is no longer of The House," himself said. "Is that what you mean?"

"No," Mãe Isis said, and laughed. "She's a servant. She does what she's told. She is the woman of Clovis. He is great-grandson of Mãe Neuza. He is son of Exú. When Democritas goes, he will be Number One. His other woman is *iemanja*. The Lady Hilariana will also be one of his women. Any *iemanja* will be his sister and mother and wife."

The O'Dancy put a hand on the jamb and leaned on a straightened arm, looking out at the dark garden, at specters, shades, denials in the blood.

"Clovis," himself said. "Unbelievable."

"Exú works among unbelievers," Mãe Isis said. "Unbelievers are his subjects. He always goes as a simple one. What is belief? It comes after the fact, for some. Before the dream, for others. And before this night, would you have listened? You saw the oratory?"

He nodded.

Mãe Isis raised her hands, let them fall.

"We shall go with you to The House," she said. "Four, that's better than one. And we go the short way. We shall wait in the house of Mãe Narcissa."

Himself went out to the gap in the hedge and stood until the light went out, and the door was locked, and three white shapes came toward him. He stood aside to let them pass and followed on the low level, skirting the kitchen gardens and the greenhouses, to the stairway up to the garage, and every step with little in mind except Divininha, and Clovis, one and the other. Clovis, now that the mind had space to measure, could easily be the monster in sheep's clothing. There was ever a smile in the eyes of the man, that might be mistaken for good humor, but the men under him were far from taking liberties, for he was quick with boot and whip, and he was known to be a knife fighter, and all those, besides a way with animals, made him a good Number One without any flourishes. He could certainly drink, but not at work, and he also was known to have an eye for the wives of other men, though no trouble had so far come of it. A simple man he had been at the beginning, but he showed real shrewdness in many things, though that might be normal growth of one going into the prime, and yet his rise from the coffee plantations, into cotton, cattle, and transport, and up to the Number One post and undoubted successor to Democritas had been without a word of comment from anybody.

But.

There was something about him, some thorn that caught an instinct, a certain slime in the glance, a walk that could be mistaken for the horseman's, pigeon-toed and short stepping, but it was far more a stilt, a picking up and putting down, as if hoofed. He drew a Number One's pay, which was ample, and he owned a string of fine riding horses and cattle ponies, and a car, though, of course, his mam and grandam had left him money. He also owned a bar down at the village, and perhaps other property, all evidence of ability.

Himself caught up with the three women.

"Tell me," The O'Dancy said. "If this Clovis is what you say he is, why does Democritas permit him in my employ?"

Three smiles seemed to whiten the night. They all stood on the steps to breathe easy.

"Dem will keep him close until he shows sign," Mãe Isis said. "It took time to find out. But he'll do no harm. He fears Democritas. Mãe Nueza was grandam of Ephemia, too. That's how he was taken on. He's nothing, beyond the spirit. He knows where the power is. Democritas and the saintly father, they'll take him in a cloud one day. Then he'll go under the cross. After, he won't be anybody."

"Won't be anybody," himself said.

"Just plain Clovis da Souza," Mãe Isis said. "Nobody. Not Number One. Nobody."

They went on up the stair, between strelitzia clumps and camelias, and in that scent the wave came, crushing, closing the eyes, and no going on for that moment, knowing it was time to think of Divininha.

Three simple women had passed judgment on another. They spoke from the simplicity of their hearts. They were good women. None knew it better than himself. Their opinion at other times in other matters might have been passed by without so much as a sneer. But in the matter of Divininha they held premium of authority. They were women and they knew their own.

It seemed strange that so many years could go by without any thought of her, except that she was at The Inheritance. Or, if other thought intruded, a mere conjecture about what she might be doing. And invariably a disgusted turning away to consider something else. She was simply another human being on earth.

So, the weeks, months, years.

They might just as well have been divorced, but there was no wish, certainly no intention in the heart or soul of himself to marry again, and she kept her promise, never said anything, and so it went on.

It had been more than three years since they had last met, at a reception given at The House for foreign visitors to the O'Dancy Foundation. Hilariana did everything, and himself was merely asked to attend or not, as he wished. As it happened, one of the delegations had been arranging a loan with the bank and he flew down with them, not as host or owner or even as a welcome guest, but just as somebody happening to drop in. But then, of course, everybody confused issues and crowded to congratulate himself on a magnificent institution and a remarkable daughter, and Divininha had taken his arm, beautiful as ever.

She wore creamy pink worked in pearls, and with that deep bronze-brunette hair and the diamonds there was no other woman in the room except Hilariana, in apricot with emeralds and that red hair.

"Now, darling," she said in a good, loud, plenty-of-champagne voice. "Why don't you tell these dear people the truth? I mean, for a change."

"I'd prefer you told them," himself said, half guessing what might be coming.

"Well, everybody, listen to the bone of contention," she said, patting her midriff. "He loves his daughter so much he's got nothing for his wife. And his daughter hates him so much, she's got nothing for anybody except a darling Jap and he's not here. Between money and hate, the Foundation and everything else go along splendidly. As you've seen. Now, all sit down, and I'll show you a local version of a *candomblé*. It's of the country, but not of this state, in origin. But it'll do. Right? Music."

Rather than drop his arm, and himself careless, she walked him to the small gold chairs and sat beside him, for a moment, and left without a word. At that time he should have had the sense to go. Discomfort was about the place. Hilariana was nowhere near. Everybody seemed to be wondering if Divininha had been joking a little too far along a pipe of champagne, or if she said what she meant, and if she did, why himself could sit there. He could have told them. He was disinterested in her, in them, in all their opinions.

The *candomblé* was better than any other himself had ever seen, good as any ballet, finer color, rhythm, mass movement, more sheer use of the body and control of muscle than most. Girls danced, whirled, almost shook their heads off in simulation of trance. Men leaped, turned in mid-air, bounced, drummed their feet, all in motions of the trance.

But himself was suddenly and freezingly aware that they were, in fact, in trance.

All of them.

From childhood, himself knew too well.

A group in scarlet came down the stairway. Under black capes with scarlet linings, they wore red jersey tights. The men were bearded, mustached, with golden horns stuck to their foreheads. The women wore horns reaching over their heads. Under scarlet paint none was soon recognizable. But the legs of Divininha were not to be disguised.

The O'Dancy kicked back the chair, turned all the heads, and walked out in the middle of the floor.

"Now we've seen a *candomblé*," himself said. "That's how they used to act up north in the slave days. I'm glad Mrs. O'Dancy Boys made it clear it doesn't go on here."

People were shouting and the dancers were clawing his arms, but Januario put the lights on at the back, and the scarlet group on the stairway stood there.

"You make a fine picture," himself said, and began clapping. "Thanks for a gruesome entertainment. You did well. Next time, let's have some cattlemen and the guitars. It's healthier. Besides, they're better dancers. I don't like this devil's business."

Everybody in the audience stood to applaud. Many of the girls were carried off, some were dragged, and the dressed-up people on the stairs went out.

Hilariana never mentioned it. From that night to the moment, not a word from Divininha.

The shock was to be told that she was a "good" woman. Himself knew what was meant in the mind by those words. But most ever known about her pointed to the opposite.

"Wait," himself called to the three a little way in front.

They waited at the top of the steps, breathless.

"What do you mean exactly, when you say Divininha is 'good'?" himself asked quietly, for voices carried.

They took time among themselves, showing whites of eyes in darkness, and teeth smiled in the night.

"She wants to do only good," Mãe Isis said quietly, too, but certain. "She sends children to school. Got teachers here. Two nurses this end, two the other, always traveling. Children's hospital. Toys for all of them. Picture books. The wives of the men working in the mountains, she sends them up every week, brings them back.

Got a savings bank for the children. Nothing she won't do. Ask for anything, if it's good, she'll say yes."

The other two nodded and hm-hm'd agreement.

"Isn't she of the *khimbanda?*" himself asked.

"Like the Lady Hilariana," Mãe Felicia said. "Now you know, you can cure."

"I'll have help in it," himself said. "Now there's this. How could I tell the difference between *Umbanda,* and a *candomblé* and *khimbanda?*"

The three laughed high in their throats.

"Ah, Master, you mean *macumba,*" Mãe Isis said. "You could tell only that *Umbanda's* the White Way to God and Jesus. *Khimbanda's* the black, to Exú. Skulls, and blood, and horned heads. *Candomblé,* that's the way everything's done. With the drums."

"*Candomblé's* the ritual, is that it?" himself asked.

"They turn it how they want," Mãe Palmyde said. "A *candomblé,* that's the place where they beat drums. People just enjoying themselves. *Macumba,* they don't work White or Black. They couldn't work White. But the Black's bound to get them. That way, everybody gets caught."

"Everybody," Mãe Isis said. "Caught before they know it. But they don't know it. They never know it. Exú is in them. He tells them. The Touch is on them. They're caught."

"Caught," himself said.

"Yes, caught," Mãe Isis said. "You can't go in trance just to enjoy yourself. Exú's waiting there. And the *orixás.* All they need is a hole in the wall. Then they get in. You don't know it. Perhaps never will. But they work. You work for them. In trance or out, you're caught."

Standing on the steps talking to three women almost the same age as himself, among all three of them not one tenuous fancy of the exigencies himself had passed through, yet until the moment, himself, of self-righteous patronage, might have gambled a fortune that their lives were open pages in large letters.

No great onset of self-confidence came in knowing himself thoroughly, disgracefully mistaken.

In basic matters of living and thinking, they knew more than himself, had more grasp of immediacies, more knowledge of right and

wrong, and all without an hour of formal instruction or any training except of The House.

They were truly of Brazil. They felt, they sensed, and they knew,
with help only of their kind, within sanctuary of the Church.

"I'm obliged to you," himself said. "We'll talk more often."

Three white smiles stayed in the night, and three white shapes
turned and walked on, across the paving but not toward the
Women's House.

"Where will you go?" himself called.

"To the church, Master," Mãe Palmyde said beyond the fountain. "We'll wait there for Father Miklos."

"It's the oratory that needs the cleansing," himself said.

"The church, first," Mãe Isis said in a voice that denied doubt.
"The bodies must be put back in the walls. But after Father Miklos
has been in."

"Explain yourself," himself said, and the fountain's cold marble
came gratefully in grip. "How do you know the bodies were ever
out?"

"Because it's always been," Mãe Felicia said. "Every time they
come here they empty the tombs. And we call Father Miklos and
he brings the men to put them back. Then we clean."

"Nobody'd tell me," himself said.

"Ah, Master, how much would you believe?" Mãe Palmyde said.
"Without seeing, what do you believe?"

The voice came out of darkness from a throat he had known lifelong, but the question held the substance of all the seconds of his
time on earth, and with the thought came a rage that himself was
also in a body, and one day, in a moment, that helpless rattle of
shrivel and bone could be taken out by the children of Satan, or
put back by the Faithful, and never a word to say, or, if they were
all like himself at the moment, none to raise voice or hand from
lack of knowledge or witlessness, or purest ignorance, yes, they,
pretending so much.

"Stay here," he said, and passed them. "Let me see what's to be
believed or not."

The steps wound down, for the church was cut into the hillside
where a cavern had been, and the gate led to a flight of stairs and
the sacristy door, and around, to the font, and the nave. The plan

was part of the mind of himself and his feet took the steps without guide or light, down the flight toward the sacristy. Incense blew strong from the open gate, though not the incense himself had ever known, but another, sweeter, that wrinkled his nostrils.

At the font he stopped, held.

The church was lit by candles in sconces around the walls, on the altar, and in the four small private chapels, and the gold roof reflected light from flying cherubim and seraphim in clouds about the Virgin Mother enthroned in the sun's rays. But the clear gold was hung in spider's webs. Yards-long falls of cobweb hung in dark clouds. Goats' skulls were stuck where the web draped, and human skulls weighted the falls to the backs of pews, and the skins of cats, goats, snakes, hung about the walls, and chicken feathers, wings, legs covered the floor.

The saintly figures were gone. In their places almost life-size statues of the demon gods clawed, grinned, pranced, and Satan gestured on the altar, crowded about by scarlet two-headed beings on two bodies, male and female joined at the waist in one pair of legs, and the female arms reached hands to the phallus, but the male hands stretched down between the thighs.

The door to the vault was open. Incense blew from the bowl on the top stair.

Slowly, himself became used to candlelight and the shadows of cobwebs and he bent, looking over the backs of the pews to the other side of the church.

In a long line all the cadavers of the family had been taken from the coffins and stood up, in groups of their children, with candles burning at their feet, all wreathed with speckled chicken feathers, and hung about with strips from the skins of animals.

Grandam Jurema's skull made lasting screech through missing teeth, and a hang of white hair spread a frozen wave over a winding cloth stained by red earth. Grandams in silk shrouds were about her, all in fall of black plaits, white plaits, and several with fair hair, and mops of black hair, and some shaven to the bone, with earrings larger than their ears. Grandam Aracý's face shone smooth over temples and cheeks, and the lips said oh to frame perfect teeth, and all her sons and daughters and grandsons and daughters and all the children made a crowd about her. Grandam Xatina, in silk still gleaming, wore the colored feather wreath that thankfully hid her face, among the crowding heads of the family of her time, and her left hand spread in a skeletal fan, but the thumb of the right hand poked between the first and second fingers, and the fist rested over the heart. The Mam stood in the lilac dress bound about by the muslin that had tied her wrists, but the fair hair, a myriad thanks to the Mother of Jesus in Her mercy, was over the eyes. From a corner of vision himself saw the leaden glint of Fransisca's sheath, and all dearest flowers to her memory now, but the courage was not in the heart to look direct.

Kneeling there, himself knew they were most intimate part, the scores of them, and all the others on the staircase, all the glares from hollow bone, all the candlelit grins, all were part of himself, of his blood, sharers of his name and common inheritance, and all of them Christian, whether Euro or Indio or African, or any interbreeding of the three. All had been baptized in the Light and the Word, all were remembered by name in family prayers in the holy place where now they stood in quietude of ghostly shame, and about them all an olid blight of putrefaction, all disturbed by tacit permission of himself, by lack of guardianship, neglect of duty, and by usurpation of attitudes presumed superior that were only brutally, passively ignorant, and himself a product of the rotting womb a few steps away.

In that silent company once of happy, chattering, singing people, of children born and loved, and women adored, and men made dear by devoted women, he saw himself, though not with them, but out, up, on the hill, under the sixth granite cross, part of them, with his name in the same prayers, now and at any time helpless victim of Satan's human tools, to be stacked by evil will against a wall, decked with feathers, splashed with blood, desecrated in shadow of cobweb and the skulls of sacrificed animals, all before the altar of God, in defiance of grace, in obscene contempt of salvation, or any respect for the dignity of death or any simplest decency. No voice was in him, no breath to speak or will to curse, or any desire to pray.

Himself was soul unborn, unblessed, imbrued with vice and moiled in grossest rags of remorse.

Numb, mute, he pulled himself upright, and walked to the font, and around, and up the stair.

Outside, he stood against the breeze to breath the living draft, he, that agglomeration of vital atoms that time would turn to dust, himself, the spirit to be judged, and both of them vested for a little while in The O'Dancy, citizen, employer, patriarch.

And traitor.

In sum, no more than any of those down below, in part, far less.

Three white shapes waited on the turn.

"You were right, and God help me for a footstool creature," himself said. "Don't go near."

"Father Mihaul and the men are on the Long Steps," Mãe Isis whispered. "Walk below the cross, Master. The Touch is on you."

In the darkness he saw the bend of each white-sleeved arm behind their backs, and knew the thumbs would be in the fists.

"Would you pray any harder if I told you I didn't care?" himself said, and walked on. "I'll think of myself when the decency is part of us, again. I'm a drowned one, in nothing. I've no age, and no wish."

He heard them weeping, and the fountain's spray whispered over, and the night wind in the rhododendrons sighed across his footsteps, and the roses breathed beneath the arbors, and the air beyond the massing white of camelias was alight and a prayer floated there in a single voice. A chorus was stronger, and over the top of the Long Steps a crucifix shone, rising, and torchlight flared on the white habit, and white clothing massed, walking on, praying powerfully, in unison.

Behind the jacarandá he waited, and watched the scores of chanting men in white procession beneath the torches cross the lawn toward the church.

Himself fell on the bones of his knees, and put hands palm to palm, and wrung the fingers.

But no word was there. Only The Mam's bowed head, and the black stares of the grandams, and the scarlet horror perched on the altar were in mind, or in sense, and the rest was memory of putrefaction.

Anger was cold in himself that dear dust could be so mishandled, defiled, brought to merest servitude of Satan and the colony of hell, and the church they had revered lifelong used as stables for Black Sanctus and the reign of fiends.

A man padded along the path in the long stride, stone to stone, carrying a staff, running on.

He got up, himself a tired one, and empty, no more, and walked in darkness toward The House. Yet as leaves burst as swords from the sprouting cactus, anger broke the passive grief and trees and shrubs, yes, the very grass itself turned crimson.

30 The O'Dancy reached the gate while the man jogged, jumping from stone to stone, flashing the torch, a glittering ball in silent bounce. The light shone full, blinding, and the man stopped.

"Well," The O'Dancy said. "Who is it? Turn off that thing."

"A pardon, Master," the voice said in heavy breath, and the light was not. "I am Euripedes Silvestre da Cunha. I bring the gift of Ahatubai."

The light shone again, and a fist held up a longbow all en-flowered along the haft with orchids intertwined in the string.

"A son?" The O'Dancy shouted. "She's borne a son? Now God be praised, and how is she?"

"Well, Master," Euripedes said. "She begs you will bring Father Miklos. He was born early. He's strong. I heard him."

"Come with me," The O'Dancy said, and held the gate open. "Januario will look after you till I've finished a few matters. What more do you know of the Lady Ahatubai?"

"Nothing, Master," Euripedes said. "I was youngest, and I can run. The truck was out for the doctor."

"Two hours or more ago," The O'Dancy said, and passed a light hand over the flowered haft. "Was it her father who thought of this? Who sent the longbow?"

"The mãe of Ahatubai," Euripedes said.

"Jurema," The O'Dancy said, and nodded. "What did you see on the way here?"

"Many in white," Euripedes said. "On the other side, like a morning mist."

"Detergent," The O'Dancy said. "Go with Januario."

The longbow held faint scent of flowers, gentlest reminder that the arrow is sometimes only love's, and Januario's eyes opened, shining the wide grin of other joy, known, felt, that cannot be spoken, the same wild, secret joy that filled The O'Dancy.

"A first-born," he whispered, and fell on his knees, hands out to touch the haft. "Ah, Master. We prayed for this time. We prayed. We are answered. A first-born son."

He took with delicate fingers a flower from the haft, and kissed it, and undid a jacket button and put the rose above his heart, did up the button, crossed himself, kissed his fingers, and raised his face and flung out his hands on straight arms.

"We have no altar to rest the harbinger," he said, a broken prayer.

"It will go in the case and Father Miklos can sprinkle it when the boy is baptized," himself said, and took out the keys. "Take Euripedes downstairs till I leave. Telephone the heliport. I shall land at the house of the Lady Ahatubai. Come to me in the Leitrim Room."

Himself carried the longbow in both hands up the stairs, and stood, putting a fist on the shoulder of Grandfa Leitrim.

"One of your own," he whispered. "I swear it. Myself'll present him to God in our name. If I die before he's a man, I'll leave him guarded by the best. If he goes wrong, it'll be in the blood. If he's right, it was in the pain of his mother. And the prayers of his father. And God the Father, help me now."

The corridor seemed alive with the grandams. Their faces came to him and he looked into their eyes, passing them, knowing, perhaps, what they were thinking, as if the bodies he had just seen crowded in the church were speaking, each in her own voice. The keys jingled on the ring, and the glass door opened. All the longbows, signal of first-born O'Dancys, dressed in dusty flowers with the fallen petals in little wrinkles on the floor, and the bunches of everlasting flowers, heralds of eldest daughters, hung from spurs nailed up by Grandfa Phineas, and his longbow was first, hung there by the father of Grandam Nahua, cacique of the Tupi, peacemaker between the pioneers and his people.

The O'Dancy bent to go into the case, and moved the bunch of flowers which marked the birth of Breonha, first child of Divininha, and hung the longbow so that the orchids' petals were free, and stayed there for a moment. Three times in his life he had been inside. Once for Daniel. Once for Breonha. Once for Stephen. But

Stephen's should not have been there. He was not first-born, but first to live. The children of Tomomi were registered in her name, and all were born outside The Inheritance.

The son of Ahatubai was truly The O'Dancy, first-born of first mating.

Himself knew why Januario had kissed and kept the rose.

Ahatubai's almost purely Indio mother, Jurema, was married to Alcides, of an Afro-Portuguese family known since the days of the pioneers. A first-born son of hers by The O'Dancy could only be a sign from on high that The House was thrice blessed and thrice secure. In the mind of himself the plans were in being for the festival of baptism, the guests, the hospitality, decorations, gifts.

But sadness came deep in thinking, though without will, of Divininha. There was no fear of what she might say or do. There was great unwillingness to hurt the woman she hid, had ever hidden, perhaps since the death of Breonha, that little bundle in lace, crushed in the fall of her nurse down the stairs of the Women's House, and Vanina raging, shrieking through the place day and night, and nothing to make her sleep until Dr. Gonçalves ordered her pinned while he injected the drug. That, too, might have been start of the habit.

Himself shut his eyes to it, and locked his mind while he locked the case, and went down to the Leitrim Room.

The five men stood together before the fireplace in cool air, as if they had decided to go, and they looked around without a smile.

"Sorry I kept you," himself said. "But there's a plane'll take you into the city, and you can catch an early one to Brasilia without much trouble. Did you have all you wanted?"

"Thank you," Young Carvalhos Ramos said, though in dryish temper. "We're sorry we dropped in like this. But it's possibly the most serious matter we shall ever have to deal with. Sir, we hope you'll think it over without being too prejudiced. I know it sounds, well, false, I suppose. But it isn't. After all, it's our duty to protect people. Not to throw them dreams. That's what this Agrarian Reform Movement is. A phantasm. If we can control it, we've got a chance of doing something really constructive for the nation as a whole. If we don't, I mean, if we let the present reformists have their way, we'll have a dictatorship here. By the proletariat. There won't be any private property. There won't be anything. Not even anarchy. Even anarchists have to think, or else they find themselves becoming imperialists. Our lot, given a piece of land to breed on, will do that. And very little else. They certainly won't think. They're not trained or schooled to. No plan, no concentration, no discipline, no authority. Chaos within months. The idlest nation on earth."

"Very well," himself said, and sat down. "What's your own plan?"

Young Carvalhos Ramos stared at him, and half turned to the others, and thought better, and sat on the arm of the chair.

"We've got nothing worked out," he said. "But after yesterday's speech, the writing's on the wall. The whole of the north will go reform. So will most of the south. When that happens there won't be parliamentary representation. There'll simply be a block vote and a steam roller. This place will be cut up. You may not be able to own as much as your youngest laborer. If you're paid for it—that's if—what'll it be? Bonds? Not worth the paper and print. Money? There isn't enough to pay one per cent of the value. A share of the harvest? What harvest? Who's the co-ordinator? By what system of controls, values? Currency? They tell us they've got the answers. Nobody's seen them. They want to alter the Constitution. That gives them the right to appropriate. Question is, will you allow it? If you do, this place is no longer yours. If you intend to fight, why not join us? Why play their game? You make yourself a sitting duck. You're helping to make Brasilia into a real Little Moscow. Aren't you? Can there be any doubt?"

The others nodded, and seemed to be waiting for somebody else, or something else, or anybody or anything else.

Suddenly in the mind of himself there was warmth of compassion for all of them because, at last, they were brought to realize that their comfortable world was in danger of disappearing, and there was little in their minds or spirits to prevent it. The voting urn they all had eulogized as symbol of everyman's freedom was about to become their private cup of gall. Election oratory, noble phrases, slogans no longer held power to persuade a mass of unschooled voters, and all the free wine or beer, rum or sugar brandy would certainly make willing drunkards, but not supporters. The vote would go to the man promising free land, a house, milk and honey, world without end, forever and ever, amen. The spook of that Euro invention of Something for Nothing at last was about to achieve substance in promise of votes by the million.

Himself had sudden access of other sight, but momentary, not truly clear, not even fully apprehended, but merely perhaps touched to the mind's own retina, of Daniel, a little younger than the general age of the group, standing there at one with them, moving in the same crowd, part of the same fashion, a vice-president of O'Dancy Enterprises, or general director, or perhaps a senator, might be ambassador—no, now wait, take the fangs from your heart —well, anyway, one of them with the same problem, him and those gray eyes, and the red hair, and perhaps four or five, or how many fine children somewhere about the place, yes, and listen to what he might be saying, or perhaps the words were in the mouth of himself.

"Tell you what I'll do," himself said. "I won't come out for agrarian reform. It's a pretension hatched by burglars. What I'll do is offer to buy a tract of fiscal land on the other side of the river, here. I'll raze the present village, and I'll build a town for five thousand men and their families. They'll have a hospital, parks, transport, cinemas, sports fields, everything they need for a full social life. They'll have schools of agriculture, forestry, conservation. I'll supply all the agricultural machinery necessary for them to learn how to become productive farmers. Each student will have his own piece of land big enough to support a family with profit. Successful students will take possession of that land. They'll farm in common with their fellows. The crops will be decided by competent authority. They'll be sown, grown and harvested in common, and the proceeds will be divided share for share. A railroad will take the produce into the city. The plan can be copied all over the country. If there's money to pay for appropriated land, then the same money will build those agro-towns. Little Brasilias, not Little Moscows."

The five looked at each other, five blocks of solid doubt, or incomprehension, the same. They had the eyes of men struck by a bullet, aware of disaster, but disbelieving.

Lycurgo was first to shake his head.

"Sir," he said, in slow search of words. "Believe me, I know. Agrarian reform is a magic pass. It means free land. It doesn't mean work. Agrarian reform carries the promise of the new Christ. But without the sweat. It means you simply walk to a piece of land, and it's yours. You build a house. Four poles, a rush roof. It's yours. Now do as you please. That's what agrarian reform is in most minds. Of course, others have other ideas. But when the vote puts it through, they'll discover their mistake. You can take a horse to water, but there's no guarantee he won't kick you in."

"I feel Lycurgo's plan has real merit," Arruda said. "Come out strongly for agrarian reform. That's the most important. There's no need to go into detail."

"Naturally not," The O'Dancy said. "Most of us can't read or write."

"Isn't that the best reason for trying to protect them?" Young Carvalhos Ramos said. "They're being victimized. But if we can only get control, we'll be able to give them the solid help they need. We'll have time to find out what we can do."

"It's become a crisis very suddenly," Teodoro said, and polished his glasses—hahhh!—and squinted through the lenses with the ferocious glare of a general seeing an entire campaign, the while blind as any bat. "I agree with Lycurgo. Any suggestion of school, or work, and we're finished."

"It's the gift of free land, that's what we're up against," Nelson said. "As practical politicians, we have to deal with it. I must say Lycurgo, as usual, put his finger on the weakness in your plan. Sweat. School. Somebody giving orders. Hopeless. No. Agrarian reform is very simple. In very few words. No explanations. No footnotes. There's your land. Take it. All you have to do is vote for the right man."

"We've got to be that party," Young Carvalhos Ramos said, and hit the arm of the chair. "That's why we came here. We need television, radio, newspapers, billboards, mobile units. Everything the imagination can rig up that'll swing the vote to us. If we can get enough of the common vote our way, we're safe. At any rate for a few years. In that time we could even try your plan. But would it work? How many would go there? All you're promising is a free roof they'll eventually have to pay for, and work. That's a dangerous combination."

"But, you see, I'm not suggesting I'll accept 'anybody' or 'they' or anything so transparently stupid," The O'Dancy said. "The only people I'll accept are Indios. The original people of this land. The naked people. The people you don't give a damn for. People I doubt you've ever even thought about. But there are millions of them. And they're Brazilians."

They were looking at each other sidelong or under the brows, short glances, sizing the effect, except Arruda, and he stared, hands in pockets, looking down at his shoes.

"I agree, to some extent," he said. "I've got some property up there. But it'll take years to train them as far as wearing clothing. How do you start?"

"It's a red herring," Nelson said with sharp impatience. "This is politics we're talking about, not anthropology. You've got to find a way of winning an election. It's no use going off at tangents. Political lives are at stake. Political parties could disappear. Do you realize that? Most of us won't elect a single member if we don't take absolute precautions immediately. The campaign's got to start now. That's why we're here."

"If you could promise outright support," Teodoro said, almost supplicatingly. "I believe we'd pull it off, sir. It's going to be the most difficult thing in the world to take this bone out of the dog's mouth, don't you see? Because it all sounds so simple. Vote to alter the Constitution. Then vote to appropriate. There's your land. Walk in. You're the owner. It's mother's milk. The people they're appealing to are the basic element of the nation. They've got the most votes."

"They're not by any means the basic element," The O'Dancy said. "I've told you who they are. Naked Indios. And their children. Those children will be adults in ten, twenty years' time. Producing what? Nothing. The nation's poorer in men and women, poorer in produce. They're not even statistics. Doesn't it worry you?"

"But we can't go combing the banks of the Amazon or rummaging through forests looking for a lot of filthy Indios," Nelson said, pink in the face, though perhaps he had drunk too much. "This business is on top of us. It applies to a quite different class of people. People who could produce a lot more than they do. Earn more, if they worked more. They're hopeless because they don't earn enough, and prices are going higher every day. Those are the people you're going to talk to about Indios?"

"Just a moment," Young Carvalhos Ramos said, and held Nelson by the arm. "You clarify nothing by shouting, you know. I sympathize with The O'Dancy's idea. It could work a miracle, that is, given time. But in that time, an election will put the reformists in. Away go your land and your property, sir. Nothing anybody could do to stop the rot. Its democracy. Parliamentary edict. Army and police in support? It goes through. Where are you? Not here, and probably not even with a square meter to call your own in São Paulo."

"A pretty picture," The O'Dancy said. "But nobody's going to say I put my name to deception. I'll tell you what's wrong. You see, you're not Brazilians. You've no thought for Brazil, this glorious animation under our feet, here. You're simply Euro transplants. You're out for yourselves. Grab, and it's yours. To hell with the rest. Especially 'filthy' Indios."

"I'm not sure you ought to say that," Arruda said, bright, a little pale. "So far as I'm concerned, you're quite wrong."

"You've done very little except sit on your arse and spend your grandfather's money as your father did," The O'Dancy said. "I can tell you what you've done. I can tell all of you exactly what you've done. What you've got. Who your women are, and their addresses. If, of course, you wish? Now, I'll tell you what I'll do."

Men were shouting below, but faintly, and somebody ran down the far wooden stairway, and there was silence.

"I'll find out what that was," The O'Dancy said, and touched the bell. "Now, this agrarian program. If it's for the appropriation of fiscal land, I'm a hundred per cent in favor. But they'll have to build their training centers before they start giving away the earth. That's the first thing. New cities, where men and women can live decently while they learn how to earn. They spent billions on Brasilia. They can spend more on Little Brasilias. Planned by the same architects. Financed by the World Bank, and ourselves. If we need, and we're bound to need, credits for roads and railroads, perhaps the Alliance for Progress'll help us."

Nelson put his hands behind his back and turned to Young Carvalhos Ramos.

"Worse than Kubitschek," he said. "I've had enough, if you have."

"Apparently you haven't done much thinking about the surpluses resulting from that sort of intensive farming," Teodoro said. "Prices'll go into the ground. They'll be plowing it all back again. Haven't you had enough of that?"

"Construct your market," The O'Dancy said. "Millions are going hungry. The United States is giving the stuff away. All right. If it should fortunately come to that, why shouldn't we?"

"We aren't making any money as it is," Nelson said. "You're simply building into national bankruptcy."

"What you're building is another Cuba," The O'Dancy said.

"That'll pass," Teodoro said, and pulled his jacket down in confident discomfort. "They won't stand much more of it. Any more than we would, here. Anyway, they've got too much to fight here. Too much industry. Too many earning good wages. Got their own houses. No. Not a Cuba. But a Brazil given over to the demagogues. No man's property his own. Is that what you want?"

"No," The O'Dancy said. "I want this nation, that's an entire continent in the bounds of one land, to realize its superb possibilities in a second, purely Brazilian gesture. The first was Brasilia. The second ought to be the Little Brasilias. It could be a light to the world. And the perfect answer to the Russian experiment. They only pretend to give people liberty in everything. Except in thought and action. That's by executive order. Is that what you want?"

"But, Mother of God, that's what you'll get here," Nelson said, arms out, almost bent double.

"Wait," Young Carvalhos Ramos said, and held up his hands. "We seem to be on the same road, but not in the same direction. Supposing we adopt this idea of Little Brasilias. Very well. This means a gift of fiscal land. That doesn't hurt anybody."

"Except world markets," Teodoro said. "Remember the surpluses."

"Deal with it when it comes," Young Carvalhos Ramos said. "Now. Thousands of men taken into Little Brasilias. With their families. How many millions left out? Millions, that is, with the vote. Who's going to win an election? How many Little Brasilias can you build between now and the election? One? With your own capital. How many by vote in the Senate?"

"None," Lycurgo said. "That's a scheme of billions. Who's going to guarantee it? Where's the money going to come from? Print it? What's going to happen to the cost of living?"

"What's going to happen to us at the next election?" Nelson said, at the wall. "Somebody tell me that."

"You'll be sent to hell," The O'Dancy said. "That's what you deserve. You've thought for nobody except yourself and those like you. After this, you might think about Brazil."

"What have I ever done against Brazil?" Lycurgo said, and opened his hands. "All I've done is build. I've helped to build one house into a village. More than once. And many a village into a town. Why should Brazil or anybody else be angry with me?"

"You've done too much for yourself," The O'Dancy said. "That's why you find yourself here. Asking for help."

"And what have you done for Brazil?" Nelson said over his shoulder. "Whatever it is, it's paid you in billions. Who are you to talk?"

"Brazil's a hell for Negroes, a purgatory for whites and a paradise for mulattoes," The O'Dancy said. "I don't know who thought of that, but I agree. I'm a mulatto, and I find this a paradise. I'm unworried about yesterday. It's gone and it was good. Unworried about tomorrow because it hasn't come. Unworried about today because God is my Father. His will be done, and I will do as He advises. What I have done is produce coffee, and cotton, and sugar. I've helped to build cities. Roads. Communications. Light and power. Provided some of our basic industry. Capital for marginal industry. Port facilities. Schools. Scholarships. What have I done? What have you done to earn the right to ask the question? What are you? A lawyer? You make a business of lying from dawn to midnight. You must, to earn a living. No wonder you need mistresses. Somebody has to provide the spiritual cotton wool to soak your filth. One woman alone would die of poison. What have I done? In truth, nothing. Brazil's done everything for me. She's my mother."

Januario tapped, and the white gloves fidgeted in eye line.

"Well?" himself said. "What was all the noise downstairs?"

"Some of the young men and women, Master," Januario said. "Most of them are leaving."

"Whiskery little humbugs," Nelson said. "Came in here and wanted to start a session on the hi-fi. Twist? The African spice in them? Ought to be shipped back to the Congo."

"I told them we were busy," Young Carvalhos Ramos said. "Serena packed them out. There's one with sharp nails. By the way, there were some people here when we first came. In the corridor. In fancy dress, I thought. All in red."

Lycurgo nodded, turned down his mouth, a mountain of dolor.

"I wish I had something to dress up for," he said.

"Support my reform bill for a hundred Little Brasilias to be built on fiscal land," The O'Dancy said. "I'll back you with everything. And we'll win."

"If you'll permit me," Young Carvalhos Ramos said, and held up his hands. "A hundred Little Brasilias. Five thousand men and their families—did you say?—in each. That's five hundred thousand taken care of out of how many millions?"

"A hundred to start," The O'Dancy said. "Let's say, it'll take six months to finish the first hundred zones. Any reason why the second hundred shouldn't be started immediately after? And a third hundred? Fourth? Fifth? We need a populated land. Each town is center of its farming area. When a thousand of those towns are built, you're going to want a thousand more. Then a minimum of ten million families will be settled on their own land, sowing, harvesting, earning. Put that to the voters. Put some teeth in it. You'll see if they'll vote for it. We're hardheaded from the Euro. We have visions from the Indio. Shrewdness from the African. Sometimes one gets in the way of the other. But we can laugh. Or play maracas. Suggest that the men who made fortunes building Brasilia can make larger fortunes out of Little Brasilias. We steal, but we create. Sky's the floor of paradise. It is robbery?"

"It has virtue," Young Carvalhos Ramos said. "It's the time element that worries me."

"My town will start being built tomorrow morning," The O'Dancy said.

Nelson shook his head, beating his hands behind his back, still staring at the wall.

"Agrarian reform," he said. "Two words. There's your vote. No use talking about a sense of humor. And maracas? A rattle of beans in empty bellies. Pocket and belly. That's our people. Two words. Agrarian reform. That's all."

"We can think it over," Teodoro said. "I like the idea. There's a good deal of opportunity there."

Arruda shrugged.

"I'll go with anything that's got a chance," he said. "I like the Little Brasilia idea too. But what about the cost?"

"How about the cost of a nice, comfortable revolution?" The O'Dancy said. "Everybody in. General paralysis. World loss of credits. How much? You'll have to think about it, as it is. The Army's not all that safe. Sergeants, for God's sake, sending directives to the Government? Sergeants?"

"Letting them say what they think's better than clamping down," Lycurgo said. "Gets rid of a lot of steam."

"Save it for the laundry," The O'Dancy said. "And if they could think, they wouldn't be sergeants. They'd be earning a living. In any case there're too many of them. Waste of time and money. The least trustworthy part of the nation."

"You'll be glad of them if ever there's a coup here," Nelson said.

"They'll be the fire power for any coup," The O'Dancy said. "We've several soldiers in the family. Anything else you'd like to talk about?"

"I think we know just about where we are," Young Carvalhos Ramos said. "I'll let you know later what sort of feeling there is."

"I'd like a quick word with you before you go," The O'Dancy said. "I'll see you all off downstairs."

Young Carvalhos Ramos turned to the others, but as if thankfully they were on their way to the door.

The O'Dancy waited until Januario's white back went out and the door snapped shut.

"Your son killed two men last night, I'm told," he said. "He's in deep trouble with drugs, and so forth."

"My son?" Young Carvalhos Ramos said.

"By Kyrillia," himself said. "Why don't you own him?"

Young Carvalhos Ramos sat down, without hurry, and took a cigarette from the box, and flashed the lighter.

His face was longer than his father's, but the same adamantine quality was in the hard, dark eyes that could be kind, and could smile, that now stared without a blink, making himself blink twice as much in wondering how he did it, until there was memory of an African great-grandmother.

"First, Kyrillis is not my son, he said, through cigarette smoke. "I'd like to knife that into you. He is Kyrillia's son. By your son, Daniel. The proof, if you require it, is in your strongbox in my office. Only myself, Dr. Gonçalves and Father Miklos, so far as I know, are aware of the details."

"Why have I never known about this?" himself asked.

"It happened when you were out of the country," Young Carvalhos Ramos said. "At that time, you were oftener away than here. Kyrillis was born in the city."

"Why should Madame Briault lie?" himself asked.

"That was the rat?" Young Carvalhos Ramos said. "She hates Kyrillia. That's a fine girl. She was strong-minded enough never to say a word. Went through it all. It seems you're willing to believe anybody before those who've served your interests almost with their first intelligent breath."

"I regret it," The O'Dancy said. "I do. But what was the woman's object?"

Young Carvalhos Ramos shrugged.

"Why don't you call your wife?" he said. "Ask her. Wouldn't it be because Kyrillis is heir to The O'Dancy Inheritance? Who'd want that?"

Instantly, in all horrifying certainty, himself was aware that the other white woman in that room with Hilariana could only have been Divininha.

Shaven, daubed in red and white spots, bloodied, cut.

Divininha.

"I accept what you say," himself said. "Inquiries'll clear it. Will you defend Kyrillis?"

"You've told me that lawyers spend their lives earning a living by lying," Young Carvalhos Ramos said. "I've had to do a great deal of lying for you. And bribing. You acquiesced in the lies. You paid the bribes. You now accept my word that I am not Kyrillis' father, and you ask me to lie in his defense? Knowing that you can buy him out of trouble? Expecting me to do the buying? And afterward accusing me?"

"I suppose I could find somebody else," The O'Dancy said. "If he's his father's son, it's my duty."

"Undoubtedly," Young Carvalhos Ramos said. "But the lawyer will have to lie and bribe. On your instruction? Who is, in effect, the liar and briber?"

"Who's the prostitute, who's the customer?" The O'Dancy said. "Or should it be 'client'? Sounds better. All right. What do you know of *Umbanda, macumba,* and *khimbanda?*"

Young Carvalhos Ramos put out the cigarette with two, spaced jabs downward into the dish, and stood, running his fingers around the waist belt of his trousers, looking down, head bent, still with the same stare of dislike.

"I know nothing about them except what I've heard, and that's too much," he said with felt restraint. "What I wanted to say was this. I'm just as much a mulatto as you are. A couple of generations back. Even then, it's a loose use of the term. Indio blood cuts the mulatto. It's all right. I know what you mean. But I don't like your remarks. We use the law as our clients desire. The client pays. It's his responsibility. But as a citizen, when did you ever complain of winning by 'legal' cheating? Or bribing? If Kyrillis is convicted, who'll you blame? Him, as a murderer? Or his lawyer, for losing the case? You have a number of cases coming up. Shall I be the lawyer according to the law? Or shall I win those cases?"

"Win the cases," The O'Dancy said. "That's your job."

"By lying from dawn to midnight, and by bribery," Young Carvalhos Ramos said. "Those are your instructions?"

"My instructions are to win," The O'Dancy said.

"By lying and bribery," Young Carvalhos Ramos said.

"If you don't, the other side will," The O'Dancy said.

"Exactly," Young Carvalhos Ramos said. "While you're building your Little Brasilias, why don't you try building another type? Affecting the law. And its operation. Why don't you let this Kyrillis go on trial and let the evidence do the talking instead of money?"

"I don't feel like making him the meat in any arena," himself said. "That's why I asked if you knew anything of *Umbanda, macumba* and *khimbanda*. If you take this case, you'll have to know a great deal. To argue."

Young Carvalhos Ramos shook his head.

"I've got a good mind to resign," he said. "Everything. Walk out, clean. I'd be a naked chicken within hours. I know it. And for what?"

He buttoned his jacket.

"I'll think this over," he said. "Rough session tomorrow. I need some sleep. I haven't been home for three weeks."

"You're not worried about this boy?" The O'Dancy said.

Young Carvalhos Ramos walked a couple of paces toward the door.

"No," he said without turning. "I'll show you a file. He's certainly not alone. We seem to be breeding a certain type of wild pig, here. That's a slander on the pig. They're always natural."

"You've three children," himself said. "Are you disappointed?"

"It isn't time to be," Young Carvalhos Ramos said. "But if you put all three in that crowd out there, you'd never tell the difference. It's not a question of youth or vitality. I had plenty of both."

"Hard judging," himself said.

"If there was evidence of any brains," Young Carvalhos Ramos said. "My son doesn't want to follow me. Study interferes with the life he wants to enjoy. They permit me to pay the bills, well, yes. One girl's aborted. Eighteen. I'm sick of them, and so's Ormilda. She often asks what we've done to deserve it. Children seem to have changed."

"You're only one couple," The O'Dancy said.

Young Carvalhos Ramos shook his head, not in denial, but in fatigue.

"Too many pleasures available," he said. "Anywhere. Films, television, swimming pools. Life's like a huge fairground. Anywhere you look. How does a boy preserve his brains? I don't know what to do for him. No use sending him to the farm. He'd run away."

The tragedy seemed to form before the eyes of himself. Creonice —sleep on, in peace, now—must have been well in mind before his twelfth birthday, and how many women had taken time and substance since, though if there was harm, no memory was left of it whether physical or mental, and since young men and women of the day certainly could not be using themselves more, or oftener, then by the same standard, they could not possibly be coming to any great harm. Yet, one item, easily the most important, had saved himself from becoming a waster.

Old Mr. Carvalhos Ramos, that wise one, had put him to work.

Long before himself finished school, half a dozen jobs had been learned never by any order, not even by persuasion, but simply by quietly being told what he was to do, always to the end that he might be fit to take charge of The Inheritance. There was early deference to authority, for The Tad had never been a man to brook any nonsense. Old Mr. Carvalhos Ramos took advantage of that training and left the rest to God and blood.

But in Young Carvalhos Ramos, that early training was missing. Apart from that, there were not in his youthful time the roads or motorcars and there was certainly not the mixing of sexes. A youth had to find his own diversion, but only after proper time for study.

Himself never remembered any nonsense with Daniel, for the boy was told what to do.

Young Carvalhos Ramos had never known, because his mother fluttered and his father was busy with affairs. The boy entered law because it was expected. He married Ormilda, a wealthy girl, and the three children grew in a time of asphalt roads, airplanes, sea resorts, and motorboats. Himself was forced to wonder what might have happened if those pleasures had existed in his young time, if he would have gone to work, if he would have been so tractable. There was a doubt. There was hardly blame to the children. The toys were there, but they were never taught to earn them. They took them, all of them, greedily, as children.

"Did you never put any of them over your knee?" himself asked. "A thrashing does a power of good."

Young Carvalhos Ramos laughed, the derisive, short one.

"Too late, now," he said. "Anyway, I was never a believer in that sort of thing. I don't think it does any good."

"Well, now, tell me," himself said. "I owe a great debt to your father. Did you, yourself, want to be a lawyer?"

Despite tiredness and impatience to go, Young Carvalhos Ramos showed surprise that might have been fear.

"What makes you ask a question like that?" he said, and licked his lips, and took out his handkerchief to wipe his mouth. "There are many times when I'd throw it all down the nearest drain, certainly. I'm not so many years younger than yourself, you know. Soon, I shall retire. I believe my son's going to be a television announcer. That's as far as we go."

"What are you going to do?" himself asked. "I mean, when you retire?"

"What I've always wanted to do, just lie on the sand and listen to the waves, and watch the gulls," Young Carvalhos Ramos said. "That's all. Nothing else. I think the Little Brasilia scheme's got a chance. I'll do my best. Don't come down, please."

"Nobody leaves this house and myself not on the doorstep," The O'Dancy said, and led the way. "I'm sorry you're so downcast. How long have you been feeling like that?"

"Years," Young Carvalhos Ramos said. "I wanted legal diplomacy. The Hague. Ormilda didn't. So."

"Anything I could do?" The O'Dancy asked, going downstairs. "If it's a word in the right place?"

"Thank you," Young Carvalhos Ramos said. "I shall soon retire. Thank God. And speaking of thrashing children. Did you ever use that method with your daughter?"

The O'Dancy shook his head.

"In so many ways, you are honest," Young Carvalhos Ramos said, and held out his hand. "Good night. It was a pleasure to be here again. What a glorious place it is."

The others were already in the car, and they reached out their hands, but only Lycurgo made an effort to open a side window.

"If this place was mine," he said loudly, over the good-bys of the others, "I tell you, by God, where I'd put that agrarian reform. I don't think you're right to give anybody a chance. Stamp them in the mud. After all, who are they?"

"All millionaires," himself said. "Every one of them's a millionaire. That's a little mystery you can try to solve on the way. Why would multi-multimillionaires and a chorus of wealthy landowners want to run the risk of having their own properties appropriated? Good night, everyone, and God lift the wings of you."

31

The car curved out toward the airfield, and while himself walked up the stairway a plane tested its motors on the runway beyond the trees.

"The second plane of the Lady Serena's party," Januario said. "She is waiting for Mr. Kyrillis at the pool. Master, that was the noise. Moacyr and Gilberto were trying to catch him."

"I'll deal with it," himself said. "When the maids get here, keep them downstairs till I call. See there's plenty of hot water."

Himself went across the garden to the cabaña. Only a few lights were on among the shrubs and everything was a disagreeable pale greenish color. For some reason Young Carvalhos Ramos came in mind, with deep sorrow for a good friend. Undoubtedly the fellow was in need of help, though perhaps it was too late to do anything even if he permitted the attempt. There was no question of financial trouble. His law firm was possibly the most influential on the continent, and the social position of Ormilda made their house a meeting place for all the somebodies of the day. Yet he wanted to throw it all down the drain, and just listen to the waves.

So many were like him.

Many of the men nearest himself, all wealthy, all in the highest position, were only waiting to throw up what they were doing and just listen to the waves, a debility that until the talk with Young Carvalhos Ramos himself had never quite understood. But in the man's face the reason was plain enough, though it might have been cruel to tell him.

The best of the earliest training himself had enjoyed unaware came to flower in the lap of The Mam, and in company of The Tad and Father Miklos.

The Faith was in himself with his first solid food, and in such strength that there was no getting it out. Whenever there was doubt, or a vexation, then Father Miklos resolved it, not by any long speeches, but simply by pointing out what was wrong, and then what was correct to do according to the Faith, and in that way himself was taught to think in terms of right and wrong, and if he ignored what he knew to be right, there was no surprise or resentment in himself when things, in fact, went wrong.

Himself was ever expectant they would, and when they did, he knew how to put them right.

That was only the smallest part of the Faith.

Young Carvalhos Ramos had none, not any, or any church, or any priest to talk to, and so the cheapest and best mental treatment known to mankind was denied him. There was nobody to confide a secret worry, nobody to share fears, or moods when all foolishness was possible, or hatreds, or simply the euphoria that came of knowing he could do what he wanted with few to deny him and everybody, except the few, to encourage.

"This ridiculous pilule," Father Miklos said, taking the head of himself between cool hands, and shaking. "One day it'll be rattling about in a box. And then powder. Where will your Self be? You don't care? But others do, you see. Because what's in it now, the true Self, will be elsewhere. It's my business to see it's in its proper place. You silly sheep. You little ram. Jumping about in my flock. If I were a true shepherd, wouldn't I lock you up? But I can't, you see. I can only tell you. That's my responsibility. Will you make it an onus? Will you not try to be what The Mam and Tad expected? Do you think they're unaware? Think again."

Childish stuff, yes, for a child, but still a gift that brought lifelong riches. In some part of himself the mark was made, a sense of right and wrong was rooted that grew with the moments of time on earth, not to be ignored, ever the ready help in stress, always to be thought about with gratitude for the devoted givers whose single purpose in living was sanctified in the love of God for Man.

"You see, men don't have a great deal of time to go to church if they're not priests," The Tad said, down there in the grading shed. "Of course, we go at the proper times. But we have The Mam behind there, you see? Now, she prays for us when she thinks it's necessary. And if we miss a time or two, or if we're fishing, or riding out early, or seeing the herds somewhere, well, we know we're excused till we get back, you see, because we know she's put everything right. We've nothing on the conscience. I'd be willing to bet you, even while we're standing here, there's a beautiful prayer going up for the pair of us. And don't you feel the better for it?"

It was the finest, warm feeling.

But it was not in many lives, was not in Young Carvalhos Ramos', not in so many others'.

Was not in Divininha. She had grown as a pagan.

Not in Hilariana, out of The Inheritance in the young years, all unknown brought down in the stews of necromancy.

Or Serena.

"*Culpa mea*," himself said out loud, crossing the short grass toward the pool. "*Culpa. Culpa. Culpa.*"

Not because the little thing had no respect, did not believe, was not a churchgoer, but because in later years, at times when the spirit failed there would be no Rock for her to rest against, no assurance of help, no light, no faith to sustain. A little one crying in the wilderness because himself had left her to nurses and governesses, and a cursory period or so with what the school report called religion, and all because Lys's parents and grandparents, harshly not of the Church, had insisted she be brought up outside any clerical influence, and himself, resolved at any sacrifice to take her, agreeing. She had to spend certain weeks in the year with them in the first few years, but the grandparents died, and then Lys's father. The mother was never the one to care. But then it was too late, and Serena was settled in a "progressive" school, which seemed to mean she was allowed to do as she pleased, and she certainly did, that is, outside The Inheritance, or beyond the eye of himself, which perhaps was why they were never so close as he would have preferred, if at times she seemed no less than alien. She made it a matter of a French mother, French birth, and spoke loudly of a decided choice in all things French, with a youthfully distant and ever smiling contempt for Brazil, Brazilians, and anything pertaining, an attitude that more than once had infuriated himself into ordering her out of the room. She had a passion for *la grandeur*, a notion she had never succeeded in putting into plain speech for his benefit, and she spoke French with the lofty accent of those sent from On High to teach rude humanity, and chose to mouth her own language in a fashion to assure her audience that at least one of her roots, incontrovertibly, if not incurably, was Gallic.

The more he thought, the more himself recoiled at the shambles made by an expensive school of a spirit and brain that with other training could have had some use in the world. There was time yet, but the Rock was not there, and in himself was no hope that she might change, or grow into a woman, perhaps a mother, with any real power over those around her comparable with that of most of the grandams, or The Mam's.

Yet, while himself cast the balance in her disfavor, thought came of responsibility in himself for Divininha and Hilariana and the truly criminal shambles on The Inheritance, worsening by the year, and year after year and all under the nose of himself, Rock and everything else thrown in. Perhaps the impact had taken some of the shock from having to recognize Kyrillis, that neglected one, as direct heir to The Inheritance, eldest natural son of a deceased first-born.

The hackles came cold in protest, in denial.

Instantly then, himself wondered if Hilariana knew, and had told Steb, and the two between them made a pact to split the place usefully, rather than see a bad one, or at any rate, one with the markings of a bad one, simply throw it away.

He folded his hands and stared at the sky, but no prayer was in himself, no word, no syllable, only barely, almost defensively, the thought of praying.

Without the spiritual exhaust of prayer, he realized the emptiness of those without knowledge of the Rock.

Men were moving about at the pool, and glassware clattered in the bar. Ney was nearest, piling chairs, and he came at a whistle.

"Where is the Lady Serena?" himself asked.

"She went with the others in both the cars, Master," Ney said. "Nine, in all."

"No word to me," himself said.

Ney shook his head.

"Finish here," himself said. "Be ready to help at The House. Tell the others. You'll have three days off and triple wages."

The sky was dark with cloud, and there was no distant line of mountains, no deeper darkness of plantations, no glint of the river, but only the dark night space and a sense of height.

It was only a few steps to the top of the Long Steps, but before he reached the ramp, on the first rise he stood staring, almost not believing.

A nebula of white groups lit by candle flicker waited, silent, without movement, all down the stair, each face looking up as though toward himself, and below, in the pasture, a long white procession walked in the ragged flame of torches, and white light shone from the cross carried in front.

Brother Mihaul walked alone, a small figure just behind, and the white balloon of Democritas moved between a line of women in front of the main body.

Still the prayer was not in himself, no word entered the mind, merely the desire, and above all, a soreness of thought that Serena could have gone without leaving at least a message. It was not lack of consideration that hurt, but only a peculiar discourtesy, which himself had become aware seemed endemic in those without knowledge of the Rock.

Himself watched the procession reach the foot of the stair, and walked away, clear and cold in the mind, strong in heart. No feeling was in himself, not anger, or tiredness, or disappointment. Everything was frozen into one mold.

The House, and all in it, had to be cleansed in the same mood as plowmen go early into the fields, one thought superate, to finish and earn the supervisor's nod.

A short cut back to The House led through the small cemetery among Grandfa Phineas' first plant of shade trees, where many a cousin was buried among older retainers. Flowers and shrubs almost hid the graves, and paths went from one circular fountain to another and out to a paved square, and a memorial tablet carved with all the names. In darkness that showed almost no difference between sky and trees, light seemed to flicker where normally there were flower beds.

A whiff of incense destroyed a thought that the gardeners might have put up a shelter. Nearer, light shone from cracks between boards, and he walked to a hut of fair size, but the door was locked. Two kicks, and the hinges broke in sudden flash of many candles.

A wooden cross, taller than himself, leaned out of the ground, with skulls pinning a drape of cobweb from each arm.

Dishes of food, onion rings, mandioca flour, meats, rice, made a regular pattern on the floor in front, among bottles of wine, and neat heaps of chicken legs and feathers piled behind, with the carcasses of headless goats, and skinned monkeys, perhaps, glistened flayed, pinkish limbs. In one corner, an iron effigy of Satan held trident and irons before a pile of white stones. In the other, a rack of strange tools perched on another pile, though none of the stones could have been found on The Inheritance. Packets of matches, bottles, dozens of candles, cigars, and boxes of incense filled the corner nearest the door and over all was constant movement from a squatting of giant toads.

And filling all the floor space the skulls stared, some white, some moldered, some with hair and flesh still on them, many of friends known in childhood and since, looking up in horror, or in adoration, at the one skull in hang of long gray hair on top of the crucifix, that one, Mãe Nueza.

Himself stripped paper from a packet of candles and went outside, holding a lit candle overhead, spattering grease through the flowers to the nearest grave.

The stone was tipped aside, the casket was open, and the skeleton had no skull.

If rage and sorrow were self-consuming, neither was in himself, and yet the thought was alive that one or the other might have been proper. Instead, there was mild surprise that tears with less taste than sweat were running into the corners of his mouth, reminder of those years ago in thinking of The Mam. Around the walls he groped, looking for a space to start a fire and burn, but the breeze was strong in gusts, and all the candles went out. Inside the hut, any thought of having to touch sacred bone in all reverence to put them safely outside, and then set fire, and the heart failed.

Perhaps the eyes of himself were more used to the light, for other detail cleared.

The far wall flourished long black braids, and a brush of pale yellow hair. Bowls of red and white color were on the floor, and a knife, a scissor, a razor, stone, and saucers of flour, grit, incense.

The long switch of red hair shining from the right arm of the crucifix could only have been Hilariana's. The other, the wondrous bronze, and almost as long, must have been Divininha's.

He reached across, kicking plates and bottles aside, careful not to disturb the skulls, though the toads were leaping, and took first Hilariana's, and then Divininha's, one weight in each hand, and went to the doorway, and again he looked at the cross.

Yet again the prayer was not in himself, but only a confession that had no words, that scarified, and tore, and then the rage was in him, but weak, shaken, and he could laugh while he kissed the hair, one kiss, a touch for each, but words were choked in ruin of grief. Out, to the darkness, the cool of night, and blessed air, and the switches blown to liveliness in the gusts, and himself blundering into shrubs, and back to the path, and then the guiding light of the Coffee Room windows, which seemed to strengthen even the bones within himself.

White-clothed figures seemed everywhere in the open garden, but he called none and made no sign, and they stood while he passed toward the door of the terrace, and touched it open, and went through to the foyer, not looking at Januario and Rui and the younger men, and on, to the elevator, and up to his rooms.

Across the study, while Tavares came hurrying in to switch on lights, he went to the ironbound chest of Grandfa Leitrim, and stood there, and Tavares knew from a nod to put all his strength into lifting the lid. The top tray held most of Daniel's boyish toys, pens, chewed pencils, and neat piles of schoolbooks, and Hilariana's girlish detritus, beads and bangles, and a rag doll with one arm, dear things to the heart that never could be thrown away. In a space he coiled one length, and the other, and nodded again for the lid to be shut.

The telephone flashed a small blue light, and trilled a bar of the *uruipura's* song, a fluting Hilariana had recorded on tape, that ever reminded himself of hours along the Amazon and listening to a handful of brownish feathers in pipe unto God and all glory.

"Master, the Lady Serena told me to say she had gone to the Foundation," Januario said in a whisper, as if his fist were over the mouthpiece. "She had a message from the Master Estevão. She took two trucks. And the Master Kyrillis is in The House. I think he's upstairs. Perhaps on the third floor."

"Get every man you can find," The O'Dancy said. "Bring them in around the back. Lock the garden door to the Silver Room. Let nobody out or in. Search the house. Rope him."

Himself went over to the desk and took a .38 from the drawer. Tavares held up the crucifix, and closed his eyes tight.

"Lock everything," himself said. "Allow nobody in. Take care of yourself."

There were faint shouts somewhere and he ran to the elevator, and got out in the corridor leading to Divininha's apartment over the rose gardens.

But while the elevator door slid shut himself knew something was wrong. Incense held faint but plain. The corridor was fairly long, verandaed, and planted with flowers, lit by lamps in rattan shades that gave no real light except over green squares of card tables with a glint of ash trays' glass, shading the armchairs and the doors to the sun terrace at the end, where the way turned up the steps to the foyer.

Himself halted at the turn.

A naked male blotched in scarlet paint sprawled on the stairs.

The O'Dancy went nearer. The man lay face down, with the weight of a black cloak holding legs and feet to the top stair.

"Aristodes," The O'Dancy said, and knew himself foolish, for the eyes stared. Two golden horns were stuck to the forehead. Eyebrows, mustache and small, pointed beard of black horsehair were glued.

Two bullet wounds had bled dark puddles in the smear of scarlet paint. He must have crawled away, for paint was over the steps at the top and across the parquet inside, and the white walls were daubed and printed, and furniture was overturned.

"Divininha," The O'Dancy shouted. "Divininha, my beautiful. Are you in there? Answer me."

Somebody laughed.

Man or woman, there was no telling.

It might have come from the bedroom.

The drawing room seemed to have been splashed with buckets

of paint and the furniture's white satin covers, cushions, and the walls and curtains were horridly, redly wet, and everywhere the darker spots and pools of blood shone in the light.

Himself made sure there were no bodies in the overturned furniture, and went to the door of the bedroom. Incense smoked from a censer beside the stripped bed splashed in paint, and the crimson flared everywhere, satins and silks torn in rags, toiletries strewn, bottles broken, and the sweetly strong fumes overrode blue furls of smoke and brought a drunken sense of passive enjoyment.

A couple of steps toward the other side of the bed and himself saw the flowered silk peignoir and the scarlet-jersied body of Madame Briault lying in the corner, head against the wainscot, hands loose-fingered over the breasts, and through a curly mass of hair, a staring glint of dolls' eyes. One golden ram's horn was stuck to the head. The other lay where it fell.

"She's dead," Kyrillis said, behind there, somewhere. "So's the other. So will you be."

The O'Dancy hid the .38 in turning.

"What have you done here, you maniac?" himself said. "There's no power on earth'll take you free of this. Where's Divininha?"

"Downstairs with her friends," Kyrillis said, and leaned against the doorway.

Nothing was wrong with the fellow that might give warning. He was uncombed and unshaved, and wore a blue sweater long out of shape from wear, and canvas trousers and rubber shoes, but little else was remarkable about him.

The O'Dancy flung aside a reddened sheet, and sat down on the mattress.

"I'm not sure I'm awake," himself said. "Why did you do this? Why did you murder those men in the taxi last night? Why?"

Kyrillis laughed, and looked at the automatic, and felt in the hip pocket for a crumple of cigarettes.

There was nothing to warn of danger. He was not the screamer down at the bar, but only and coolly his usual crafty-*cum*-vapid self.

"No, well, you see, it was all very sudden," he said, and straightened the cigarette with the automatic swinging on the little finger.

"The two last night were up near the top. Bars, night clubs, hotels. They worked with her."

He nodded toward the body in the corner.

"I wanted to get in for the cut, but they wouldn't let me," he said. "I started working the small rounds about five years ago, so I thought it was time for some real money."

"Five years?" himself said. "You were a child at school."

"Surprise you what happens in schools," Kyrillis said, and lit the cigarette, and flipped the flaming match in the corner, but it was out though still smoking when it fell in the hair. "Anyway, I got my loads and pocket money out of it, and that's all that interested me. Up till now."

"Just a moment," The O'Dancy said. "Do you mean you were an addict in school?"

"Addict?" Kyrillis said, and shrugged. "I had to have it."

"But who started this with you?" himself asked. "Would you never come to me?"

Kyrillis blew smoke, leaned lower, and laughed as waking gods might, up at the sky, mouth in upturn, eyes almost under the lids.

"Supposing I had," he said, and tapped off the cigarette ash on the barrel. "Imagine your answer? No. I went where I'd always get it. Vanina. Dear Vanina. She liked little boys."

"Right, now, wait," himself said, sure of the truth. "It's terrible what you've done, but I'm sure I can help, and I will."

"You can't," Kyrillis said. "I'm going to put two in you, just as I did the others. Then I'll find Vanina. Then that other thing downstairs. Then Hilariana. Then Serena. Then me. I've got twenty-eight bullets. It's enough."

"Why Serena?" himself asked, and took tighter grip on the .38 through the folds of the jacket pocket.

"Before she's spoiled," Kyrillis said, head on one side, lighter in voice, stating the fact. "She thinks she knows a great deal. I told her most. All innocent stuff. I've got rid of everybody that tried anything. I warned the rest. They know me. They kept themselves distant. As I told them. She's the only one who's been anything like a friend. Believes in me. Defends me. Me. I'll kill her before she's made like the others. But this thing's tried to get her."

He spat at the body in the corner.

"Hilariana tried, and so did Vanina," he said. "I don't know if they did or not. She wouldn't tell. But this other thing downstairs. She did. And she got her in the *candomblé* as well."

"Which thing is this?" himself asked, though he might have wagered a million he knew.

"The Mãe Santa," Kyrillis said, as though everybody knew. "Came in this morning with the others. I was supposed to deliver the stuff last night and meet them here. But the two nabobs wouldn't let me in. Cutting their profit. So I asked for more money. On the small rounds. They wouldn't. We argued. My load was half off. I got the sweats. I was dancing on my grave. So I gave them the gun. They had a lot of money. A lot. I had to go back to get a load. The stuff I had wasn't clean. It was fresh. But I know how to mix. Better than they did. I'll make more money. But I hadn't enough clean stuff. So I came here. In the sweats. Vanina gave me a pickup. Nothing. Then she went downstairs. I couldn't get in down there. Then this thing came up. She wouldn't give me any unless I put on the paint. She's got kilos of everything. So."

He straightened the automatic.

"Why don't you put that down now, while you're in a reasoning mood," himself said. "Let's talk this out. You could take a cure, let's say, and then go anywhere in the world for the Enterprises. After all, you have many advantages. Is a drug so important?"

Kyrillis looked down at him, and lowered the automatic.

"You poor old cuckold," he said. "I've got advantages? I was offered a place with Enterprises. 'The' company. Sales clerk. Me? Sales clerk? Listen, I can earn more in one half hour working for the Foundation than two whole years as a sales clerk. Selling the stuff. Anywhere. Here. Rio. Anywhere else."

"How would you work for the Foundation?" himself asked. "You know nothing about plants, do you?"

Kyrillis laughed down the barrel of the automatic, doubled, paroxysmic, and straightened.

"What do you think they grow there?" he said. "Everything. From opium up. Work for it? Where do you think I get it? The moon? That thing in the corner did the money side. That Mãe Santa downstairs, she did some of the split. I worked with her.

She put me on to the main tap. The two last night were nothing. There won't be any case. Two bodies found? So."

The O'Dancy thought himself able to taste terror, the true taste of terror, bland as blood, in the throat, remembering Iralia, and the police chief speaking of Big Fish, and Young Carvalhos Ramos picking that thumbnail and twisting his face at an offer of a ten-million-cruzeiro reward, and every policeman aware of O'Dancy Enterprises and the O'Dancy Foundation, and Hilariana, and The O'Dancy, himself, companion of a peddler, and she, think tenderly or climb up to Christ and try not to think, strangled, and himself, yes, the innocent, and culpable, and damned.

He cleared a throat in choke of incense and perfume.

"What of Divininha in this?" himself asked.

Kyrillis looked at the cigarette, and tapped off the ash with the automatic.

"She got a haircut with Hil-oh," he said. "Joined the hierarchy. Vanina, mother of Satan, instead of this one."

He looked over in the corner, spat, and moved to the other side of the door.

"Of course, you know nothing about it," he said, blowing a cloud bluer than the incense. "You've been walking about, that's all. I forgot that most of you don't know. You'll never find out. Even if somebody told you. You're from Mars. And you enjoy life? Enjoy it? Enjoy what?"

"What had this woman to do with drugs," himself asked, and nodded toward the corner.

"She was the main tap," Kyrillis said. "I could have been her money man. She sent the stuff everywhere. She used Vanina's name. Or Hil-oh's. Or yours. Why not? Couldn't miss. O'Dancy. That's a big name. Gets things done."

"My name's been used in this?" The O'Dancy said.

Kyrillis blew smoke in laughter.

"Used," he said. "You're the power. Everybody knows it."

"Ah, but I'll attend to it," himself said.

"You won't," Kyrillis said, and looked at the automatic. "You're going with the rest. In the garbage. I feel fine, now. In a couple of hours, I won't. I had a big belt this time. There's a lot of stuff out there. I didn't know she had so much."

"What do you know of this Maexsa?" himself asked, and the .38 was pointed, hidden, ready.

"She's got *boîtes* about the city and state," Kyrillis said. "Filling stations. When they know you, you can get it. Then she's got you."

"Who's above her?" himself asked. "Who looks after her?"

Kyrillis smiled at the body in the corner.

"I can't tell you, but she could," he said. "Goes all the way up. Doesn't have to be the stuff. Every woman with a lover. Or two or three. That is, every woman with money. Every man with a mistress. Or two. Or five. Every man with money, I mean. All the girls who like girls. All the boys who like boys. All in the book. All paying. A lot of them are downstairs now. Cream of the cream."

"I don't believe a word you say," himself said.

"So?" Kyrillis said, and inhaled. "Remember, Vanina knew everybody. She was supposed to be the light. Bri-Bro happened to hide hers under a bushel. Of everything. What do you want? Cocaine? Heroin? Hashish? Opium? Coca? Marijuana? See Bri-Bro. Not Vanina? No. Why not? Because she was cold on pills for eighteen hours of the day, and drunk for two."

"And your mother's the same," himself said.

Kyrillis put out a hand, palm down, and bent it slightly side to side.

"More or less," he said. "Not quite. Getting nearer. She's planning to go to New York to start a *candomblé* there. That's where the money is."

"She doesn't need money," himself said.

"Well, no, not like that," Kyrillis said. "She doesn't need money, that's true. But when enough people have paid her enough, she'll tell them to do as they're told. That's the whole idea. A daughter of Satan. Has things to do. Must do."

He seemed to be quivering. The cigarette spat sparks.

"On whose instruction would this be?" himself asked. "And what's Hilariana to do with this?"

"Oh, I'm not answering anything," Kyrillis said wretchedly, turning his eyes up. "Not. I acknowledge John of the Skull. Exú of the Closed Road. Hil-oh, yes, *iemanja*. Exú, of the Circling Dove. The scarlet one. At the edge of the sea."

"Stop mumbling," The O'Dancy said. "What had the other fellow to do with it? Why is all this red stuff about the place? What devil's work's been going on here?"

Kyrillis raised his eyebrows to show large eyes not quite the O'Dancy gray, but the murder was there.

"Of course, the father's work," he said, whispering. "It's where most of them dressed. The dressing rooms outside and in here were all full of clothes. I tore them all up and threw them out. The one out there? Pupi? Oxosí. Of the Seven Crossroads. Urubatão. Saintly father of Hil-oh. Ah yes. And Mother."

"But for God's sake, why did you kill him?" The O'Dancy said.

Kyrillis shrugged, spat the cold cigarette on the floor, spat again, violently, and stretched his arms in the woolen sleeves.

"Why do we do anything?" he said. "I was told, that's why. They're down there now, telling people what to do. The Exú flies. *Exú pinga-fogo.* I hear you. Ah yes. You see? That's Pupi. He was called. He told me."

"Stop yelling your nonsense," The O'Dancy said. "Talk sensibly. Listen to me."

The automatic flashed a deafening rap, and the smell of powder burned the air but the bullet went in the floor.

"The next two will be my present to you," Kyrillis said, calm again, nothing in his eyes or set of the body to mark him out of the ordinary. "This thing, then Pupi. One and two. Then you, Vanina, Maexsa, Hil-oh, Serena. And me. And anybody who gets in the way. I've killed others. Like hunting. Go out in the car, wait for somebody to cross the road. That's it. That's the feeling. Metal on bone. A wonderful soft crunch. Like treading in a basketful of lots of worms. Only it's better. Especially if it's a woman. They're softer. Their titties burst."

"Bastard pig," The O'Dancy said. "Thank God. You're not whole of my family. You're what I told you down there. You're not a man. You're no human being. Subessential decay is what you are. Kill yourself. The world's richer."

Kyrillis looked at the wall mirror, smoothed the curls, jolted sideways to rest on a hip, and a lock of hair fell, and for an amazing moment he looked more woman than man.

"Vanin' and Pupi and a few others saw to that," he said. "That's why I gave him his two. He didn't want to go. He made most of this mess trying not to. He crawled. He prayed. But what I promise, I promise. I swore I would. But it took time. This is taking time too, isn't it?"

"How did Vanina see to what?" The O'Dancy said, and moved the .38 for a clean shot. "What's she to do with it?"

"Well, no, she laughed," Kyrillis said. "I'm not sure. But everybody got me drunk. Pupi sodded me."

The O'Dancy put up a hand, for nothing, and looked at nowhere, and shut his eyes in wonderful darkness.

"You don't believe me," Kyrillis said. "It's true. Every time he was here. That's why they brought him."

"Did any of this have anything to do with Hilariana?" himself asked, and saw the movement, perhaps of a hatbrim, in the doorway, a flick.

"Don't know," Kyrillis said. "How do I know? Well, I'm not sure. But what's it matter? I wasn't the only one."

"For Christ's sake, stop your drivel," himself said.

"They wanted me down there tonight, but I wouldn't go," Kyrillis said, quiet as the next, and straightening another cigarette. "That's why this thing wouldn't give me the load. So then Pupi came up here. This thing came up here. They didn't know Vanin had given me enough to stop the beat. She didn't have any more. But I let these two talk. They got one each. That started them dancing. Then they got the second. But it's a feeling. When you tell them they're going to die. And they don't want to. Don't you want to die?"

The thin leather lariat flew, falling over the suddenly screaming head and shoulders, and Kyrillis fell sideways, dragged without hope of struggle toward Gilberto, in the doorway. Moacyr jumped over the kicking legs, struck once, and the head fell, and the lariat twirled a calf bind from knees to ankles, all without pause.

"Get him down in the truck," The O'Dancy said. "Take him to Dr. Gonçalves' clinic. No noise. See me in the morning. Tell the rest of the men to stay out of sight in the men's lodging. Be ready when I call."

Gilberto lifted a bound blue sack, and went out, and Moacyr slipped the silver-handled quirt in his pocket.

"A lot of our people are coming in, Master," he said. "In white, with candles."

"Of *Umbanda*," himself said.

Moacyr nodded, turning the hatbrim.

"Let them do as they will," himself said. "Democritas knows. Tell him to send women here. Leave these bodies until Father Miklos has seen them. Tell Januario to telephone the carpenter's shop and ask for two boxes. The length of a man. You did well. Till later."

32 The O'Dancy knew that the mind of himself must be adjusted to think, calmly, of an oratory cursed in sacrilege, a crypt in desecration, a cemetery violated and the dear dust of kinsmen and women fouled by other hands and eyes, a church in nameless pollution, and a temple to Satan built and in flourish within a few yards of The House.

And murder.

But himself, without reason or feeling, but only himself, naked and in darkness, that one, yes, rebelled.

In the elevator going up to Hilariana's rooms, it seemed, in cold thought, that the death of Madame Briault and the other might pass without much in the way of prying. Father Miklos could read a service over them, and then a burial, and by the time any inquiry was under way, none would know anything about them. Oratory, church, and cemetery would straightway be put in order, with ample precaution to guard against future misuse, and when the skulls were joined to their proper bones, the hut would go in fire, and if himself had a word to say, so would the builders scream in the same flame.

Hilariana's rooms were still as he remembered, still the same perfume, though it was years since the last time he had gone in to sit on the bed and read her a story. The carpets and furniture were a little worn, but the air of comfort held, and he breathed the deeper to see everything in order in the drawing room, and on the sun terrace, with a bowlful of all sorts of sunglasses, and magazines where she had left them, and a tray of make-up, and a hair drier that he picked up and kissed, and flung in a corner. The bedroom had not changed. Still the creamy satins she preferred, a dressing table shining with the crystal he had given her year by year on birthdays, the sprays of rarer orchids she brought from the Foundation, the bedside books, mostly novels and poetry, a newspaper two days old, the dents in the dressing table's stool where use had worn the shape of herself in the satin, and a row of lipsticks in different colors, smart as a file of soldiers. But the small glass table next the window he never remembered seeing, and he went around the bed toward it.

A pace away, and the ruin was on him, piercing through and through, without touch of light or mercy.

The table held what had been in the little packet from the ship, all that was left of Daniel, set out on blue velvet, and covered with glass.

The boy's photograph was there in the middle, in laurels of gold and silver, and pieces of metal were held in place all around. One piece might have been the cigarette case she gave him. Another could have been a watch. Or a button or two.

Hilariana had taken the trouble.

Violets in the silver bowl were fresh, his favorite because Fransisca had loved them. One enormous pink rose flaunted perfection in the holder over the *prie-dieu*, and the little lamp still shone at the icon.

Himself found a way over there, and knelt, empty.

The will was not in himself to make the sign, and the words were not ready to ask for the Blessing, or for mercy, or forgiveness. No words, no movement, but only the wish, or not even that, but merely the knowledge that a prayer should be made, some kind of prayer, any prayer.

Nothing.

Only darkness, and the senses at work, and the foolish, saltless tears.

"Don't wonder because you haven't a word to say," Father Miklos said, that time, at the church when candle ends were taken from his pocket. "You stole these to light fires, didn't you? But you know there are people waiting for candle ends to give them light at night. You didn't ask. You stole. You fell from a state of grace. You can't argue. You can't deny. You can't shout. All you can do is stand there. Not a word to say for yourself. You go and talk to The Tad, first. Then see me."

"A state of grace is what you enjoy when your conscience tells you everything's all right," The Tad said. "If you haven't any conscience, then there's no such thing as a state of grace, d'you see? You knew you were doing wrong to steal these bits of wax, didn't you? Could not you ask one of the women for candles? Packets of them. I ought to be giving you the stripes of old Beelzebub. But I'm not in the way of it for the moment. Don't do it again. Go back to Father Miklos. Tell him what I said. Tell him there'll be candles for everybody from this day out. That's one bit of good it did. But if I find you stealing again, I'll not leave a decent piece of flesh whole on you. Remember it."

Remembering the other time, and Mamede tied up and thrashed with the long, thin guava branches until the skin burst, and the Grandam whispering that pain would bring the grace into her if nothing else would, and in future to keep her hands off the silver spoons and bedsheets and pillow slips, or she would suffer as her mother had, and a man would clip his knees to the head of her, and pull all her teeth, and leave her mouth a hoarsing, bloody cavern. But her mam had taken more than the eye of the Grandfa, and that was why.

A state of grace.

The O'Dancy got up, knowing that in the Silver Room was possibly the last of the Beggar's sores.

Any thought of breaking-in offended a sense of propriety against The House.

But there was no need.

Grandfa Phineas had twice hidden the key and forgotten where he put it. The first time it was found in Grandam Cybele's sewing basket, but the second time, every woman on The Inheritance was brought in to start at the rooftree and work down, scrubbing, looking for it, all the way to the outer paving. But a laundrywoman, that one, great-great-great-grandam of Januario, found it knotted in the corner of the nightshirt he never wore, and he freed her as a gift. Unknown to any, he had a key made on the end of the powder rod of his shotgun, and he told only Grandfa Shaun, and he told only Grandfa Connor, and he told The Tad, and The Tad whispered it to himself, though it was no great secret, and yet it was, for nobody else knew.

The House was quiet, except for the carpet's pile whispering back to place after his footfall.

Perhaps there were drums somewhere, felt more through the soles of the feet than heard.

Or a few lines of a hymn vagrant through the open window.

The O'Dancy went down to the corridor, and walked along the collection of arms, and lifted Grandfa Phineas' heavy shotgun off its hook. The rod pulled easily, and the key shone, and the hammer cocked smooth as morning coffee. Temptation was upon the brows of him to load it and put in a charge of nails.

"Never carry a pistol or load a gun," The Tad said. "If you do, you intend their use. What you intend is premeditate. In the act you're a murderer. Never let your willful self take your soul by the throat. If you do, you've no defense anywhere, not in this life or the one to come, or in humanity or out. From the moment, you're a murderer. A desperate, lonely one in search of forgiveness. Don't be doing it."

The O'Dancy put the weapon back, and took the .38 from his pocket and put it on the rack, and twiddled the rod in his fingers along to the Silver Room doors. The key went in without sound, turned in velvet, and the door parted without a creak, an inch at a time. Drumming was heavy and many voices in toneless mutter, bringing to mind the swift traffic of beehives, except that bees made a cleaner sound, of more edge, more suggestion of vital work. The door opened full to let himself in, and shut without noise, though nothing could have been heard in the inner din. Two yards from the door, an iron lattice backed by figured leather led to the right and a stairway down to floor level.

Light from the room glowed red.

The Silver Room had been a spacious countinghouse, and a row of iron chests made a polished line under a rack of abaci. The walls held what was left of the silver paneling from the oratory, and decks of shelves carried the trophies won by The House in horse racing and cattle shows, a mass of hundreds of pieces of gold and silver from all over the world. The floor projected over the garden, and a wide balcony under canvas made a fine place for a cool drink on hot nights, and the covered stairway brought the grounds in easy reach for a stroll before dinner.

Himself went to the top stair and looked over the balustrade through cigar smoke mixed with incense rising from two censers on each side of a tree trunk still in its foliage, planted in the middle of the room, with owls taped to the branches in constant lean and flap of wings, and doves, dyed red, in hopeless turns trying to perch beyond reach of pinions and gaping beaks. The haze seemed to shake in a hammering rumble from three drums at the side, and small rappings and beatings of other rhythms. Men and women painted red paced a short step in close circles, bent down until their necks might break, or upcast, eyes shut, at the ceiling, every mouth in move, spittle shining, hands clutching the naked waist of the one in front. At the table alight in dozens of candles near the window, a score or so in scarlet dress with black capes danced their own small jig, all of them wearing golden horns, men with beard and mustaches, women with larger horns curving down to their cheeks, among a crowd of women wearing smaller horns, all of them naked except for shining scarlet paint, all in the motions of a prance to hand clapping.

Silver walls of Jerusalem's worshipers were covered over with red sheets, but the bas-relief shapes showed in light and dark, and praying hands, even covered, yet made shadowed supplication. Bloodied goats' heads were about the floor, and a heap of slit-throat chickens feathered one corner, and the dancers slipped in reddish slime, and near the second table a group of women glossy with blood were in kiss of each other, and on the other side a crowd of men were bloodied and rod-ready for a woman. Pairs copulated on the floor in front of the long table among the entrails and carcasses of goats and chickens, and scarlet toads hopped, mice scurried, and bedraggled cats crawled on broken hind legs and mewled openmouthed. A fat woman below the long table raised a chicken overhead in shrieked invocation and brought it down slowly, and bit into the ruff, spitting out blood and feathers over the head of a woman being pulled to the floor by a man, and flung up both hands in a long howl to let the bird flap away flittering drops from a broken neck.

Behind, almost hidden in the glare of candles, a gold throne had been moved in front of the window, with jeweled curtains and baldachino, and a corps of scarlet-painted attendants, all seen in the sporadic flash of red light from braziers below the steps. The satanas on the throne wore beard and mustache, long golden horns, and a black cape, peaked black cap, and a trident flashed gold in the right hand, and a skull shone white in the other, with rows of skulls in front of the throne and underfoot.

All of them were still, as if waiting. The bodies and faces seemed carved in shining red stone against the darkness, almost part of the rank of life-size statues, male and female, and male and female torsos on one pair of female legs, told apart from the living only by the stare of glass eyes.

Below the stairway a line of women seemed to be stitching, and being sick, and stitching, but when smoke cleared, toads hopped from their hands, and others were taken from baskets, and food chewed in the women's mouths was spat into the toads' maws, and the lips were partly sewn, and more food spewed in to fill the space, and the entire maw stitched tight, and hands dipped the toads in the scarlet *urucú* paint, and flung them out on the floor to leap and slither.

Drumming rode as part of time. Rhythms altered, level softened, gained, thudded, stopped a few ecstatic moments, and the chants, moans, sighs, spewings, and the human screams and the rending shriek of dying cats wove in space, and the drums rattled and broke into a steady, headaching pulse that brought all movement still except for the owls and doves, and the cats crawling on fores, shaking openmouthed heads, and the mice in endless scurry, and the toads leaping scarlet splashes everywhere.

Satanas lifted the trident in blaze of scarlet light, and except for the pairs in the floor's red slime all the bodies turned toward the throne, straining and howling, arms raised, and the hands fluttered with the purling drums. The voice screamed, and again the bodies strained and howled, and knelt in a mass fall, and a man scooped a toad and stuck its head between the fat woman's thighs, but she made no move.

Himself knew the will to shout at them, to go into them, one by one to savage, rend, and utterly destroy.

But the eyes were upon him. A stinging was in the mind.

Time passed on a clock without sound or light, and there were no days. Will was not in himself, and no memory, no struggle, no longer desire to move, or feel, or think, or be.

"Sin," Tomomi was saying those years ago, yet so clearly, that voice, now. "What is sin? They speak of it. Sometimes. Are Catholics, truly, Christians?"

"The only ones who matter," himself said, half in the pillow, half in hair. "What's taken fire?"

"Well," she said, and turned to the ceiling. "I was reading the Bible."

"Dangerous," himself said. "Most dangerous piece of literature there is. Not for solitary reading. By ignorant Orientals."

"I am not an Oriental," Tomomi said, and gripped a handful of hair between white teeth and turned a fearful mask. "Ah. You see? I am a *brasileira*. From Santos and São Vicente. I am a Christian. I torture. I burn. I break unbelievers on the rack."

"Not in these days," himself said, and pulled her closer. "These days we don't talk about unbelievers. If you don't talk to, or about them, they don't exist."

"But I am sinning," Tomomi said, and pushed the hair away from her face. "We are sinning. What we do, is it sin?"

"Yes," himself said. "It's sin. According to some. But it's nicer not to take any notice, isn't it?"

"You are Christian, but you are nicer not to take notice," Tomomi said in the softest voice. "A nice Christian? Or a nice sin?"

"Don't get mixed up with nice, because that's a word," himself said. "It means what's pleasing. It hasn't anything to do with sin. That's an offense in the eye of God."

"You are not afraid," Tomomi said. "Buddhists have no sin. I think it is better. We have no God. It is strange to find a terrible shadow waiting beyond the sky. God. With a book. All sins in the book. So many people writing. For nice Christians sinning."

"You're using your storybook Tomi-nonsense," himself said, but a coldness was upon him. "Better leave such things for the priests. They know the meaning of sin. They have to fight it."

"They are not allowed women," Tomomi said. "A sin. Is a woman a sin?"

"More than one is," himself said. "For us. Outside the priesthood, one woman. By marriage. No more."

"And so we sin," Tomomi said. "Poor priests."

"Not poor," himself said. "They know the terror of temptation. The victory. If it is."

"If," Tomomi said. "Isn't it victory?"

"If it was me, no," himself said, and took the lobe of her ear between his lips. "I couldn't do even that little so-much if I was a priest. Between doing that and not doing it, there's victory. I'd rather do it. That's a use of free will."

"Free will is sin," Tomomi said.

"The misuse of free will is," himself said.

"We misuse free will," Tomomi said. "That misuse is sin? Would there be a world without it?"

"A world, certainly," himself said. "A pure, beautiful world. The Buddhist world."

"Ah no," Tomomi said. "No. No. Not the Buddhist world. There is no temptation in our world. Only wisdom. There is no wrong thought."

"Wait there," himself said. "Have you any wrong thought at the moment?"

"No," she said. "I have a woman's thought."

"Then let's be having no more of the other," himself said. "Do what you're thinking."

"I shall plant one more chrysanthemum tomorrow," she said.

As if coming drunk out of sleep he watched the scarlet movement, heard the shrieks, the rattle of maracas, a tinny thrash of many *agogó*, but the deep-throat flail of horsehide drums brought him away in broken struggle from dearest dreams of a loved woman and another day.

In that clear mercy, without thought, himself made the Sign, at the forehead, at the breast, but before he kissed his fingers the single scream, a female scream of exultation stopped the drums, and all the heads turned.

Toward himself.

A red, gleaming woman in many necklets that looped below perfect breasts and elbow-length bracelets of jewels came tiptoe on muscular legs toward the stair. The drums thudded, and the circles went on, and women shrieked and fell in the grasp of men.

No doubt, none, in the lines of the shiningly reddened body, in the dark, smiling pierce up at himself, in the drag of the mouth, in the fondling of those breasts, in the feet-apart thrust of thighs.

But in that moment he knew the need for frilly drawers.

There might have been part of a woman. Plainly, the remainder was half a small boy.

Maexsa raised her arms, but turned aside quickly toward the splintering noise of heavy movement near the window. The red mass up there moved backward. A moan began, and a shout, and the scarlet crowd broke in a screaming run.

White figures were at the windows. Glass broke and shattered. Drummers jumped from their places, and statues fell in smash over on the far side. An enormous serpent slid, fangs in white flash, down the steps, a slithering swift gray length of whipping coil, and the red figures screamed unheard, and the drums toppled, bumping down the stairs, tripping a woman, and she scrambled, slipped, and horror glistened bright in her eyes, and a coil lashed about her, and another, and the snake seemed to slide without movement toward the tree and pull itself and the woman in among the branches.

Paul, no doubt of it, fell, hands down, through the window, and ran the long, leaping stride, cleanly white, to the tree where the leaves showered. The balcony door splintered and broke open, and Democritas filled the doorway. The crowd on the stair stood silent, shivering.

Himself, crushed against the lattice, realized that most were still in trance, harmless, but there was no way to go through them down to the floor.

He went up, pushing a way between those at the turn, and opened both doors out to the corridor.

Ephemia and a crowd of women stood waiting.

"Get bedsheets to cover them," himself said. "They're all crazed. Have you been upstairs?"

Ephemia nodded.

"That's it," himself said. "Start work this moment. Roof to cellar. Where's Januario?"

The man waited in the door of the Leitrim Room, and himself went through the crowd of women, taking care not to touch white linen, and stood looking in at a collection of furniture in chrome and plastic that in the moment brought the hate of years.

"Take it all out," himself said. "Give it away or burn it. Move in all the original pieces. Mãe Acheropita knows where it is. At last there'll be a comfortable chair to sit in. Bring me a drink in the Coffee Room. Tell them at the heliport to be ready. Tell Tavares to bring me a clean change down here. I'm smothered in disgust. Inside and out. I'm not fit to live."

In the Coffee Room, Mãe Narcissa swung a censer trailing blue smoke, purifying a corner.

"Outside," himself said. "You can do all that when I'm out of the place. Out of church, I'll not have it scarfing over me."

"Master, the *urucú* is over you," Mãe Narcissa said, bluish through incense, and swung the holder toward himself. "You suffer The Touch."

"I love you a thousandfold more, and The Touch has no power here or about," himself said. "Puff your pretty ways when I'm gone. Out of it, now, or you'll be spoiling the drink I ever wanted."

The door shut quietly behind broad white skirts, and he waved his arms to be free of the smoke. He sat down and closed his eyes.

There were no thoughts in himself. Memory moved red, but he turned from it, from shadows. He might have slept a moment, but he felt wakeful enough. The red stain was drying in the cloth of his suit. Jacket and trousers went into the empty fireplace, and he walked deliberately to look at himself in the glass.

There seemed something new about the eyes of himself, but he was unsure what, unless it was light of an absolute satisfaction that animals were either caged or strung.

A knock brought in Tavares, frightened pale, and looking down the corridor before he shut the door. A suit and linen went on the table, and the shoes he brought over with a shoehorn from his pocket, clicking and shaking his head.

"Don't be going on, now," himself said, and laid a hand on a quivering shoulder. "Nothing here to frighten anybody. There'll never be again, I promise you."

The door swung, and Tavares leaped, but Brother Mihaul walked in, smiling.

"Well," he said, over the howling outside. "Did the skeptic learn any lesson?"

"Be shutting the door, for Moses' sake," The O'Dancy said. "Sit down. There's a drink coming. That I'm needing. Did you ever see anything like it?"

Brother Mihaul sat in the black oxhide chair, and folded the width of white habit over his knees.

"Not here," he said, in rare humor. "Of course, they hadn't got very far. They weren't nearly up to the mass. The women hadn't been brought up from the oratory. There were a number of others asleep out there on the balcony, so you really didn't see a true session. They'd only been at it a few hours. It should have gone on till the moment the Lord Christ yields the Holy Ghost."

"That's the day after tomorrow?" The O'Dancy said. "How do they keep it up?"

"They've had their practice with drugs and alcohol," Brother Mihaul said. "The trance supports a certain physical state that I suppose would hardly be possible for a mind or body in the ordinary way. I'm only sorry for the poor animals. They suffer terribly. They've no champion."

The O'Dancy held out wrists for cuff links.

"I'm ashamed," he said. "Animals mistreated. Here. It's never been. *Culpa mea.* I've a great debt for repayment. I ought to walk barefoot to a shrine."

Brother Mihaul nodded, blank.

"I'd be edified to know what good that'd do," he said. "Wouldn't you be on to your old ways in three minutes?"

"Damn it, and save your presence," The O'Dancy said. "Why'd they break the hinds of a poor cat? Will I ever be getting the hurt of them out of my mind?"

"The cat's an old friend in magic's history," Brother Mihaul said. "The debased break the hinds to cause pain. The cat's howl is prayer for release. In that prayer, and in the silence of dying chickens and the energy of quiet toads, there's a mental disturbance that's used in much the same manner as the prayers of faithful humans. But for other ends."

Tavares helped on with the jacket, and The O'Dancy set the tie in the collar, and went to stand within a yard, looking down at his brother.

"Mihaul, be telling me, now," himself said. "You believe in Satan?"

"Not 'in,'" Brother Mihaul said, and looked at the beads. "There's an existence in spirit, yes. Always was. Why?"

"While I was watching there, a moment or two, couldn't have been more, I felt myself going," The O'Dancy said. "Wasn't in my own mind. Not in the skin of me, if you can imagine that. I went off."

"You'd be safe enough considering it's what saved you," Brother Mihaul said without surprise. "Very few'd survive that exhibition and come out in their right minds. That's what the horror's for. To imprison the mind and all waking thought. Make mental slaves. I'm rather proud of you. You look wholesome enough. I'd expected a great deal worse."

Himself had instant vision of Fransisca walking the tranquil way under the fall of poinsettia, and the silver splashing up under the bare beautiful feet of her.

"I was guarded," himself said. "If you've good women in mind, they'll not allow harm."

Brother Mihaul shifted in the chair.

"I've no opinion about it one way or the other," he said. "Or if I have, it'll not be made known at the moment. Are you off somewhere, all dressed up?"

"I'm going to be giving my own son his name," The O'Dancy said. "You can witness my statement made here and now. Ahatubai is his mother. Her son's my heir. I'll have him in church before morning light."

Januario came in with the tray, and a loud pealing of a bell before he shut the door.

"Miklos is busy," Brother Mihaul said. "There's a dedicated lifetime of prayer going into every moment. You know, in a way, we were fortunate you were here. I don't suppose we could have made any sort of campaign without you."

"You'd intended to," himself said.

"We had," Brother Mihaul said. "They'd disturbed the cemetery once too many times. We'd possibly have caught them there. We might have caught them in the oratory. But nearly always we've been too late. Nothing for us but the ashes. This night, all the unfortunate women will stay in the Women's House. The men'll be in the men's quarters. They'll get a good scrubbing, first. Then I'll talk to them."

"You, or Father Miklos?" himself asked. "Who's the spiritual authority, here?"

"Miklos," Brother Mihaul said. "Beyond all doubt. But you see, we're not dealing, in truth, with the spirit. Only with a perversion of the will. When they're prepared in the spirit, then Miklos will have his day. He's waited long enough."

"But what's the explanation?" The O'Dancy asked. "If I found any of those were educated, let's say. Of any financial standing. I'd put them in court for trespass."

"How would you sustain the charge?" Brother Mihaul asked. "They're guests of your wife. Or your daughter. They'll look well in court, won't they? And they've most of them been here many times before. Why didn't you say anything?"

"I didn't know," himself said.

"Now be asking yourself, who'll believe it?" Brother Mihaul said. "Anybody? If you hadn't been present a moment or two ago, would you believe anything? What do you base 'belief' on? What is belief?"

"I think I know it well enough now," himself said. "I'm an unlettered man. I've gone a lot. I've been a lot. I've had a lot. But I can't defend what I am, except with what I have within me. I confess it, now. It's very little. I can remember a few prayers. A verse or two. The Mam's voice, and God love every moment I can remember of her. I could serve at the altar. You'd never fault me. I know something of coffee. Something of a lot of things. I know who I am. I know what I ought to do. I know what I'm going to do."

Brother Mihaul nodded, and nibbled the end of a little finger.

"Doubtless," he said. "There's a great of 'I,' is there not? What about others? Or anything outside yourself? For example, the image over in the corner. You've no feeling for it? I just caught it in this light."

The O'Dancy half-turned toward the tree trunk carved in the lines of a Madonna standing in prayer.

"That's Grandam Xatina's," he said. "What's that to do with what I'm saying?"

"Look again," Brother Mihaul said. "It's so much part of the 'I'—'I'—'I' everlastingly. Blind, except to self."

The O'Dancy looked at the figure, familiar through years, white-painted, flaky, smooth at the foot where many pilgrim lips had touched in prayer.

"Well, what?" he said. "It's there. What else?"

But something was different, a strange line, or shine, and himself walked over. The Madonna himself had ever known was no longer there in timeless blessing.

The face was palely Satanic. Set, staring, of Maexsa.

It might have been of the woman herself.

"Wax," Brother Mihaul said. "Stuck in the folds. Would you ever have noticed? And what's it to do with what you were saying?"

The O'Dancy plucked up the lemon tongs and went closer to the image, and dug into the wood beside the hair fall. The wax chipped, broke, came off in pieces, in half a face, the nose and mouth, the whole chin, and the face of the Madonna looked out.

"Well now, may The Woman forgive me," himself whispered. "How long has she been so affronted? So cursed? And The House, too?"

"You can't tell, and nobody else knows," Brother Mihaul said. "You're not looking for it, so you don't see it. And what you don't see, you don't believe. And even if you do 'see' in your own way, if you're not told to look again, what exactly do you 'see'? What you want to see? As it agrees with what you 'believe'? What do you 'believe'? On what grounds? You just said you're an unlettered man. Compared with many another, you're not. Then what about them? What do they 'believe'? On what basis?"

"Well, I suppose, what they know," himself said. "They only know what they 'know.' Isn't it so with any of us?"

"It's commonly held," Brother Mihaul said. "They 'know' what they know. They 'know' what they believe. Add them. What's the assumption?"

The O'Dancy looked at his own brother, remembering him a small one in blue knickers dabbing a forefinger into an avocado and dropping the ragged mess taken out, and bawling, looking up at Rustra with the big tears, and she, putting in a little finger and bringing out a gob that stopped his mouth, and brought silence in a gulp. Why such a memory should recur in the presence of a man in white habit, distantly affectionate, replete with cold authority, was defeating for the moment. But it was no great assurance to the spirit that one born later than himself, of less experience in the world, was closer to Eternal Truth, whatever that could be.

"Very well," himself said. "What, exactly, is the assumption? Which assumption would you be talking about?"

"The assumption that you are 'who' you are, not what you are," Brother Mihaul said, still taking bites of the little finger. "Who are you? You go back to Grandfa Leitrim. Who else, before him? Do you know? But he, too, had a grandfa. Who was he? There are families that go back in gravestones. And on paper. To where? 1200? 1100? 900? What happened before that? Whose was the seed? Which male went into a canal? Whose canal? Which male? Does it matter? We live just the same. After all, our people here have better proof of lineage than most. Their antecedents are on paper. Slave sales. We've families recorded here back to 1681. And the prices paid. All the way from Africa. Sold. They can prove their parentage even further than ourselves. Why doesn't it make them aristocrats?"

"You talk like The Tad," The O'Dancy said. "But I suppose it's money."

"To some extent," Brother Mihaul said. "Lack of interest from above's the main reason. We've seen they were roofed, fed, clothed, paid. We've considered ourselves owners. Proprietors. Fatherly patronage toward the men. The women got into a closer relationship. There's no aristocracy or system of privilege quite so savagely defensive as the one ruling in this house. Dare any woman try to take the smallest precedence over Mãe Narcissa, for example, and there'd be knives out. The woman'd either be dead, or she'd much likelier be dying of a bewitchment from the instant. And the rest'd stand about and watch her die. Not out of ignorance. Out of knowledge. And loyalty. To the people, line, clan, whatever name seems best. That's their aristocracy. Stronger than any ties we ever knew. The Africans have a true aristocracy, you see. Name and blood, yes. But it's far more mental. Of the spirit. That's the terrible worry here."

"It won't be after this," The O'Dancy said. "I'll see to it."

"Don't talk like a lunatic," Brother Mihaul said, and sat straight. "Just because you catch a few degenerates about the place, you don't think you've solved anything, do you? There are millions of them. It's alive, outside there. What's to be done for them? The churches are emptier by the day. More and more going to the *candomblé*. Of one or other kind. Doesn't it penetrate that block of yours? The world's grown as it has, faultily though it may be, within a Christian tradition. There's nothing Christian about any of this."

"Then what about your own beauties in this *Umbanda* nonsense?" himself asked.

"It won't be long before I'll have them back in the Church," Brother Mihaul said. "Then I'll die, and within the month, most of them'll be back at their own altars. What's to happen to the country a generation or two from now? What principles? What methods? Which morals? They're a matter for regret as it is, in some sectors. And getting worse. That's in a time of Christian dominance. Remove it. What, then?"

"Oh, now, come on," The O'Dancy said. "The Church is still powerful, after all. It won't die overnight."

"As it did in Russia?" Brother Mihaul said. "Except for a few, the very few, without the smallest influence, it died. It's fairly dead in Cuba. In China. In India. In Africa. Another kind of thought's taken its place, you see. How long for Europe? North America? Here?"

"But you're not saying the same sort of rot's at work," himself said. "I see nothing comparable. What's India or North America to do with us? They've little enough to do with themselves."

"You're hopping about again," Brother Mihaul said. "The rot, as you call it, is the failure of our Christian thought. It doesn't bring people to us. An act of baptism has become merely a pace into social acceptance. Into respectability. An occasion for profane celebration. Marriage? A matter of common fashion. Death? Often an orgy of tears. An emotional luxury. The Church is simply becoming a sort of convenient bus station for arrivals and departures. In between, a social center for older women. Our saints, themselves, are changing. Being made to change. Prophets have no honor in any country, much less their own, unless they're footballers or singers. In Russia and China, they've smashed the statues. They use photographs, instead. Here, well, all you have to do is to look next door. There's an altar there. Statues of all the saints, Satan in various forms. Male and female. They're simply taking what's left of the Church and using it for their own ends."

"Wasn't it The Tad told me the Church is strongest under attack?" The O'Dancy said.

"Ought to be very strong at the moment, but it's not," Brother Mihaul said. "We've lazed into a quagmire. I don't know what'll bring us out. Young fellows aren't joining the priesthood. There's no joy in the life. No belief in sacred ritual. No sense of service. They'd rather be off to football. Or out with a girl. There's no credence in the power of God. Poor Miklos goes with the holy oil and administers the unction. The person dies. These people make their submission to Exú, or whoever. And the person lives. Any doubt about it? None."

"You believe, then, with Paul?" himself asked.

"When all this is over, I'm going to sit down with Paul and find out exactly where we differ," Brother Mihaul said. "There are thousands like him. Great faith, absolute belief, but nothing for the Church. That's where we part company. It's my duty to try to find a way of bringing all these lost ones back. That's why Miklos is joining me. Will you help?"

"Yes," The O'Dancy said. "How? Mark you, I'll have nothing to do with any of the nonsense I saw this afternoon."

"Nonsense is needed to bring in the majority," Brother Mihaul said. "You'll have to put up with it for many a year after I'm boxed. You're dealing with generations of hidden emotion. Hidden in the slave quarters. They were forced to be Christians out in the open. But among themselves they became something else. Now we're building roads. The bus lines and railroads open up the country. People travel. Those emotions, those rites, they travel too. The spells are practiced even in the churches. Priests are helpless. It's everywhere. What are you going to do?"

The O'Dancy shrugged, poured another drink, and again Brother Mihaul shook his head at the offer.

"I don't know what to think about it," himself said. "I'd better talk to a few senators."

"Talk to the air," Brother Mihaul said. "At least, it'll freshen your mouth. No senator, or anybody else in public life, will touch it. They'll deny it exists. That denial and that silence are part of the poison that's going to ruin us. Will you help prevent it?"

"Tell me how you'd need help, and what sort, and I'll think it over," The O'Dancy said. "There's a political aspect, here. It's not something to be gone into without consideration."

"Not as you'd go into a woman," Brother Mihaul said. "Yet, a child results. It's publicity we're needing. The widest sort. Show them for what they are. Let them see for themselves. Hold up the mirror. Television. Cinema. Newspapers? Not so much. The majority can't read. A program of teaching unfortunates to read and write. It'll all cost money."

"*Umbanda* on television?" The O'Dancy said. "Who'd tolerate it?"

"Tolerate?" Brother Mihaul said, and lay back. "It's been on most programs since they began. What d'you mean, tolerate? What we're most in need of are men who know how to sell soap. Salesmen. Not religionists. Not crusaders."

"Those men have the soap," himself said. "What are you going to give them to sell?"

Brother Mihaul stood, and pulled the rope a little tighter about his waist.

"I've worn this habit since early youth," he said. "I'll not go down just as an onlooker. We've to show that the slave quarters are still with us. We were never out of them. And never mind whether you read or write, or what your beliefs, those slaves can vote."

The O'Dancy raised the glass.

"That's the soap," he said. "I'll help. Oh yes, I will. I know how this fits into a little idea of my own. What do you advise about Paul?"

"Leave him to me," Brother Mihaul said. "Miklos will take care of the others."

"There have been deaths in The House tonight," himself said.

"I was told," Brother Mihaul said, and in his pale eyes pity, staring, thoughtful.

"Murder," The O'Dancy said. "By a fellow who'd already murdered two others. And by his own confession, still more."

"The boy was never quite clear about himself," Brother Mihaul said. "Why should he be clear about anybody else? He's his brother's keeper when he knows the duty of a keeper. That'll come after he knows what a brother is. But if he doesn't know his own self? Why should he be careful for another? Or for a brother? What's a brother? Another piece of clay kicking somewhere about the place?"

"You're highly charitable," The O'Dancy said.

Brother Mihaul nodded.

"I know a little too much about it," he said. "You've the ageless example of this very day, have you not? Judas Iscariot supplied the coin. Peter denied. Would either of us have done any better in the same place? Given the life of Kyrillis, what would we have done? Should we not both eat bread and salt, and take his sins upon ourselves?"

"Gladly, if I thought it would do any good," The O'Dancy said.

"Then we'll be holding a sin feast tomorrow at noon," Brother Mihaul said. "We'll decide, then, what to do for him, and the rest of the family. How will you arrange about your newborn son with Divininha? What's your thought about her attitude? She's still your wife. When Miklos has finished with her, and with Hilariana, remember, they'll be different women. The women you knew."

"I'll pray for it," The O'Dancy said. "When I see it, I'll decide. As it is, Atahubai's boy's my heir."

"If not, Kyrillis," Brother Mihaul said.

"You can't have an heir in prison for the rest of his life," The O'Dancy said.

Brother Mihaul turned his back.

"You'd not consider buying him away," he said.

"I might have done many a fine hidden thing," himself said. "I'm thinking of the women he knocked down and killed with the car I gave him. He went out looking for them. He liked the 'feel' of it. Their titties burst."

Brother Mihaul put both hands to the white head and walked to the door, and stood there. His arms dropped and he fell to his knees, and his hands were loose.

"That's right," The O'Dancy said. "You pray for him. And Miklos. That's why we need you. Because we can't pray. Not I, or the families. And I doubt, the women he murdered. How could Daniel have been his father?"

Brother Mihaul caught at the door handle and pulled himself up.

"Remember we join in a sin feast tomorrow at noon," he said without turning. "That boy was a cripple from birth. Drugs. Spells. Do you know what they do to throw away a child? A knitting needle pierced his head. Will you blame the child? Or the mother? Or ourselves?"

He opened the door.

"Try to see Divininha and Hilariana before they sleep," he said. "They're entering this world again. They need a gentle word. There'll be prayers for your son and his mother. And for yourself."

"Will any free soul be uttering a word for the good man, my own brother?" himself said. "Does he need it? I'm so far away, I can't even talk to you. Could I be talking for you? Is there anything I could be saying, in the squalid meanness of me, that might put a grain more of help under your feet?"

Brother Mihaul looked back, and the face of him was like the brown-lined masks in the icons.

"Don't be drinking too much more of that," he said. "Remember you've plenty to do. Good night now, and a blessing in every thought. Until noon tomorrow."

Januario opened the door a little wider. The man could smile. There was quick scratch of scrubbing brushes beyond him.

"Master," he said. "The young Master Estevão telephoned. Will you please be sure to go to the Tomagatsu house. There's a lot of mist."

"Why didn't you put the call through here?" The O'Dancy said.

"Mr. Carvalhos Ramos the Younger cut us off," Januario said, stretching the white gloves on his fingers. "He wanted to speak to Brasilia."

The O'Dancy finished the drink.

"Very well," he said. "Where is the Lady Divininha?"

"Everybody's gone to the Women's House," Januario said. "The men are down below. They're being taken to the men's lodging. Except a few. They ran."

"Tell Mãe Ephemia I'll talk to everybody about an extra month's wages when I get back," The O'Dancy said. "Was Clovis da Souza one of the runners?"

Januario made the sign, and kissed his fingers, and nodded.

"The Devil won't save him a pair of broken legs if I lay hands on him," The O'Dancy said, and held out the tumbler. "I'll drink to the cats. And God damn the memory."

33 Mãe Palmyde stood on the top step with her arms about Zilda, two big women crying, Zilda in gulping sobs, Mãe Palmyde with silvery eyes, trying to soothe.

"Zilda," The O'Dancy called. "Find the Lady Divininha, and take care of her from this moment. You want to look after her, don't you?"

Zilda looked up in sudden smile through sobs, and Mãe Palmyde squeezed her and laughed up at the sky.

"Hair grows, master," she said. "This Zilda? She'll kill anybody goes near her. She was broken because of that hair."

"Not the only one," The O'Dancy said. "Why were you sent home?"

"The Mãe Bro cursed me," Zilda said, and swallowed. "I filled the needles with water. When I could."

"What needles?" The O'Dancy asked.

"Injections," Zilda said. "Two every day. Then she slept. Then they had a session, and whispered."

"What session?" The O'Dancy asked. "What did they whisper? Who? Come on, now."

"It was from the bottles they sent from the Foundation," Zilda said. "Mãe Bro let me use the needle sometimes. Then I pressed it out and drew in the water. Then she didn't sleep and she tried to fight Mãe Bro. But one night, Mãe Bro was watching. So I went home."

"Why didn't you come to me or Democritas?" The O'Dancy asked. "If you knew the Lady Divininha was being mistreated, why wouldn't you?"

"Who would believe me against Mãe Bro?" Zilda said, and opened the pale palms. "You'd be angry with me. Send us out. Where would we go?"

"A moment," The O'Dancy said. "What was it they whispered?"

Zilda wiped her eyes on the lace-edged kerchief around her neck.

"The laws of *khimbanda*," she said. "She was *iao* of the Seven Crossroads. In her sleep she was in trance. When she woke, Mãe Bro gave her drink and made her say the prayers. Many times I hid a crucifix. But they always found it."

"Where was the Lady Hilairana in this?" The O'Dancy asked.

"She was *iao* of the Closed Road," Zilda said, as if everybody knew. "She could have been *iemanja* years ago but she went too often to the house of the Master Paul. She loved the children. But they took her power."

"How would they do that?" The O'Dancy asked.

Zilda tipped her head, raised her eyebrows as if hurt.

"Children are in the protection of Our Lady," she said. "The master Paul and Cleide tried to make her stay with them. But she knew the Lady Divininha needed her. And she had work at the Foundation. They had sessions there."

"They," The O'Dancy said. "Who?"

"Exú of the Black Cape," Zilda said, and nodded at The House. "And the *iemanja* of the Exú Quirimbo. That mother of corruption."

"I think I know who you mean," The O'Dancy said. "If only to God Almighty I knew what you were talking about. Is everybody out of their decent senses? Do you believe any of it?"

The two turned their eyes to each other in the stare that says nothing and everything, and looked up at The House. Mãe Palmyde nodded, but slightly, and her eyes were dark, affirmative, and himself realized that a lifetime might be needed to absorb that knowledge of the occult which she carried weightless as the scent of her hair.

"Catholics believe," she said. "All people believe. The Protestants, and the Assembly of God, they believe. The Baptists believe. Others believe. *Khimbandistas,* they believe. If there is no truth in the belief of the *khimbandistas,* why is Father Miklos purifying The House? Why does the bell ring?"

"To exorcise the demons of hell," himself said, and feebleness set in the throat. "Why else would the holy man be wasting his time?"

"Then he must believe, Master," Mãe Palmyde said. "We also believe. We have cardinals and bishops. They have a name. There are cardinals and bishops among the *khimbandistas,* but they have their own names. If they have another name, is it a reason to disbelieve?"

The O'Dancy shook his head. There was no great pleasure in being offered the unanswerable. Yet far more disconcerting was the woman's sureness. Eye, voice, the comfortable way she straightened the lace collar of the white linen jacket, there seemed no doubt in her. Zilda, half as old, despite wet eyelashes, stood like a great lump of tranquillity.

But a freeze was in the neck to think of the Silver Room's crimson wilderness and the helpless condition of himself to explain it, and the calm acceptance with fair argument and obvious knowledge by a pair of women with barely a couple of pen strokes between the two.

There could be no question of burning it out of them or anybody else, or of cleansing anyone or anything. The knowledge came with the mother's milk, was integral part of themselves, immune, indestructible.

"Don't interfere," The Tad said, when Zinho was punished for beating his wife and burning her clothes. "They work for us. Very well. What they do afterward is their own business. They're not slaves. Sick, they go to the clinic. We pay. Father Miklos will attend anything else. This fool will pay a little every week for the new clothes The Mam's going to buy for the woman. Sober, the man's sorry. That's enough."

But no, it was not enough.

The hand seemed hard on the shoulder, turning himself to meet an Eye, to hear a Voice.

Himself had the responsibility, for the rot should have been seen in flagrant practice and extirpated then and there. If himself was in charge of others' souls, there was question for doubt, but responsibility for his own soul and duty toward his spirit lay beyond discussion.

"You'll find a lot of people getting embarrassed about talk of the soul," The Tad said. "Religion itself's a business for argument, or so they'll tell you. Have nothing to do with them. Be away. You've nothing in common. Get on your knees now and again. Drop into any church when you can. You'll see a lot of things with a new eye. That's the value. Never think of yourself as a great one. Fall in the press, you'll be the same bloody mess of butcher's meat as the next. Die, you'll be as cold as your fellow. You'll smell the same. Keep yourself in right order, body and soul. That way you can hope to be telling others what's to be done."

Himself was unsure which thought caused widest writhe, that of not being told by those he trusted, or the other, that in all the years he had never been smart enough to see or sense what was remiss.

But the branding iron smoked whitest in the hair of his pride, and he was unsure if he could weep with rage for himself or in sorrow for all of them, the dear dust, dragged from the tomb in puke of sabbat.

Blindness in himself, pleasured and moneyed and careless, off here and there though never to do anything so sane as finding out what was warm in the hearts of those he imagined were ever his own, if not in body or spirit, then certainly by fealty and moral duty.

A day must come, and that one kicking sand in a run toward Morenne would be wrapped in a box and taken up on the hill, but the harm would persist unto the third and fourth generation, for that was the Promise.

Swaddle to shroud, the blindness was ever in reign, that lilt of indulgence for the self, and only rarely the reach of favor for others, even nearest or dearest, down to a blight of shaven skulls and the fall of Hilariana's hair, and the bronze-silk of Divininha's, if only those, but the worst disgrace lay in the piled friz of the Negro women, for they were more sacred daughters, born to expect and needing the protection himself had ever withheld.

"God help me," himself said. "Palmyde, take Zilda to find the Lady Divininha. Look after both. Tell her I shan't be long. There's no wish in myself to see her less than the woman she is."

Mãe Palmyde laughed the white teeth and clapped the palms.

"You see the woman, master," she said. "You'll see the one on the White Side. I hear the Lady Aracý. *Oapi*, she's laughing. Yes, she's laughing, and she's with us. Exú, he's gone."

In himself was no will to ask questions. A thought burned that he should have known far more than the woman, and yet every moment he stood there was further confession that he knew nothing. Shame corroded, for The O'Dancy, that true Brazilian, should have known as much or more than anybody within bounds of The Inheritance and every thought in flight between the eyes of them.

He walked down into silence and darkness, toward the heliport, seeing lights in the cemetery and trying to remember the words of the chant in men's voices. White trousers and shirt came near, and Euripedes bowed and laughed.

"Well, then," The O'Dancy said. "Let's have some healthier talk. What are you doing, these days?"

"Finishing the fence on Eighty-two," Euripedes said. "Next week, plow One Hundred One."

The fellow walked like an athlete.

"Won't you soon be taking your father's place?" The O'Dancy asked. "When are you getting married?"

"Not until my brother marries," Euripedes said. "He's older. He'll take my father's place. I have my military service to do. I was going to help my uncle. But he sold his land."

"Why?" The O'Dancy asked. "Which uncle's that?"

"Telesphoro," Euripedes said. "He got a good price. He went to Minas Gerais."

"He's fourth-generation *paulista*," The O'Dancy said. "What's he doing, selling his patrimony?"

Euripedes shrugged.

"He got a good price," he said. "If he'd stayed, he'd starved. I worked with him four months. I had to come back. They wouldn't buy from him. And they sold for half or less. We slept under the stall. He couldn't pay me. He hated them. But he sold. It was a good price."

"What do you mean by 'they'?" The O'Dancy said. "What stall? Where?"

"In the market," Euripedes said. "In São Paulo. Mushrooms, tomatoes, celery, river fish. New potatoes, peas, beans, lettuce, how many kinds. But they put their stalls all around us. They sold for half. How can a man live? Those Japanese, they have a Mafia. He wanted to sell his stuff to them. They offered half the price they gave their own people. So? He sold. Land, everything."

"He never came to me," The O'Dancy said. "I'll look into it. No place for any Mafia here."

A white light switched on to show the way to the helicopter and the control tower's windows glowed deep green.

"Good evening, sir," the pilot called, coming near. "There's a lot of mist, but I don't think we'll have much trouble."

"Foundation, first," The O'Dancy said. "After that, the house of the Lady Ahatubai, and then the Tomagatsu place. We'll be back here in an hour, and off you go to São Paulo."

"Thank you, sir," the pilot said. "I know the Foundation, but what was the second place?"

"We'll show you," The O'Dancy said.

The pilot's smart uniform and pleasant manner were reminders that sanity did, in fact, rule in most places. A facile handling of the craft brought confidence that, if emotion and ignorance rioted in small spheres, there were others, educated and capable, which more than counterbalanced. Yet confidence was of the moment, grown in optimism, and, remembering the day's warnings, himself was unsure, though the noise of the rotors could have been voice of another prophet leading a people out of the desert, a soaring clamor rising from imagination and skill, product of love, perhaps, or of scorn, for the past.

Euripedes sat forward, talking to the pilot, looking down at blowing mist and pinpoint lights.

"So you went back to help your father," himself said. "You didn't want to stay in the city?"

"Wanted, yes," Euripedes said. "But I couldn't do anything. I got more money at home."

"We have our uses, then," himself said. "Is that where you'll stay?"

Euripedes looked at the instrument-board lights, and turned a child's face.

"I wanted to learn television," he said. "We haven't got one. But I've seen them. That's what I'd like to do."

"Have you had the schooling?" The O'Dancy asked. "Don't I remember you were always better with a catapult?"

Euripedes nodded.

"But I don't have to read to build a television," he said. "It comes in pieces. Learn to put them together. Everybody wants one.

I'd have a shop. A car. I'd work to bring my mother to the city."

The O'Dancy sat back.

The boy was seventeen or eighteen, in flame of notions far beyond the scope of his brain or hands. But in the set of the head was some bursting quality of the young Daniel, perhaps only the boyishness, or an apprehension of thought in shyness unexpressed, though the pain in the voice was itself an issue.

"Very well," himself said. "You'll never say I didn't give you a chance. Start at the factory on Monday. Be ready to leave tomorrow night. Isn't your mother happy where you are?"

"They'll soon be pensioned," Euripedes said. "They don't want to leave the house."

"No reason why they should," The O'Dancy said. "They've worked hard. I'd never permit their being moved."

"It has a big stable," Euripedes said, over the bump and sway of flight. "And a garden. My mother's garden. Mr. Clovis might want it."

"Mr. Overseer Pereira is in charge of housing," The O'Dancy said. "What's he to say about it?"

"Mr. Clovis will take his place," Euripedes said.

"I'm surprised everybody knows except me," The O'Dancy said. "Isn't he a relative of the family?"

Euripedes turned down his mouth, looked here and there, and nodded, and it fell, then, that he was great-great-great-grandson of Mãe Nueza.

"Of my mother's," he said. "He hates us. We are Catholics."

"Ah," The O'Dancy said. "And isn't he?"

Euripedes shook his head, but slightly, looking down at the darkness, reaching to touch the pilot's arm, pointing over the silver swirl of the river.

"That's the house of Ahatubai when we come back," he shouted.

"Is he not of this *Umbanda*, or some such?" The O'Dancy asked.

Euripedes looked into swaying, roaring darkness. At odds with the quick, tooth-shining shout of a dearest wish, the boy's silence brought a prickle at the neck. A colder feeling of surprise came in wondering why himself should feel a creeping sense of terror at mention of a mere cattleman, slimy-eyed, laughing sidelong, stilting, whatever he might be.

"*Khimbanda,* isn't that it?" himself shouted. "Come on, now. What do you know about it?"

But plainly the boy knew a great deal, because in sudden light it was clear that one of the girls in the little room at the oratory was sister or cousin, one or other, of his own family.

"Nymmia was also to be *iemanja* tonight, was she not?" The O'Dancy said.

The boy nodded, looking away, stretched out, not at the rest but watchful.

"If she's gone so far, why haven't you or your mother and father?" The O'Dancy asked. "How can there be one, not others?"

Euripedes sat up, and half turned, hands between his knees, nodding.

"That's it," he said. "There must be one. There wasn't anybody else. She takes it from us. There's no other way."

"Explain what you're saying," himself said. "What is it that makes a fine, sensible girl like Nymmia shave her head and play with demons in hell?"

"Master, it's not us," Euripedes said, and his eyes showed whites up at the pilot. "It's in us. Brought down to us."

The clumsy hands made signs in the air.

"Tell me how," The O'Dancy shouted. "How do you know?"

Euripedes looked at darkness, and his body shook denial, and he sat up.

"The *orixás* come," he said. "They must be answered."

"But you say you're Catholics," The O'Dancy said. "What's *orixás* to do with children of the Holy Mother?"

"They are the same children," Euripedes said. "We die. The *orixás* guide us."

"How often do you see Father Miklos?" The O'Dancy asked.

Euripedes barely shook a head, part of the heaving night, lit only by the whites of his eyes that stared without a blink.

But the meaning of that stare was part of the blood stream, a warning.

"Let's see, now," The O'Dancy said, while the helicopter banked and swayed. "Why did you bring me the longbow?"

"Ah, Master," Euripedes shouted, and covered his face. "I want to learn television. I don't want to think of other things. If you are watching and listening, *ai*, happy and comfortable, what is anything?"

"Speak of *orixás*," The O'Dancy said. "What has Mãe Nueza to do with this?"

"She comes herself," Euripedes shouted. "My mother speaks to her."

"Your mother is sister to Mãe Narcissa," The O'Dancy said. "What is she to the mother of Ahatubai? To Jurema?"

"She is *babá*," Euripedes said. "*Ialorixá*."

"Saintly mother?" The O'Dancy said. "Jurema?"

Euripedes nodded, and his eyes were live with fear.

"Then what's Ahatubai?" The O'Dancy shouted, and dragged him near. "Tell me."

"She is *iao*," Euripedes said. "She could be *iemanja* next year."

The O'Dancy pulled a fistful of cloth.

"Why did you bring me the longbow?" he said, and shook the fellow. "Tell me, or I'll throw you out."

The pilot turned, switching on lights.

"Over the Foundation, sir," he said. "Landing, now."

"Do you carry arms?" The O'Dancy asked, and let go a shaking bundle. "Keep an eye on this one. I'll be in there only a minute or two. What do you have?"

"Red rockets, and a Very pistol," the pilot said. "I've got an automatic rifle for emergency."

"Give me the automatic," The O'Dancy said. "Do you have a beam light?"

"Certainly, sir," the pilot said, and switched gear. "Any trouble, please remember me."

"Keep an eye out," The O'Dancy said. "Any shooting, race for The House, and ask for Brother Mihaul."

"You're expecting trouble, sir?" the pilot asked.

"I'm ready for it," The O'Dancy said, and climbed out. "Hover around the building. If you see anything red going in or out, give them a brush."

Lights were on behind the green and blue glass windows and shadows moved. The helicopter roared and rattled up, turned over the river and came in. By that time, himself was on the stair, gun slung over the right shoulder, taking it steady toward the crest.

The foyer reflected inner light, and two full sacks leaned against the wall. Pressure of a knee barely went into them. Both were tight packed with leaves and sprigs. Remembering that neglected one, he kicked both sacks on the floor, and the green stuff falling out showed truth. They were all fresh plants of hemp and coca, and other bundles of leaves unknown.

The door swung wide and a scarlet one came out, seeing the fallen sacks, and the shadow of himself against the far glass wall, and the door puffed air, and the red one ran screaming.

Himself listened a moment, but there was only the noise of the helicopter somewhere near. The door opened automatically, and himself went in, seeing the magazine on the divan where Hilariana had left it that morning, and through to the first plant room. All the beds were torn up, black earth piled on the floor, no green tip showed, or in the next, or in those on either side, but only black earth in spill. The morning's green array was gone.

Quietly up the stairway The O'Dancy went, cold in blood to kill, ready.

But the upper rooms were all cool, all lit in strange tones of light. Beds of tall plants labeled in Hilariana's print glowed deep greens. The helicopter made a tremendous noise outside, and shook the windows in sudden descent.

Himself unlocked the terrace door, even worried about the change in temperature, and went out in the air. The screaming, a whisper under the surf of the helicopter, seemed to be on the other side of the building. Dark figures ran out, across the grass, over flower beds to clumps of trees, but the light grew brighter and the rotors' roar blasted, and the helicopter came around the corner like an enormous flashing insect, and the white searchlight showed the ground in small detail, and leaves blew and fronds bent and flower petals frittered. The light caught running scarlet figures, a group, one falling and scrambling up, none turning to help. Light brightened whitely as the craft neared, lowered, pressed the trees flatter, snapped branches from trunks, ruffled the grass into a paler green, and seemed to squeeze the little scarlet figures double, and a few fell, and lay still, and others ran beyond the white circle and the craft swung after them, and they were caught in the light, strange scarlet shapes, thin-legged, arms waving, crook-fingered against darkness perhaps on the rim of the cliff.

But then they were gone, and the helicopter sang over the river and the light's white ball became a moving cloud.

The O'Dancy walked down the stairs in darkness, to the first floor, and down a flight to the rooms in black light, or red light, himself was unsure which, but there was no light to see by, and the electric torch cut a white cone over beds scraped over the floor, and more sacks, full and tied. The rooms went on underground, but the doors were locked. A light shone in Hilariana's room in the office annex. The desks were all tidy, filing cabinets were closed, air-conditioners were turned off, and, walking down the glass-walled corridor, himself wondered at the size of her accomplishment, which once had seemed a schoolgirl's dream, and tried to think of any reason why a woman of such mind and character should want to degrade herself with evildoers, not innocently or by stealth, but openly, deliberately, even to debasing her body and smirching its beauty.

Perhaps there was fault in himself for not keeping closer watch. But himself knew too well what might have happened had he dared try to interfere. Yet, the rot must have started during the young years, when he should have known every moment of the day exactly what she was doing and specifically what she was learning. Instead of reading those pretty stories he should have been asking what was in her mind. The pleasure had always been his own and cherished, of going in there night after night, the bereaved father and the motherless little princess, a thought kept delicate as the heart's own whisper.

Even then, the monsters must have been in grimace nearby, though all seemed calm and dear and devoted. Yet in that apparently ordered silk-and-satin paradise might have been start of an inability to see in others what he failed to see, or avoided trying to see in himself.

"That Nip bitch gets everything," Fransisca screamed, crouched in the corner. "You've never thought of me. You've never given a second's thought to anyone but yourself. I'm blind. Isn't that it? I'm blind. I don't matter."

"Who put that ugliness in mind?" himself said. "How does a beautiful one become so ugly?"

"There's nothing ugly that isn't part of you," she screamed. "Everything ugly you put there. You see it. You hear it. It's ugly. Your Nip isn't ugly, is she? She isn't blind. Ah, Virgin Mother, why was I born blind?"

But then, the words, almost the tone, were the same later on, the night Jaci begged of himself a place to live as a wife.

"You could come and go and I'd never ask a question," she wept and pleaded. "Never, never. We could be happy for those hours. I swear it. I want babies. I adore the thought of babies. We could have wonderful babies."

"No," himself said in one of too few sane moments. "It'd never do. I'm on my knees to think of the harm I've done. I'll make up for it. But living together's impossible."

He ever heard the crumple of her body on the floor.

"Black, black," she screamed, and tore the bodice from her dress. "That's why. It's the only reason. It's why we can't go anywhere. You can't take me. Black, black, black. Ah, Christ's Wounds and Blood, why was I born black?"

No words to deny, no hope of succor, but as in grief one desire rampant, to fall into the self's own grave, and in darkness thatch a roof for quiet death, and there cross the hands and feet to wait the Manger's Light and Resurrection.

"HILARIANA FRANSISCA ARACÝ O'DANCY BOYS," the plaque said in raised letters.

The door pushed open.

Papers were over the floor, drawers taken out of the desk, chairs toppled, a long table tipped over, and a pair of bare brown feet behind.

The night watchman, younger brother of Moacyr, looked over the top of a sacking gag. One rip and it came off, and the long scissors cut the binds on hands and ankles and the rope tying his arms to the heating grille.

"Ah, Master," the man wept, as a small boy. "I tried to break them but I wasn't strong enough. I can't stand up."

"Rest there, now," The O'Dancy said. "Wait till the blood comes back. Who was it?"

Heitor tried to bend his wrists.

"A dozen of them," he said, looking down. "I never saw them before. Men and women."

"How were they dressed?" The O'Dancy asked, and gave him a cigarette.

"I didn't notice," Heitor said, and drew a ragged breath.

One slap knocked the cigarette out of his mouth.

"They were all in *urucú*," The O'Dancy said. "They were all *khimbandistas*. Isn't that it?"

Heitor rolled over, weeping, trying to straighten bent hands and crooked feet.

"We'll die," he gibbered. "The *ialorixá*, she told me. One word, you'll die. Your children. Your house will burn. Your cows. Everything. Ah, Master, The Touch is on me."

"The only touch you'll get is my boot," The O'Dancy said. "On your feet. There'll be more to say tomorrow. Father Miklos will come with the cross. Are you of *Umbanda*?"

Heitor shook his head, looking up, almost smiling.

"My wife, yes," he said. "I, no."

"Then how did you keep this job?" The O'Dancy asked. "Did you know there were *khimbanda* meetings going on?"

Heitor barely nodded.

"Everybody knew, Master," he said. "But my work was down here. I never went upstairs. I come on at six and go off at six through the back. I watch the fire control and the thermostats. I never had any trouble till tonight. I was on the floor before I heard anything."

"You didn't know any of them?" The O'Dancy said.

"Only the *ialorixá*," Heitor said.

"Why did you know her?" The O'Dancy asked.

"She came before many times," Heitor said, but not plainly.

"You told me they were all strangers," The O'Dancy said. "Did you see anyone else you knew? Remember the cross will be here tomorrow. *Khimbanda* died tonight in the holy water. Who?"

Heitor tried to kneel and fell.

"Ah, Master," he groaned. "Master, The Touch will be on us."

"Clovis, isn't that it?" The O'Dancy said. "Clovis da Souza. The Number One. Until an hour ago. Now? Nobody."

"Nobody," Heitor said. "Nobody?"

"When the cross comes here to cleanse tomorrow, less than nobody," The O'Dancy said. "Lock up here, and go home."

"Ah, but Master, I can't," Heitor said. "Pineapple has budded. Coffee has flower. The Lady Hilariana would grill my balls."

"So," The O'Dancy said, and laughed. "You know the lady's temper. It's as well."

The money in the clip made a wad.

"Here," himself said. "Drink a good bottle with me. Have no fear. *Khimbanda* is cleansed. There'll be no more."

"But the Lady Hilariana cut her hair," Heitor whispered, kneeling. "With the others. Out there. This afternoon. The children saw it."

"Children," The O'Dancy said. "Which children were brought here?"

"Many from the families," Heitor said. "They were brought in the trucks. Everybody working here."

The O'Dancy took him by the shirt to lift him.

"Who ordered the trucks?" himself whispered. "Who?"

"The Mãe Jurema," he whispered, and blood sour on his breath. "From Alcides. For the children's picnic."

"That's tomorrow," The O'Dancy said.

"Today they had an extra feast," Heitor whispered. "Tomorrow is Judas' Day."

The O'Dancy let him fall.

"Tomorrow?" himself said. "It was today."

Heitor looked up, and shook his head, and looked at the calendar behind the desk.

"No, Master," he said. "Within the strike of the clock. Tomorrow is Judas' Day."

No doubt the man was right.

A confusion, no less.

A clock turned backward or sideways, was there any difference, no honest man might pick between them.

Mass the night before was anniversary, and the cathedral alight in orchids for Fransisca, the unmarked and calm one, taken those years ago, and himself drunk then, and raving doubtless, and drunk the night before, and to hell, regardless, but forgetting there was another night to go before the leaden sheath lay on the bier at The House.

But the days came as ever, each one further away and nearer, each with its own drip of poison, all in vagrant whiff of rot, eating a strict share of the clock, folding in a right stretch of the winding cloth, and himself a lost one, in wander between here and there and this and that, and none to tell him until Tomomi, and all sheaves of her own glory in thought of her, pulled him on the tight rein that brings salt warm in the mouth.

That day at the beach house, and himself taken as a child, and bathed, and kimonoed, and slippered and she in black for the first time he could remember, for she was ever the one for color, and taking him by the hand, and sliding the door and standing there, not offering to go in.

A girl knelt at the table.

Michuko, a finely graceful one, a kiss of all fresh flowers in thought of her, calm and gentle as a nurse, yes, until the brook ran full, and she raged and drowned.

"Wait, now," himself said. "Why?"

Tomomi bent the beautiful head.

"There are needs," she said in the small voice. "You leave me alone in the bathroom because there are needs. A man also requires to be left alone. Do you wish to live dead? A man is alive only in his function as a male. When he ceases, he is no longer himself. Do you think I wish to see you in such a condition? I am no longer as I was. I have sparks in my head. My body is numb. It is my time. It is not your time. Michuko has my mouth, my hands, my heart. Be at peace."

Tomomi.

So.

Yet even she forgot that the needs of the body should be in balance with the needs of the mind, and Michuko and the others had nothing, apart from the beauty of themselves, that, once taken, fell in thought as dry leaves whispering trite memory, rustling together in echoes of regret.

"You can't take a sensitive woman and throw her aside," Father Miklos said. "There's hurt to the spirit and soul. And there's bound to be corresponding hurt to your own. You don't go free, whatever you think. That bruise is in time itself, and it'll spread and stain you. You can take that look off your face. I'm used to talking to rustics, is that it? And you're such a man of the world? Top Set, isn't that what you call yourselves? You've got a brute's gut and a cynic's venom. The sneer makes you nastier. Come and talk to me when you're in healthier mind. You're grimed with the small filth of indolence."

Heitor stood, leaning against the desk, rubbing fingers and wrists.

"What were they looking for in here?" himself asked.

"Don't know, Master," Heitor said. "They didn't get much chance. Somebody shouted up there and they ran. Will the Lady Hilariana come in tomorrow? I was to go off for the day. And the day after. The children's picnic. I don't see mine very often."

"I'll send somebody," himself said. "Will you be safe, now?"

"I'm locking up after you," Heitor said, and hesitated. "It's true about—about Number One?"

"True," The O'Dancy said. "My hand on it. Good night, or good day, whichever clock you use."

"Good night, Master," Heitor said. "Go with God."

"I hope I'm let," himself said.

The door shut massively, electric bolts snapped in place, and the man was left in peace down there. Himself wondered at a life spent in sweeping and polishing floors and cleaning windows and adjusting boiler valves and whatever else the man did, day after day, through months and years, rarely a detail different, always in that subdued light, forever among desks and chairs used by people he never saw, part of the most progressive institution of its kind, and yet with a head full of fear, ready to believe in the strength of a curse, quailing before the promise of a half woman smeared in red paint and only because she or it was of *khimbanda,* which from birth had set a horror in his mind and in others.

The helicopter still circled. The rotors came nearer while himself set the automatic cloture on the door and went out to the steps, flashing the torch. The searchlight went on and off in signal, and the craft set down on the concrete lid of the reservoir.

The rotors were almost still, and himself ready to walk in, and the underground stairway erupted scarlet figures, leaping, somersaulting, swinging machetes in quicksilver whorls, almost up to the craft, nearly as far as himself, but the pilot switched gear and the craft went up in a thunder of air. Himself ran back out of the disc of the searchlight, and the pilot tipped the craft side to side, threatening to take heads off with the edge of the blades and the scarlet figures fell on the concrete in whisps of white dust and crawled away, running out in the darkness toward the garage.

The O'Dancy shot a burst high to help them, and walked behind, signing to the pilot to follow. The garage roof showed over the shrubs, and the pumps were lit. A truck and two cars without lights were in the roadway and the shadows clustered, entered, doors closed, and the truck went away with the cars blowing dust behind.

Nothing moved across the yard, and two cans of gasoline from the storeroom made a fair weight.

"God's death," the pilot said, giving a hand. "What was that, sir?"

"A few having a game," The O'Dancy said. "Do you believe in Satan?"

"Never given it much thought," the pilot said, busy with gears. "That youngster, sir, I didn't see where he went,"

"All's well," The O'Dancy said. "This is one of the times I'm glad we've no paved roads. And only wooden bridges. Put down on the other side of the water, there."

34 They flew through the dust cloud of the vehicles, crossed the width of water beyond the first bridge, and came in low over the second, where the river looped. The craft settled, and The O'Dancy took a can of gasoline and strolled over the timbers, pouring a soak into the main struts. Dried branches made a fuse, and the flame caught, flared, and the flooring exploded in a great ball of yellow sparks.

"Now we go back to the other bridge," The O'Dancy said. "Our playful friends can spend a night with the insects. We've an admirable variety here. Tomorrow they'll go in comfort to the prison. I was ever a great believer in extravagant courtesy toward guests."

Dust was still heavy from the vehicles' passing when the second can soaked into the timbers, and flame blew in showers of sparks. Up, over the treetops, the far bridge burned high, and the dust cloud moved toward it.

"Caught in the middle, and that water's most inhospitable," The O'Dancy said. "The house of the Lady Ahatubai, be so good."

"Any idea who they are, sir?" the pilot asked. "I never had a bigger shock. A lot of them fell in the river, there. I didn't know it was so steep."

"Daniel's Flight," The O'Dancy said. "It gives me the greatest satisfaction. They got a good wash, if nothing worse. One or the other, I'm nicely easy."

"I could lose my ticket, sir," the pilot said, a little hangdog.

"You could," The O'Dancy said. "You'd doubtless be consternated to know how many tickets have been lost because people insisted on opening their gaps. Silence is ever the dearest music. And never less than a prayer."

"I'm praying, sir," the pilot said, and banked. "Somebody down there's got some sense. They've got lights."

The craft bumped, ran a little, and braked.

"I'm still a bit curious about that red lot, sir," the pilot said. "Some of them looked like Negroes to me. Well mixed, anyway. We'd be better off if they were all poisoned. I don't know what they'll do with most of them."

"I know what'll be done with them," The O'Dancy said. "Just what'll be done with you and the rest of us. We'll all be allowed to breed out the poison. If that's what it is. Then there'll be no need to open the Gates. We'll all be born inside them."

Three men hurried, hats off, and made the short bow. Newspaper torches crackled and sparked.

"Where is Alcides?" The O'Dancy called, and went toward them.

"He is at The House, Master," Thuriel, a head tractor driver, said. "Ahatubai has given light to a child."

"That's why I'm here," The O'Dancy said. "One of you, go before. One behind. You, with me. Then we shan't fall down any holes."

"There are no holes, Master," Thuriel said. "Snakes, perhaps."

"Holes don't crawl away," The O'Dancy said. "Why aren't you three at The House?"

"The mist kept us here, Master," Thuriel said. "It's been thick since sundown. Alcides went this morning."

"Euripedes found a way," The O'Dancy said.

"He was taken to the crossroads in the truck by the young Master Estevão," Thuriel said. "Nobody else was here except the nurse. She also went with the young master."

"Who attends the Lady Ahatubai?" The O'Dancy asked.

"Her mother and some of the women," Thuriel said. "She has everything. And great joy. He is a bull. A stallion of the night. A male. His foreskin was longer than the cord. An assassin. A ravisher."

"Where was the young Master Estevão going?" The O'Dancy asked.

"To the house of Tomagatsu," Thuriel said. "The cars have passed all day."

"Why with the truck?" The O'Dancy said. "Where's his own car, and Megistes?"

"He is at The House, Master," Thuriel said.

"You mean at the House of the Twelve Apostles," The O'Dancy said.

"Nothing is hidden from the master," Thuriel said, showing smooth eyelids. "It is possible."

Jurema stood at the door in a laced white dress and apron, tall, thin, barefoot, lamplight in glint on gold-rimmed spectacles. The hair was still black, tidy, tight in a knot at the back, and she wore a flower behind the right ear, a necklace of monkey's teeth, and a bracelet of black and red berries and seashells.

"Ah, Master Arquimed," she whispered, and prayed both hands below her chin. "The house is yours. Ahatubai's a mother. A wonderful son. Fat. Master Estevão delivered him. Dr. Gonçalves wasn't here. The Virgin was with us. He is safe."

"Pity Alcides isn't here to drink with me," The O'Dancy said. "Where is she?"

The room's air weighed with incense and the odor of parturition. Three candles whirled moths.

Jurema led to a small room in crowd of women around the walls. One candle burned a long flame under the shuttered window.

Ahatubai smiled dark on the pillow. Her braids reached farther than the dark hands. A woman rocked a basket on the far side. Jurema pointed, and all the women went out in white whisper.

"Well," himself said, and took the soft fingers to kiss. "Is there ever a time that a man has less to say?"

"I prayed for a son," she whispered, and her eyes seemed even larger than in memory, brilliant, wholly calm.

The basket creaked, and Jurema folded a trailing shape and came around the bed wrapping a shawl.

"Young Master Estevão was marvelous," Ahatubai said. "I didn't need Dr. Gonçalves. It was so easy."

"You should have gone into the clinic as I told you," The O'Dancy said. "Why didn't you want to?"

"Here, in my mother's bed, where I was born," Ahatubai said. "That's what I wanted. You see? I wasn't mistaken."

Jurema threw the shawl on a chair and held out a wad of wool. The O'Dancy pressed the hand on the bed, and turned.

"I'll have Father Miklos here," himself said. "Everything shall be put in order. I'll not say I forgot you. But things slip the mind. We have to be forgiven. Show me the boy."

Jurema held aside a piece of lace.

The child slept.

Negro.

The O'Dancy put out a hand to touch the warmth.

In distance, over the crash of waves that filled the spaces between the toes with sand, and stung the eyes and rumored in the ears, the voice of Ahatubai spoke of weight, and the hours of sweat, and her disappointment in one child and not twins or triplets, and Creonice smiled, stretching the nipples, and Morenne breathed long, and shook, and Lua ran the pearls through her lips, yet himself saw the child, not Euro, not Indio, but Afro to the pink palms.

"That's not my son," The O'Dancy said. "He's nothing of me."

Jurema held the child tight in both arms.

"But, Master," she said, with the paler, brighter, thinner smile. "This is the son you waited for."

"Nothing of me," The O'Dancy said. "I throw true."

"He has the red hair," Jurema said, and Ahatubai bloodied her throat with the rageful breath.

The curls were faintly a darkish red, but the hair bristled against a passing caress.

"Don't be saying it to a man that's spent a thankful life with women in fine use of henna," himself said. "If I look, I'll find fingers stained, here, and a pot and a package. That's a wash of henna. It's no red hair. Will you be showing me the gray of his eyes?"

Jurema looked over the top of the spectacles, a smile still, but a deep hate.

"You deny him," she said.

The O'Dancy reached over the head of the bed and set a finger on the crucifix.

"I deny him any place in my family," himself said. "I was ready. He would have come with me. Anything of myself in him, yes. But where am I in this? Look at him. What part of me? Why did you send me the longbow?"

Ahatubai screamed, stuffed the sheet in her mouth, bit, tore, screamed in the throat.

"Is not Euripedes the father?" himself said, but certain. "Let it rest. You will be well taken care of. Father Miklos will be here to arrange baptism and marriage. I'll see that Euripedes shall have what he wants. Good night, now, both."

Himself walked through quiet women in the front room, and out to the garden, along the path toward the white light of the helicopter.

"The Tomagatsu place," himself said. "Do you carry any whisky with you?"

"No, sir," the pilot said. "There's a flask of brandy in the first-aid."

"Open it up for an outpatient," The O'Dancy said. "No wounds. No contusions. A slight rupture of the subliminal spleen is what it is. Trying to make a fool out of a born one, that's impractical. Here's to henna. It's been put to better use, I'll say that."

Brandy warmed cold notions, but that was all.

Himself, alone, no longer brightened by thought of a first-born son, living the moments until the sixth granite cross went up on the hoist. No hand or tenderness, no perfume in the silken rebel sweet of hair behind the neck, between the breasts, in the navel, yes, wait now, nothing of that, and nowhere for himself to be.

An emptiness of days without a woman.

"But is there none except yourself?" Brother Mihaul said, that day when Young Carvalhos Ramos read Fransisca's will. "Do you never think of anybody else?"

"If I put both eyes to it, no," himself said. "If there's nothing for me, then there's nothing."

"You're a selfish man," Brother Mihaul said.

"God forgive me, I am," himself said. "It's the way He made me. Thou shalt have none other God but Me. I believe that. Am I not formed in the Image?"

"I doubt your way of it," Brother Mihaul said. "All of us enjoy the same day. It's us who employ a clock. A ridiculous idea, no more. We were formed, yes, and in the Image, yes, but isn't it the image of a thought on the sixth day? 'And God saw everything'— remember everything, not everybody—'that He had made, and behold, it was very good. The Lord God formed man of the dust of the ground, and breathed into his nostrils the breath of life. And man became a living soul.' Are you still sure about that Image? Did you never eat a little man made of dough with currant buttons in his waistcoat? Wasn't it a fine image of yourself?"

"Mockery," The O'Dancy said.

"Learn to read," Brother Mihaul said. "Don't rest your weight on the words of your wish. Try a little thinking for a change. Every word ever uttered has been translated. Every thought transmuted and transmitted from age to age. Nothing dies. Everything except the spirit returns to enrich the original dust. Why are you so insistently selfish? Are you not a little man of dough holding on to currant buttons? Would it make any great difference if you gave them all away? Greater love hath no man. Do you mouth yourself a Christian? Never mind the Church. Should we mention honesty?"

"I know what's right and wrong," himself said. "I'll keep to what's right when I may. If I've to go wrong, it'll be for a good reason. I'll make amends one way or the other. Or I'll take the Judgment."

"That's not alternative," Brother Mihaul said. "That's certainty. Currant buttons won't placate the Wrath."

"Don't talk to me as you talk to laundrywomen," The O'Dancy said.

Brother Mihaul slapped the arms of the chair and laughed a thrummer up at the ceiling.

"I remember you with your trousers full," he said. "The Mam slapped you. A dirty boy. Were you never a dirty boy? Was there never a woman taking care of you from the day you were born? Were you ever anything else but a dirty boy? In need of a laundrywoman? Why would I be talking differently to them than to you?"

The pilot turned, and the craft banked.

"Tomagatsu house, sir," he said. "There's a lot of water."

"Take that dark place," himself said. "It's a lawn."

35 All the house lights were on, and those in the garden and underwater came up on a slow switch diffused in many colors among the shrubs and forests of miniature trees, though the greens of all the pools blurred everything in milky tints and the place seemed to float. A hundred small lakes were set in a garden built on the flat about the house, all in the same square line, if some were longer, or set a little farther apart, all conforming to the general rectangle of the property, making an area of coolness on hot nights, and a reservoir for the dry areas below the hillside. The house had been raised on six shallow steps in purely Japanese style, with a wide main door in the middle, walls of windows framing a magnificent view in any room, and an orchid house on the roof.

While the wheels touched, the main door slid open, and the family stood for moments in silhouette against the foyer panels, until the glass-brick stairway flushed in pale pink light, and all the kimonos gleamed clear color. Simão and Ini came down the steps to bow, and kneel, and all the girls came behind, to take off his shoes, and pinch the toes of his socks to fit sandals, taking off his jacket and helping on with a kimono, all in handclaps and little songs, and embraces and kisses from so many that even if himself remembered their names there was no time to say them, though perfume stayed from many women and gave splendid comfort.

"I kept you waiting," The O'Dancy said. "I've no excuse."

"You honor the house of my ancestor," Simão said, and stood aside. "The family is here to savor the grace of your presence. We were at prayer for the day of our founder."

Up, among a laughing crowd, and himself aghast to think of neglect in having forgotten the anniversary of old Tomagatsu, that one of active hands and kindly soul, and all white chrysanthemums to his memory, greatest friend to himself, if, in the end, coldest enemy.

A thought of Tomomi held in tight claws, set the long teeth, brought the water it ever did, the warmth of her mouth, a sooth of satin hands.

Her blossoms were everywhere in long white vases.

Himself in the small, secret oratory within, prayed not to break, not to falter, and heard in reward the subtle whisper of her skirts in dearest farewell.

Farewell, yes, and the head of himself bowed and blind.

"A glass of something, I'm sure, will do a great deal to ease your fatigue," Simão said. "Champagne, perhaps, or whisky?"

"The Creature," The O'Dancy said. "There's been a tremendous lack of it all day."

The men were coming in, most in black ceremonial dress, some in gray, a few in mauve, others in flowered greens and red, and they stood about and bowed low.

"I'm going to bless my lips with a drink to one of the three finest men I ever knew beyond my own blood," The O'Dancy said, cross-legged at the low table, and lifting the heavy tumbler. "He came with the noble heart God gave him, and he left us with the same heart made nobler. And an empire. That we all enjoy. Inoyushi Tomagatsu. Second father to myself. With love."

Everybody knelt while himself drank, but when the tumbler touched the table, everybody seemed up and drinking, and the girls were settling on cushions in any space they could find.

"He'd never do it today," Cheiko Tomagatsu said. "The banks would murder him. He'd never pay off the mortgage."

"*Yanquis* didn't control the economy, then," Kiminobu said, and sniffed his whisky.

"They don't control it now," himself said. "You created that one to excuse yourselves."

"We can't excuse the power of the dollar," Izumi said. "It controls everything, even the price of our own money. How do we defend or control or excuse that?"

"Stop dealing in dollars," The O'Dancy said. "You use dollars? You want dollars? You prefer to save dollars? And then you curse the North Americans. Why? For having the dollars?"

"But sir, they are colonizing us," Eitaro said. "Every investment, every smallest dividend is further hold on the economy. We can't move without their consent. Isn't it so?"

"You've colonized here," The O'Dancy said. "This estate is a colony of your own country. You're wearing your country's dress. Why don't you use your country's money?"

"Our country is Brazil, sir," Kiminobu said. "We're using Japanese capital, certainly. We'd have very little here without it. But it's small compared with the *yanquis*. We're Brazilians. They're not. We resent their interference."

"But has it not been a healthy interference?" The O'Dancy asked. "Without it, what would you have, here? Isn't this a growing country?"

"Not as much as we'd like, or as fast, or in the right way," Simão said, in a flash of spectacles on the other side of the table. "In the day of our ancestor, the whole world began to waken. The discovery of gold. Cheap money. Now it's a high rate of interest. The price of everything goes higher because even the beggar wants more to buy more. Interest has to be paid. Not inside the country. Outside. What should help to create growth here goes into other pockets. Outside. Those pockets dictate. We must live in a dollar economy whether we like it or not. We are convicts in a dollar prison. But we use cruzeiros. Nobody seems to have thought of substituting dollars for cruzeiros. Naturally not. It would ruin many a profitable business. Profitable, that is, outside the country. But we need to adopt the dollar as a currency. Or else we are simply a milch cow for any foreigner."

"You'd like it all your own way," The O'Dancy said. "But the only way we've got as far as we have is by help of the dollar. Will you deny it? Did your own great ancestor not see it? Isn't all his capital in dollars?"

"Question of taking advantage of a favorable market," Toyashi said, older, quieter than the rest. "It won't always be advantageous. That day is certainly coming. When the people are sufficiently angry to accept communism. From absolute impatience."

"It's a charm of a word," The O'Dancy said. "A lot of us are charmed into having a different meaning for it."

"Marxism or Leninism or Stalinism will do," Izumi said. "It's all the same. Small critical departures, that's all."

"Would you mind telling us the difference?" The O'Dancy said. "The word frightens you. It ought to frighten others. Isn't that it? Anybody here read the works of Marx?"

Everyone rested in stillness of kneeling color, most faces behind spectacles, eyes at the table, hands hidden, waiting. Parchment in sliding doors glowed behind them, and in a corner, a spray of white orchids bloomed from a bare branch.

"With proper hesitation I shall say I have," Simão said. "For my degree. Yes, I found nothing of value."

"That's no concern of mine," The O'Dancy said. "But did it never strike you? If the Ten Commandments hadn't been promulgated, and if Christ hadn't lived, there might never have been a Marx. He had the opportunity of living in the peaceful heart of the capitalism of his time. He took advantage of that peace. What peace was it? It was a Christian peace. Without it, all things in proper place, Marxism would never have been heard of. He had forerunners. All products of a Christian society. All in the thick of the fight between what's God's and what's Caesar's. Most of them on the side of Caesar. Isn't that the root of the argument between Moscow and Peking? The shadow of the cross divides them. Moscow always knew Christianity. Christ was ever alive there. Whether you like it or not, He leaves His light. He marks men's minds. Peking was never in the same Christian way. That's the real difference. They're backward in time. The decent Christian ethic is what they lack."

Again the stillness, the silence, and in the other room, a thought of Tomomi's blossoms, heavily lustrous, speaking their own language that she knew and whispered back to them, that entered into the mind of himself as tender knives and wounded with pleasure, and yes, every dropping tear a jag of ice.

"But, sir," Toyashi said, and bowed. "There are other religions. Other beliefs. Not always in agreement."

"True," The O'Dancy said. "Very true. I'm not talking about religions. I'm talking of Marx. Some would like to make it a religion. But the poor man couldn't see into the future. He looked at his own side of things a hundred years ago. The world's changed since then."

"Sir, perhaps Marx changed it," Toyashi said, and bowed again.

"We know the world has changed. But for men living in poverty, nothing has changed. They are still hungry. And their families. They don't know Marx. Their families don't. But others do. Others talk. The ideas of a hundred years ago are still valid because the poverty is still the same. Hunger tastes the same today as yesterday. Empty bellies have no history. They are, in fact, history. Everything else is bare record or surmise."

"You talk like what's-his-name, Hiroki," The O'Dancy said, and looked about the room. "Is he not here? I'd a wish to see him."

"He shall attend you tomorrow," Eitaro said. "Without fail."

"Aha," The O'Dancy said. "So you've put some obedience into him, at last, have you?"

Everyone seemed to smile, looking down.

"He is in Santos tonight," Eitaro said, and lifted the glass. "He is addressing a meeting. He is trying to prevent a general strike. He may not succeed. But if he weakens the will of a minority, that will be a success. If he persuades a majority against the strike, he will become the most powerful spokesman for labor. Then you will see progress."

"A further exploration of blackmail," The O'Dancy said. "I know the sort."

"No, sir," Toyashi said gently. "He is not a believer in the strike as a weapon. He believes in working. Work harder, more hours. Produce more for each hour. Illustrate theory by practice. Production, savings, accumulation, investment. That is his belief. It is difficult to persuade the unschooled. Especially, the unschooled in the higher places of government."

"But unschooled in what?" The O'Dancy said. "In Marxism? You might just as well blame me for being unschooled in Buddhism. I've no interest. Looking at your navel, or thinking about a lotus is as sensible to me as Marx's 'to each according to his needs.' Who's to judge? Have we heard of Courts of Need established anywhere? The needs are certainly there. Who'll supply them? If every need was supplied, would anybody do any work? Would bricks ever be carried? Logs sawn? Trucks driven? Rooms swept? We're all off in a fine dream of words, here. But it was written some time ago 'by the sweat of thy brow,' and it's still the truth. But the princes of Marxism are floating about in yachts. All of you came down from the loins of a laborer. You wouldn't say you'd done so badly, would you?"

"I think we shall do better," Simão said. "Of course, we can't fight preponderant capital. But we're arranging ourselves. When our social order is sufficiently strong, then we can hope to control at least part of the economy. With benefit to the rest. We need officers in the Church, in the police, in the Government. That will take time. But every day brings it nearer."

"Wait, now," The O'Dancy said. "You mean the Christian Church? The Roman Church?"

"It is the most powerful sociological force," Eitaro said.

"That's all?" The O'Dancy said. "Force?"

"It controls a certain broad class of thought," Toyashi said. "In that sense, it could be called a force."

"I'll go so far as to agree with you," The O'Dancy said. "If I've understood correctly, the long-term plan is to put people in the right place, and then start a national drive. Governor of a state or two, chiefs of police, a bloc of politicians, a cardinal or a couple of archbishops, a peppering of industrialists and bankers, you think you'd have an edge, is that it? I believe you'd have a disappointment in the Church, to begin with. You've to remember brain and spirit in the generations after you. You're forgetting a carnal Adam and Eve. They're not statistics. Not dead things on paper. Remember you're dealing with a living Church, or you make a paramount error. The Church deals with a soul. Start thinking of souls before you dream of control. Or it'll blow up in your face."

"Sir, the Church, that's Christian," Eitaro said. "Other religions have their place, surely?"

"In Brazil there is place for everybody," The O'Dancy said. "I'm warning you not to pervert. Any thought of 'using' the Church politically is sacrilege. You'd rouse an open hatred. You'd be unwise. As unwise as you are at this moment in some of your trading policies. You'll get your fingers chopped off."

"We must use our brains," Izumi said. "Others build with or without Alliance for Progress funds. We shall take any advantage of their mistakes. Do you deny us that?"

"I deny nothing," The O'Dancy said. "But I don't like the suggestion that you've got a Mafia here. It's a piece of nastiness that Tomagatsu didn't bring with him."

"Nastiness," Kingore said, from the side. "Sir, why do you use such a word?"

"It fits," The O'Dancy said. "You'd better put it about. Apparently, you're trying to run the market in fruits and vegetables and fish. Undercutting everybody else. Forcing them to sell out. It's smart business, but there's no profit except hate. Other men work and sweat for a living. And they have the right to sell at a fair price. And it's their country too. Why do you give ordinary people excellent reason to hate you?"

"They'd hate us in or out of any reason," Simão said. "We were never slaves, that's why. That's the unspoken reason."

"I wish it had remained so," The O'Dancy said. "The slave committed no crime of his own. He was prisoned into it, and a word labeled him. But he ever remained a soul sweet in the eyes of God. Some say the Russians and Chinese are all slaves. They're happy to say so. And aren't you trying to make a few slaves of your own? Here, in what you call your own country?"

"We use what there is," Taizo said, from the back. "It's a seasonal business. Green stuff rots. Fish rots. We had to put capital into freezing plants. Because anyone can grow a little of this and that, is it a reason to saturate and cheapen a market after we've provided the basis? It's that basis which creates the market."

"If you were Brazilians working in Japan, how long would you last?" The O'Dancy asked. "Never mind that you were born there. How long? A Brazilian Mafia in Japan? Ridiculous, isn't it? But we're Christian, and patient, and we suffer fools. You're the fools to take advantage. Tomagatsu never did. He was ever himself. He never contrived. He was *daimio*. Why aren't you?"

"We have no aristocracy here," Taizo said. "Of cash, yes. But we all rank the same."

"Poor soul, poor mouth," himself said. "That's the pride of freed slaves. A great deal different from the pride of free men. You've taken tone and color from some of the people you're hoping to master. Pride sits easy, or it cripples."

A sudden marvel of light in thought of Divininha, magnificently, beauteously nude, and the glorious hair a bronze whirl in a turn of the head.

"Darling, I was thinking," she said, and cool breath of perfume from the bath towel. "What about pride? Did you ever give it a thought? I mean, Fransisca's pride. Even before she knew about Tomomi? Or Tomomi's pride, let's say? Before she found out about this one and that. We won't bother about my pride. Before I found out about Lua, and a few more. What about pride? Did you ever think of it?"

"What brought this on?" himself asked, in bed with the newspapers. "A new soap or something?"

"No," she said, rubbing the back of her neck as if she loved it. "I was wondering why Tomomi destroyed everything. Photographs, for example. I'm taking Amoru to buy a really blanching birthday present. I don't believe a more exquisite girl's ever lived. In every way. I wish I'd known Tomomi. Anything like Amoru?"

"In the heart of her," himself said, secretly, serely miserable. "Outside, no. Tomomi was only half her size. Black hair. I must have taken hundreds of photographs. And there's not even one."

"Why do you think she threw them away?" Vanina said, and sat on the window seat. "Amoru thinks she hated the family because they hated her."

"There wasn't a dram of hate in body, soul, or spirit of her," himself said. "She wanted to go lonely. I know it now. Because she lived lonely. She devoted herself to an idea. To be a *brasileira*. Isn't that all? Didn't she destroy any likeness of herself so that her children wouldn't have an idea of her beyond memory? Why would I disturb it?"

"Why don't you talk about it?" Vanina said.

"I go hysteric inside at thought of another word," himself said. "We're twenty, thirty, forty years old only once, thank God. We've the machine and we use it, and excuse ourselves."

"If you found another Tomomi now, would you take her?" Vanina asked.

But he threw off the papers in rustling clouds, and laughed, and she laughed as if she wanted to cry.

"I'm not shaved and I'll scrape you raw if I kiss you," himself said. "Talking about pride, just now? Where's your own, to doubt?"

"I don't," she said, and made a long tube of the towel and tucked it behind her back. "I ask, would you take her? Would you regard us both as one woman? You'd make a preposterous error if you did."

"Not so much an error as a miracle," himself said. "I'm out of competition."

"Don't believe that, either," she said, and went to the door. "Are all women simply one woman for you? Is that how you excuse yourself?"

"No question of excuses," himself said. "If I've wanted the grace of a woman, I've gone into her if she'd let me. If she didn't, that's the end of it."

"How would you feel if a man had the same thought about Amoru," she asked. "Or me? Sauce for both geese?"

"You can't go into a woman unless she wants you to," himself said. "Or if she's so weak she can do nothing more. I never tried either. If she's not mentally with you, the body's nothing but a rubber bag. If she's helpless, that's worse. It's meat."

"Such delicacy," Vanina said.

"If there was ever willingness, I never scrupled," himself said. "That's the scatter. If I ever knew at the time, well, I don't know. But when it starts, everything else goes with it."

"Are you suitably penitent, darling?" she mewed, in the doorway. "A little aimless canter along Via Crucis?"

"No, hell," himself said. "But I know I'm talking a strict neck here, you see. I'm talking the way I know I ought to be talking. If I'd lived the same way, I wouldn't be anybody I am. Fransisca might still be alive. You wouldn't be taking Amoru anywhere. She wouldn't be born. Now, is that the answer, or not?"

Divininha half-closed the door.

"Breonha had to die," she said, ghosting another world. "She'd have been far more beautiful."

"I'll shave an hour before time," himself said in plea. "I ought to kiss you. Not just because I'm penitent. A bloody fool is what I am. Did I ever know what to say? Does anybody? Isn't thinking hell enough? When you know it's all going from you, God damn it."

Yes.

Quietness knelt in the room, and the family waited.

In color, in white walls, in the little *sake* jugs, all so like the wondrous years at the beach house.

And yet not.

"Now they speak of higher taxes," Yoichiro said. "The cost of living doubles every six months. Wages are going up eighty per cent by law. Soon, they say. How long till they go up another eighty per cent? A hundred per cent? And higher taxes. Who pays?"

"Will I never be away from politics or finance?" himself asked a lovely shadow keeping light away kneeling at the left.

"But why should you?" she said. "We listen. I shall tell my sons I heard you. I kiss your voice."

All the men called approval, and the maids went about with the *sake* jugs and whisky.

"It's the price for the Alliance for Progress," Toyashi said. "But whose progress? More taxes, more money drained from our pockets, more loans from the banks, and the bankers ask for a higher rate of interest. Outside investors have the benefit from higher dividends. The cleanest industry is loan of money on interest. But who'll collect the taxes? That's the weakness. There aren't the people. A man schooled enough to collect taxes can earn more in commerce. Unless, of course, he accepts bribes. In which case, in a couple of years, there'll be a new class of millionaires."

"You don't believe there are honest men among us?" The O'Dancy said.

"Many honest men, sir," Sessue said. "They have plenty of money."

"You are all honest men," The O'Dancy said.

"Among ourselves, it is better," Simão said, and bowed.

Perhaps a mule brayed far off, but there was no true sound except the breath of himself, and thought was alive that some phrase of relentless enlightenment should be thrown among all those faces, though if words were ready, there was wonderful space between them and the hook of the tongue, for the Creature had wasted no time.

Himself smiled, instead.

Everybody laughed in movement of color, bared teeth, flashing spectacles.

A moment's long joke.

Ah yes.

"Wait, now," himself said, looking at a dish of sugared fruits. "I wanted to talk to Koioko's father and mother. Koioko and Estevão. There's the marriage I'd wish for myself. Should we make an appointment for a day next week to discuss the business side?"

Izumi bowed.

"Sir, I shall telephone," he said. "She ought to be here."

"They do as they please these days," Mayaki said. "Why is that? I never dared."

"Wrong side of the family," The O'Dancy said. "Tomagatsu women always did as they pleased. Because of one. Tomomi."

The beauteous shadow at the side put out an arm and gentled the head of himself into a shoulder, and if the perfume was not the same, then to hell, the arm was strong to protect, the breast was soft, and the will was there to be the woman and wondrous lovable, but a shadow, no more than a shadow of that one gone the years before, and even the Creature's spinning vacuum took no pain, dimmed no memory of small smiles in the half dark, sound of the comb in long breaths through black hair beyond parchment walls, tap of wooden soles bringing honeyed tea, pressure of knees on the mattress, cool hands, a hot towel, arms in mondial enfoldment, cradle whispers in Japanese she never translated which seemed to pour from a waterfall in the heart, and a cat grace of satin muscle that set open lips in a shoulder and there trembled.

"Taddles, darling," Serena said, just above, somewhere. "Please don't be angry, will you? We've been looking for Stephen and we can't find him anywhere. We tried to get to Ahatubai's, but the mist's so thick. But we got here. He didn't. Where do you think he can be?"

"Wait, now," himself said, and left the warmth, and sat up. "Stephen, is it? He left Ahatubai's a couple of hours ago. Why's he not here?"

Serena waved a finger against offer of a drink, against invitation to sit, and looked down at himself, fingers locked under her chin, a blue-toweled column tied at the waist, and the loveliest head in the room bound in a blue-checked dishcloth.

"He went to meet Koioko," Mayaki said. "She took flowers. In the Jeep. Then they were going on to The Inheritance."

"We were waiting for them," Serena said. "They didn't come, so I thought something might have happened at Ahatubai's. We went there for nothing."

"You didn't hear about the child," himself said.

"Oh yes," Serena said. "He told me on the phone. He was rather funny, I thought. 'If that's The Tad's, poor old Mendel'll be revolving all night.' And we were quite sure it was yours. For some reason. But her mother wouldn't let us see it. Taddles, where's Kyrillis?"

"Where the harm'll be taken out of him," The O'Dancy said, and covered the tumbler against another pour. "Wait. What's this about Estevão? Stephen. Koioko. Where are they?"

"Koioko went to the shrine this afternoon as her grandmother did, and her mother," Izumi said, and bowed. "With flowers, sir."

Again the silence, and Serena standing there, hands under chin, looking down.

"What, then?" The O'Dancy said. "Did they elope, or have they bundled somewhere? I'd not blame them. I was ever the one for initiative."

"Taddles, it's hours, and he told me to wait at the cabaña," Serena said. "He was going along the river road to meet Koioko and then go to The Inheritance for some music, and back here."

A silence of so many people.

The O'Dancy put aside the tumbler.

"Wait, now," himself said. "I don't understand any of this. Tomagatsu's buried not a minute's walk away."

Serena held her face as if it might break, and half-turned.

"Sir," Simão said in bright flash of bowing spectacles. "It's for the day of the O'Dancy's veneration of the Lady Aracý. The O'Dancy Shaun. My ancestor always filled the love seat with her favorite flowers."

"The love seat," The O'Dancy said. "Which one is that?"

"Oh, Taddles, the one by the river," Serena said with the big tears. "The one he built for her."

"A reflection from his mind," Simão said. "He remembered the shrine below Fujiyama."

Somewhere beyond the humming, golden vacuum of the Creature, somewhere apart, and cold, in a place so far away, a wide-horned skull turned whitely in flamelight and spider smell heaved in perfume of dirty women.

"Let's out, now," The O'Dancy said, and struggled to be up. "I'm disgraced in the blood that I forgot the day of my own Grandam. Let's out."

36 Voices called, hands tried to hold, Serena's tears begged, but the sandals were kicked off, the kimono flung aside, and stones were unkind to the feet, but finding a way through the green gloom of the lakes took all other feeling away, and the pilot came to show a light and no man more welcome.

"Find the river," The O'Dancy said. "Go to the hill of crosses, first. Have you enough in the tanks?"

"Everything's in order, sir," the pilot said, and gave a hand up. "Only thing is, this mist."

Green water flashed in tinted cloud, all yellows, pinks, blues, and the house passed under, and dark treetops plumed, and the pilot turned for the river. Long rolls of cloud spread white across part of the lowland, and the river shone beyond, a blink, a scroll of light, and dark pasture, darker squares of sugar cane, paler plots of banana, ranks almost in detail of pineapple, and glints of water among the rice paddies near the river.

The hill humped dark against the sky, a little too far away to see the crosses, and mist rolled and furled, a bridal veil.

"I've a prayer in the deep belly of me," The O'Dancy said. "If I could get it out. Except I might pray and then curse the prayer."

"How's your faith, sir?" the pilot asked.

"As good as your own," The O'Dancy said. "What makes you inquire?"

"We're flying here strictly on faith," the pilot said. "If you weren't the boss, I wouldn't take her off the floor in this weather. Especially down here. This wind can change any moment and blind us. I'm not too well acquainted with the ground. So if we hit something, forgive me and good-by, sir."

"Good-by, it is," The O'Dancy said. "And if it is, to hell with it. I'm no fatalist. I don't believe things happen because they do.

I'm no believer in 'to be, or not to be' which I ever thought the silliest cavil of them all. If you don't want To Be, get on out. If you want To Be, then get on with it. The rest is driveler's poesy. And there are too damn' many drivelers. You'll ever find them in front of a looking-glass. Admiring what others never saw. Helpless bastards."

The river swirled beneath, lucent in the night, a glint here and there, a glitter now and then, enough to tell they were over running water.

"Go low," The O'Dancy said. "Find the island and keep on. The hill's beyond that fog, there."

He switched on the searchlight, focused in a wider beam, hung above the white rolls pouring like milk underneath, and suddenly came into darkness, where leaf was in shadow on the ground, and a path glowed red, red earth rising, and falling away in a rasp of power, and space.

"That's the hill, in front, sir," the pilot said, as an afterthought. "We nearly hit it."

"What you don't meet, you'll never miss," The O'Dancy said. "Go over the house, now, close as you can. Watch the coco palms. They're tall."

As if land came to an end, the glowing earth hid beneath the ragged edge of the swarm, moving, circling, never still, like pitch in bubble.

Spiders spread all the way from the house to the path up the hill.

"Something moving down there?" the pilot asked, and touched the searchlight into strong focus, just long enough to see the jumping mass in horrific mill, and turned mournful eyes.

"I omitted to tell you," The O'Dancy said. "I believe the Lady Koioko Tomagatsu's down there. And my son, Estevão."

The pilot sat straighter, focused the light in a wider beam, and swung the craft over the rise going up to the cemetery's flat paving at the top. The crosses stood in a long line dark against the sky, and then, taking light, were suddenly, sharply, granitically green, smiling in the night.

The swarm almost covered one side of the hill, a ragged black

stain against earth and grass, curving around below the main
stair leading up to the vaults.

"There's a truck, sir," the pilot said, and banked to turn about.
"There's a Jeep there, too."

The Jeep lay on its side, and the truck stood dark with an open
door, both swarmed black. The pilot took the craft low enough
to see the spiders in monstrous detail and the rotors caused fright
or the dust annoyed, but in a moment the vehicles were clean,
and, hovering, they made sure, but in silence, that the drivers
were gone.

"Thank God the Father," the pilot said in a blowing breath. "I
thought that was it."

"Are you believer in God, then?" The O'Dancy asked.

"I've been too near it many a time not to be," the pilot said. "I
never thought this sort of thing happened."

"You live too near the city," The O'Dancy said. "Isn't that smoke
around the front, there?"

Bluish clouds mixed with whiter river vapor, and, flying below
the level of the crosses, the pilot turned wide toward the entrance
gate on the far side, and the stone rail of the stairway took a
golden line from flame. The swarm made a black ribband over the
lower steps, and stopped at fire spreading through the grass and
flower beds on both sides.

The pilot went up, above the shaft of the Leitrim cross, and
the searchlight shone in waving white, and Stephen had his shirt
off, standing on the roof of the vault, and Koioko jumped up and
down, hands clasped, openmouthed on the paving below.

"I'll use the flat just beyond," the pilot shouted. "Take the
automatic, sir. Spray them if they come over the edge."

The craft bounced, braked, and himself hopped out, but if the
paving looked smooth, it had sharp edges, and Koioko had to come
most of the way herself, and fall into open arms. Stephen trotted,
putting on the shirt, holding the jacket in his teeth. The pilot
pulled Koioko up, and himself followed, and Stephen crawled in,
and the craft swayed off.

The searchlight's circle took in the edge of the paving, and the
spiders hopped, forelegs raised and spread, the dozens, hundreds,

thousands, and eyes held vicious points whitely myriad in the black, hopping, hopping.

Koioko sat beside the pilot, Stephen behind her.

"Did you enjoy the evening?" himself said while they turned along the river.

"I am not brave," Koioko said. "They were in my veins."

"No braver in this world," Stephen said, and put a hand on her shoulder. "I was only worried the gas wouldn't hold out, or the lighter wouldn't work. We'd have gone in the vault and shut the door. Hoped for somebody to find the truck tomorrow."

"I ran into them," Koioko said. "I tried to take the Jeep to the top, but I hit a rock. I had to jump, and it rolled down. Then it was getting dark."

"I prayed when I saw the Jeep," Stephen said. "I had just enough time to get the gas, that's all. Thank God they all move together. That slows them."

"Well, then," himself said. "How do you feel about them? You were a little opinionated this morning, were you not?"

"We'd have been taking the children there for the picnic tomorrow," Stephen said without looking around. "I didn't know there were so many. They were jumping in the flame. What made you come down, Tad?"

"Koioko was late," himself said. "You were supposed to meet here. Answer the question. Would you let them live?"

Stephen shook his head.

"Exterminate," he said. "I'd be glad to take charge tomorrow."

"I'll be down before noon to see it was done," The O'Dancy said. "Not because I distrust you. But I like to sleep peacefully in the afternoons. Before that, I have a little verminizing to do of my own. So we'll be busy."

"Did you attend the house of Ahatubai?" Stephen asked without looking back.

"I did," The O'Dancy said. "I promised I'd take care of her and the eventual husband."

From the back of his head the boy was smiling.

"I wanted to stay to hear the run of conversation," he said. "She'd had a child before. It probably went on an altar, somewhere."

"*Khimbanda*," himself said.

Stephen nodded barely.

"That's the other vermin," himself said. "How'll it be exterminated?"

Stephen turned all the way about.

"Not until we grow a little," he said. "That child born today, he'll be part before he's away from the teat. And how many others? Today, tomorrow, it goes on. Nobody gives a curse. If they do, they keep quiet. That's why I'm with Uncle Mihaul. Bring it out in the light, train it, school it. That's partly why Koioko's going to be my wife."

"What's the other part?" himself asked.

"I love her," Stephen said. "All the more tonight. We'll marry before I go. Then she can come with me."

"Koioko," himself said. "Is there any pleasant little piece of property you happen to have the light of your beautiful eye on?"

"Yes," she called over her shoulder. "Stephen."

"Pardon, sir," the pilot said. "Tomagatsu house or The Inheritance?"

"The Inheritance, please," Koioko said. "I must see the Lady Divininha. She needs me."

"God love the heart of you," The O'Dancy said. "She does. You see her, first. I'll see Hilariana. What in the name's to be done there? Or is there anything?"

"That's why I'll work with Uncle Mihaul," Stephen said. "If some clever one ever injects a political idea into that movement, and it passes into the trance state, how would you prevent those people from voting as they were told? *Umbanda's* nothing more than the most primitive Christian worship. The casting out of evil, cure of sickness and the raising of the supposed dead, that's the heart and soul of *Umbanda*. Now introduce another Christian idea, that the poor shall inherit the earth, for example. If you take it a step further, you're near a communist state. What's to stop it?"

"Pardon, sir," the pilot said. "You don't believe there's any real danger, do you? I know all about *macumba* and that nonsense, but that's only some of the blacks. If they got out of hand, don't you think we could deal with it?"

"We're as handy with guns and bombs as most," Stephen said.

"There's plenty of wire to make prisons. But martyrs die for a faith. *Umbandistas* will die without a murmur. Gladly. They don't acknowledge death. It's the beginning of a better life. It's birth into the world they want. The one they inhabit when they're in trance."

"But isn't that a type of hypnosis?" the pilot asked, and plainly not in accord. "Drunk or doped, out of their normal habit of mind? Which isn't much more than animal, to start with. Is it?"

"Isn't it?" Stephen said, light as cotton fluff. "I'm one. A number of my friends. Mostly professional men. I know a few in the Air Force, too. Animal?"

The pilot shrugged, banking toward the heliport lights.

"First I've heard of it," he said. "Can't be too many."

"We don't need ostriches in this country," Stephen said. "There's one in all of us."

"And don't be so almighty about the blacks," The O'Dancy said. "Most of this land would still be jungle without them. There wouldn't be much of a town anywhere. Take away the blacks and their issue, what's here?"

"I don't want to harm any feelings," the pilot said, going over the field, from his voice anxious to placate. "But it doesn't help much to start the talk about color, does it? We haven't the problem here. At least, not to compare with the *yanquis*."

"Whether they like it or not, it's in the open," The O'Dancy said. "We pretend it doesn't exist. But it's worse. It's hidden."

"But just talking about it doesn't create the problem," the pilot said. "There's no proof, is there?"

"What color are the politicians, or anyone else, here?" Stephen asked. "When have you seen anyone black in charge of anything or doing anything worth while?"

"That's educational," the pilot said instantly and confidently. "There's certainly a school problem. They don't call us under-developed for nothing. But one problem isn't two, is it?"

"Two hundred, plus," Stephen said. "No schools, no scholars. No scholars, no hope of training. No training, no social advancement. That's two hundred separate and distinct problems in three clauses, plus. And in most parts we lose more than half of every thousand births, the majority black or mixed."

"And in a couple of hours we'd be over the territory of naked Brazil," The O'Dancy said. "Millions. Uncounted. Can't be too many, didn't you say? How many do you want? Talking doesn't create a problem? We're too frightened to talk. Too ashamed to acknowledge them. Because they're picturesque? Or poor relations? We're giving a lot of high-sounding advice in the councils of the world outside, but inside our own bounds we've no advice for ourselves. And we resent it from others. Especially the *yanquis*."

"Nobody speaks of love," Koioko said in the small voice. "It's not only the men. There are women and children, too. Talk and laws and politics, that's all very well, but it frightens. We need love. We have so little. We hate so much. I hated those spiders. But they live their own way. How else should they live? Some hate the blacks. But why? Because they live? Or they wish to live as we do? We make them to be what they are. We manufacture their misery. It's not how many schools we must build to produce what. It's how many we must build before we absorb the hate."

"I don't hate anything," the pilot said, almost a complaint, and switching off. "Any hate I've ever noticed was good-humored, anyway. No blood. Not many bruises. A lot of shouting. But they soon get tired of it. Cup of coffee cures a lot of it. The rest isn't very important."

"Thanks for the flight," Stephen said, helping Koioko down.

"We owe you a lifetime of gratitude," she said. "I shall offer prayers to St. Christopher for you."

"Thank God for the *yanquis*," The O'Dancy said, patting the body of the helicopter. "One of you, be back Sunday afternoon to take me in."

"Yes, sir," the pilot said. "I hope you didn't mind my having a word?"

"Glad you did," The O'Dancy said. "You've to listen to the way a man opens his head to know what's inside it."

Stephen and Koioko waited beyond the control tower's beam in darkness that showed The House lit basement to attic, bright in every window, and a glow of greens, pinks, and blues from lamps among the trees and shrubs in the garden.

"I believe Mihaul's right," The O'Dancy called a little way off. "If it's let go, the silk-shirt boys won't bother their arses about it.

The comfortable jobbers'll never care. There's to be a lot more than we're thinking of doing. Koioko, would you prefer I spoke Portuguese?"

"I am learning English," Koioko said, tightening the arm about Stephen's waist. "I have a teacher."

"I'm the one to listen to if you want it right," The O'Dancy said. "I don't suppose The House was ever cleaner than at the moment. Will it not need another cleaning next week? Never mind the rooms are cleaned every day. Will we ever be sitting comfortable again? I'm not even sure I'll use the Silver Room after this."

"It's splendidly clean at the moment," Stephen said. "You've plenty to keep it so."

"Were there not plenty before?" The O'Dancy said. "A Houlihan's own shebasset is what it was, with or without them."

"But then you need someone at the top," Stephen said. "Vanina was ill. Ill, mentally, physically. There was nothing spiritual there, so we'll not discuss it. Now it'll be all that different. You'll find a different woman. You'll have to be patient. She won't remember a lot of things. I'll help, there."

"Trancing off, again," The O'Dancy said. "If I could understand what you mean, exactly. Shame's me, how do you enter trance? What is it? Do you know it, or welcome it, one or the other?"

"Both," Stephen said, and put his arm about Koioko almost as though he, and not she, needed protection. "It's like being washed away in a sea of warm electricity. No pain, or fear, nothing. Then it's a time you don't want to do without. You want to return. A feeling of power, but over the elements, alone. It's certainly a tonic for the physique."

"You don't remember anything?" himself asked.

"An impression of complete peacefulness," Stephen said. "After the first few seconds, no memory of anything tangible. Might not even be as long as that. And coming out's just like leaving a warm bath. A few thoughts, tenuous perhaps is the best way to tell you. But they soon go. Memory doesn't seem to apply even as much as in a dream."

"And it's the same with these *khimbanda* people?" himself said.

"No, and it's just as well to get that firmly in mind, first," Stephen said. "*Umbanda* means, roughly, one body, of one discipline, in one direction, or one way. Essentially it means worship of the one God through the one Holy Ghost. *Khimbanda's* the opposite. A lot of people find it easier. They prefer the pleasures of the body. They forget they have to pay. There's certainly a form of the trance. Drunkenness is a simple form of trance. Delirium tremens is a deeper, hallucinatory form. It's simple to evoke a state of trance when everybody's doing the same thing to the same rhythm, for the same, self-willed reason."

"How far is Father Miklos in this?" himself asked.

Stephen laughed, and Koioko leaned her head back, up at the clouds.

"Every priest who's ever raised a monstrance knows the state of trance, or he wasn't much of a priest," he said. "The Church long ago ruled against the trance in public. Too many pretenders. Too many charlatans. Father Miklos has studied *Umbanda*, *macumba* and *khimbanda* for most of his life because he's had to. He knows nothing's going to be done by edicts. I believe I'm the first in the family he's ever talked to about it. The early Christians didn't root out paganism by ignoring it. The Church isn't going to do any good by threatening. But it's serious in more ways than religious or moral. How many days have I been to the clinic here, and nothing to do except clean a cut or give somebody a shot of serum? But the *Umbanda* meetings are full. All taking cures from the mediums. They most certainly do cure. They have the power. It's a strange thing to see. The miracle in our time."

"It's the artificial insemination I don't like," The O'Dancy said. "Using a woman like an animal. I've no regard for it."

"That's nothing to do with *Umbanda*," Stephen said. "The woman wants insemination or not. African women want white children. There's no doubt about it. They love the black, of course. A lot of them are fanatic about mixing. But that's oftener to obliterate what they truly feel. They want white or paler children. Talk to Cleide. She'll tell you. But that's not a matter of *Umbanda*."

"Have you tried to cure in a state of trance?" himself asked.

Stephen walked slower, and Koioko put her arm about his waist.

"No," he said. "It would be unethical, first. But then, I need to know more about the mind. I want to know exactly what a 'trance' is. What happens in the mind. What forces are brought into use that until the moment seem nonexistent. But they do exist. They are there. And they're extremely powerful. I'd like to be able to explain why a normally intelligent father should go on his knees to a fifteen-year-old daughter and ask her advice. Because she's in trance? A body occupied by another spirit? What is a spirit? Is the Christian theory correct, or have we forgotten something at some time? When we die, we go to be judged. Is that correct? Then why are 'spirits' free to enter bodies in trance? Were they released from Judgment? If one, or thousands, why not all the millions of dead? So many whys. So far, some comfortable theories. No substance."

"You've marvels of problems," The O'Dancy said. "I'll know the solution before yourself. That's, of course, if cinders can know anything. The moment they fold the hands of me, I expect to start a smolder. What's Koioko think, here?"

"If you had not come for us tonight I wouldn't be thinking," she said from under Stephen's chin. "If someone had not the idea of a telephone, you would not be there. If Santos-Dumont experimented with something else instead of cutting wings from canvas, there would be no airplane and possibly no helicopter at this time. What do I think? I think he must do as he thinks. There is no other thing to do."

"I'd like to know why I've never been in trance," himself said.

Stephen looked, and stopped in the middle of the path, taking his arm from Koioko.

"But, Tad, we've done nothing but pray you never would," he said. "Think, now. You know the altar ritual of Mother Church. But a woman's body was the only real temple you were ever comfortable in. After the day was over, in the tired moments, or the weak moments, didn't you go to the bottle and women? Did your mind hold anything else at those times? Wasn't a rhythm established? That's the *khimbanda* way. Most people are unaware of it. But the *khimbandistas* go further. They establish a ritual based on the Church's own, and a dress, ornaments, the prayers, the rhythms. The mind succumbs. There's no memory. Simply the experience of what passes for pleasure in common prolonged into exhaustion. That's the lowest form of the trance state, but it's very deep, and basically evil because the subconscious mind becomes accustomed to vice. It loses all the defenses of the civilizing process. It becomes capable of any crime. There's no conscience."

"Then how did Clovis da Souza last so long?" The O'Dancy asked. "I never saw much wrong with the fellow. A little sly, perhaps."

"It was known from the beginning," Stephen said, not offering to take the hand Koioko held out. "How could any of us do anything if you wanted to take his part?"

"Hell, I wouldn't," The O'Dancy said.

"Ah, hell, sir, but you would," Stephen said. "Before today, would you accept anything you disagreed with? People were afraid to talk to you. You screamed at them, didn't you? You broke everything. Smashed, burned. Then you were sorry. For how long? Poor Hil-oh. That's what really started her. That night. We tried so hard with her. I was too small to do anything much."

"Will you blame me for what's happened to her this day?" The O'Dancy said. "Myself knowing nothing about it?"

"You smashed her wedding presents," Stephen said, and no more than a whisper. "Everything ready and you come back drunk. That's the night she had to be given morphia. And that's what started everything else."

"I'm willing to leave it," himself said. "What did you know of Madame Briault?"

"Little," Stephen said. "She had a bad heart condition, I know that."

"Useful," The O'Dancy said. "And what of Kyrillis?"

Stephen took Koioko's hand.

"Psychopathic," he said. "Once a male's acted the female there's nothing much to be done. There's always danger of reversion. Drugs are a deadener. Not a cure."

"And Serena," himself said.

"Nothing wrong, there," Stephen said. "Hardest head in the family. She looks delicate. And that's all. She knows what she wants, and she'll get it. Her way. She's got a lot of you in her. In about forty years' time she could be our first woman president. Make me a bet?"

"I wonder will I be let live another forty years with enough brain to know what's around and about?" himself said, and limped over a stone. "I'll have these paths paved, too. Every road and path in the place asphalted. 'Will I not go sock foot and equable into my own house, then? Oh yes, but I will.' But I wasn't at all in equability under those crosses tonight."

Stephen laid a hand on the shoulder of himself.

"Many a fine day, yet," he said. "What shall I tell The Mam?"

"Say I'll be with her," himself said. "Why were you never able to do anything for her, poor girl?"

"For the same reason you didn't," Stephen said. "I didn't know till it was too late. In any illness there's a crisis. I knew I had to wait for it. That's why I've hung about the place these months. And thank God I did, or I wouldn't have met Koioko. Don't worry any more about The Mam or Hil-oh. It won't take long. *Khimbanda*'s a sickness of the soul, no more. You have to catch them in high fever, as it were. Cleide's probably in trance at this moment and Grandam Aracý's in full control of everything. If she needs any help she can call the other Grandams. They're all ready. When she's finished, there'll be no more *khimbanda*. Unless you permit it."

"If I didn't stop it before, it's because I never imagined anything of the kind," The O'Dancy said. "How am I to know after this? Am I ever to be on hands and knees looking for *urucú*, or plucked fowl and cigars, for God's sake?"

"Leave it to Uncle Mihaul and Father Miklos," Stephen said. "They're sterner men than you know. The Mam and Hil-oh can do a great deal. Then there's Democritas and Ephemia. Efram. Scores of others. You haven't a single worry."

"Why must I forever depend on others?" himself shouted. "Am I such an ignoramus? A drooler among my own people? I'm The O'Dancy. I'm the one responsible. I'm the one to say yes or no. Everybody off in a trance and talking to this one and that, b'God. Why not myself out of all of you?"

Stephen took his arm away from Koioko and stopped again. The lights from The House lit one side of his face, and a gray eye, paler than most, and a right, reddish tinge in the hair.

"Tad," he said quietly and gently. "Gather your mind. Think away from everything, now. Calmly. Remember through your days. Were there never times you had pains in the body, in the muscles, in the head? When you had strange thoughts? Strange, beyond drink or tiredness. When you took yourself off to a doctor, and there was nothing wrong beyond a pill or two? Remember, now. Did you?"

"I did," himself said. "Many times. Nothing wrong with me. But I felt terrible."

Stephen slapped his hands together.

"That was the *orixás* working in you, preparing you," he said. "But they could never bring you into the final state. You stopped it. With drink, or exhausting yourself with anything off the street. Once make up your mind, and Paul and Cleide'll bring you in. You'll be the happier."

"I'd like to know how," himself said, and felt truth in the blood.

"You'll begin to live on two levels of consciousness," Stephen said. "The one you're used to, that's this one, and the other you'll be sent to, that was always your own if only you'd known about it. Most of the people on The Inheritance are far more advanced as human beings, more adjusted to this life, and happier—whatever meaning you prefer for the word—than you are. If you are meant to be a medium, meant to carry the Spirit, you'll be unhappy in body and mind till you do. It's the true discipline."

"I don't trust what you say," The O'Dancy said. "But I'll be looking into it. You've lived a third of my own time. You came from seed at secondhand from me. But you seem to know a great deal more about living?"

"I studied medicine, so I know more," Stephen said. "Koioko's studied obstetrics and infant nursing, so she knows more. I've been *Umbandista* since I was six. I know more. Better than that. I'm certain."

"But how will I go into a church again?" The O'Dancy said. "If I'm trancing and crawling about the place, how will I have a prayer in me? How will I meet the Eye?"

Stephen took himself by the shoulders in a son's strong embrace.

"Ah, Tad, don't you ever try to understand?" he said. "Try, now. What's born in us has to come out. Isn't it so? When it's out, when racial memories, and centuries of cruelty, and the despair of generations are put at rest, then there's Mother Church waiting for us. Hasn't every priest worthy of the Love passed through the fire?

Doesn't he pass through every day of his life? Is temptation such a small business in a man's time? Does he never have to crush and destroy the gentlest and dearest within himself? The sweet, the heat, the wonder? Does he not? Is the spirit no more than a word? Have we spoken nonsense all our lives? Are God the Father, the Son, and the Holy Ghost simply patterns of speech? Nonsense? Some think so. Some enter the Church with nothing more than baptism. Some enter through pain. Some go to church as a habit. Others, as a duty. But when we go to church, we'll know why we must go. We'll know because we passed through the other, and earned the right. Mother Church isn't just architecture and ornament and a mumble. Isn't it a place of the spirit, guarded by men and women under constant pressure of temptation? Are they such mild souls? Don't they live in a body? Is the body so dead? We, and how many others, have the African and Indio in us. We were praying to God Almighty in our own way a long time ago. Christ came here with freebooters. With murderers, and slavers and thieves. Our people were sold and resold. They were never themselves. But their appeal was not unheard. They took strength in other climates, beyond the physical. We in this day have to enter there. We must remake the maps. Reorient. Bring as many back as we can. And when all of us enter Mother Church we shall know why we are there. It will be for a reason. Until that time, we shall be lost children, looking for a family."

"Why did you not become a priest, yourself?" The O'Dancy asked.

"Medicine's my priesthood," Stephen said, and took Koioko's hand. "We have work to do together. So many issues. So many confusions. But there's time, even though they speak of blowing up the world. Let them. At least, we know we don't depend on this life. We have a duty here, that's all."

"It seems only five minutes ago I was holding you in Grandfa Phineas's red shawl," The O'Dancy said. "And here you are, talking such a way I'm unsure if I'm stood on two feet or on end. Or even which day it is for wandering in sweet bad luck, myself sock foot and bleared, here."

"We're an hour or so into the very day of Judas, and he'll be patron, and brother, and defender before the Judge of every traitor and murderer and thief to the end of time," Stephen said, and put his arm about Koioko, and she turning to lay a smiling head on his shoulder, and in the tip tilt of closed eyes, again that yearn—O MAVRONE!—for Tomomi, and Fransisca smiling there somewhere, and ever a thought of Divininha, yes, Vanina, waiting in that extra world himself knew so little about. "It was this day, all those years ago that he climbed Golgotha and chose himself an olive tree, and looped a rope and jumped straight-armed down toward the lights of Jerusalem. The bitter juice of his tears are still in the olive's fruit. We eat an olive, we pray with Iscariot, and while we spit the stone, another sinner's lightened of a hindrance to enter In."

"There's no shadowest doubt you'll be The O'Dancy after myself, and it'll be made plain to those who matter," himself said. "Will you ever be eating an olive, then, and remembering one beneath the sixth cross up there?"

"I will," Stephen said. "But there's many a fine day, yet."

"I'll be in need of it, anyway," The O'Dancy said, and took Koioko against himself, and put a hand on Stephen's shoulder. "Do you not find great fortune for us that a woman's the marvel she is? Have you never thought what it might be if she were created some way else? Or if she thought about us with less than the heart of a mother? And are we not doing our talking in a sweet morn that's been gifted us? Will you look at The House, there, quiet? Every flower in sleep, to the root. Myself a happier one, except there's grit I ever hated in the teeth of me from the dust of those blades. Shall I complain a little more, then? Why would you not be telling me I was doting in the wrong day?"

"Is it any use if the mind of yourself is made?" Stephen said. "And does it matter? Sometime or other, you'll find out. It saves the bellowing."

"Bellowing, is it?" himself said. "Imagine that. Ah, son. I've been a bad father."

Stephen smiled, and wagged the red head, but slowly.

"No, sir," he said. "You were a man of your time."

Date Due

MAR 4 '65			
MAR 2 3 '65			
MAR 2 '66			
MAY 19 '69			

Demco 293-5